**Novels in series order**
*Off The Edge*
*Over The Line*
*Out of Time*
*Ecuador*
*Nemesis*
*Remilious*

# Remilious

## Two Women an Unbreakable Bond

**RS Perry**

ISBN (Hardback) 978-1-989938-19-5

ISBN (Trade Paperback) 978-1-989938-16-4

**ISBN (Paperback 6x9) 978-1-989938-15-7**

ISBN (Large Print) 978-1-989938-14-0

ISBN (e Book) 978-1-989938-17-1

ISBN (audio) 978-1-989938-18-8

Remilious

Paper back, exclusive rights, CA.

Copyright © RS Perry

Published by Penelope Ltd.

Back cover: author's photo taken by Ruth Ottman.

 Formatted with Vellum

*$H_5N_1$ is no longer just a whisper on the wind ...*

*To those who sounded the alarm before the world was ready to listen—and to those who will fight the next battle when it begins.*

"It was paradoxical—the loss of love and companionship contrasted with the loss of an archenemy. His mind had worked through the past month as much as he was capable. Rehashing, reworking, and rethinking would only contribute to the destruction of the present and those around him."

Jim Johnson

Contemplations

Pedro, the Mexican Yaqui boy with chestnut eyes, burnt sienna skin, and dark brown hair, had seen his family and friends murdered as he watched, paralyzed by fear and helpless—all in a life of fewer than seven years: his mother, father, brothers, sisters, and dog Rosita, and then his newly adopted mother, Heather, murdered at the hands of Najma.

Only days ago, his life had begun to feel normal with Heather. He had started to accept her as a friend and teacher. After the murder of his family in Mexico, he was living a new life on the ranch that she shared with her partner Jim. Pedro had begun school, where he had made few friends and many enemies. The enemies were easy for him to make with his Latino ethnicity in an Eastern Washington ranching community. Even his name, Pedro, brought narrow-minded comments. Intolerance was a way of life. In direct contrast to the ingrained prejudices of the ranchers were the westside "Coasties", the 'elitist' urbanites who were slowly invading the ranchers' home turf with their hiking clothes and oversized log houses. At the ranch, the young boy was taught values corresponding to the educated, tech-garnered wealth, erudite big city coast culture, which further failed to ingratiate him with his school contemporaries.

*How much could his strength of character stand?* wondered Jim. Besides being out of place at school, Pedro had watched Najma brutally murder his family and the woman he had begun to accept as his mom. Motionless,

Pedro sat next to Jim, his blue-eyed, tall, thin adopted father, feeling both fragile and strangely content, fused between events in time. Inside, he was overjoyed to have Jim close, and Najma gone, and equally afraid that his new dad, friend, and protector would be taken from him like all the others. Soon they would be *home,* at the ranch, and he would be in bed with his memories.

Lola, his Yaqui self-appointed guardian who had valiantly tried to save him both from the cartel and Najma, was now an American citizen thanks to the influence of Colonel Jim Johnson and his boss General Crystal. Was it safe to think of Lola as his "mother" and call the colonel his father? Lo, Heather's nickname for Lola, would make him breakfast and dinner, and life would be normal. Old Man Shuskin, the past transient, the phantom of the woods, brought to the ranch by Heather, would be his grandfatherly companion, feeding and working with the animals together, just as Ben, the teenaged ranch hand, would be his new older brother. Roy, the ranch caretaker, would teach him to ride and rope and myriad fun cowboy things and be his uncle. All of them, his newly pasted together family, would support him. There would be, however, a gaping hole—Heather—who had created the ranch's warmth and vitality.

It was Jim's ranch, his name on the title, his before he had met Heather. Nevertheless, the spirit of the Wolf Canyon Ranch had become that of Heather, the llama lady, as she was both fondly known in the valley by a few and sarcastically called by the horse packers, many ranchers, and the bulk of his school classmates. She had filled the gap left by the loss of his birth mother like a warm weather front rushing into a cold void. Now she was gone, too.

Jim felt his son's pain as he watched Pedro sit on the co-pilot's lap, inattentively holding the cyclic as the chopper continued to push westward through the crisp blue winter air. He wondered, as he often did, how the young boy would dislodge those memories. How much could a fledgling human endure? *How will he ever cope with all the death he has seen?* He forced his mind away from the questions he might never resolve. His thoughts wandered to Heather, and for a second, he allowed himself to ask himself how *he would cope.*

Then add another death, Najma, the devil lady dying only feet away from the boy. One, however, Jim hoped might ameliorate Pedro's pain. *Could a six-year-old really find pleasure in a killing, even his mortal enemy? Would it put an end to the suffering he had endured? The fear he had lived with?*

Is he like me or who I have become? Is he capable of embracing the pain and continuing? Is that the synergy I felt for him the moment we looked into each other's eyes during the skirmish, the battle with Najma at the hacienda in Tubutama, Mexico? *I've always been different from others in my ability to handle death and grief.* Jim had long known he differed from most of humanity. Both in his thoughts and interests. *Could Pedro be the same? Can I do for him what my grandmother did for me?*

Intellectually, he had had an interest in philosophy and art ever since his grandmother had given him a copy of

Will Durant's *The Story of Philosophy* and another on Picasso's art. Both, when he was on the verge of being a teenager, twice Pedro's age. The lessons learned from reading those philosophers' ideas changed his life and cemented his thoughts, removing any desire he might have had for organized religion and giving him a respect for knowledge.

The book's gift was a mystery to him. His grandmother knew he was beginning to find religion distasteful, even though she wholly embraced it. *Or is there something I don't know about her?* he wondered. Neither the adult Jim nor the boy Jim had ever understood why she had given it to him. What was she telling him? Was it more than to keep an open mind? Was she telling him to embrace more than one theology? More than one way of seeing the world, as Picasso had attempted. Or was it simply that he should think as others had before him? Or was it not to think as they had? Another enigma he had never resolved. The two books were incongruous with her religious side. Despite his evolution away from religion and its ardent beliefs, he never lost his lasting love and respect for her. She had become his mother and his friend, as Heather had become Pedro's.

Jim missed her, his faux mother, and often wished she were still living so that she could know he had turned out okay. Not in the religious sense, but rather in his differentiating between the good and evil in the world. *Or would she abhor what I do?* He had read the Durant book she had given him, as a boy and later as an adult, several times. The book spanned the ancient philosophers to the modern and their ideas and quotes, which had become his moral compass. One chapter he had read more than the others and remembered a smattering of quotes from Arthur Schopenhauer. As he sat watching Pedro, one entered his thoughts: "Mostly it is a loss that teaches us about the worth of things."

Jim's affection for Pedro had been immediate a year ago when they were under fire from the cartel at the Mexican hacienda. Not being sure, during the last few days, whether he had lost his adopted son to Najma's vengeance cemented his understanding as to just how much Pedro meant to him. By both almost dying, only feet apart, they had something they shared. Something that many fathers and sons would never share. They had come together not by a shared biology, but through their shared experience, an inherent respect for each other, and a natural liking that had evolved into a special caring. Schopenhauer had been right...loss teaches us to value what we have. And Jim added his thought that life is not only about losing but also gaining.

New beginnings.

In the past, Pedro would dream, wish for, and demand being at the controls of a helicopter. This time, as they cruised toward the Cascades and Heather's grave, he barely noticed. He sat next to his father, not caring about flying, not saying anything, and not seeing the countryside as it slid beneath them in a blur. Jim hadn't tried to make him talk before moving him to the pilot's seat. But he had kept his arm around Pedro and reveled in having him close, having him alive. Thoughts of Heather coursed in and out of his mind. She would at least be happy that Pedro was safe. She would be if she were here.

As they floated over the eastern Washington scablands, Jim decided it was time to distract Pedro, and perhaps himself, from their emotional realities, their thoughts of death and evil. He gently lifted him to the back seat between himself and the sleeping Major Brush McGuire. 'You see all those dark rocks below? Rocks with soil washed away, leaving them exposed?'

Pedro listlessly looked up at Jim. Then he slowly, as if reluctant to have his thoughts interrupted, looked out the window. 'I see.'

'In a minute, when you look out, the black basalt rocks will be gone and there will be huge sand ripples. They are way too large to tell that they are giant dunes when standing on the ground. From down there, they look like undulating hills. The scale is big. You need to be high up looking down to recognize what they are. They were caused by a flood, long ago, racing from the northeast tip of Washington to the Pacific Ocean.'

'Where flood come from?' as he reverted to his comfortable—but incorrect way of speaking—the pidgin English Heather had worked hard to eliminate.

'An ice dam broke near the Idaho border that had been holding back a large lake.'

Pedro didn't understand and didn't respond. Jim decided to postpone saying more. He squeezed Pedro and gently turned his head so they could read each other's eyes and perhaps see a little into each other's minds. 'Both of us can teach each other lots of things. For one, I have always tried to learn Spanish. I'm still pretty lousy.' He almost said, piss poor, but he tried to keep his military jargon locked up around family and civilians. 'Do you think you would help me learn to speak better?'

'Sí. Sure, I teach you.'

'I'd like that, son. It might take you a very long time.'

'Posiblemente, you not so good,' said Pedro with a slight grin. The happy face, even if only momentary, was enough to let Jim know that through all the death and loss, he would come through the turmoil intact.

'We're safe now. We have each other. Together we will make a good life. Earth can be a good place.'

As much as Pedro respected his new father, his mind questioned the Earth as being a good place. *The rocks, plants, and animals are, he thought. Many people are not good, and some are worse—evil. The devil lady killed my family and Rosita.* Tears welled in his eyes as he thought and looked at this man who had taken him in, rescued him, and become his friend and father.

They held each other's gaze for several seconds. Pale blue eyes to Pedro's deep brown, trying to understand each other's thoughts. It was as if Pedro was verifying that he was safe, that Jim could be his father, that life would be okay and not a horror show, and that no one else would disappear from his life. Was it possible that the future could be good and full?

They would soon be home. A home without Heather. One that would never be the same for either of them without her. Still—it was their home. Their thoughts merged into the steady rhythm of the helicopter's beating blades.

Jim wondered how Pedro would be affected by being at the ranch, where Heather was now buried under the small plateau above their house. *For me, it's always best to embrace the bad head-on. But is it the best way for Pedro?* Jim nodded imperceptibly. 'Time answers some questions,' he said out loud into his mic.

Both Pedro and Brush looked at him.

'Questions?' asked Pedro.

'Sí, muchas preguntas, pocas respuestas.'

Pedro looked down while moving his head from side to side and said, 'Muy mal, papá. Ese mal acento. That bad accent.'

'We're even,' said Jim, smiling. We'll learn together.'

With the darkness of their thoughts interrupted, Jim lifted his adopted son off the seat to the floor so he could see the cockpit and the view out the windscreen toward the approaching mountains. 'Do you want to be upfront again? You can fly us home.'

# Chapter One

'All's okay here at our Idaho preppers enclave,' said Glenda into her mic, sitting in the command bus affectionately known simply as the *Bus* 'Pedro seemed fine when he left with the Colonel, at least on the outside. They're in the air. Forty minutes till they arrive home at the ranch. It makes sense that Jim wants to get him back to a normal environment as quickly as possible.'

'It'll be difficult,' added Sheilla as she slowly turned in her chair 350 miles away from Idaho and several stories below ground at the Biological Warfare Center, 'Won't it? Being back so close to where Heather was murdered?'

'There's no other choice; it's their home. Pedro will have the animals and friends. Perhaps being close to where she was killed, he will embrace grieving instead of concealing it. I don't think it will do him any good if he keeps it inside.'

'But look at what he must already be keeping inside: Mexico, his whole family killed in front of him.'

Glenda shook her head. 'Really hard to imagine what is in his head after all that. I'm glad Brush is flying back to the ranch with them. He's going to help as much as he can, take the burden off Jim so he can pay more attention to Pedro.'

'I just can't imagine how hard it will be for him. Is there anything I can help you with finishing up the crime scene in Idaho?'

'We've got it covered. And you will have a ton of reports to write. But thanks for offering. I'm just looking forward to seeing Brush under everyday circumstances and being with him again.'

Sheilla ran her fingers through her long auburn hair as she listened. After Glenda mentioned Brush, Sheilla's thoughts drifted to Martin. She began to understand Glenda Rose's feelings for Brush when Glenda said, 'I hope I can get there soon, too. I always miss him, my big guy.'

The General, who had not said a word but was listening on the phone, said, 'As long as no emergencies pop up, I'll make sure you have time with the Major. Can your staff manage the cleanup?'

'They're a good team, General, although we're all eager to finish up and get out of Idaho, not just me.'

'You can chalk up another successful mission and this one terminating Najma's reign of atrocities. You were the right choice to handle it. You too, Sheilla. I'm proud of you both. If you are certain the staff can handle it from here—

Glenda, get your 'budinsky' on a chopper in the morning. Take a few days' downtime at the ranch with the Major.' He almost said, 'with your big guy,' but he couldn't bring himself to add personal comments.

*Budinsky? I'll tell him sometime that it's not a "d".* 'They can handle it, but I feel responsible and think I should stay.'

'Don't underrate your team. From what you say, Kitty and Brees can handle the final cleanup fine. And it isn't only about that,' he added. 'More people at the ranch will help take everyone's mind off what happened to Heather. And you deserve downtime. Take the time before something else requiring you pops up on our radar.'

'If that's an order, sir, thank you.'

'It is, and, as I said before, I'm proud of you both. Well done.'

'Thank you, General,' the two women said nearly simultaneously.

'Keep me informed, and ah, Merry Christmas to you both.' With that, Will Crystal hung up. Sighing, he began to look through the stack of CIA reports on his desk. There was never an end to trouble in the world. Holidays were no different from any other day. *All our meddling, reacting, and promulgating events; is there a positive benefit in the end?* he wondered.

'Have to get back to work here, Sheilla,' said Glenda, 'but what's this I hear about you and Martin?'

'There's nothing.'

'Sheilla Mary McCarrick,' said Glenda.

'Okay, okay. There is nothing so far. That's the truth.

Yeah, I think there could be.' Then she relented. 'He makes me feel all gooey inside. I've never felt that before. I was starting to feel like I was frigid when it came to men.'

'Embrace it, girl. Don't let it get away if inside you know it's real. Brush makes me feel that way still. I don't see it changing.'

'Thanks, Glenda. I appreciate talking to you. Maybe we can talk more later; I have a mountain of paperwork to do.'

'Same here, but tomorrow I get to play cowgirl and pass the drudge work off to Kitty and Brees. Sayonara gal.'

Sheilla smiled and did one quick spin in her well-lubricated swivel chair. Then she stood up and headed back to the team in the operations room. It would take them the rest of the day writing reports. All except the two computer elites, Misa, who, along with Vidya, had negotiated exemptions from report writing when the General recruited them to the Biological Warfare Center. They kept computer records of their contributions however they wanted. Never having to indulge in the drudgery of after-mission reports. *Those two had negotiated a "sweet" deal,* thought Sheilla. And the General never regretted what he had offered to recruit them. Their tech and thinking value became more obvious with each BWC mission. The world was moving toward technology. The Biological Warfare Center fully embraced it. Sheilla doubted that the two computer whizzes' importance would decrease as time chugged into the future. *Why didn't I negotiate something to get me out of report writing?* Nonsense, simple answer: *I was a lowlife and felt that way in the FBI when the General gave me an out to come here. Now it's different. I'm a supervisor and respected. What more could I ask for? Hmm, maybe one more thing.* As she walked down the hallway, humming, she thought of Martin and how her role in life had changed from a dispirited FBI analyst to being a trusted, important member of the staff, and perhaps even loved. She opened the door to the operations room. Fred, her soft-spoken lead computer engineer, looked up.

'You look happy.'

Sheilla chuckled and said, 'Just glad to have a good ending. No one killed, at least none of our people, that is. Let's get these reports done and put an end to Najma. What's her last name? I never think of her other than by her first name, N-A-J-M-A the evil one: The Snake, La Serpiente, the Devil Lady.'

'It's Hussein, Najma Hussein,' said Fred. 'May she never rest in peace.'

# Chapter Two

'Hey, Sheilla, it's Glenda. I thought I would check in with you one last time before leaving Idaho for the ranch and Brush. It's been a pleasure as always. And as much as I like to work with you one-on-one, I admit I prefer it better up here in the fresh air with the sky and stars above me rather than down there with you cave dwellers.'

'You must really feel that way, saying it again.'

'Yep, I guess I do. I think about you and the others down below having all that dirt piled above. It leaves me feeling a little claustrophobic.'

'From my experiences up there with you know who, I feel safe and secure down here, buried several stories underground with a military fort above me.'

Glenda thought about Sheilla, Vidya, and Misa, in their below-ground high-security vault. The desk jockeys far removed from their bloody experience at the hands of Najma and the cartel in Mexico. *Perhaps I can see why they like it down there. Sheilla is happy with her job, spinning in her swivel chair, long auburn hair lifting, focused on a problem much like the Sufi, in their whirling meditation ritual,* imagining the show she had once seen somewhere or other. *I wonder if Sheilla's ever seen the swirling dervishes? Maybe we can see them together sometime.*

Najma had been the devil reincarnated. She had become, however, something that all of them had in common. Sheilla, Heather, and the others being held captive, and now her new romantic interest, Martin, who had endured the same fate at the woman's hands at the cartel headquarters in Tubutama. Then there was Jim, Lola, and Pedro's experience at the same place. A shared inglorious bond.

'Okay. I have to get on with finishing up here. I'll be ready in a couple of hours to happily follow the General's orders and leave here to join Brush at the ranch. I just wanted to check in with you before I left. Call Kitty or Brees if you need anything.'

'Will do.'

'I was just thinking that the prepper cult would be very envious of you, Sheilla. Their bomb shelter seems inconsequential by comparison.'

'I feel pretty lucky to be here and have the General as a boss. It was considerate of him to want you to be with Brush. He's turning into a regular softy,' said Sheilla.

'He's got a heart, but I wouldn't go quite that far. He expects a lot, we give a lot, and he knows when we need a reward.'

'Yeah. He's a good boss, isn't he? I guess we both owe him for pulling us out of our FBI quagmire.'

'Second, that thought,' said Glenda. 'Talk later. I gotta tidy up with my crew, then get my 'buttinsky' on a chopper, as the man so eloquently put it. I suspect he was using that in a military way about moving my rear end said with a 'D' instead of with 'T's'. Sometime, we'll have to let him know that buttinsky means a person who butts in, not a bud in,' said Glenda.

'I'll leave the in-sky talk with the General up to you. A little personalized slang doesn't bother me.'

'See you soon sometime in the New Year, I hope,' said Glenda as she clicked the off switch while turning to look at her team.

Sheilla spun around and around in her chair. Her long hair imperceptibly lifted with the centripetal force. The last few days had been a whirlwind chase of Najma across Washington state to Idaho and eventually to the preppers of Idaho. *Take a deep breath and get the report writing over with,* she thought.

Brees, Glenda's third in command, took her headset off and turned to her boss, 'Everyone but forensics, SWAT, and the investigative team is gone, and us five of course. The investigators will be retracing her route to make sure there are no other unfortunate people she killed along her travel route. They will be busy for days, but that has no effect on us. SWAT will stay if you think we need them.'

'Yes, I want them to,' said Glenda. 'This area and maybe some in this compound are as hostile to the FBI as it gets. It's just a precaution. And for that matter, some are probably not so fond of your black skin either, Brees.'

'Hmm, I did notice the prepper clan looking at your voluptuous curvy self, strawberry hair a little different than they looked at me, like I was a smudge on their environment.'

'Well, not all of them are the brightest that humanity has to offer. It's a different world here than in D.C., or for that matter, in the western part of the other Washington.'

'Yeah. Two hundred years and only slight changes in some areas of the county. At least I'm not plucking cotton. Okay, SWAT stays and the forensic team leaves. The investigative guys and dolls should be here soon to start their backwards journey retracing her path. Hopefully, they will finish up here muy rapido, so we can leave, and they can hit the Najma trail.'

A light blinked, and Brees put on her headset. 'Roger that,' as she set her headphones on the counter. Brees closed her eyes and sat back in her chair, feeling exhausted.

'Take a break, Brees,' said Glenda, 'get a couple of hours, sleep in if you want before I leave. We'll be fine here. Kitty will be done interviewing the compound's members soon.'

Brees stood up, raised her hands above her head, stretched, yawned, and started to walk away. She turned, 'Thanks, but don't let me sleep any longer than two hours. Chen, Sept, you got that too? Oh, by the way, that was the recovery crew saying their ETA was 1300. The forensics team radioed in when they arrived at the airport from the Seattle field office and should be here in a few minutes.'

'We'll take care of them. Off you go, gal. One of us will wake you in a couple of hours.'

'You promise?'

'No, I don't promise, but remember, you're the only one who didn't get any sleep last night. If nothing is happening that we can't handle, maybe, perhaps a few minutes longer even, okay?'

Brees rubbed her eyes. 'I guess I need it, thanks. Don't forget the trackhoe,' said Brees, desperately wanting sleep and still reluctant to leave.

'Got you covered, now get going. Pleasant dreams.' *Lucky to have Brees and the others. I'm going to hate losing them back to the FBI*, pondered the ex-FBI agent, Glenda. *I'm glad I'm not going back.*

'We've got her covered,' said Chen. Let her sleep for as long as she needs. I don't have any tech problems to deal with at the moment, so no problem watching over her stuff while she gets some Z's.'

'We'll let her sleep a few minutes longer. She'd not like it if we let her sack out too long.'

Her mind switched back to the job of finishing up and getting out of here and to Brush, 'Chen, trackhoe, now.'

'Sure, boss.

Glenda rolled her eyes. 'When are you going to stop calling me "boss"? You know I prefer you call me by my name.'

'I think it suits you. And you are the boss and, if I might add, a good one compared to what we are used to.'

'Trackhoe is rolling into the compound,' said Sept.

'The recovery team and the investigative team should be here in a few minutes. Get someone to direct the trackhoe driver to the meadow and have the recovery team meet them there. They might find something interesting in Najma's ride after they dig it up,' said Glenda.

'Happy to do it myself,' said Sept. 'I need to get outside. I could use a little of this mountain air.'

'No such luck, buddy. I need to discuss some things with you, Sept. So, Chen, you direct the digger crew.'

Glenda looked over at Chen, their lead technician, who nodded and twisted her lips in one of her many enduring facial expressions. 'Show them where to go and come right back. Wait. Change that. Better that you stay, and Sept and I will walk down with them, and we can talk on the way there and get him some that cool air. We'll be close if you need us.'

'How long do you think it will take then for forensics to wrap things up?' asked Chen.

'Hard to say, me thinks maybe later tomorrow. With forensics out of here later today. The car the preppers buried will get excavated pretty fast, so forensics can do their thing. The unknown is how long it will take for the investigators to get the full story down on how Najma ended up here before they hit the road and start backtracking her movements. Grab your coat, Sept, let's go.'

'What are they going to do with her body?' asked Chen as Glenda, followed by the tall, thin Sept with his always perfectly combed hair, headed for the door.

'Coeur d'Alene probably has an indigent burial program.'

* * *

Jim stretched his long legs as far as he could in the rear seat of the Huey. Pedro had climbed into the front and squeezed in next to the co-pilot. He looked at his watch. A watch he never tired of, at a cost of less than forty dollars. Lightweight, nylon band, plastic case, large numbers, not digital, and lit by pushing the stem. When the battery died, he purchased a new one: the same model or as close as he could find. As he looked at the Timex, he calculated they would arrive before sunset in about twenty minutes.

Brush pulled his muscular body up from where he had sagged in his seat and rubbed his fingers over his short hair. He squinted out the window as they sailed over the wide, slow-moving Columbia River. 'Fifteen minutes, twenty minutes, eh,' as he studied Jim before looking toward the cockpit. He looked at Pedro before turning and giving Jim a thumbs up. Jim nodded.

Brush's thoughts, as they often did, turned to Glenda. *She is one capable lady,* he thought. *And one sexy lady, too. Those double D's, she's as desirable and perfect for me as it gets.* An image formed in his mind of her smile, her strawberry hair, and the three tummy scars from Najma's bullets at the Space Needle. Some would consider them ugly, but he liked them and considered them survivor badges. Then he jumped reluctantly back to the present. 'What's the plan?' he asked.

'Stop at the house. Say hi to Lola and let her see Pedro is safe. The pilots can get some refreshments. After, maybe we'll fly to Methow State and bring the Enstrom back up. Weather looks stable. It might be a good distraction for Pedro.'

'No skis on the skids of your little chopper?'

'The blade wash from this bird should blow most of the fluffy stuff away. We'll check to make sure.'

Brush guessed what Jim was thinking. Bringing the helicopter up avoided driving by the Secret Meadow and Heather's murder site. 'Staying slightly removed from where she was killed by flying over might soften the impact on Pedro. Maybe for all of us.'

'Thinking so,' said Jim.

'Maybe leave him at the house while we go down, or you both stay, and I'll drive down and fly the Enstrom up?'

'We'll let him decide. We'll both have to face up to passing the spot where she was killed sooner or later. I don't think Pedro knew about the glade before. Only Heather and myself. Our secret...' Jim's thoughts moved for a few seconds through mental images of the time they had spent there, made love there, and when they had named it 'Secret Meadow'.

His eyes and thoughts shifted outside as the ground rose below them. The helicopter traced a path over the Loup Loup Pass, which was only a mile behind the ranch. The pilot flew straight over the curving road. They descended into the valley as the road dropped away. Where the conifers stopped, and the sage and rabbit brush took hold. The pilot, with Pedro holding on to the co-pilot's cyclic, nudged the chopper northwest toward Coyote Ridge. Below was the approach that Najma had taken on foot in the early fall, in her failed attempt to kill Jim after the cartel attack on their house. The physical wounds she had inflicted on him in Mexico had healed, except for a few errant nerve endings that fired pain signals at random times.

Jim said into his mic attached to his light green David Clark headphones, 'Approach the house from the east. Drop straight over the ridge, not up the canyon.' He would avoid flying over Secret Meadow this one time, with its memories of his and Heather's special times there and now her death site. Avoid it, at least for the first thing Pedro would see arriving back at the ranch. After Lola and seeing the house, if Pedro chose to go to the airport, they would fly over the area. Hopefully, Pedro would see the special, loving parts of his home before being reminded of the murder site. At the very least, today, Jim reflected, was a day of retribution, not one of them getting killed. Jim and Brush had survived the day, as had Pedro. Najma, their long-term 'nemesis', had not.

Jim toggled the talk switch, 'When we touch down, I'm going to take Pedro into the house. Give us about ten minutes and then come in. Lola will fix you coffee or a snack before we fly back to the airport. We'll get you fueled up. You do a twilight to Ft. Lewis.'

'You got it, Colonel.'

Pedro had his hand on the cyclic, following along with the pilot's movements. Even though the pilot was control-ling the helicopter, he played the game, letting Pedro pretend like he was the one flying. Maybe deep down the boy knew he wasn't really controlling the chopper and decided to let go, saying to the pilot, 'You have the controls,' just as he had been taught by several people, including Jim, Brush, and Will Crystal. After letting go, he turned to Jim. His eyes had lost their sadness, and his lips curled upwards shyly at the corners. It was not a toothy grin. Not a wildly happy smile. It was, however, one that deeply moved Jim. Pedro conveyed everything he needed to. It said many things all at the same time: I'm fragile, I'm strong, and it will take time, but our lives will go on and we will be okay.

He turned back to the front, took hold of the cyclic, and the pilot said, 'You have the controls.' Pedro responded, 'I have the controls.'

The pilot and Pedro descended. Moments later, they flew a few feet above the pine trees lining the top of the ridge, slowed, turned down into the canyon toward the big barn and the old homesteader's cabin, made a loop, and swung up toward the house.

'Flat spot in front of the aspen trees. Break the crust with the skids and then hover a bit before you touch down. Blow some of the white stuff away. We want an LZ for later,' said Brush into the mic.

'Gotcha.'

Jim looked toward the main barn and didn't see anyone. Snow swirled in all directions as the pilot used the skids to break the icy crust before lifting a few feet above and hovering for several seconds before touching down on the exposed frigid ground. Brush climbed out and opened the front door. The blades turned slower and slower as if putting an end to the last few days. The co-pilot passed Pedro into Brush's arms. Pedro kept his eyes closed and held Brush tight for a second before Brush set him on the frozen grass. Pedro held Brush's hand on one side and his dad on the other as they shuffled through crusty snow into the trees and up the steps that led to the octagon deck below the side entrance to the house. The side door swung open as Lola stood perfectly still, then as fast as the short, stout Yaqui Indian could move, she rushed toward Pedro. She grabbed him in her short arms, saying, 'Estás bien!' She looked up at Jim with tears trickling down her face.

Seeing her tears, it was the first time Jim had thought about life changing for her. With this new ability to express emotions, surely hope would follow. She had not had an easy life. She had been hardened by misery and pain; thanks to the cartel, she had learned to expect little else from life. There were never thoughts of a future until Najma had brought Pedro into her life, and perhaps now she was allowing her tears as a statement that her future, their future, held hope. Her mothering instincts rose to the surface. She had lost her son, but perhaps she could save this boy. She had tried to save him at the cartel headquarters. Her inept but well-meaning attempt to escape from Najma and Guillermo's hacienda luckily coincided with the appearance of Colonel Johnson and the Special Forces' surprise attack.

Life for the young Mexican boy and the Mestiza woman with Yaqui blood had changed from cactus and desert to mountains and snow. Good had followed the bad.

The ranch gave them a new life. One that proved, however, that life would still come with its tests. Both had survived the losses of their families in Mexico. Lola's son had been consumed by the cartel gang and later murdered for a reason unknown to her. Surely there could be no more disasters after Heather. The return of Jim and Pedro, along with the news of the serpent's death, brought hope and tears for a better tomorrow.

They stepped inside through the tall wood-framed glass door. Entering an island of warmth scented by burning aspen. Through the window wall, sparse clouds floated above the distant mountain panorama. Lola bustled around, wiping a tear from her face, prodding Jim and Brush to sit in the sunken living room. Trying in vain not to let emotions dominate her. She couldn't stop them: a sudden burst accompanied by snorts escaped her resistance. Once the emotional upwelling burst into the open, her days of pent-up worry and despair were expelled, and she felt reborn. She cast continuous furtive glances at Pedro, her worry turning to happiness.

Jim had never seen her smile this much. And then tried to recall if he had ever seen her smile before. Her round face was punctuated with upturned lips and eyes. Her teeth showing. *Always the stoic, round face. I really don't remember seeing her smile before,* he thought.

The rear hall door clattered closed. Everyone turned toward the sound. Carrying a stack of wood so tall that it barely allowed his grizzled face to be seen was Old Man Shuskin. He stopped. Pedro ran toward him shouting, 'Grankin.' Shuskin's mouth dropped. The wood tumbled to the floor. Pedro ran to him and wrapped his arms around the old man he had learned to love. Lola rolled her eyes, tut-tutting as she grabbed a broom.

'Pick up now, Tom,' as she marched sternly toward them. 'Big mess. Put wood by stove. I no time for this. Mr. Brush needs his coffee,' as she neared the old man and boy, clucking and shaking her head, Pedro, leaving one arm around Shuskin, placed his other arm around Lola and pulled her into a three-way embrace.

Brush looked at Jim, 'Tom?'

Jim shrugged, 'No idea.'

Lola, twittering, pulled away, quickly brushed away a stray tear that was not lost on Tom, and while trying to sound stern, said to him, 'Pick up mess, Mr. Tom.'

Shuskin didn't let go of Pedro and only reluctantly let go of Lola as she wiggled free. The old transient nick-named long ago the *Old Man of the Woods,* and to some the *Phantom of the Woods,* had found a life that he had never dreamed possible. He would cling to it, just as he was embracing two of the most important remaining people in his life. Shuskin had worshipped Heather, his llama lady, whom he had secretly watched in summers past in the mountains. She was kind and gentle. Men were different. At first, he had feared Jim. Males, especially ones who were physically larger, had always represented a danger to him in his previous life as a vagrant on the streets of Seattle. After months, however, the tall blue-eyed Colonel had moved from fear to timid acceptance. Pedro, on the other hand, provided meaning to his life. Shuskin didn't know why he felt the way he did about

Pedro. His background didn't provide the mechanisms to decide such things. The best description was somewhere between a friend and a pal who physically could not hurt him, and an equal with whom he could be himself. A grandfather and grandson relationship. Something he had never experienced before.

Lola admonished Shuskin again and clucked at him about the wood mess. She had said many times to Heather, 'No like him, tell old man stay away from house.' Now she cooked for him, mended his clothes, and during the last few days talked to him, commiserated with him about Heather's death and Pedro being kidnapped at the hands of the "Serpent Lady." Over the past few months, the small woman's stubborn manner softened to the old man. They had both been rescued, just as Pedro had, by Heather and the Colonel. Their shared experiences brought them closer together, as it had for Pedro and Jim.

'Pick up wood. I clean up. Pedro, help Tom. Tell me what you like to eat?'

'Are you hungry, Grandkin?'

Shuskin nodded.

'After floor clean, all go sit in living room,' she said as the pilots knocked on the glass door.

'More men,' she chided attempting unsuccessfully to frown. Pedro, go let in.'

'More to feed, many men,' mumbled Lola as she happily shuffled into the kitchen.'

Jim caught the old man's attention and motioned for him to come over. Shuskin looked down and hesitated while his feet started involuntarily to move toward the Colonel.

'Sit with us.'

Shuskin sat on the long tan leather sofa, looking ill at ease.

'Have there been any problems with the animals?'

'Ah, no, sir.'

'Can I ask you something?' said Jim. 'Is your full name Tom Shuskin?'

Shuskin nodded.

'Would you like it if I called you Tom? And I would like it if you called me Jim. There's no need for the sir.'

'Same for me, Tom. Call me Brush.'

Shuskin, who was still feeling emotional about the happiness he felt finding his young friend alive, contrasted with the loss of Heather, choked back tears. His eyes reddened. When he was a transient, crying or showing weakness would leave him vulnerable. He was adjusting to his place here, his first home in years, feeling more comfortable each day; nevertheless, memories of his old life were hard to dispel, just as they had been for Lola.

He managed to keep the tears at bay. To Jim and Brush, it was apparent that he was struggling with his emotions, and they liked him more for it. The two pilots sat down on the sofa. The one next to Shuskin turned slightly and gave the old man a brief nod. Pedro ran over and jumped onto the chair with Jim. Lola brought coffee on a tray and one orange Fanta for Pedro. Five coffee mugs drifted steam toward the high pine wood ceiling, thirty feet above.

Jim, Brush, and the two pilots each took theirs, Pedro the Fanta. Lola pushed the tray toward Shuskin. 'You take.' Tom, the reinvented Old Man Shuskin, reached up slowly and took the mug. He couldn't help himself as a lone tear emerged and descended to his cheek.

Jim introduced the pilots to everyone, as Tom Shuskin looked down and tried as hard as he could not to shed another tear.

'Tom, it's good to hear that there were no problems with the animals. Thank you for taking care of them,' said Jim, and before he could ask more, Pedro shouted, 'How is my baby, Blue Suede Shoes?'

'Jumping around the field,' said Tom, uncharacteristically, perhaps buoyed by his emotions.

'I want to see her.'

'It's okay with me, as soon as Tom eats,' said Jim.

Pedro looked at Shuskin, waiting for his answer. Tom waited for Jim to nod his approval.

'It's up to you two,' said Jim.

Shuskin nodded as he sipped his coffee and tried, unsuccessfully, to brush away another tear.

'Ah Tom,' said Brush, 'I'm sort of used to addressing you without a first name.'

The Old Man of the Woods, aka Old Man Shuskin, not wanting Brush to see the tears that he now seemed unable to stop, looked down at the floor.

Brush gave it a few seconds and said, 'Tom is a nice name, but I have rather gotten fond of calling you Shuskin. What do you say, eh? Do you mind? I would be happy to call you Tom if you prefer.'

Shuskin shook his head slightly.

Brush, not knowing what that meant, added, 'You tell me anytime if you would rather go by Tom. Somehow, calling you Shuskin seems natural, a special name.'

The next morning, Jim sat in his bedroom lounge chair, ready to catch up on the news. He dialed Maria Dakine on the sat phone.

'How are things in warm, sunny Colombia?'

'Warm and wonderful. The only thing I miss is the white stuff at Christmas. Great to hear from you. I'm so glad Pedro is safe. Everything is fine here. Well, lots of problems. What else should we expect trying to coordinate with the government, rebels, and the World Health people? All being solved little by little each day, though. The virus is still spreading. But at least we seem to be staying about even with it.'

'What are your stats?' asked Jim.

'We've had one death in the FARC compound—I can't think of them anymore as rebels; they've become friends, almost family. Thirty-seven have died in other villages. Mostly vulnerable older people and two children. At last count, 1142 are or have been symptomatic or in the early stages. That's a rough number. While we have good numbers in the compound, it's problematic in the villages. It won't get worse here with everyone in the compound vaccinated, except for one or two holdouts. Obviously, it's not the case elsewhere. When the infected prisoners were released, they dispersed to lots of villages in all directions. It's impossible to track them all down. WHO is quarantining and inoculating, but things will stay worse for a while and then hopefully start to get better.'

'So far, there are no pox cases outside Colombia. World Health tracked the Rio tourists down and inoculated them before symptoms started. They're in Europe and are being held in quarantine to make certain.'

'A few of the infected prisoners dispersed to larger towns farther away. Probably even some will get on a plane and spread the virus. It won't be a big deal, since if one of them manifests symptoms in a foreign country, everyone who has been in contact or remotely close will get inoculated.'

'Makes me wonder what might happen in the future if a virus with a high fatality rate, one we have no vaccine for, and unlike smallpox, has a short latency period— equals a serious, big-time pandemic. Unimaginable devastation.'

'Yep. It's the vaccine and the seven-day plus latency time that allows us to stop it.' It is quite surprising that we have kept so much smallpox vaccine considering Variola major was declared eliminated.'

'Accidental good planning. How's Jago?'

'Promoted, I think. A rising star in a disbanding rebel organization. Yet I think he is pleased. He left for the Amazon with a small group to recover the helicopter.'

*And the gold they hid by it,* thought Jim. Well deserved.

'Lobo and Cherry?'

'Lobo went with Jago, and Cherry is sitting right here.'

'Tell her, hello.'

'She says hi back, and she asks how you and Brush are?'

'Tell her we're both fine.'

'Jim, you mentioned you might come down this way with Pedro. Are you still thinking about it?'

'I need a few days to see how he is doing. Let him settle in and pass some time.'

'Professional advice,' said Maria. 'Take all the time you need. No need to rush decisions, Jim. Oh, I received a strange call today. Remember Professor Iglesias from Rio?'

'Zarita, of course.'

'That's the one. She called today. Things are calming down in Rio. She said that a local paper had published several hideous photos of people infected, and it scared a lot of people. She also asked after you. And then she surprised me by asking if she could pay a visit here.'

'Any reason she would want to come?'

'I asked her the same thing. She said that she had never been that interested in Orthopoxviruses, but since this outbreak originated in her lab, she has been reading up on them. She has some vacation time coming, and while a bit unexpected, she would like to spend it with us in Colombia. She offered any assistance, anything she could help with.'

'It's up to you, of course,' said Jim.

'I don't mind, really. I pushed her a little more, and I got the idea that she wanted to help, but it would be a unique experience after our detective work in Rio, and I have a feeling she would like to bump into you.'

Jim hesitated. Zarita is an interesting, accomplished woman. It didn't matter. He was nowhere close to thinking beyond Heather, and he might never be. *In my line of work, I shouldn't even have a relationship.* He shook his head. The admission to himself that he wasn't interested in Zarita, or any other women, filled him with a strange sense of peace. Heather had been his only passion and would remain so.

'How much longer are you planning on staying in Colombia?'

'Possibly another month, maybe longer.'

'I hope we can visit before you leave.'

'That would be great, and I think it would be good for Pedro. These are sweet, down-to-earth people. I've grown very fond of them. I've told Cherry she should visit us up north sometime, but she would have to take off her bandoliers. Besides the Ecuadorian Amazon, she has never been out of the country.'

'You could take her sailing.'

'I said that to her. It would be fun. We've become quite close. Do you think that the country would allow a rebel in?'

'I think with friends in high places like the Veep, the director of the CIA, she won't have a problem getting travel docs.'

'Okay, I won't discourage it then.'

'I'll give you a heads-up before we come down, assuming we can or do. I am thinking that maybe sooner might be better. Pedro seems okay, so far. However, I don't see how he can be fine after what he saw. I worried about him after what he witnessed in Mexico and now Heather. He seems to compartmentalize, keeping it inside.'

'From a professional point of view, that is most often not good; time will tell.'

'He's overjoyed to be back and to see Tom.' Jim gave it a second until Maria asked, 'Tom?'

'It turns out that our lone man of the woods has a first name.'

'Surprises never end.'

'As far as coming down is concerned, I think it best to let him deal with a ranch without Heather for a few days or maybe weeks before traveling down. Visit you and the FARC, and after, there is a little girl I promised to visit in the Amazon.

'Anytime, Jim. I never had any doubts that you would rescue Pedro. I'm glad he is safe.' Then Maria uncharacteristically choked as she said, 'I'm so sorry. I'll miss her. It hasn't been a very good Christmas for you.'

# Chapter Three

The cargo ship slowed in the dark. Shimmers of moonlight and stars winked on the undulating sea. The quiescent water slumbered and slowly heaved, as if asleep as a small boat quietly plowed the water toward them. Max turned his flashlight on and off four times. The wooden boat, not more than twenty feet long, had bright yellow, blue, black, and red paint. Cigalle squinted during the last flash, as he thought he saw an eye painted near the bow.

'Colorful little buggers,' said Max, who was originally from the smaller Maltese island of Gozo. 'They're called, "Luzzus." The traditional fishing boat of the islands.'

'Stands out,' said Cigalle. 'I don't want to be seen. All those colors make it a target.'

'The bright yellow and red only show up if a light shines on them. There are hundreds of them in the harbor. When that little boat pulls in with dozens of others, they all look the same. It will disappear like a water droplet in a rainbow.'

Cigalle never understood half of what Max said to him on their voyage. Even so, he liked the man. The two made an incongruous pair as they voyaged from the Libyan port of Tripoli to just outside Valletta's Grand Harbor in Malta. One had dark skin clinging to bones, the other had an olive round face and a protruding overfed stomach.

The luzzu bumped the side of the cargo ship. Max grabbed the line that was tossed up and secured it to a cleat. He lowered a rope ladder over the side as two men lowered a small crate with ropes to the wooden boat.

'Vjaggi sikuri.'

Cigalle shook his head.

'It means safe voyage, my friend,' said Max.

In my language, 'Nabad galyo. Lasoco insha Allah,' said Cigalle, as he unsteadily climbed over the side onto the wobbly rope ladder and climbed down.

Max shrugged; he didn't understand a word of Somali any more than Cigalle did Maltese. The word Allah, however, was clear enough. Max, like most Maltese, was a Catholic.

Max leaned over and said, 'Don't be spouting that Muslim lingo on shore. It won't help you stay under the radar.'

As Max listened to the luzzu's soft chugging diminish as it moved toward the edge of the harbor. He opened his cell phone and dialed. After providing a code, he said, 'He's on his way to the ship.'

* * *

They woke to golden jeweled light refracting in the crystalline snow. They visited the animals, and Pedro spent a gleeful time playing with Blue Suede Shoes, Bobby Sox's ninth llama cria. Glenda arrived from Idaho. They, the makeshift family drawn together through hardship, like, and love, lost themselves in the ways of the ranch. Lola cooked. The sun hovered just over the mountains as the winter afternoon wore to a close.

'Pedro, let's go to Winthrop for an ice cream cone.'

'Ice cream, it's cold out, Dad.'

'Best time for them.'

'Well, can Tom go?'

'Sure, if he wants, we'll stop by his cabin.'

They climbed into the Suburban. It was still in all-wheel drive from its last trip up the snow-packed canyon road. Jim twisted the dial back to 2wd. Traction control was a hindrance when going downhill. Jim had wanted a day to pass before taking Pedro down the road and passing *Secret Meadow. The ice cream is an outing and partially an excuse to test our feelings*, thought Jim. With Shuskin in the car, he wondered if it might have as much of a negative effect on the old man who had adored Heather. It probably would. They all had to do it sometime. They might as well get it over with. He wasn't as worried about himself, although he was not looking forward to being so close to what had been their special secret place, the place that had turned into Najma's killing ground. If he and Pedro were going to keep the ranch, and they were, it would be something they would both have to get used to.

Jim stopped with the tires slipping on the hard-packed snow outside the old homesteader's cabin that was now Tom's home. The old man poked his head out of the door and walked toward the car.

'Come on, Tom,' Pedro giggled at Shuskin's new name. 'Get in the back. We go for ice cream cones.'

Shuskin peered in the driver's side window, seeking Jim's permission.

Jim rolled the window down, 'Let's go, Tom. Get a coat before the ice cream melts waiting for us.'

'Funny, Dad.'

'Get in, will ya?' shouted Pedro.

Shuskin smiled, albeit shyly, showing his repaired teeth, and opened the back door.

They looped around the meadow, over a slight rise, and then along an ice-packed, long, straight flat dubbed the "Speedway" before the road descended steeply. At the bottom was a fork where they could drive right up and over the sand hill or left following the road along a creek and the leafless aspen grove. It was not customary to snow-plow the upper sand hill loop, so there was no choice this time of year with the deep-crusted snow on the upper road. Besides, both roads ended up at the same place near the wooden bridge that crossed over the creek with 'Secret Meadow' hidden feet beyond.

As they came around the corner where the upper road descended and met the plowed road, it was only a few hundred feet to a small bridge that passed over the creek and brought them close to their Lilliputian meadow. Jim was not sure what he would or should do as they drove by. *The reason we liked it was because it was hidden, our special place,* Jim reminisced, which would not be for the last time. They all knew it was there, just yards away, even if it remained obscured by trees and brush. He glanced at Pedro, who showed no outward emotion. He seemed frozen. Abruptly, Jim did something he had not intended. He stopped the car just after they rattled over the eight-foot-wide plank bridge.

He turned to Pedro, who was looking down the road and avoiding the meadow. Jim misinterpreted Pedro, who was trying hard to see if there were any glass apples on the old homesteader's tree. He concentrated, willing himself not to think about where Najma had hit him before killing his newly adopted mother. As hard as he tried, an image of her lying in the blood-red snow transposed itself over the frosty apple tree.

'It was one of your mom's favorite places. In the spring, we can gather some of her favorite flowers and leave them there.' Pedro turned to his dad. A tear rolled down his cheek. He said nothing. Jim looked at Pedro, concern in his eyes, feeling his pain, understanding his pain. He gently reached his hand to Pedro's cheek and nudged away the tear. He wanted to say something else, but he didn't know what to say. Perhaps it was good that Pedro was letting his feelings show. He put the car in drive, and they moved past the scraggly apple tree.

'Stop, stop.'

Jim feathered the brakes on the packed, snow-covered

road, stopping just past the old tree. Pedro opened the door and jumped out.

'Come out. Both.'

Jim walked around the car, and Shuskin opened the rear door and stepped down. Pedro was standing in the snow under the apple tree, pointing. 'It's a glass apple. You remember, don't you Tom? Mom showed us.'

Colors danced from the icy surface as the ghostly iced apple transcended their sadness.

# Chapter Four

Martin and Bertrand moved toward the sofa in the General's office. It had become their daily custom. The General sat in a wing chair as his PA set down a tray of coffee for the General and Martin, and Earl Grey tea with milk for Bertrand.

'Najma, finally, is a closed book,' said General Crystal, wistfully thinking about BWC where his adventures with Najma had begun. *I wish the same could be said for my time at the CIA,* a recurrent thought. He had reluctantly left BWC to be the CIA's director. 'Let's get to it. What's the state of the world today?'

'There is one item in particular,' said Bertrand, 'that I want to bring to your attention on this fine winter morning. Martin's group has been tracking a Somali after various intercepts suggest a possible terrorist threat aimed at Europe.'

'We, so far, have little information,' added Martin. 'We are trying to make sense of it, build a story. A Somali male, possibly a courier or smuggler. With an unidentified link to Mossad.'

The General raised an eyebrow. 'New one for me: Israeli intelligence partnering with Somalia?'

'Our thoughts exactly,' said Martin. 'We don't know much at this stage. A few intercepts, which are in your briefing, and a Somali with unknown cargo got dropped off this morning outside Valletta's main harbor in Malta. It appears he's headed to a cruise ship, leaving today, that will work its way around Sicily, up the Italian coast, stopping in Sardinia, Corsica, and Nice, with a final stop in Marseille. Then it picks up new passengers for Majorca, Spain, and Portugal, then heads across the Atlantic to its home port in Antigua.'

'This is one big ship,' added Bertrand. 'Nearly six thousand people are on board. It was designed for the Caribbean and is making a special voyage through the Med after repairs in Malta. A newish crew, many not experienced, makes it an easy target if he is smuggling.'

'Smuggling what, where?' asked General Crystal.

'Unknown really. Too little information yet,' said Martin. The only reason we brought it up to you now is, according to our source, there's a biological slash terrorist element. Nothing much to go on, but I thought you might want to pass it along to the BWC.'

'Martin, liaise with Sheilla and keep me informed. Leave Colonel Johnson out of it and anything else, for that matter. He needs some downtime.'

* * *

The luzzu's bright colors were duskily illuminated by a flashing green light at the end of a stone breakwater and a red light on the other side. Red and green alternated every few seconds, absorbing into the boat's other colors while intensifying the reds and greens. It carved through the smooth surface with its quiet four-stroke outboard motor attached to the side. Just beyond the breakwater, shadowed limestone cliffs reached into the night sky. The rocky peninsula's natural limestone, crowned with illuminated limestone-block buildings, several with multi-colored lights. The buildings, the walls, and the breakwater were all constructed from the same tan-yellow rock, the only building material readily available on an island where few trees grow.

The architecture shaped by the cream-colored stone created a pleasing appearance. It made the Maltese Islands' structures homogeneous, warm, and texturally stunning. To Cigalle's left, jutting out on a point, was the harbor's guardian from the time of the Knights Templar— Fort Saint Angelo. Its limestone walls also rose ominously into the dark sky, mirroring the Valletta side of the harbor. The fort, on a center peninsula, was flanked by two prominent points: Senglea and Kalkara, known together as the three cities. The fort that protected the harbor in the days of the Knights of Saint John was confusingly called by two names: Vittoriosa by some and Birgu by others, depending on what name you felt like calling it on any given day. The truth: the peninsula is Vittoriosa and the city in the center of it is Birgu.

Each of the three ancient "cities" was surrounded by

hundreds of small boats, mostly tethered to multicolored plastic floats. As they rounded the fort and entered the harbor, Cigalle looked in awe as gleaming super yachts came into view, lined up along the shore below the fort. Several long lines extended from their bows far out into the harbor to six-foot-diameter floating balls. Their sterns, tied to the shore, lined up one after another. Cigalle had never seen boats so big, and he wondered who could own such things.

On shore, in several directions, were massive floodlit churches. They dwarfed even the 300-foot yachts, but not the fifteen-story cruise ship tethered next to the cliff on the Valletta side. It towered almost as tall as the dusty yellow limestone rock and block wall supporting the base of the city.

The luzzu skimmed around the fort, far below Valletta, before turning into the channel separating Vittoriosa and Senglea. The first superyacht, a black-hulled, glistening 240-foot boat, dwarfed their luzzu. It made Cigalle feel as small and insignificant as perhaps it made its owner feel powerful. As they passed the black ship, its hull shimmering with the city lights, several more yachts came into view, many longer and taller. On the opposite side of the harbor from the monster ships were small boats tightly packed and anchored by bow and stern lines tied to plastic containers: bleach bottles, milk jugs, plastic Coke bottles, and empty motor oil containers.

The luzzu slowed and turned, squeezing between sister boats, before blending into the flotilla, just as Max had said it would. Max, who had befriended him, unknown to Cigalle, was one of several informants paid by various intelligence agencies. Malta was as close to North Africa as it was to Europe. It was a natural location to bridge the two worlds. Max's position on a cargo ship that plied the waters between the two regions put him in a unique position to report illicit trade or shipments, or on rare occasions, as Max suspected, possible terrorists or smugglers such as Cigalle. He liked his dual role, from which he gratefully received a CIA and other supplements to his income.

The luzzu nudged its way to the stone sidewall. Cigalle, and the two dark-haired men who had not uttered a word, lifted the trunk onto the stone-paved walkway. *The whole place is made of stone,* thought Cigalle. The two men put the trunk in the back of a dark-green Suzuki soft-topped jeep-like Vitara before motioning Cigalle to get inside.

They drove down a deserted narrow street, their car dwarfed by the stone walls of the old city. Boats and empty café tables lined the water's edge. The roadway seemed to be more of a passenger walkway than a street for cars. It reminded Cigalle of small market towns in Somalia. When they weren't separated from the break-water by out-of-the-water boats, chairs, and tables, they were only feet from the water's edge and the myriad small Maltese boats swinging in the harbor on their makeshift buoys. On the inland side were cafés with chairs stacked for the night and grand stone staircases leading up to an ancient village.

They drove around boats perched on blocks, some

being repaired or repainted along with a few decaying derelict boats, deserted to the elements by owners who either abandoned them or were long gone themselves. As they passed through one oversized arch that looked like part of an old castle, contemporary sheets of glass met the hundreds of years-old stone housing a boutique hotel. The narrow roadway became a street as they drove past several closed shops, then up a hill packed with parked cars on both sides. A sandwich board abandoned to the night on the sidewalk said "Fresh Lampuki." The dorado was a popular catch when it migrated past the islands in the fall. This time of year, the sign might better have read "Frozen Lampuki."

The street went through another stone façade reading Saint Helen's Gate. They picked up speed as the road descended the hill before passing through a long tunnel, circling a roundabout, and then a mile-long divided highway before they slowed as they entered another smaller harbor road. Sitting alongside the edge was the massive cruise ship. The top parts loomed above them, rising over 200 feet, almost to the base of the ancient city of Valletta.

# Chapter Five

'This looks like an Old West town in the movies, Dad.'

'It does, and the city ordinances prevent anyone from building anything that doesn't look like it.'

You mean, 'Everyone wants it to stay looking like it does for the tourists.'

'That's exactly right.'

Jim pulled into a parking spot on the street just past the Duck Brand Restaurant.

'Ice cream time,' shouted Pedro.

They walked down the sidewalk, crossed the street, and stepped up onto a weathered boardwalk. A café with outdoor tables and umbrellas wrapped up tight for the winter was nestled in the back, about thirty feet away. Three locals sat talking, bundled in heavy coats. Sitting at another table, sipping steaming paper cups of coffee, two coasties, wearing REI hiking clothes, braved the cold weather under the hazy blue sky. Jim, Tom, and Pedro walked together around some empty planters and turned right toward the ice cream shop's entrance. Pedro stopped short and moved closer to Jim.

A stocky, pug-faced boy about six inches taller than Pedro came through the door licking a strawberry double-scoop cone. He looked at Pedro, sneered, and said, 'If it ain't that little brown baby-boy spic. What are you doing here? What makes you think you can come here?' asked Butch, looking back toward his father for approval.

Jim put his arm around Pedro and said, 'Let's go inside and get our ice cream.'

Butch didn't move. He just stood, blocking the door. Old man Shuskin had known lots of belligerent and mean people from his life on the street. He felt some comfort being near Jim, but he did what he had always done—hid from trouble. As he backed up until he bumped into a large man and started to tremble.

A man inched up close behind the boy, he was wearing a blue plaid shirt, jeans, and cowboy boots. He had the same wide features as Butch.

'Stay put kid,' he said in a slurred voice. 'Let's hear this here, *Coastie's* answer. You gonna answer it now, right?'

Another man with beefy hands and a rough two-day beard over a weather-worn face walked up on Jim's left and stood about six feet away. Jim sized him up, not liking what he saw. A rough character. He was far enough away that Jim ignored him and turned back to the man who was apparently Butch's father.

'Go ahead, Pedro. Step around him. Pedro looked up and reluctantly moved in front of his dad and started by

Butch. Grinning, Butch moved sideways, blocking Pedro, who looked back at his dad, not knowing what to do.

Butch's father, now facing Jim, was about the same six feet in heighth. He was wider, with broad, grizzled facial features. His flat nose and cheeks were covered in blue spider veins from years of heavy drinking. Jim moved in a little closer to the man and said, 'My name is Johnson. What's yours?'

'That ain't what I asked you, *Coastie*. You didn't answer my boy's question. That there's rude.' The rough-looking man smiled at his friend's comments and stepped a foot closer.

'Was there a question?' asked Jim.

'He said this here little brown shit was a spic, and he had no business being here in this town or country.'

The rough-looking man said, 'Spic and shit all the same color. Worth about the same too, I reckon.'

Pedro started to shake.

'If it was a question, not worth answering.' More of a statement and, I'm guessing, one the boy learned from you.' Jim could feel the man tensing. His knuckles pulled into a fist. Right-handed, and so was his buddy. Jim swiveled his head a few degrees to the right, keeping Butch's father in his peripheral vision. He didn't like surprises from the rear. He was too late as he first caught a flash image of Old Man Shuskin visibly shaking and standing wide-eyed, frozen in place, just as a third man circled his chest with two beefy arms, pinning Jim's arms. Beer breath permeated the cold air.

Butch's father pulled his right arm back and said,

'Ain't no place here for spics, or llama lady tree-huggers, or smart-ass *Coasties*. This here's country is fer men.' He wound up for a big right hook. No worry about telegraphing it, since his big brother held Jim from behind in a bear hug. Making a show out of his wind-up, Butch's father moved his eyebrows up and down twice and grinned at Jim with tobacco-stained teeth.

As the man pulled his arm back for what would be a vicious punch, Jim did something that he had learned early in the army's basic self-defense courses. He raised his boot up the leg of the man holding him, scraped it down the big man's shin, and slammed it on the arch of the brother's foot. The blow was enough of a distraction that the man loosened his grip. Using gravity and his weight, Jim dropped a few inches out of the man's grasp and shifted his body to his left. He turned his fist underhand and drove it back into the brother's groin. He could have softened the blow, but he didn't.

Jim was angered by these men who had bullied all their lives, passing uncouth views on to their children. Combined with Heather's death and Pedro's kidnapping, any sympathy he might have garnered for these rednecks evaporated.

Pedro looked toward the street and saw Brush and Glenda and weakly yelled, 'Help!'

Brush shrugged, putting his arm around Glenda's waist. 'You're not going to help him?' asked Glenda. 'We'll see, beautiful. Let's walk over a little closer.'

The few people standing outside the café by the tables stood frozen. They stayed out of other men's affairs, and that reasoning allowed them to rationalize not getting involved with the three notorious brawlers.

Jim couldn't see the man's face, but he was familiar with the sick feeling coursing through Butch's dad's brother's veins. His testicles were not only hit, but later, everyone would hear that one had been ruptured by the blow.

Butch's dad's roundhouse punch arrived. The timing was off. It was high, and Jim was now low. Instead of hitting Jim, he hit his brother square in the nose making a crunching noise as the man fell back onto the gray weathered planks, his weight shaking the deck.

Jim pivoted to his right and instinctively covered his groin with both hands. He lifted his left foot and drove his Lowe boot into the man's right knee. It made a noise between a crack and a crunch as Butch's dad's kneecap moved out of the femoral groove, fracturing it along with the patella. Butch's father would always walk stiff legged, with lingering pain to remind him of this day. If his son was smart enough, he would learn that fights were unpredictable. You never knew how good your opponent was. There was always someone more skilled, something his father had not added to the boy's limited knowledge bank.

The rough man stepped in just as Jim stood straight. Jim stood relaxed, with knees slightly bent, his left foot forward. The man had been in enough fights to know not to telegraph the punch. He drove his fist straight in like a piston. No wind-up. Putting his muscles and body into the blow, his oversized knuckles zeroed in on Jim's nose and upper lip.

Jim shifted his head to the left as the beefy fist skimmed past his right ear. The man's momentum carried him forward, shifting his weight onto his forward left foot. Jim swung his right foot around and behind the man's ankle. He had choices to make: to win, to disable, or to kill. Jim knew he could kill the man, and he was angry enough to do it. There was no question, however, about what he would do with Pedro and Butch watching. Putting the man down was enough. Pedro didn't need to see another person die.

Jim took a middle choice. Instead of laying his forearm across the man's chest and pushing him over the fulcrum made by his foot, Jim placed an open hand just below his throat and none too gently shoved him backward. A modified jujitsu move. The man's right foot and leg were caught by Jim's. He was off balance and easy to push to the ground. He pivoted back over Jim's dark blue boot like an upside-down pendulum. He went down hard. His skull hit the plank decking with a sickening thud.

Jim knew from experience that the harder the surface, the more lethal the move. Instead of pushing the man's head up with his palm and then propelling his head to the ground, he chose the more compassionate position. Nevertheless, he caused more pain than if he had propelled him over more slowly from the chest. This suited Jim's mood.

It was a lucky choice. The off-balance body went down with little resistance, his head slapping into the wood planks. There was no give as his head hit a board directly above a joist. Another cracking sound. This time, a skull.

Butch's ice cream cone fell from his hand. It landed with a splat upside down. He pulled his arm back to punch Pedro, an easy target, who stood stock-still in fear and disbelief. Three men lay on the wooden walkway. The rough-looking one lay silent while the two brothers moaned and cursed. Pedro didn't move. He didn't even see Butch's fist coming toward him. Brush's arm reached over Pedro's head, stopping the fist with an open hand.

Butch dropped his gaze and looked down at his father. Confusion contorted his face, and tears rolled down his cheeks. Brush let go of the boy's fist and pulled Pedro back to him. Butch's lips moved. He looked at his father. Brush thought he heard him say, 'That'll teach you,' but he wasn't sure.

With Pedro safely tucked against him, Brush said to Jim, 'Having fun without me, eh?'

Jim turned to Pedro. 'Take Tom inside, son. Get yourselves cones. I'll be in shortly.'

Pedro almost said no. He didn't want to leave his dad's or Brush's side, but he was in too much shock to disobey. He walked back and grabbed Shuskin's hand.

'I'd like one too,' said Glenda.

'I'll be in a minute,' said Jim.

Pedro and Tom hesitatingly stepped over Butch's father and around Butch. They stepped into the warmth of the ice cream shop, a famous store with over eighty flavors.

Someone had called the sheriff when the ruckus started. Sheriff Jay McKenney walked up to Jim with his deputy trailing behind.

'Colonel.'

'Jay.'

'What just happened here?'

Before Jim could speak, Glenda said, 'Sheriff, we witnessed the whole thing, and there are a couple more people outside the café that did too. How about letting Jim go in and take care of his son, and we'll give you a rundown first?'

The sheriff rubbed his chin as though he were stroking a goatee. 'Well, okay. I know these three. They cause me trouble all the time, so I expect it was their doing alright. You three are all best pals; you might not be the best ones to tell an unbiased account.'

'Sheriff.'

'Ms. Stuart. It is nice to see you again, by the way.'

'The Major is the Colonel's friend, but don't forget what they teach you in the army—don't volunteer, keep it simple, and always tell the truth. Truth and honor. And you know me from a few days ago. You'll get the straight story. Besides, I expect you'll use proper procedures and take everyone's statements individually. Obviously, none of us would have time to concoct a story.'

'Yeah, I knew that. I was just considering how it would look to the judge when these boneheads go and get themselves some slick attorney and sue. Good thoughts to keep in mind along with using, as you say, good procedures.'

The deputy put his radio in its holster and said, 'Sheriff, those boys have been in the Six-Gun Saloon. The bartender said they drank three beers each. They weren't drunk, but they were pushing some tourists toward a fight when they left.'

'Go back on over and take a statement before anyone leaves the saloon.'

The sheriff looked at Glenda, who had only days before been his boss when the task force was in town searching for Najma. 'Figured that's where those boys had been. The bar is where they mostly spend their time. First, Ms. Stuart, lets you and I sit for a spell, and the Major here can give a statement to Willis as soon as he gets back. Willis, before you go to the tavern, get the witnesses' over yonder names and phone numbers, and tell them to stay put. Check their ID.'

'Got it, boss.'

Glenda turned toward Jim, who gave her and the sheriff a slight nod. 'Let me know when you're ready for me, Jay,' he said as the local ambulance pulled to a stop out front, its siren winding down.

Jim looked at Pedro's school antagonist, Butch, thinking the boy didn't have much of a chance in life. He turned away and went inside. A minute later, he opened the door, holding out a new strawberry ice cream cone to the boy.

'Better wait inside where it's warm. We can call your mother.'

For a second, Jim thought Butch was going to swipe the outstretched cone away, but instead, he reached out and took it.

# Chapter Six

A metal-grated walkway spanned the water from the shore to a sliding door, which led into the bowels of the ship. A man stood fidgeting on the deserted street as the green Suzuki drove up.

The ship's upholsterer held out his hand. 'Money now,' while he scanned nervously in all directions.

Cigalle expected the demand. He reached into his coat pocket and passed over an envelope he had been given containing 5,000 euros. The cash represented more than ten months' salary to the ship's Libyan assistant upholsterer.

'Hurry,' he said as he walked over the catwalk onto the ship.

The two men with Cigalle went to the back of the Suzuki and opened the tailgate. The upholsterer appeared from the ship's hold and waved frantically.

They followed him to a storeroom full of upholstery material and sewing supplies. 'Put it there,' he said, pointing to the side. The two men put the chest down. The ship worker moved some boxes and supplies on top of and in front of the trunk.

'You,' pointing at Cigalle. 'Haste, Taejal, Taejal, follow me.' He waved toward the door and told the two Maltese to leave fast. The two men shrugged, walked back outside, and drove off into the night. Cigalle was led into a compact cabin buried in the lower deck, where the workers, who never met passengers, lived and went about their jobs, working endless twelve-hour days, seven days a week.

The man closed the door. There was a cardboard box sitting on a small table. Inside was an oval loaf of bread wrapped in clear plastic labeled David's Bread, miscellaneous fruit, a bottle of strawberry jam, peanut butter, instant coffee, salami, four tins of tuna, and a large bag of potato chips. Cigalle looked in the small refrigerator: a carton of whole milk, six bottles of Pepsi, a squeeze bottle of salad cream, a red cabbage, and seven onions.

With water from the small sink, and a kettle to boil it, he would drink and eat well during the five-day journey to Marseilles. He was not accustomed to this much food. A narrow door opened to a tiny toilet. He would rather have the chest in his room if only the ship's upholsterer had not said a customs officer could enter and go through his belongings. The man said customs officers would not look in the small storage room, and immigration checkers would not check workers while in the EU zone.

Cigalle was receiving 7,000 euros to escort the chest to Marseilles along with two bottles of soda. His family was given 1,000 euros in Somali currency before his departure.

A fortune to them. Cigalle had learned both French and Somali as a child. He had been offered the courier position, not because he spoke French, an official language of Somalia. It was because his sister's boyfriend's older brother was a member of the Egyptian Islamic Jihad. The EIJ needed to recruit someone who would not be identified as a terrorist.

Barwaaqo knew his girlfriend Shara's family was poor and would jump at the chance for so much money. If Cigalle did not return, the family would have no way of finding out what might have happened to him. Barwaaqo, on behalf of Egyptian Islamic Jihad, would also tell them that Cigalle had taken the money and run off, and it would be dangerous for them to try to find him. The EIJ and their al-Qaeda partners would do what they could to locate him. The family would not be able to go to the government even if they knew anyone who could help. They would be admitting that Cigalle was part of a terrorist organization. Barwaaqo wondered why all the talk when they could kill the family and keep the 1,000 euros.

Cigalle was told that the trunk was loaded only with some old statues packed in sand. It was a ruse in case someone thought Cigalle had something valuable and tried to rob him. A thief would think the fake artifacts were what he was smuggling, and customs officials would not take any interest if they were inspected. He also was given two bottles of Pepsi-Cola. They contained the same virus that was multiplying in Cigalle's blood. Unbeknownst to him, he was carrying a viral strain that Dr. Jelle

Visser wanted. Each was insurance for the other in case something happened to the bottles or Cigalle.

The doctor in Tripoli told him that a well-known research hospital in France wanted a sample of an African disease, but they were being prevented from obtaining it. They were willing to pay a lot of money, which was why Cigalle was needed and being paid so well to bring the bottles with the sealed disease to France.

'You get a free cruise and food, along with a fortune for your family. The doctor had an empty Pepsi bottle and showed Cigalle how the samples were stored inside. They had a glass container at the bottom that was sealed. The Pepsi, he said, would be safe to drink if someone opened it. He gave Cigalle a long lecture on what to do if someone took an interest in the Pepsi bottles or questioned him.

Dr. Egal then told Cigalle that he needed some inoculations. 'Do needles scare you?'

'I do not like them, Doctor.'

'It will be safer for you and better if you are questioned. Here is a card with the shots I am giving you.'

'Many shots?'

'Only two injections. They will not hurt much. You may see some redness or swelling afterward. If you do, it might become itchy. Do not worry.'

'They are for hepatitis and one other. See, it says so here in French and English: hepatitis A and B. Roll up your sleeve.' He swabbed Cigalle's arm and filled his syringe with the contents of a vial. 'You will be safe now from these diseases when you go home, and the French authorities, if they ask, will let you pass as you have been inoculated. You will need a second inoculation, which you will be given before you return home.'

Cigalle smiled at the cot in his cabin, *better than a dirt floor,* as he remembered what the doctor had told him. The two Pepsi bottles were now in the small refrigerator where he had been told to put them. The cot was comfortable. He would eat some food and lie down. First, he locked the cabin door. Soon, he was full. Not something he was accustomed to in Somalia. After the day-long voyage on the cargo ship with Max, he was getting used to a full stomach. Minutes later, he was fast asleep.

# Chapter Seven

They managed to drive through the main gate in twilight and past Secret Meadow without saying anything. It suited Jim as he didn't want to think about what had happened there any more than Pedro did.

'I want to stop at the barn and see my baby.'

'It's almost dark, but sure, Shus ... Tom can check on the other animals.'

As they turned up the road to the barn from the cabin, an arm reached out of the vet room window and waved.

'That arm belongs to Roy or Ben unless Lola came down to the barn,' said Jim.

'No way. She never come to barn.'

Pedro had the certainty of youth. Jim, conversely, expected the unexpected and was not surprised when it happened.

Tom sat silently, as was his custom. Especially around Jim. That hadn't changed, but Shuskin was starting to feel more comfortable with the Colonel. The just-shy-of-six-foot man, slim but muscular, had protected him in town. Saved all of them. He had given him more things at the cabin than he could ever remember having in his life. The Colonel asked for nothing in return. He was even paying him to work, which he would have been more than happy to do without pay in exchange for the cabin. He had little use for money. Even so, he carefully hid the bills in a tin on the shelf. He had taken the money out twice now and lined all the bills up on the table to admire them.

'My bet's that it's Ben. What do you think, Tom?'

Shuskin sat, not knowing what to say.

'It's Ben. I know it is,' said Pedro.

Then Shuskin smiled with his new white teeth and said, 'Rosie.'

Jim turned around and glanced at the old man of the woods. There was a heartfelt sincerity in how he said, "Rosie." He was displaying genuine affection for Jim's tawny coarse-coated Irish Wolfhound.

Brush and Glenda were driving behind them in the mechanically functional, twenty-year-old, battle-worn dark green Dodge pickup. Feeding 1,500-pound cows when they jostled for their hay left deep dents and undulations along both sides of the truck.

Jim pulled to a stop, and Pedro jumped out and ran into the barn, yelling for Grankin to hurry. Rosie started to follow Pedro into the barn. Instead she turned, and stood looking at the Suburban, waiting for Jim.

'Steering feels wobblier than the last time I drove this thing,' said Glenda.

'You ever check the gas mileage on this?' asked Brush.

'I think it was over half full when we left. By the time we got to Winthrop, it was below a quarter tank.'

'The gauge is off near the low end. It never shows less than a quarter tank. You might have run out if you hadn't filled it up. When I first purchased it and drove over the hump, I ran out of gas on this side of the pass and had to get Roy to bring me fuel. Small tank and the gearing doesn't get you very far. Not to mention the faulty gauge.'

'Something tells me it was its last drive over the pass. Never make it again,' said Brush.

'Didn't make it the first time.'

'Besides, the way it looks, it might scare people,' said Glenda.

'Once upon a time, it had a pretty clean body until we used it for feeding and the cows bashed it, but it still has its good points. No worries about door dings when you park in town.'

'Let's see what's going on in the barn,' said Glenda. 'Then I'm ready to sit down for a while and smell Lola's cooking. Have a glass of wine. Whatcha think, big guy?'

'Sounds like a plan. And did I mention, I'm glad you're here?'

'That's a me too. Thanks to Will.'

As they neared the door, they could hear Pedro's excited voice. 'Yeah.'

'He conked all three of them?' asked Ben.

'Guess what, Colonel Johnson, you've got a rep now,' said Glenda. 'How're you going to handle that?'

Jim opened the door. Ben stood holding a baby bottle with a small-sized nipple, and looked up smiling, 'I was about to feed the fawn when I heard you driving up, so I stopped.' Standing, tapping its feet, and nudging Ben's leg with its nose was the tiny, rescued deer fawn.

'Me, me,' said Pedro. Ben handed him the half-sized bottle full of cow's milk.

The fawn immediately presented herself and aggressively grabbed the small silicone nipple.

'What are you going to call her?' asked Glenda.

'Tinker Tot,' said Ben.

'We named my baby llama too,' said Pedro. 'Her name is Blue Suede Shoes.'

'Interesting name,' said Brush. 'For short, you can call her BS or Bull ...'

Glenda elbowed him before he could say it, gave him a look, shook her head, and changed the subject. 'He sure slurps that down. Don't I remember hearing something about them imprinting on people?'

'Fortunately, it probably won't happen this time,' said Jim. 'This little girl had enough time with her mother.'

Pedro giggled.

'We have a llama who's imprinted,' said Ben. 'Rocky.'

'We found him at a horse farm,' said Jim. 'He was with Bobby Sox and her daughter Tulip and another male, Tulip's son Darby. Our first llama purchase was the four of them. They're all still here. Heather wouldn't hear of getting rid of them.' *Even the irascible Rocky,* he thought, thinking fondly of the life they had had with the animals.

'So, he's imprinted?'

'Both the males were imprinted. Darby, though, is friendly and loves to eat any sort of food you feed him.

He's big, so he can be a little pushy because he likes to be close to you. Rocky has a different personality.'

'I think I can guess what Rocky's attitude is like,' said Glenda. 'His name says it all.'

'He's unpredictable and dangerous. The people didn't know any better and cuddled them from the moment they were born. An imprinted llama doesn't know if it's a human or a llama, so it treats llamas and people the same way. The problem seems to be if the llama has an aggressive or nasty personality, and Rocky is one of those. A naturally surly guy. He attacks and spits at people just like he does the llamas. He can hurt you if he charges and hits you with his breastbone.'

'I guess they gave him an appropriate name,' said Glenda.

'He knocked the vet out,' said Ben. 'Rocky flattened him, and when Murray went down, he hit his head hard and got knocked out.'

'I was worried that time,' added Jim. 'He's had a concussion one too many times. When I revived him, he kept saying over and over, 'Jim, what are we doing today? Where are we?' Over and over. I met his wife on the main road. She called the hospital to alert them. On the way there, he didn't remember he was in the car. He opened the door at sixty miles an hour and started to climb out.'

It was obvious that Ben had not yet heard about Murray's death. Jim had decided not to add to Pedro's grief by telling him that Najma had killed another of their friends. Murray, the local vet, was more than just a friend to Jim and Heather; he had almost become extended family.

'What're you going to do with Rocky?' asked Glenda.

'You could eat him, eh?' suggested Brush.

Everyone stared at him.

'I wasn't serious,' said Brush, smiling.

Glenda grabbed his hand and said, 'Let's head up to the house and sit by the fire before you have any more ideas.'

'Ride up with me. Ben can bring Pedro and Tom up in the Dodge. If you can get Rosie into the truck, bring her too.'

As soon as they left, Ben said, 'I want to hear all about what happened in town. You seen it too, Shuskin?'

Tom nodded. Still, he said nothing. Not that he felt as though he couldn't talk with Pedro and Ben. They were not the same as the adults. The ones in authority. He didn't want to say how scared he had been. 'Pedro was closer,' is all he would say.

'It happened fast,' said Pedro. 'Three big guys. One grabbed Dad from behind. Then, BAM! POW! He was groaning on the porch boards. Then Butch's dad, BAM! On the deck too. Then the last. A big ugly guy out cold on his back. He was still out when they took him to the hospital.'

'Wow,' said Ben. 'Did you see what he did? We could learn.'

'He saved us,' Shuskin blurted out.

Ben and Pedro stared at him.

'Brush saved me from Butch,' said Pedro. 'I didn't see his fist coming at me.'

'We gotta get a-going,' said Ben. 'We can come back and feed the rest of them there critters later. I want to hear more on the way up to the house.'

'Now I understand Mama telling me to talk right,' said Pedro.

Ben cuffed him on the shoulder as they walked out to the truck. Ben and Pedro exuded confidence in their walk and thoughts, thinking they might have Jim as a teacher fast-tracking them to warrior status.

Shuskin wanted nothing to do with learning to defend himself. He knew from long experience how to make himself invisible: make yourself small, shrink into the shadows. Even so, he didn't always escape unscathed. If it hadn't been for Jim, he might not have escaped tonight.

While the Colonel had always made him feel nervous, those jitters were subsiding more every day. Then tonight he had been their protector. And Mr. Brush probably could be too. *He has always been nice to me.*

Shuskin continued his thoughts; *Maybe he will keep me safe.* Still, he was a little confused, in that he knew the man could physically hurt him if he chose to. But he could also keep others from hurting him. He realized that instead of being afraid, he had a guardian angel to keep him safe. Maybe even two. But Shuskin's life left him uneasy with trusting people. Pedro, Ben, and Lola were different. He felt no threat from any of them.

* * *

Cigalle was sound asleep until a long, sonorous blast of the horn announced the cruise ship docking in Marseille. Minutes later, there was a knock on his door; the first knock since they had departed Valletta's Grand Harbor. The upholsterer motioned with his hand to follow.

'Wait, I need to pack my things.'

'Make it fast.'

'It will only take a minute.'

Cigalle opened his small rucksack and loaded the contents of the refrigerator, including the two Pepsi bottles. He stuffed the rest of his meager belongings in and followed the man into the hall.

They walked to the same loading door and the same metal walkway.

'Where is my trunk?'

'Go outside, turn left, and there is a van waiting.' The man turned quickly and disappeared. Cigalle did as he was told. A woman stood by the side of a silver Peugeot van.

'Bonjour.' She opened the sliding door and motioned him inside. Using the sun and the shadows, Cigalle could tell they were driving north. Ninety minutes later, the van stopped at an ornate black iron gate. The driver got out, took a padlock off, and unwrapped a heavy chain, drove through, and reversed the process, closing the gate. They drove on a little-used narrow road. Sometime in its past, it had been gravel. Through the seasons, the gravel had mixed with clay, grass, and moss, leaving a greenish track through the woods.

Five minutes of driving, and the track emerged into a

meadow, which transitioned into a lawn surrounding a gray stone castle. Cigalle had never seen anything so big. Then the woman opened the sliding door, and they walked to an enormous door with an arched top surrounded by stone carvings. The heavy wooden door opened seconds before they arrived.

Another woman said, 'Monsieur Warsame, entrez s'il vous plait.'

'Merci,' answered Cigalle with his perfect Somali French.

Three men wearing white lab coats stood a few feet away. A thin man with an odd protruding stomach, thinning sandy brown hair, and bright blue eyes stepped forward. He was about the same five-foot-eight-inch height as Cigalle. Other than their height, there was little comparison between the two men. Cigalle had short, curly black hair with a slightly receding hairline. He was thin, nearly gaunt. His inky dark skin contrasted with that of the pasty white skin of the man, as did his deep-set black eyes compared to the odd man's blue eyes.

Cigalle had seen many people in his home country with similar protruding stomachs. An aid worker explained undernourished people use their muscle tissue for energy when there is not enough food or fat. The stomach muscles weaken and allow the intestines to push forward. It was especially common with children. *This rich Frenchman could not be undernourished?* wondered Cigalle.

'I would like to introduce Dr. Jelle Visser,' said the woman. 'The doctor speaks Dutch and English. I understand you do not speak Dutch, so we shall all speak English. Other than Dr. Visser, the rest of the house staff mostly speak French. You will be comfortable speaking to them.'

'I am pleased to meet you, Mr. Warsame. Let me introduce you to my assistant, Heinrich. He speaks French, German, and English. Please follow me. We are moving the trunk into our laboratory. While we walk, perhaps you would be so kind as to explain the meaning of your name. I understand that many African names have meanings.'

'In my country, we do not often use surnames. My papa had one simply for convenience when he worked with Westerners. An optimistic person, my father decided on the name Warsame. It means bearer of good news.'

'Very interesting,' said the American-trained doctor, rubbing a hand over his thinning hair. He had a slight lisp, followed by a laugh that seemed to stay inside him, vibrating in his bowl-sized stomach paunch.

# Chapter Eight

Jim walked up the hall carrying a three-foot-long log balanced on his shoulder. Brush was close behind with two smaller-diameter logs. Jim laid the log on the smoldering embers. Small red plumes jumped from the hot cinders, flickering up the bark, and just as abruptly, disappearing. The oversized log slowly settled into the glowing remains of its disintegrated predecessor. Flames started their dance in earnest up the sides of the rough ponderosa bark, bringing a golden glow to the room. Brush set the two smaller pieces on the side of the mica-schist ledge.

As Jim pulled the wire mesh across the opening, Glenda said, 'That is definitely a grand fireplace. I've never seen one that big before, other than in movies with old castles and mansions.'

The fireplace had become a major undertaking when Jim built the house. He had spent hours with Ben finding and loading the right-sized rocks from the steeper hillsides

100 meters below the meadow and what had become Tom Shuskin's cabin. A local stonemason had agreed to construct the two-story stone wall. It formed one side of the living room adjacent to the equally tall glass window wall.

As heat soaked into the log, the flames blazed and reflected off the tall windows. The reddish yellow reflections on the glass only partially obscured the view of the snow-capped mountains that rose high above the lower valley in a spectacular panorama. The windows were unobstructed by trees where they faced the mountains and Oval Peak. On the left side of the living room, and opposite the fireplace, was an equally tall, but less wide window wall. Its twenty-foot double-pane windows would have let the house heat up in the summer if it were not shielded from the sun's rays in the summer by the leafy aspen grove. Through the glass, the seasons marched from verdant summer to autumn's golden yellow as the leaves trembled, as if anticipating the winter's cold. A few shriveled brown leaf corpses tenaciously clung to the sapless branches allowing a filtered view of a frigid Coyote Ridge.

As Jim gazed through the windows, his thoughts drifted back to when he, Duane, and Craig had set them in place. He had ordered two dozen three-by-eight-foot uncased insulated windows from a manufacturer. The three of them had built wood grids using three-by-four-inch fir wood. They sealed the windows into the wall grid. Making for the spectacular view down the canyon.

'How did you ever find this place?' asked Glenda.

'A bit of a long story.'

'Let's hear it.'

'The short version is I drove over from the base to see what the east side of the mountains looked like and what might be for sale. This was the first place I looked at. I spent the night camped back below Wolf Mountain. The view was, as Heather later said, knock-down gorgeous. Then I drove around for a week looking at properties, almost to the Idaho border. At each property, I compared it to here, and by the end, it was clear that none were even close.'

'I'm surprised it took you a week.'

'Truthfully, I think I knew right away this place was special but wanted to give others fair consideration. Through the years, we looked at dozens of places from Arizona to Montana, and nothing ever came close.'

The mention of Heather caused a stillness in the room. After a pause, Jim continued, 'Whenever we got back here, it was always the same. This place was the best. I think we needed to remind ourselves just how special it was.'

Lola stared out the window and crossed herself. The crusty, snow-covered canyon fell toward the valley, reflecting pinkish orange as evening approached. Slowly, amber swaths with rose-red tails faded to charcoal-gray as the first two planets and then the brightest stars of the Milky Way punctuated the night. The flames of the fire continued their dance as if in support of the changing color-symphony.

'Venus,' shouted Pedro, walking into the room.

'How you know? A bright star, no?' asked Lola.

'Dad told me.'

Lola turned and looked at Jim as if saying, okay, Mister Colonel, how you know?

'If you look closely, Lo, stars twinkle because they are so far away. Planets like Venus don't, as they are so much closer. Venus along with Mercury are closer than Earth to the sun and set just behind it.'

'There's Mercury,' shouted Pedro, proud of his ever-increasing knowledge as he pointed low on the horizon before sitting down on the floor and calling Rosie to his side.

'Brush, Glenda, are you thinking about doing anything for New Year's Eve?' asked Jim.

'I hadn't thought about it,' said Brush. 'Holidays have always taken a back seat for us.'

'We'll celebrate Christmas next year.'

'Let's hope,' said Glenda.

'I was thinking about taking a trip with Pedro to Colombia and the Amazon. What do you think, Pedro?' asked Jim.

There was no answer. Everyone looked at the silent Pedro; he was sound asleep with his head on Rosie's chest.

'He's had quite a day,' said Glenda. 'Out cold. What are you thinking?'

'I need to do some work at BWC. I thought maybe we could all go over together, including Pedro, and watch the New Year's fireworks.'

'Sounds fine to me,' said Glenda.

'You're thinking about heading south after?' asked Brush.

'Yep, maybe in a couple or three weeks from now. A week at the BWC and then another one or two here. I think everything will be fine with Roy, Ben, and Tom, but what would you two say to hanging out here for a while when we leave for Colombia?'

Brush looked at Glenda, who shrugged. 'Feels like our second home, anyway. How long do you think for?'

'No special time, just as long as you wanted.'

'Sounds like a plan, then.'

'What plan?' asked Pedro as he sat up, rubbing his eyes.

Jim walked over, scooped him up, and said, 'Say good-night. I'll tell you tomorrow.'

'You have an update on the Somali? asked Bertrand.

'He was collected from the ship and followed north to a French castle called Château Noire, six kilometers east of Aix-En-Provence. I should have more details soon,' said Martin.

'No idea what the bio threat might be, or even if there is one?'

'Nada. Nothing yet.'

# Chapter Nine

Jim immersed himself in the BWC's projects and felt he was on top of what the labs were working on. He looked for discrepancies in the approach the lab was taking under Barbara's leadership. He found nothing significant. The single largest worry he had was always the same: microbes that would enter the human population in the future. *Are we prepared as well as we can be?* Barbara walked in as he contemplated whether they were overlooking any important issues.

'Colonel, did I interrupt you?'

'No, not all. I'm just mulling over our same old concerns, what we're doing, and if we are missing anything.'

'The big question, the unknown,' said Barbara, raising her eyes to the ceiling.

'At first, I wanted to bring myself up to speed with the lab's research projects and then to see if we could improve on any of those. And I couldn't. Then I drifted into thinking about zoonosis and what comes next.'

'Hmm, there's nothing seriously bad since the 1918 flu,' said Barbara.

'It's like waiting for a volcanic eruption. Could be decades or tomorrow.'

'Wouldn't it be nice if we could predict which virus might jump from the mammal or avian population, which will become our nemesis? That's what we're here for, isn't it? If you need me for anything, page me, and please say hello to Doc Dakine for me.'

'I will. I'm ready to head home. Spend a day or two before we leave for Colombia and Maria, and then the Amazon.'

'I haven't seen the outside since early morning, but the weather doesn't look good for flying through the mountains. I don't suppose that will stop you.'

'Not supposed to clear over the hump for a couple of hours. I guess I'll sit here like a VFR pilot and wait it out.'

'Excuse me. What pilots?'

Jim chuckled, 'Visible flight rules, VFR, are not allowed to fly in the clouds or at night. If the visibility on the east side of the mountains is low, and that's rare. It wouldn't make any difference taking off in the gunk over here. It's always surprising; rain and clouds coming from the west, backed up to the mountains, and then when you crest the mountains, it's endless blue sky and sunshine. That's normal, but just not today.'

'So, if you can fly without seeing anything, only using

your instruments, why can't you land over the mountains or the hump, as you call it?'

'Mountains block the radio signals, and little airports don't have electronic landing systems.'

'I'm happy just to stay here. Okay, safe travels, boss, both flying over the peaky mountains and when you head south.'

'Thanks, Barbara ... thanks for the great job with the lab. We're lucky to have you. We always have been.'

'Appreciate that, Jim. If there's nothing else, I'm needed to keep Nus corralled. The guy is still bonkers, and I've grown to love him.'

Jim raised an eyebrow.

Barbara was half-turned to leave and started laughing, 'Lower the brow, sir; you know what I mean—total chaos, brilliant in the extreme, and the man has zero sex appeal.'

'Agree with you there. Better you than me interacting with him. See ya.'

*Think. Before I leave, there must be something I haven't thought of. A new danger, a better solution. Something the labs should be working on,* thought Jim.

*Think. Rehash the basics:* nasty bugs jumping species must come from somewhere, a mutation in the human or non-human population. Viruses need to hijack a cell's machinery and don't survive long outside cells. While bacteria live by the millions in many niches outside of warm bodies. Many thousands of species live in soils, oceans, and lakes, all biding their time, multiplying every minute, waiting for a genetic change that would allow them a new home and the comforts inside a mammalian host.

Ebola kill their host in days. *Highly transmissible, but with a long incubation period,* Jim said to himself. *How would a terrorist alter it, allowing airborne spread instead of bodily fluid contact or shortening the incubation period? Same-o same-o. No new insights.* As was usual for him, he couldn't let it go. The questions were in his head and didn't want to be put to rest. *It's my job not to miss anything.*

A hundred percent death rate with no cure was rare, at least so far. The rabies virus was a known exception. Once you develop lyssavirus symptoms, it is ninety-nine percent deadly, a near-perfect killer, with no cure, and nothing can save a person. Before symptoms manifest themselves, a few shots stop it. After symptoms, it was movie-monster time, hydrophobia, your infected brain turning you into a zombie.

While emerging zoonotic viruses were a concern, the BWC's primary research was directed at viruses already in the human population and how they might mutate: Ebola, rabies, and AIDS; or bacteria: like anthrax, brucellosis, and the plague; even parasites: toxoplasmosis or trichinosis engineered by either governments or terrorist groups. A new virus jumping species into humans had the potential to be lethal, but an existing virus engineered was certain to be. The variola virus they were dealing with in Colombia might have been the world's big-time killer years ago, but today it was easily defeated by vaccines if administered during its ten-day incubation period. Before vaccines, the several days between infection and symptoms were the reason that allowed the virus to reach pandemic proportions.

Russia tried and failed to manipulate the gene code and engineer a short incubation period. If they had reduced it from ten days before symptoms to twenty-four or forty-eight hours, the ancient killer could regain its title as the "world's greatest killer."

Few have to think about the dangers the world faces from natural or engineered viruses. Everyone at BWC knew that it was only a matter of time before a virus created worldwide havoc. *A small snippet of DNA or RNA causing millions or hundreds of millions of deaths.* Jim shook his head, trying to dispel the thoughts. The same ones he had always had, *ad nauseum*, he said to himself.

'Okay, I'm leaving,' he said to no one, as he stood. *Home, see how Pedro's doing, say goodbye to the ranch, and ... Heather.* He let out a long sigh. Jim didn't know that all these worries coursing through his mind, as he sat there wasting his mental energy, getting nowhere, were already in motion eight, nine time zones to the east of BWC in southern France.

Bertrand and Martin walked to their usual places and sat down. Coffee, tea, and milk were already on the long, low, polished walnut table.

'Here's the first report, General,' said Bertrand. It's not

extensive, but it provides some background material. It's Martin's team's work, so I'll let him give you a summary.'

'They met the Somali at the Marseille port, and French Intelligence followed them to Château Noir. It's apparently a magnificent estate owned by a Panama corporation. It's a front for the real owner, André Boucher, the CEO of Remilious Group. Full background on both him and the company is in your file. It's a large French biomedical firm, which you might have heard about when a few months back, they were denied FDA drug approval for a new drug that they hoped to be a possible cure for Alzheimer's.'

'I remember reading about the drug trial. If I recall, there were questions raised about data being falsified.'

'That's right,' responded Martin. 'I'll get to that in a minute. First, the finance types analyzed the company's finances and background. The results are also in your brief. In short, Boucher, the CEO, is the company founder and the largest shareholder has a net worth estimated between one and two billion dollars. Since the Alzheimer's drug approval fell apart, Boucher has been scrambling to get the company's lines of credit extended, and the word is—he is meeting resistance from the banks, and Remilious is having cashflow problems. One more thing. The company appears to have been pushing an egg-independent influenza vaccine that has not been considered worthwhile by their investment bankers.'

'So, what's he up to?' Bertrand asked while he gazed at the ceiling. 'Seems risky smuggling a Somali into France. There must be a reason. Go on, Martin.'

'Okay. Back to the FDA. A source there said their investigation showed that the results had been altered to suggest a better finding. The drug might have been efficacious; however, the data changes did not allow the FDA to consider accepting it.'

'They investigated, and then what?' asked Will.

'Nada,' said Martin. 'They dropped it.'

'Suspicious. That's all,' said Bertrand. 'Whether Boucher knew the data had been faked and was unethical is an open question. The immediate mystery is why they would want to smuggle a Somali to France with links to terrorists. It doesn't fit together nicely.'

# Chapter Ten

'Fucking A,' said Dr. Dakine as she read a note passed to her.

'Maria, you shock me,' said Cherry, smiling at her new friend.

'Sorry, this is bad news,' she said, glaring at the fax she had just received.

'No need for sorry. I am proud for you. You speak with passion.'

'Your English is improving, and mine is deteriorating.'

'What this means, deteriorating?'

'In this case, the opposite of good—something falling apart.'

'So maybe now you tell me what you read?'

'WHO is sending someone whom I find difficult to get along with.'

'Who is sending someone?'

'Not who but the WHO, the World Health Organization.'

'Sí. Sí. I no like them. All think they special. Running around making everyone feel stupid.'

'They can be a touch arrogant. They're pussycats compared to this bitch.'

Cherry grinned, 'I like the new way you talk.'

Maria sighed, 'This woman really bothers me because she is both such a pain in the ass and at the same time brilliant.'

'Why they send her?'

'She's obnoxious and effective. When there are unknowns, she's WHO's secret weapon.'

'Why they need a weapon? Okay ... I remember what you say. Why "do" they need a weapon?'

'A thinking weapon, not a military one. One that looks at problems and finds solutions no one else sees. It's just that she is so rude. She drives me nuts. I enjoy being here now, with you and the others, it's easy. A simple happy way to live. It's the way life should be. When she shows up, things won't be the same.'

Maria sat silently for a long while and said, 'Everyone is inoculated in the camp, but for some reason, we are losing control in the towns and villages. The cases are growing. There were so many prisoners infected. They dispersed in all directions. The infection rate is increasing faster than we can inoculate. Imala Smith almost has second sight when it comes to assessing epidemics.'

'I no understand. We give everyone shot and poof gone.'

'Maybe, if we had enough vaccine and enough people to administer them to everyone. Trisha's calculations show there should be fewer people with symptoms than we are seeing. There are two methods we can use. Inoculate millions until no more cases appear. Even with teams and more vaccine arriving daily, that will still take a very long time, and many people will die. There is a better method of aggressive case finding. Isolate and seal off the infected persons, then inoculate every possible person they may have been in contact with. That technique worked well in Nigeria back in the 1970s.'

'Where this Nigeria?'

Maria loved Cherry's curiosity when she asked these sorts of questions. She and Cherry, for some strange reason, had become close. It might have been only that they were two females forced into close contact. Maria realized there was more to it than that; as dichotomous as they were, they naturally liked each other. An odd friendship: Cherry the guerrilla received her education "on the street," and Maria was educated at a top Ivy League school followed by the University of California Medical School San Francisco. Cherry wanted to know things about the world. Maria happily did her best to provide explanations. At night, they sat around campfires, sang, and sometimes danced. Maria felt as though she was a different person being here. Cherry craved information; Maria craved happiness.

It was not a one-way street. Cherry taught Maria many things—Maria learned a great deal about the culture, plants, and drugs, including cocaine, and Cherry had even shown her how to use her AK-47. Guns were something that Maria was philosophically against, especially in the

United States. Why should every nut be able to own one? Cherry, the guerrilla fighter, rarely went anywhere without her personal weapons: knife, automatic rifle, and sometimes bandoleers crisscrossing her breasts as they had been when they had first met in the jungle.

Cherry and Maria, opposites as they were, had not only grown accustomed to each other, but were increasingly fond of one another. It felt natural for them to spend their days together, with Maria working on controlling the pox and Cherry helping where she could, which was especially useful when dealing with the FARC, where she commanded respect as a fighter.

Maria's Spanish was improving daily. The formal grounding, she had received at Yale now blossomed into daily use, necessary to communicate with the rebel members who did not speak English, while Cherry was improving her understanding of English. The two switched back and forth, not often mutilating sentences by speaking Spanglish, but rather sometimes speaking English and sometimes Spanish. Both benefited equally in improving their language skills, and they hardly noticed which language they were speaking anymore.

There was something free and open about living with the FARC—none were pretentious, few had personal belongings—still, they were individuals in the way they adorned their uniforms, talked, and behaved. There were leaders, but not bosses or castes. They all knew their worth and duties, working together both to survive and support the community.

It differed from anything Maria had experienced, and

she liked the way it made her feel. Her mind drifted back to the pox. Technically, it was not her concern now. WHO had the lead outside the rebel compound? She could leave anytime, as her mission for the BWC was over. The compound occupants were safe, but she couldn't bring herself to leave—she wanted to stay.

'You say okay for me, I make this woman you no like disappear.'

Maria looked at her new friend, feeling their different worlds. At the same time beginning to see their likenesses. No longer feeling any sense of disbelief at Cherry's nonchalant attitude about eliminating someone Maria didn't like. Puff woman gone; she would say without a second thought.

Nusmen was torn between working on his special prion project and a puzzle: the origin of the smallpox from Colombia. He loaded the pox into the Polymerase Chain Reaction hopper for the third time. He was certain that the sample was the virulent 1975 Bangladesh smallpox. It had been sequenced in the early 1990s. He wanted to check the DNA one more time; something was bothering him.

The PCR machine began its steady work of exponentially increasing the quantity of the double-stranded DNA. Nusmen had a fondness for the simple device and would have sat patiently watching, imagining the rapid enhancement of the DNA inside it. He reluctantly got up.

He had samples in a mass spec that he needed to review. It was the proteins he was analyzing in the MS that were causing him to doubt this was the smallpox strain he had thought it was. The mass spectrophotometer would confirm the amino acids, allowing him to identify the proteins and the strain.

What was troubling him was that he was no longer sure that it was the Bangladesh smallpox strain. It would take days to run full sequences, but he had enough information to guess that there were more base pairs than the accepted 186,102. What he needed to know and understand were the pathogenic proteins. Anyone else would have dismissed the variances. Nusmen's obsessive nature required him to have everything in perfect order.

'Sheilla, can you have Nusmen call me?' asked Maria.

'Yep, okay. How are you doing down there in Colombia land?'

'The truth is, I like it here. These people live simply. It's something we're missing in our society.'

'Like what?'

'It's a big family, cohesive. They live together, fight and die together, sing around the campfire—they're happy —I'm happy.'

'You are coming back, aren't you?'

'Sure, it's just that it's comfortable here. I'm trying to figure out what we're missing in our society. It seems sterile to me now, full, and rich here. Maybe communes are like this.'

'Similar to what Colonel Johnson and Neilly said after they worked with Jago. Okay, so what's up with Nusmen? Why do you need to talk to him?'

'I want to know what he has found out about variola. Its strain. Understand it.'

'I thought it was all settled.'

'I'm not an epidemiologist, but the stats are off to me. Our control of it and predictions are not accurate. It a mystery. Hey, and a special favor, can you have Katarina do a profile on someone for me?'

'Sure.'

'It's a WHO rep that's on her way here, Imala Smith.'

'Is it urgent?'

'As soon as you or she can get it to me, I'd appreciate it.'

'Okay, and I'll make sure Nusmen calls you today.'

'Thanks, Sheilla, much appreciate it.'

Sheilla stood with her hands on her hips. 'Nusmen, you didn't call me back when I paged you.'

'I'm busy. I have experiments. I ...'

Sheilla cut him off. 'Do I page you all the time?'

'Ahh, No.'

'When I page you, it's important. You answer me. Do you understand?'

'Okay, okay. I need to get back to work.'

Sheilla reached down and pushed her pager as he walked away. Nusmen's pager buzzed. He looked at it irritably and kept walking.

'You stop right there. You get it through your head that I'm your boss, and if you don't do what I ask and when I ask, you won't work here anymore. Don't test me. The General will back me up. And so will Colonel Johnson, no matter how valuable anyone thinks you are.'

Nusmen stood fidgeting, thinking this was the second time a person had implied he was valuable.

'I, I don't understand.'

'It's simple. Don't walk away from me. Answer me immediately when I call or page. And show up at debriefings. Do your work, which you are brilliant at. You are the main, first, most important research scientist here.'

'You think so? But you just said you'd fire me.'

'There's more to being useful and brilliant. You need to be socially responsive and answer your damn pager.'

Nusmen looked confused. His Adam's apple bobbed up and down.

'Look, never mind. Get back to work, but you answer me when I call you. Look at your pager. It's why you have it. Who just paged you?'

'I dunno.'

'Well, look.'

Nusmen pulled his pager off his belt.

'It's you. Why ...'

'What do you do the next time your pager buzzes? It's simple. You see who it is and call them back, pronto. Now get back to work, but first, you call Dr. Dakine and tell her what you know about the variola virus.'

'That's what I'm doing that's so important. It's what I gotta get back to. Something doesn't add up.'

'Call her first, and then you can get back to work. Got it?'

Nusmen tipped his head forward. His uncombed hair straggled over his face. With his head down, his protruding Adam's apple was obscured by his chin. He nodded, 'Okay, I understand, I guess.'

'Good.'

Nusmen turned to walk away.

'Nusmen.'

'What?'

'Call her.'

'You mean like right now?'

'Well, Mr. Warsame, we have good news for you; please sit on the exam table, and we will do a quick few tests. You may possibly have some illnesses from your home country. We have excellent medical facilities here, so we shall discover what they might be and provide you with medicine for your family back home.'

The two men walked in behind Heinrich and closed the door. One walked a few feet to the wall and stood by a rolling gurney.

'Please, Mr. Warsame, lie back and roll up your sleeve.'

Cigalle looked at the other two men in their white coats; the one standing by the door had oversized square hands, large feet, and a thick neck. He did not look like the medical personnel he had met in Somalia. He looked at Heinrich, who was a blond Aryan, a stereotype of the "ideal" German male. He swiveled his head to the odd-looking doctor. Visser smiled and nodded, motioning for him to lie back on the exam table.

Dr. Visser tied an elastic band around his bicep and felt the crook in his elbow for a vein. Satisfied, he undid the band and inserted a winged butterfly device with a twenty-gauge needle. A small amount of dark red blood appeared in the attached tube. The doctor nodded, showing his pleasure.

He attached a vial to the other end, and blood filled the collection tube. He repeated the process until he had seven vials. He extracted the butterfly while holding a cotton ball to Cigalle's arm. 'Hold this with your finger.' After tapping it. He reached over and picked up a small glass vial from the tray and inserted a needle through the rubber seal and withdrew the clear solution. Chuckling, he injected it in Cigalle's other arm.

Cigalle watched the doctor's strange belly jiggle as the room blurred and he drifted into unconsciousness.

The two men moved the gurney over and lifted Cigalle onto it before wheeling him down the hall and into small room. Dr. Visser followed. He took Cigalle's other arm and inserted a PICC line and hooked it up to an IV attached to a liter bag hanging on a chrome post.

'Cover him up. I don't want him dying of cold. One of

you stands guard and pages me if he starts to stir. I want him sedated but alive.'

The blazing fire enveloped everyone in a blanket of warmth.

'My face feels warm,' said Pedro, 'but the back of my neck is cool,' as he placed his hand on his cheeks. 'It feels good.'

'Nothing like a warm fire on a cold wintry day to relax you,' said Glenda, sipping a glass of ruby-red Malbec wine. 'I love this wine, Jim. It has a fuzzy, soft feel. I don't like tart or fruity wines.'

Jim said, 'I have always wanted to go to Mendoza, Argentina where they make this Malbec.'

'Just like I used to want to go to Alaska,' said Brush.

'And since we went to Alaska, you replaced that thought with a Venezuelan tepui desire,' said Glenda as she snuggled up to him, holding his bicep with her hand.

'Yep. I do at that.'

'What's with Mendoza?' asked Glenda.

'It's sort of like here, east side of the mountains. It's in the rain shadow, except it's the Andes blocking the bad weather,' as he looked out the window wall at Oval Peak in the starlight.

'You were about to tell me something I already know— with one big difference—the Andes are much taller than that peak or any of the Cascade mountains.'

'And you can bask in the sun and go skiing all in the same day,' added Brush.

Glenda looked inquiringly at Brush.

'Jim and I have discussed this before, eh.'

They laughed, talked, and relaxed. The flames dwindled, making occasional soft pops as they eventually extinguished one by one, leaving pockets of glowing orange coals.

The light in the doorway where Maria and Cherry sat shifted to a rosy glow.

'Let's go outside and watch the sunset,' said Maria. 'A vino tinto would be nice,' as she grabbed a bottle and two glasses.

They sat outside, watching the activity in the camp. Friends walked by, some stopping to chat. Some stopped to sip their wine. Cherry disappeared inside and brought out another bottle. The time passed as the night sounds set in, and the camp quieted. The stars were brilliant, sparkling above. Maria felt happy and content. She began to wonder if she would leave. *I could be a doctor here and do what I trained for*, she thought, closing her eyes.

'Dios mio,' shouted Cherry. Others appeared and stared at the full moon as a crescent started across its face. Everyone stared as more people emerged.

Cherry stood with her mouth open, looking at the moon as it turned red.

**Remilious**

'What is this? I never see before.'
'Wow and wow,' said Maria. 'I have no idea.'

# Chapter Eleven

P edro was curled up, sleeping again. The full moon lit the Cascade peaks under a gray flannel sky. As Glenda looked, a shadow appeared on one side of the moon.

'Are we having an eclipse?' asked Glenda.

'I forgot all about it,' said Jim. 'It's a special one, too.'

'Special, how?' asked Glenda.

'Let's watch, and I'll explain. There won't be another one like this for about twenty years.'

Jim got up, stretched, and walked over to Pedro, rousing him.

'There's something unique happening. You will be almost twenty-seven years old before you see this again.'

'I never be that old.'

'I hope you're wrong. Come on. Let's go outside where we can see it better.'

Earlier, the sun had turned from yellow to orange while the log fire dwindled to red embers; a night of warm colors while the moon took on a ruddy-red cast as the Earth covered it in a full eclipse.

'I've never seen anything like this,' said Glenda. 'Is this normal?'

Lola came outside. 'What you all do outside? Cold out here. Then she covered her mouth with her hand. 'Malo, is bad no?'

'No. It's not bad. It's rare.' Jim put his free arm around her and pulled her to his side, just as he had done Pedro moments before.

'Look,' said Pedro, 'the mountains are turning the same color as the fire.'

'The moon only does this during a total eclipse, which is pretty rare in itself. The light is scattered like it is in a sunset. It's called a blood moon since it turns red. But more than that, this is extraordinary, as the moon is close to Earth in its orbit this time of year, making it a super moon, and in January, a full moon is a Wolf Moon. This is as good as it gets combining all of them; the Super Moon and the full Wolf Moon during an eclipse becomes the Super Blood Wolf Moon.

'Wolf like our ranch,' said Pedro.

'That's right, son,' as Jim pulled him close against the chilly night air.

'I go inside,' said Lola. 'I no like the bloody moon. Bad omen.'

Jim heard his sat phone ring inside. 'I'll be back.'

'Hey, Maria.'

'I called you because I knew you could shed light on

this. No pun intended. I know it's an eclipse, but please explain the color to me. I hope I didn't wake you?'

'It's fine. Everyone's outside watching. I'm glad you called,' as he stepped closer to the tall glass side door where he could see.

'Before you tell me about the moon—are you okay? Is Pedro, okay? Everyone else?'

'We're all good except Lola, who moments ago informed us that the bloody moon was a bad omen.'

'I hope she's not right.' There was a long pause, and Jim knew what she was struggling to say or not say about Heather. Maria and Heather had remained close friends through the years after their college days as roommates.

'I understand, Maria. We both feel the same. Better than trying to put it into words.'

'Maybe you're right.' They were silent for several seconds. 'Now tell me about the bloody moon!'

Jim walked back outside, inhaling the cold night air, and said, 'Do you remember studying Rayleigh scattering in your pre-med science classes?'

'If I did, I've forgotten.'

'Well, that's what causes sunsets and sunrises and the same for the Blood Moon,' Jim said, before he repeated much of what he had told Pedro, Lola, Glenda, and Brush.

'Quite the confluence of events: close, full, and eclipse. It's special, and for me, it's nice to have it happen here with the FARC. Then she hesitated again and said, 'I'm glad we could talk at the same time, too. It's good to share this with you. I keep saying this, Jim, but it's true—these are lovely people. They are gentle and have come together and formed a community. I understand more now about blending in with a group and without possessions. We learn to accept people for who they are and not for what they have.'

'I liked them too,' said Jim.

'Are you able to visit soon and bring Pedro?'

'I hope so. I think he needs a few days to adapt. Adjust to being so close to where she died.'

'Do you think you can adjust, Jim? It must be very hard for you, too.'

'It is. In truth, I'm looking forward to getting away with Pedro.'

'It will be nice to see you both. So, are you going to come here for sure?'

'Yes. It will be nice for Pedro, and to see Jago, Lobo, and Cherry again.'

'After all your adventures in the Amazon, they feel like you are part of their team. One of the first times they have embraced a guerrilla Notreamericana, or a North American warrior with your skills at least. Say hi for me to Glenda and Brush, and Pedro too.'

'I will, but you can say hi yourself. I'm feeling a tug on my shirt. Getting a bit cold out here. Say hello to Maria and we'll go inside.'

'Dad, say "it's" getting. Mom taught me'

'You're right, son. Now say hello.'

'Hi.'

'Hi, Pedro. Are you taking care of your dad?'

Pedro's loss of Heather and his dad rescuing him from Najma, then the fight — he couldn't bring himself to play the child's word game. 'We take care of each other,' he finally said, and handed the phone back to his dad.

Jim watched Pedro walk toward the door. 'One last thing, Maria, besides a full-time cook and nanny, we've adopted someone else.'

'Lola is taking care of you, is she? Who else? I got it. You mean the old man, the transient with the new choppers?'

'Yep, and he has a first name: Tom.'

# Chapter Twelve

After Maria read the first paragraph of Katarina's profile of the WHO rep, Imala, she set the papers on the table and contemplated why she had such difficulty dealing with the woman. *It's no wonder I find her difficult, but why can't I handle that?* She thought about it for a minute before glancing up at the sky. Then the thoughts of Imala were displaced by those of the Super Blood Wolf Moon from the night before.

The top of the document contained a note to Maria from Katarina: Phew, quite a personality combination. This woman will be a handful for you. Good luck. Maria decided to read the profile from the beginning:

Profile: Imala Begay, Female, age 38 – 'Classic Narcissist and Bipolar'.

As a narcissist, she craves drama and chaos. She treats people without empathy and as objects. When they are of no use to her, she discards them. She is not a psychopath.

And she has no interest in power or money. She feels she is entitled to do whatever she wants. She will act immorally or even illegally and will later justify her actions as necessary. Imala Begay has an IQ of over 150. As smart as she is, she graduated in the middle of her class at MIT and Caltech. She is a Native American, which appears to have no relevance to her psyche, other than Imala means strong-minded, which fits. Her personality defects prevented her from achieving better grades or honors. As you already know, she is rated as a brilliant problem solver. Perhaps a math savant. She is single, with no known relationships, which is typical, as she would say she has no time for anyone besides herself. She is heterosexual and occasionally picks up a male for sex. Complicating her narcissistic disorder, she is also bipolar. She feels a certain invincibility. What makes her tolerated by WHO is her capacity to delve deep into problems with extreme focus, combined with her underlying number-crunching ability; she finds patterns in epidemiological issues others are unable to. Some think she has second sight. Your issue is how to handle her. My recommendation is the least amount of interaction with her as possible. She will think she is superior to you. Arguing with her is fruitless. Provide data, but limit comments and opinions. In short, keep quiet. Whatever you say will have little benefit for you.

Maria pondered the differences between rational and irrational people. She understood rational individuals always assumed logical arguments could persuade others. She had come to accept that this was far from true. She learned to limit her discussions with people to those she thought were rational. Having a normal conversation with someone like Nusmen was impossible. However, Nusmen was a lovable pussycat compared to Imala. Take a deep breath, girl; you'll be able to deal with her. Try to keep Cherry in check. She shook her head, wondering ... *how she could ever explain Imala's death at the hands of Cherry.*

* * *

Dr. Visser picked up the old-fashioned push-button phone on his desk. The interruption irritated him as he had just started to review Cigalle's blood tests.

'Yes.' He answered in a surly voice before sitting up a little straighter. 'Monsieur Boucher. It is nice to hear from you. How can I help you?'

'Visser. You can help me by stopping your play-acting. I know you have a negative attitude about me, and I couldn't care less. It's your scientific ability that makes it worthwhile for me to put up with you. I want your thoughts on the VLP and the DNA research. We are reaching a critical time. François just told me that there are problems with the DNA plasmid immunogenicity.'

'There are problems,' answered Visser. 'Nevertheless, it has strong points. It's easily manipulated, safe, and, well, relatively safe. It might be the best direction to take if the problems can be overcome. Currently, it requires several vaccinations to be effective. I read the reports and data daily. So far, your Marseille labs have not figured out a way around that weakness. The virus-like particle's method may be the last one left standing.'

'François is sending a full report. I want your opinion in writing and on my desk by 6:00 a.m. tomorrow morning.'

The phone disconnected. Visser said, 'Klootzak, bastaard.' He rolled his eyes. 'A redundant bastard too; 6:00 a.m. is morning.'

He dialed Heinrich. 'I want you to talk to François and coordinate a report as to why the VLP is a superior technique to the DNA plasmid method. I want the report he has apparently been writing and your report on my desk by 8:00 p.m. tonight.' He laughed. Ha, 8:00 p.m. tonight.

'Fick dich, Arschloch,' mouthed Heinrich as he hung up.

Dr. Jelle Visser slammed the phone into its cradle just as angry with the extra work as Heinrich was. He let out a sigh as he looked at the blood results from his new African lab rat and promptly forgot all about the call.

The famous André Boucher needed Jelle for his plans, since there were very few of the researchers who would consider going along with the heinous course they had planned. Dr. Visser and Dr. Heinrich were not only integral to the plan, but they had originally suggested it to him. Now that the billionaire had gone along, there would be no backing out. Boucher was the boss. But Visser and Heinrich could blackmail him anytime they chose unless Boucher could find a way to dispose of them.

For now, the unstated leverage Jelle had over Boucher

meant he could carry on with his pet project without interference. Unless, of course, Boucher was caught infecting chickens and people in the U.S., then the walls would come tumbling down. Visser had never been able to pursue his adolescent interest before, but with Boucher's money supplemented with the EIJ, it became possible. No matter that even Heinrich thought Visser was whacko over his zombies and his latest interest in voodoo zombies. Now, with Boucher and the Islamic jihadists, he had the resources, with the laboratory and company, to pursue his juvenile fetish, regardless of what anyone else thought. He had his first guinea pig—the Somali.

Boucher didn't know about the Somali. His only concern was about his child—Remilious. *A manageable partnership in crime,* Jelle thought. Boucher needed the unprincipled scientist's help to save his company, and Jelle needed his money. Visser's concern was indulging his fantasy. The Middle Eastern jihadists didn't care about money. Still, they, too, added to Visser's research with both money and connections. Their motivation was to disrupt and cause pain to the Western non-believers. What Dr. Visser wanted differed little from his zealot backers: he wanted to see the terror in humanity, while his backers wanted to cause terror to humanity.

The project had nucleated in his thoughts years ago. Just idle curiosity at first. Much like the one Nusmen had when he first developed the antibiotic-resistant strain of *Staphylococcus aureus* as a student at Harvard—Visser would find Nusmen interesting.

As he studied the Somali's blood results, he couldn't

help wondering why some things excited one person and not another. His older brother had loved all horror films. When Jelle was a ten-year-old, he and his brother had watched, on their old TV, two movies back-to-back on a Bela Lugosi Saturday night movie marathon. They both had an impact on him until this day. One made him shiver and cringe, while the other left him joyous and happy. The strange happiness that *White Zombie*, the 1932 black and white movie, aroused in him, and the other, which still frightened him to this day, even to say its name; *Dracula* perplexed him.

Fortunately, the 1931 *Dracula* had been shown first. It was sort of like taking medicine and then getting a piece of cherry pie. Zombies saved his mind from the blood-sucking Transylvanian vampire. Zombies were not scary in the least to him. In fact, they represented what Jelle thought of most people. The world was overpopulated with idiots who mostly thought they were unique members of society, special individuals, unique in the world—*hah*, he thought, *braindead followers, all of them.*

Over the years, he collected or recorded on his VHS every zombie movie made. While he loved *Day of the Dead, Dawn of the Dead, Night of the Dead, City of the Dead*, and especially *Night of the Living Dead*; he always had a soft spot for *White Zombie*. No one played the role like Bela Lugosi.

He forced his thoughts away from zombies to the interesting but still less interesting vaccine methods they were working on. Boucher needed his plan to save his company. Jelle needed Boucher's plan to succeed so he could continue his fanciful research. If the company went under, so would Jelle's pet project. *Both plans were achievable,* he thought. *Boucher's keeping his company from going tits up. Mine is making a statement on this earth about what I think of the human race.*

# Chapter Thirteen

Jim spent the three weeks after the Super Moon going back and forth between the ranch and the BWC. He hated to be separated from Pedro. There seemed to be no alternative if they were going to be away for several weeks, maybe even months. He needed to ensure that the labs projects and focus were in good order. Since he couldn't find any justification for taking Pedro into the lower BWC levels, he engaged a military chaperone on base. Once they had flown over in the Enstrom, Jim had an MP from the BWC's ground floor office give his son a tour of the base. Pedro wasn't that interested in sightseeing. But it didn't take long for the MP to discover that Pedro was crazy interested in helicopters. They spent the rest of the day on the field, in the flight shack, and in the repair hangars, which they repeated on several occasions. Pedro never seemed to tire of watching and learning from the mechanics.

Jim finally called it quits when he was satisfied that he

could add nothing more to the lab's agenda. Tomorrow was Lola's birthday, and it would be Pedro's and Jim's last full day at the ranch before they left for Colombia. He had spent much of the previous week discussing the lab's goals with Sheilla. She would be in charge while he and the General were absent. Of course, General Crystal would fly out as often as he could and would always be available by phone or for a video conference. The CIA was his current responsibility, and General Will Crystal always honored his duty. However, the BWC was and would always be his passion.

At first, Sheilla had been a little nervous about being entrusted with this much responsibility. Those insecurities fell away as Jim pointed out that it was never the person at the top who made things run at the BWC, but the many exceptional people. Sheilla was not a born leader; rather, she was a skilled problem solver who had learned management skills on the job. She would look after the center and be supported by the key staff: Dr. Milton, Misa, Vidya, Mark, Fred, Katarina, Kramer, and even Nusmen.

It would not be that much different from when Jim was away in the field and the General in D.C., he told her. She would not have to become involved with the politics outside the lab. That was still Will Crystal's job. Missions were Jim's. Nothing, in reality, was changing, other than one important thing. Sheilla's value was being acknowledged as she was officially given the title of temporary BWC director. It was a long step from her unrecognized skills and entry-level analyst job at the FBI.

Jim flagged another issue, something they had not had

a problem with in the past, which meant to Jim it was something important to consider: security. He wasn't worried about their computer security—the lab was fortunate to have the most skilled IT personnel available—except for being infiltrated by a foreign government or even the U.S. government's agencies like the NSA or even someone within the CIA. Jim and the General had had many discussions about the impact of politics on the lab. If something should happen to the General—and control of the BWC fell into the wrong hands—it could be a dangerous situation depending on what their motivations were. The mission of the BWC was proactive and defensive. A bad actor could easily change that purpose to create biological weapons.

Even with as much trust as Jim had for Sheilla, he did not disclose his and the General's embedded security person. Since the inception of the Biological Labs, Kramer had been their mole. Sheilla was only aware of the visible security team, and it had been decided to keep it that way. With the technology changes moving at a rapid pace, Jim felt the lab's security procedures needed a thorough evaluation. General Crystal and Jim intended to do so later in the year.

Another issue—Sheilla had never had a PA or assistant of any kind. She had Mark and Fred, who often assisted her, but only during missions. It appeared now that she should have a full-time PA, whether she wanted one or not, and whether she would know what to do with him or her or not. Glenda had mentioned Brees glowingly. Brees, for her part, could not think of anyone she would rather work with than Glenda and the BWC. They had discussed it. It wasn't to be. Brees was social and had her friends on the opposite side of the country. The idea, however, had caught hold, and it was decided that Sheilla needed a high-caliber personal assistant. The search was on in the CIA and with the staff at BWC. Jim hoped they would find the right person before he left for Colombia with Pedro.

Jim and Maria talked on their satellite phones several times. They worked out a list of supplies together that would make both her and the ex-rebel's lives easier. Maria was a doctor and, of course, she thought the compound needed lots of medicine and medical instruments. 'I want things that will be useful for the community. Not stuff that will become personal possessions.' Maria was adamant. She hadn't needed to be. Jim had understood where she was coming from.

Jim had Sergeant Williston organize several crates for Maria and the FARC. Maria had mentioned one special request. The time she had spent with Cherry had gravitated many times to discussions about countries, cultures, landscapes, and animals.

'Jim, could you bring some books for Cherry? Jim thought he knew exactly what was needed. He had a love of travel books that were geared more toward images rather than individual hotels, guides, and transportation. He favored DK and Insight guides. The contents were about the country, the people, and places, not only hotels and restaurants, with lots of photos. They didn't become outdated as quickly as other guidebooks. Less useful if you wanted current information about hotels and more useful if you wanted to know more about the culture, cities, and natural history of a country. DK and Insight guides had only a few pages at the back about transportation, accommodation, and details that would become antiquated as time passed.

After Maria's request, Jim left the BWC in a government car under gray, overcast clouds and drizzle. He drove north on Interstate 5 to Olympia and parked at Barnes and Noble.

The travel section was empty, with no shoppers browsing the shelves. He pulled the books halfway out that he thought would be interesting for Cherry, so he could keep both hands free while browsing. He had selected so many that he asked a clerk to find him a stocking cart to carry them to the checkout and take them out to his government sedan. After loading the cart, he added a selection of books about mammals, mountains, deserts, and the ocean. He wanted a *Larousse Encyclopedia of Animal Life*, but it was out of print. He decided he would take his copy for Cherry. He was especially fond of the book and hoped she would be, too. *Eventually*, he thought, *I'll find a replacement at a used bookstore.*

Peculiarly, the drizzle and grayness, typical of winter in the northwest, left him feeling strangely content. Earlier, he had called Pedro at the ranch, as he had every day that Pedro had not accompanied him to Fort Lewis. Pedro reported that all the animals were happy, and the skies were blue. Jim's thoughts turned to the dark side that often shrouded him as he remembered Heather lying in the blood-stained snow.

He sighed as the BWC's oversized hangar door lumbered open. Sergeant Williston stood near the plane he and Pedro would fly in with the supplies for Maria. Williston was wearing dress greens. Even though Jim knew his record, the ribbons, campaign medals, and multiple gold hash marks, the Sergeant First Class Army patch, a big yellow First Air Cavalry combat patch, airborne wings, and blue combat infantry badge were an impressive sight.

Sergeant Williston snapped a salute as Jim got out of the olive-drab car.

'All loaded, sir.'

'Thank you, Sergeant. I've got some boxes in the car to add.'

Williston waved two men over and directed them to secure the car's contents in the plane.

'Wearing your dress greens, you must be going somewhere?' asked Jim.

'Top is hosting brunch at the club. No one told me what it was about.'

Jim knew exactly what it was for. He and the General had agreed that Sergeant First Class Williston deserved a promotion to Master Sergeant. Both were pleased with how well their new logistics sergeant had adapted to his position. He was about to go to a ceremony where the base Sergeant Major would hand him his new stripe.

Jim flew back to the ranch immediately after their conversation. He would not get to congratulate Williston after receiving his official promotion. However, he had left a bottle of champagne with a note attached addressed to Master Sergeant Williston. The lab had been lucky to find this good of a replacement for their deceased friend. Williston had fit right in. It felt as though he had always belonged to their group. Even so, Jim wondered if gains could ever cancel out the loss of their old friend who Williston had replaced.

Jim moved out of his thoughts as he focused on the ranch and the snow. For the last day, it had been as if he were debriefing himself. Getting a grasp on reality and what had led to where he was in the here and now. Reliving everything that had happened. He could do nothing else. He could not change the past. The future would be what it would be. He had to deal with the present.

It was a clear winter's day. An assortment of fluffy faraway clouds hovered atop the snowy peaks of the Cascade Mountains. Over the valley and the ranch, there was only cobalt blue. *A low-pressure system,* thought Jim. *No high-pressure haze.* It was a blueness engulfing this part of his universe that matched his feelings.

He climbed the hill above the house and dropped his foam chair onto the snow-crusted slice of flat area. He wore an old blue down coat he had purchased in the first REI store in Seattle in 1971, and a black polar fleece stocking cap. His hands were warm in heavy dark blue ski mittens. The chair separated his green Eddie Bauer rain pants from direct contact with the crusty snow. It was only a little below zero, but sitting still for minutes, close to an hour, perhaps longer, as he intended, would allow the cold air to eventually seep through the layers to his skin.

His mind turned momentarily to a hike he had made several years ago. He had been underdressed while hiking. The temperature had been in the twenties. However, he had stayed warm from the exertion. As the evening wore on, huddled, sitting still around a campfire, there seemed to be no thickness of clothes that could keep out the bone-chilling cold. He expected the same cold that mirrored his mood today to seep through his clothes as it had done that evening in the North Cascades.

He was on the knoll above the house. The flat spot was as hidden from view just as their Secret Meadow was. The knoll was obscured from the house and those below. However, there were no trees or shrubs surrounding it like had been the case at their special meadow. Both special places with their own distinct realities. Only sage, rocks, and one lone stunted *Pinus occidentalis*: Heather's favorite tree species. West toward the Cascades, Oval Peak, another of their favorite hiking destinations, rose majestically into the sky. The small plateau felt miles above the house. In reality, it was only 100 yards above. Wolf Mountain was blocked from his view behind by the micro-plateau that was sculpted from the hill. Lower down the same hill, Jim had carved out a flat spot to build their house.

The tiny invisible plateau, sliced out of the ridge, and hidden from below, had become a graveyard. A baby llama years ago had died in his arms on an ice-cold day, much like today. Not knowing what to do with the soft-coated black llama baby, he had climbed the knoll and arranged the lifeless infant facing west toward the mountains, leaving it exposed to the elements, birds, and animals. Bits of its skeleton remained scattered about in the dirt and plants when the spring brought warmth and the snow melted. The only thing he knew for sure about the infant llama and its return to the natural environment was that something had not carried it off as a coyote might have.

This is what he wanted for himself: not to be buried in the dirt of a cemetery, but to be left on the "consecrated" natural soil of a mountaintop. Brush knew his wishes, and if his buddy survived him, Jim knew he could rely on his best friend. They had made a pact to do what each wanted in death. Brush had made Jim's part of their agreement easy. He said, 'He couldn't care less what happened to him when he was dead.' Jim would get his mountaintop, and Brush would get his whatever. Jim smiled whenever he thought about his buddy's couldn't-care-less attitude.

After the baby llama had been left here, both he and Heather had found the small plateau a fitting place to leave a few special animals exposed to the elements. A ranch was a never-ending cycle of births and deaths. It was the natural order. The only nonliving entity below ground on the plateau was Heather. It had not been hard to arrange with General Will Crystal, expediting the necessary permissions. Getting her physically below the iced ground had been the larger problem.

This would be Jim's last visit to the knoll for several weeks, or maybe many months. He didn't cry or weep. He sat stoically facing the western mountains, his mind swirling with memories. Oval Peak rose majestically above the Oval Lakes, where they had camped, swam, and hiked over the years. He harbored no illusions or mysticisms about Heather being with him as he sat in contact with the same ground that touched her lifeless body. While memories of her were scattered throughout Wolf Canyon Ranch, this spot was, at least in this moment in time, more poignant than any other.

Despite the gruesome reminder of sun-bleached bones protruding from the snow, they had sat here many times, joined with the memories of their past animal friends. She had once said the plateau left her feeling like an eagle on a treetop.

He thought of her smile, her lithe figure, her green eyes, and how desirable he had found her. Images plied his memory. Summer images when she wore loose shorts and oversized T-shirts with nothing underneath. Her winter smiles. Her longing look before they made love, and her indescribable rosy-cheeked look of satisfaction after. In all the time he had known her, he could truthfully say he had never desired another woman. Maybe he never would.

It was paradoxical—the loss of love and companionship contrasted with the loss of an archenemy. His mind had worked through the past month as much as he was capable. Rehashing, reworking, and rethinking would only contribute to the destruction of the present and those around him. There was nothing for it now but to do it—go on—stay in the present and relegate the past to a memoir his mind would read in an endless loop. Making sure Pedro would have the life he had not experienced so far as a child. He was confident that there would be no emergencies that Glenda, Brush, or Neilly could not handle. He needed to leave, Pedro needed to leave, to put time and distance between the past and the future. The General would respect what Jim and Pedro needed, and barring a world disaster, leave them to recover.

He ignored the cold seeping through the seams of his clothes, up from the frozen, iced soil through his padded chair. The air was so clear he could see details of Oval Peak and the Cascades beyond. From his vantage point on the plateau, he couldn't see the Methow Valley, which was blocked by the ridge that rose between Beaver Creek and the valley. A steep ridge, which in the past had been climbed with mules and aptly named: Balky Hill. Not seeing or hearing civilization was one of the special things about the ranch. A shallow grade descended from the house to the homesteaders' cabin. A small rise beyond the cabin and before the flattish "Speedway" obstructed the view of the lower canyon and Beaver Creek unless he climbed the ridge above him.

He and Heather had always chosen to walk to Coyote Ridge on the opposite side of the canyon. They never questioned why. But above him, there was another ridge: "No Name Ridge." It rose above the western side of the canyon. Coyote Ridge was a favorite, perhaps since it rose more steeply; one felt as though they were far above the canyon, the barns, and animals below. The terrain on the other side differed from the canyon. It was a wide undulating basin of sage, blue bunch grass, and mounds extending to the Loop-Loop Pass Road.

From either ridge, the speedway and parts of the lower canyon were visible. Balky Hill not only blocked the Twisp and Winthrop River valley from view, but it also buffered the busier valley's noises. Fortunately, the gravel Balky Hill Road was not a favorite of the bikers. Otherwise, the throaty growl of unmuffled Harleys might have rumbled their way up Wolf Canyon to where he sat.

Jim pulled off his blue ski mitten and extracted Heather's notebook from inside his coat. He intended to read and look through every page, ones she had made notes on, drawn on, written poems on, and pressed meadow flowers in. The booklet was her special treasure. A happy place to share her thoughts and observations. Jim wanted to be part of those thoughts and feelings with her this one last time. It was his way of both keeping her close and saying goodbye.

# Chapter Fourteen

'I no want to leave house,' said Lola with hands on her hips.

'It's your birthday and the tradition here is that we take you out to dinner. Pedro, Ben, Tom, and Roy are all going to be there.'

'It too cold. Warm inside. I stay.'

Jim knew he was in a losing battle.

Lola didn't move or say anything. Her mouth was tightly shut, and it looked as though it would remain that way. Jim wondered why she was so adamant. *Was she developing agoraphobia? Possible,* he considered. She hadn't left the house or its immediate vicinity, to his knowledge since she had arrived at the ranch.

Lola didn't know why she didn't want to leave either. She hadn't thought about it. No one had asked her to before. There was a part of her that felt if she left, she might never return. Maybe she just didn't want to change her daily routine. One she was happy with. Perhaps she was simply afraid to go outside. She switched her gaze from Pedro to the door. 'Ghosts, many ghosts,' she said so softly that no one heard.

Jim was becoming uncertain that he could convince her. Pedro had a different idea. He knew they were not going to a restaurant. Betty Lou and Loretta had cooked a birthday dinner at Betty's house.

'You take care of me like a mother in Tubutama, then you my aunt, and now my mother again,' said Pedro. He reached up and took her hand. 'Dad, please get her coat and gloves.'

Lola took one step forward. Calling her mother was too much for her to bear. She folded. 'Please, Colonel, need hat too,' she added as she stood watching Pedro with his large brown eyes.

Jim chuckled and smiled his way down the hall as he retrieved her winter clothes. He had never even seen her wear them after Heather brought them to the house.

It was a six-mile drive to Betty Lou's. Jim had put the far back seats up in the Suburban. Ben rode shotgun with Pedro and Lola in the back. At the cabin, Tom climbed in and squirmed to the back third-row seat. They stopped and picked up Roy at the main gate, who jumped in and sat next to Lola. Tom Shuskin liked being by himself in the back. He could see everyone. No one was too close. He had a great view and felt like a king being chauffeured.

They followed Beaver Creek Road to Highway 20, turned right and then left onto a side road. Up a county-maintained and plowed canyon road with scattered houses and small ranches along the way. Near the end of the road was Betty Lou's and Duane's house built on twenty acres. Directly across was Loretta's and Craig's home. It was hard for Jim to think about it in any other way. He had visited Duane and Craig and their families so many times. Two more losses thanks to Najma and the cartel. Craig was Najma's first victim when she crossed the Canadian border with the terrorist group that had been intent on blowing up the Seattle Convention Center. Duanne was killed in the attack on Wolf Canyon Ranch led by Najma and the Sinola cartel. Memories of two of his favorite people. Ones he would never forget.

Jim turned into Betty Lou's drive and circled to the back of the house. The screen door opened, with Loretta standing next to Betty Lou.

Pedro scrambled out from behind Roy and said, 'Come on, Birthday Girl.' Shuskin brought up the rear as they walked inside to the smell of coffee, warm air, and wood smoke.

Betty Lou had left her Christmas tree up. The needles were starting to fall. This had been her first Christmas without Duane. She could not bring herself to take it down. It didn't seem like a birthday ornament; however, it added a refreshing bit of color to the tan and brown leather interior.

Pedro let go of Lola's hand and ran over to the sofa. 'Mr. Brush. How you both get here?' as he looked at Glenda Rose and Brush.

Brush said, 'The red hunk of metal parked out back.'

'I thought it maybe was Betty Lou's,' said Pedro.

'It's our new truck. Do you like it?' asked Glenda.

'Sí. Es muy rojo!

'Adds a little joy to the white stuff,' said Glenda.

'Lola,' said Jim. 'We decided to have a little birthday celebration for you before we have dinner. Is that okay with you?'

'You, boss man. I do what you say.'

*Uh-huh,* thought Jim. He stepped over and hugged the short, round Yaqui woman, who had had a hard life and tipped her face up toward his. 'Happy Birthday, Lo. You have a home here with us as long as you want.' Then he turned her to the others as they sang *Happy Birthday to You.*

'Better her than me,' whispered Brush.

'Shush, lover.'

Betty Lou went to the card table and pulled off a cover. At least a dozen presents sat on the table. Jim had to nudge her over to them. She was overcome with all the presents and opened them slowly. They waited patiently. Brush rolled his eyes at how daintily Lola peeled each paper wrapping from the presents and received a 'Don't you dare say anything' look from Glenda.

'Lola. there is one more thing for you.' Jim handed her a brown envelope about an inch thick.

'What this?'

A chorus erupted, 'Open it.'

She carefully unsealed the envelope, not knowing what it could be, and extracted a glossy blue folder with a gold-embossed seal wrapped in tissue paper. Pedro fluttered his fingers, 'Go on, open it.' With the meager reading skills she had just begun to learn from Heather, she stood mouthing the words as she said them to herself. Her mouth opened as she pressed the papers to her chest before falling back into Duane's well-worn recliner.

'Congratulations, Lola.'

Lola let the folder and papers fall to her lap and buried her face in her hands. Betty Lou and Loretta looked at each other as tears descended both their cheeks seeing the effect the document had on Lola.

'You American citizen now. Just like me,' said Pedro.

Lola looked up, red-faced. 'How you do this? I no go out of house. Afraid I get arrested if I leave.'

'Let's just say the General has some influence in Washington,' said Jim. 'You are safe here, Lola. You don't need to worry anymore. You can do what you want. Now ... are you ready to eat someone else's cooking?'

There was no answer, she couldn't get words out, as Jim watched for the second time, as tears streamed down her brown cheeks while she clutched the folder to her chest.

* * *

'There is nothing particularly new to add to the report,' said Martin.

'True,' added Bertrand. 'Even so, it doesn't mean we can't start constructing a meaningful story.'

General Crystal nodded and said, 'Let's hear it.'

'A short recap of what we know: a wealthy businessman in financial trouble, most of his assets are tied up in Remilious Group, he has personally had to guarantee bank debt, they smuggled a Somali male into France and brought him in through an unused back gate to his estate. The company has or has had two drugs they pinned their hopes on. One was in the U.S. pipeline. The Alzheimer's drug was rejected by the FDA. It was projected to be a real profit maker. The second, a universal or pan vaccine for $N_1$ viruses, is not in the pipeline yet but close. It might protect against as many as sixteen $N_1$ viral strains. From what I hear, it has a lot of potential, but nothing like the Alzheimer's drug had.'

'The pan vaccine would inoculate against any $H_1$ flu?' asked General Crystal.

'That's what the intelligence reports I read said,' answered Bertrand. 'It would be a big advance and Boucher's fortune would rise. But his company might have problems with the FDA after the company's history of faking data. It might be a hard sell.

'Strikes me as a little odd. As you say, big potential if it could be done. No one has before, and a non-targeted vaccine doesn't add up to me. Martin, check with the BWC and see what their opinion is.'

'My next question is why smuggle someone in from Somalia? Risky at best, and then bring him in through a back gate. The answer must be something illegal, or? Why take the risks, and spend the money to keep it a secret? How is it related to his troubles with the bank, which, by the way, have gotten worse since yesterday?'

'How so?'

'Another large U.S. firm with a lot of clout has been getting the ear of Boucher's banks and stopping them from coughing up funding. The word from our Wall Street contacts is that they want to take over his company on the cheap. They could push him out completely or buy his shares at a substantial discount. It's all about money and they are, as usual, ruthless when someone is in trouble. Boucher's back is against the wall.'

'Conclusions, Bertrand?' asked the General.

'He needs to do something fast, and it needs to be dramatic. Faster than getting the $N1$ pan vaccine in the pipeline, which could take years, even if it is eventually approved. I think for us the Somali is a key. We need to know why he was smuggled in. So far, my best guess, and it's nothing more than a guess, is that he wants something that he can't obtain through the normal routes or health agencies. That seems obvious. Best guess, it has something to do with the company's virus development drug, but why the mystery?'

'Terrorist plot, maybe?' suggested Martin.

Bertrand shook his head. 'Doesn't make sense.'

The General stretched both feet out and leaned back. 'I don't see how the Somali and Boucher tie together. Other than people in his position with power and money can become unpredictable. What do you want to do, Bertrand?'

'Martin is going to continue to dig into the connections. There isn't much we can glean at this point. We'll see what his team finds, and we can discuss it tomorrow.'

* * *

'I think we are wrong,' said Heinrich. The data all points to the fact that the better approach is DNA Plasmid. The issues we've had with needing multiple vaccinations seem resolvable. If I'm right, it is easier, cheaper, faster, and safer to develop than using Virus-Like Particles.'

'Get the data and your report on my desk by 8:00 pm, and I'll call you if I have questions. If there is a unique way we can solve that problem and patent any of the processes, we would have a happy boss,' said Jelle.

'What do we get out of it?'

'You mean, what do you get out of it?'

'Look, Heinrich. I want to continue our side research, and you want to make money and be impervious to Boucher firing you. We need a plan to ensure we keep our leverage over him.'

'Our vaccine research saves his company - makes him richer - and we get nothing?' asked Heinrich with astonishment.

Visser smiled. 'We shall see.'

* * *

Martin and Bertrand walked into the General's office, followed by an aide with the usual tray of biscuits, tea, milk, and coffee.

'Good morning, gentlemen. Shall we review the daily briefing before we continue our speculations about the Somali?'

'There's not a lot interesting in the daily briefing, but

possibly there is in what Martin has discovered. If it's okay, let's discuss that story first.'

Martin looked at Bertrand, which pleased the deputy director. Martin always had good skills. After Martin's thumb amputation in Mexico at the hands of Najma and his escape from Guillermo Vasquez's cartel fortress, they had become close. In the Somali's case, Martin had discovered something significant. Instead of jumping right in and going for the glory with General Crystal, he was being respectful to his superior and let him take the lead in informing the General.

'Martin's investigation has dug up some interesting points. He came to me with what his team had discovered last night. I'll let him tell the story.'

Martin was well pleased that Bertrand would let him tell what they had found. In truth, he expected no less. Bertrand contributed enough on his own and didn't need to take credit for those who worked for him. That humility brought him loyalty and affection from his staff and now Martin.

'Cigalle's sister's boyfriend, has a friend who is a member of Egyptian Islamic Jihad.' Anticipating the General, Martin continued, 'That is not necessarily surprising in that part of the world since nearly everyone is connected to some rebel group or other. Here is a detailed report on EIJ.' Martin set a thick folder on the coffee table.

'Where this gets interesting is the connections of EIJ to al-Qaeda. Again, something expected because the technical leader of EIJ is Ayman Mohammed Rabie al-Zawahiri. We've known for the last two years that al-

Zawahiri formed an alliance with Bin Laden. They've known each other for years since before they were both kicked out of Sudan.'

The General sat up a little straighter, sensing this was going to get interesting.

'We've tagged him as the responsible person for the attack on the U.S.S. Cole last October.'

'I thought it was Bin Laden?' asked Will.

'It's what we originally thought. Our most current information is that we were both working together. We also have him designated for the embassy attacks in 1998. Where this starts to get even more interesting is—the sister of our Somali—Cigalle has a boyfriend who is part of a faction that we have traced to Egypt and right to the top with al-Zawahiri.'

'Part of a top-level al-Qaeda operation,' Will Crystal mused while he rubbed his chin.

'Exactly, and one that appears to lead to both Bin Laden and al-Zawahiri.'

'What's the evidence?'

'Circumstantial at this point. The connections in Egypt led to a professor at Cairo University. Along with the State Department, we have been investigating their connections as they have been attempting to form research partnerships with a molecular biologist postdoc in the U.S. Hold on to your hat for this, from the University of Washington Microbiology Department. Jim's alma mater. He is currently working on a short-term research grant at Scripps Institute since the State Department did not fund the work with the Egyptians.'

'Why decline it? It's not uncommon to work with the Middle East. The NSF and the State Department routinely fund cross-cultural research.'

'True, but not with a professor who is linked directly to a terrorist group. The SD declined the research proposal, and the FBI is investigating the postdoc.'

The General raised both eyebrows as he looked at Martin.

'If we had known, we would have done the opposite. Monitored the postdoc and got him the NSF grant.' Will shook his head. Martin continued, 'We've started on the Egyptian side. We have surveillance on Ayesha Mustafa, the professor, and we are trying to trace her contacts.'

'You will, of course, bring the BWC into this now with the molecular and microbiology connection?' added Bertrand.

'The short answer is yes,' said Will. 'Martin, you liaise with Sheilla McCarrick at BWC.'

'Certainly, sir,' said Martin, feeling ecstatic about the turn of events.

'All this is very interesting, but what the heck does it have to do with Boucher bringing the Somali to France?' asked General Crystal.

# Chapter Fifteen

'It is nice to have you back, Jim,' said Maria.

Jim nodded, 'I see why you like it. Like summer camp. No TV, a fire, cool, not cold, nighttime air.'

'I think Pedro likes it so far, too.'

'He has immediately taken to everyone. More than I would have hoped.'

'You think it's because he feels at home speaking Spanish?'

'Partly. Also, maybe it's neutral ground for him.'

'What are your plans, Jim?'

'I'd originally figured we would stay a week. We've already been here eight days.'

Maria reached over and took his hand. 'It's good here. Real people. There's the nicest old man who has helped me ever since he first volunteered to be vaccinated.'

'I know the feeling. It's a bit like an army bivouac. A large community group embedded with a nucleus of friends. It's not easy to always be around people all the time, but amongst the crowd, you can still relax and be on your own, in your own space, when you feel like it.

'Much like growing up with a houseful of siblings, I suppose,' added Maria. 'This is something I have always wondered about, and we never had time to talk about—'What made you decide to adopt Pedro?'

'Well, he was on his own with no one. I was wounded. We ended up right next to each other during the shootout, and there was this immediate simpatico. Lola had been trying to sneak him out of the cartel compound. Najma was there, and we were taking heavy fire. If we hadn't taken them with us, the cartel probably would have killed at least her or, worse, forced the boy to kill her, and his future would have become that of a cartel soldier.'

Maria smiled, 'Look at you now. You've nearly adopted a whole pack: Old Man Shuskin, Lola, and maybe Ben too, who I think is a really nice kid.'

'Ben is taking care of Loretta. He works hard on the ranch, and I think he likes it,' said Jim. 'But I think Loretta is the right one to adopt him if anyone does. She has no one after Craig died.'

'So, does he think of her as his mother? Do you think she will officially adopt him?'

'More like an aunt, and truthfully, I think he thought of Heather as being more of a mother. He likes Loretta and feels responsible for her after Craig's death, but it was Craig and Duane who he was close to. As much as he talks about you, Maria, after you took him sailing, perhaps you should adopt him.'

'Great mother I would be. I'm always off somewhere. Used to living alone. I confess I felt comfortable with him when we were all up in the mountains camping,' Maria almost said after he escaped from the terrorists and Najma. *Starting now I'm going to delete that woman's name out of my vocabulary.* 'It started with him telling me about the wilderness. Him being the teacher. Then everything flipped. When we exhausted back-country lore and got back to the psychology of people, it became my turn to coach him.'

'Heather mentioned something about that. I got the distinct impression Ben had a lot of respect for you.'

They both glossed over Jim's speaking of Heather again. She was gone. They needed, as they often did, to mention her while trying not to let it hurt.

'It seemed to be an easy time we had sailing together. I'd like to see him again and spend more time with him. We might always be united after him being stranded and almost killed by ...' she said to herself, *alright I'm stuck saying her name, hopefully for the last time,* Najma,' she said, disgusted with herself as she said the name. *Final time though. I want to bury thoughts of her. I don't want her in my head any longer.* 'Anyway, I think Ben's doing fine where he is, and I would not make much of a mother.'

'The way he talked about loving that day with you out on the boat, I don't think it would take a lot of cajoling on your part to get him sailing again.'

'I'd like that too. Perhaps when we're all back up north, you and Pedro will go too.'

Jim smiled at her. Heather had always been picky

about choosing friends. *That is, if you threw Nusmen out of that mix,* thought Jim. Maria was an attractive, accomplished woman in so many ways, and he understood why Heather had liked her so much.

'That's a deal. You let me know when. I'm sure Pedro would love it.'

'You got it. Spring and summer are coming up. A good time to go, maybe even all the way north to the San Juan Islands.'

Changing the subject, Jim said, 'It appears you have added a real friend here with Cherry.'

Maria chuckled. 'Yeah. I admit I like her. I just have to make sure she doesn't terminate the WHO rep as a favor to me. It was very nice of you to bring her so many books. There's been one in her hand or open on her lap ever since you gave them to her. Our conversations have changed as her knowledge increases. I should have asked you to bring an encyclopedia set. She's asking me things I don't know. Before the books, a question might be, 'Where's this place, Botswana?' Now she wants to know which Botswana park would be best to see zebras or elephants in. She asked me last night why parts of the Skeleton Coast are off-limits. And I've never heard of half the animals in that *Larousse Encyclopedia of Animals* you brought.'

'I couldn't resist giving her my copy and then discovered a new edition was just released, so I can replace it. I especially like that book and have looked at it a lot. And it surprises me every time I find an animal I've never heard of. So, you're not alone.'

Maria reached over and touched Jim's arm as she gazed into his eyes. It was a look of caring, not sympathy.

'I'm off to my cot, Colonel. I'm getting so used to it; I'm wondering if I'll ever be able to sleep on a mattress again.' Maria stood, then bent down and kissed him on the cheek. 'Night, night. Sleep tight and all that.'

Misa and Vidya appeared in the door of their BWC rooms, affectionately called the cave by the rest of the staff, and walked into Fred's computer group room. Eleven techs sat busy at their computers along with Sheilla, who walked up and gave Misa a quick hug and then turned to the others.

'You've received background information on Remilious Corporation. It's a large biotech company with operations in several countries, with its headquarters outside Marseille. A Somali national was smuggled into the private château of the main stakeholder, Boucher. There appear to be connections to al-Shabaad, al-Queda, al-Zawahiri, and Bin Laden. Everything we know is in your summary. Let's get busy and put the pieces of the puzzle together.' She looked toward Misa and Vidya.

Misa continued, 'There are a lot of threads to follow. Fred has assigned you individual tasks. Vidya and I will be working on resolving technical impediments. They're a big company with lots of expertise. Our first problem is their Peer-to-Peer Tunneling Protocol. PPTP is designed, obviously, to keep communication private, and keep people like us from snooping. It will be a trick to penetrate it. In our favor, we've got some experience using it here in our internet communications.' And then added, 'as you all already know. Fred, do you have anything to add?'

'As Misa said, there are a plethora of threads. The CIA is working on this simultaneously. That's no concern of ours. Our primary focus, at least initially, will be on discovering the Somali's connections to al-Qaeda and EIJ. The second will be on what Remilious companies' interest is in the Cigalle's association to the terrorist organization, including the professor in Egypt and the postdoc at Scripps Research. Third, the company has financial problems. See if there's a money trail. That's possibly the motivation for the involvement with the Somali. Let's filter out the chaff and find out what's going on. First report in one hour.'

'Kids, listen up,' said Misa.

'Hey, it's the old-timers telling us to listen up,' said Jason.

'Pipe down for a sec and pay attention.'

'Woo-hoo now. Bossy aren't we?' said Jake.

'Alright, alright. We need to hack a PPTP. Are you two interested?'

'We're always interested in the impossible,' answered Jason.

'Vidya just sent you what we know. Any ideas, guys?

'As cool as us dudes are, the only way to find a vulnerability is in the encryption packets,' said Jason.

'One way, maybe,' said Vidya.

'Back to you in a bit,' said Jake. 'We'll look at the protocols. I remember hearing that the NSA had found some vulnerabilities.'

'What do you think, Misa?' asked Vidya.

'First, we need their company's encryption algorithm. Then we start testing for weaknesses. I'll do that. Since you're the expert CIA hacker, find out if they have gotten into Remilious's system or similar. They want to be the only ones keeping secrets, so I'll wager they've spent some overtime breaking transfer protocols. What do you think about seeing what the NSA has accomplished breaking PPTPs?'

'You think they would share with the head of the CIA, the General?

'They're territorial. I doubt they would.'

'Are you considering hacking the NSA, too? I know you're good, Vid, but I feel sort of lucky that the CIA hasn't tumbled to you hacking them. Or at least they haven't let on that you did. Finding a backdoor was different with the Company. I think we should have Sheilla ask General Crystal, and then, if they won't cooperate, we do what we have to,' added Misa.

'The problem with that approach is that we alert them we are interested.'

'Hmm. Let's think on it a little. I want to hear what the Huachuca juvies have to say.'

'It feels good to be working with them again. I liked it

when we were a team back in the days and calling ourselves the Wolf Pack.'

* * *

General Crystal sat thinking he needed to see his labs. He pushed the intercom. 'Sandra, I'm flying back to the BWC tonight. I want to be there tomorrow by 0600.'

'I'll arrange it.'

'After, get James Taylor at the University of Washington on the phone.'

The General hesitated and didn't hang up.

'Anything else?' asked Sandra.

'No, no thanks. I was just thinking.' Will pushed further into his chair. Mulling the information over they had about Remilious. *It's good timing,* he thought. A mystery is just what I need right now. He sat up and dialed Sheilla on the secure line.

'General, hi.'

'I'm flying back later this evening and will be on-site at 0600.'

'It will be nice to have you back,' said Sheilla. 'We're full speed ahead with the Remilious questions.'

'Let me know what you find when I get in the air. I'll get Martin's report before I leave.'

A tingle flowed through Sheilla at the mention of Martin's name.

* * *

Boucher sat at the head of a glistening, oversized oval walnut table. There were two vacant gray leather chairs out of the sixteen. The room was Old World traditional with dark wood paneling. Behind Boucher was the most impressive painting in the corporate collection. A 1919 Monet oil in the Nymphéas series. It was relatively large, nearly four feet tall by six feet wide. It dominated the end of the boardroom.

A roll-up slide and video screen hung open on the left side of the room. No one had yet touched their upside-down crystal water glasses or their briefing papers that were all perfectly arranged in front of each person. On the opposite side from the screen was a massive, eighteenth-century ornate fireplace.

No one stirred. Boucher, wearing a meticulously pressed off-white linen suit and a dark green shirt with a matching tie. He was clean-shaven with glossy, perfectly groomed blackish hair, slim, and fit for his fifty years of age. He was a demanding boss and prone to sharp retorts with board members who disagreed with his plans.

The board members' received paid travel from their home ports as well as 200,000 euros for attending four meetings and a two-day annual conference. While most of them did not need the money, the amount was still sufficiently large to make a board position with Remilious as lucrative as it was prestigious. That is until now. Rumors were rife in the world's financial centers that Remilious was about to fail.

Boucher had faced many obstacles in his climb to power. This would not be the first time that he had been tested. He looked down the table at the four women and ten men present and then at the two empty chairs. Before the meeting, he had received resignation letters from his long-term chief financial officer and the son of the chairman of one of the largest banks that had been backing Remilious.

He cut through the silence, 'At the bequest of our consortium of bankers, I have replaced two of our board members. The consensus was they were not effective.' *At least that is what I will feed to these bozos, he thought.* 'It was a necessary step for them to continue to underwrite our loans.'

No one said anything. His statement had caught them off guard. The assumption had been that they had quit a sinking ship. Now Boucher was telling them that the two had lost the bankers' confidence, which implied the bankers were still supporting the company.

'In the report, sitting in front of each of you are the recommendations of our biomedical team. Both our research into finding a pan-flu vaccine and our ability to ramp up production using DNA plasmids will make us the world's leader in the field.'

He now had the rapt attention of the board. All of whom only minutes ago were weighing the lucrative money they received for such limited work against a hit to their reputations if Remilious went into receivership under their watch. All were powerful and successful; even so, each knew better than to say anything until Boucher indicated they were free to do so. Boucher had selected them all carefully. They had their esteemed reputations, which added to what he wanted for the board's éclat. But Boucher knew they were all weak beneath their superficial appearance of authority. That was the only thing he cared about. He was not interested in their opinions. The only thing he needed from them was to approve whatever motion he put in front of them.

Boucher watched Daphne Ariel Bisset, the savviest board member and the most likely to challenge him today. She was the wealthy founder of a hedge fund domiciled in Paris. Before the short, dark-haired, perfectly styled Bisset could comment, Boucher continued, 'I need three things from you at this meeting. First, in the papers in front of you is the refinancing plan. It requires your approval. You received those yesterday so as to have time to review them for this meeting. Second, your approval to proceed with our building non-egg-based vaccine stocks was also explained to you in advance. And third...'

Daphne Bisset cut in, 'We only received these documents late yesterday. Surely you do not think we can approve something without more time to evaluate it?'

'I expect just that. There is nothing particularly new in the documents. The financing is merely an extension of our current credit lines. If I may continue, the last item needing approval is welcoming our new CFO. She is waiting outside the room for you to give your approval. Then she will come in and answer any financial questions you might have.'

Boucher expected that Bisset would be the one to challenge him and had purposely left the third announcement of the new CFO until last. He also knew that Bisset was a fighter and a feminist. She had pushed her way to the head of her hedge fund with cunning and competence. Consequential to his plan, she had ties to one of the financial institutions he needed to continue Remilious' loans. Boucher wanted her support to convince the German bank to remain a lender. If they did, the other banks would fall in step behind them.

Daphne Bisset was canny, but in Boucher's opinion, her feminist side left her vulnerable. To his thinking, he had just played that card masterfully, announcing a female CFO. More important was the reputation of the new CFO as a past head of the German Federal Reserve Bank. He would have them all, not just Bisset, on his side as soon as he mentioned her name.

'Who are you proposing?' asked Daphne in a less assertive tone.

'The second page down in front of you has her biographical information.'

Almost in unison, the fourteen board members lifted the top page and looked at the new CFO's biography: Gabrielle Albrecht. A few read the bio contained on the page, while most looked up at Boucher with astonishment. Any thoughts some of them had had about resigning evaporated. Ready to join them outside the room was one of the most prestigious people they could think of.

'This is incredible,' said Bisset.

'I see no reason to leave her waiting in the hall,' said Frank Miller-Wilson, the head of a large energy company. 'I have no reservations in seconding your motion to add her as Chief Financial Officer.'

'And as a board member,' added Boucher. 'Her compensation package is generous, as you can see in the pages below her credentials. She is worth it to us at this moment in time. Any objections?'

'All in favor?' asked Jean LePen, the board secretary.

There was no dissent. All sitting at the oversized table approved her nomination.

'Note that the board, with unanimous approval, appoints Ms. Gabrielle Albrecht as Chief Financial Officer and as a board member,' said LePen.

Boucher was pleased. This had gone exactly as he had planned, instead of his having to convince the board that they were not going to collapse into bankruptcy, which would devastate their stocks and options. They were so taken by surprise by the new CFO appointment that they were dazed. Boucher would save the company, their board remuneration, and their wealth. With the information, they were already planning to call their investment advisors and increase their positions as soon as the meeting broke up and before word leaked about Gabrielle Albrecht. A few felt panicked after having expected the demise of the company and had reduced or sold their Remilious stock. Brokers would be receiving orders in the name of their daughters, sons, ex-wives, and various offshore companies to purchase. Boucher was counting on this as the insider buying would leak and would cause further buying by outsiders.

For those who were not U.S. citizens or residents, U.S. Limited Liability Companies acted as their tax-free vehicles. While the U.S. government was always busy disparaging "tax havens," few Americans knew that the U.S. was a top tax haven for non-residents. Millions of LLCs were registered in Nevada, Wyoming, and Delaware. All earning tax-free interest and capital gains in bank and brokerage accounts.

The door opened for Gabrielle Albrecht. Most of the board had never met her, but they all immediately recognized her face from her hundreds of appearances on news interviews and G-20 meetings. Her reputation was indisputable. She was here and would resurrect Remilious' status. Not because she was being well paid and felt like doing Boucher a good turn, but rather because Boucher's security investigators had discovered something Ms. Albrecht had kept private her whole life—she was a lesbian and did not want it made public. She had stayed in a secretive relationship for over thirty years with the same partner. Gabrielle was, to most people, unattractive, with short dark hair, stocky, bushy eyebrows, and graying crooked teeth, which could have been straightened as a child if her parents had thought it worthwhile. What some would say, unflatteringly, an ugly duckling. It was assumed that her dedication to finance, combined with her looks, was why she had never married.

Boucher had, of course, blackmailed her with the information he had found. It did not turn out as simple as he had perceived. She did not want the public to know the secret she had carried throughout her life. She was a deeply private woman. If she was exposed, however, she had long ago accepted that she could live with it.

Boucher quickly learned that while he set out to blackmail her, the tables had been turned. Albrecht had the power to keep his company afloat. She was a savvy politician and immediately understood what his game was. Besides protecting herself and her partner's personal life, she also understood that her reputation would be the first step in saving Boucher's company. And being saved is what he needed. No matter the cost.

# Chapter Sixteen

Brush took his eyes away from the mountains, reached over to the side table, and passed the secure bag phone to Glenda.

'Good morning, General.'

'It's about time you started calling me Will.'

'I forget sometimes. What's up, Will?'

'Nothing certain. We have an investigation at CIA concerning some possible terrorist links to a French company. I'm leaving D.C. tonight for the BWC and would like your input tomorrow. Martin is leading the investigation on CIA's end. He thinks we should get someone on the ground. With your investigative skills, I thought you might add to the discussion.'

'Where?'

'Tomorrow, BWC.'

Glenda looked at Brush and mouthed, 'He wants me at BWC.'

'I need some flying time in my Huey. And the weather

looks clear. I'll pick you up at the ranch house at 1100,' and the phone went dead.

'Noticed he didn't say us,' said Brush. 'Means he's probably going to snatch you out of my life for a spell.'

'Maybe, Big Guy, but we've had a pretty good time of it since Christmas. I've enjoyed spending time here together. First time I've ever delivered a cow.'

'It's a calf, baby. Not something I've done much of either. Good thing Roy is around. Guess it's okay learning some new tricks.'

'We got the rest of the day.'

'Ben's here to watch the cows and feed the llamas. I have been thinking about going up the big hill behind the house. I always thought it looked like a natural ski run.' Brush smiled at her. 'It's your birthday in two days, though. Got a feeling you won't be here. Lola and I planned something for you, so let's do a little hike and make it your b-day celebration tonight.'

'We don't have our skis here. And you know I don't care about my birthday. But it's nice of you to remember. I've got a better idea than checking out your ski hill.'

* * *

'While I'm gone, Martin, you pursue the Somalia-French connection. You've found out enough to know that there is a problem that we need to solve. Something is going on. I feel it in my gut. Keep Bertrand informed. Eric, if there's anything in the presidential briefing I should know about, call me immediately.'

'Any new developments on Eileen Skinner?' asked Bertrand.

'It's not firm yet,' answered Eric Sands. 'Her lawyer is negotiating. My best guess is she will get off light for the help she gave us in taking down the rogue drug operation and then continue to assist the DEA with information on the cartels and lower-level Mexican government players.'

'Let's talk about Remilious,' said General Crystal.

'We've been able to get a technician hired in their vaccine research lab, and we just received this from French intelligence. They have a new Chief Financial Officer. It should be hitting the wires about now.' Martin paused.

'Don't keep us in suspense,' said Bertrand.

'It's a shocker. The Honorable Gabrielle Albrecht,' said Martin.

'The ex-head of the German Bundesbank?'

'One and the same.'

'Doesn't fit,' said Bertrand.

'That's what our European financial analyst says too. Talking to him gave me an idea. The public perception is the company is in trouble. Now they add someone with an unimpeachable reputation, which implies maybe they aren't in that much trouble. There'll be a lot of interest in trying to figure out what is going on. Should we try to arrange for a financial investigator and see if we can glean some information about the Somali? Between the lab mole and a finance guy we might learn something useful.'

'Embedding a person is always a good idea, but it's hard to see how someone there for only a few days is going to get worthwhile information about the lab projects, or smuggling, spending their time with the in-house financial wizards?' queried Bertrand. 'Why not search backgrounds and find someone in need of money or with some buried secrets?'

'We've been doing that and will continue, but I like this other idea better. Big Wall Street firms make the markets. They want to know what's up, so they can sell or buy, or as my guys said, hedge. Lots of money at risk. We send someone tied to a known hedge fund or ETF manager, and the company will be compelled to open their books.'

'You think they will give someone straight financial answers?' said Eric, more as a statement than a question.

'No one expects them to. Technically, it doesn't matter. It's not what we'd be after.'

'Of course,' said Bertrand. 'Important fund investigators will get the red carpet. It might shed some light on the mystery.'

'Work it out and get me a plan,' said Will.

'I have a concept, but not the who.'

Will looked at him quizzically.

Martin shrugged. 'I anticipated you might say that, sir. Whoever we send has to represent a financial heavyweight. One whose opinion will elicit fear and compliance. We have one of those in our back pocket.'

Boucher knew that enlisting Gabrielle Albrecht was only a temporary move. His current cash flow was nowhere close to what the company would require to pay its bills and salaries. A few months at best, and then he was out of options. The extension she had convinced his bankers to provide came with an increased credit line, albeit small and short-term.

He needed a breakthrough and time to put the plan he had worked out with Visser into action. But first, he had to light a fire under his research lab's director, Dr. Murray Blackwell. The thin, tall, forty-year-old dark-haired Ph.D. and M.D., a graduate of Imperial College London, sat stiff-backed in front of him.

'You've read my opinion on the vaccines?' said Boucher.

'I'm not sure I agree Virus Particle is the safest bet.' *Is he getting this from that screwball, Visser?* Murray wondered.

'We need to pick one and focus on it,' said Boucher.

'What we need is to focus on the right one. Is Dr. Visser's laboratory group working on this now too?'

'No.'

Dr. Blackwell had never fully understood what Jelle Visser was researching. But then, it really was none of his business. Visser had nothing to do with Remilious' Marseille lab that he headed. But what's the big secret? He could probably walk into a competitor's company's and get more openness than he got about Dr. Jelle Visser from Boucher.

Boucher might be his boss, *but he didn't know squat*

*about the science,* he thought to himself for the thousandth time. *Stupid opinions ... as long as he keeps signing my paycheck, which might not be all that certain from what I hear.*

Boucher only understood enough about the vaccine research to get by with unknowledgeable people. He often purported that what others told him was his own original thinking, such as the report that Visser had provided this morning.

'Explain why VP should not be our choice.'

'It frequently requires multiple injections to elicit an adequate antibody response.'

'The new research indicates otherwise,' said Boucher assertively.

'What new research? I have not seen enough data to be convinced,' responded the ever-cautious virologist, Dr. Blackwell.

'We don't have the luxury of time. Remilious must become the leader in non-egg-based vaccines. We've been farting around for years, and we need a win now. You are the tops in your field. Use all your powers of reason and intuition and get me an answer this afternoon by 1700.'

'I can only guess.'

'I want your best guess. And it better be the right guess. Both our futures depend on you making the correct one.'

'I don't like this. I'm a researcher, not a gambler.'

'Both our incomes depend on you being right. Give me an answer at five this afternoon.'

Boucher walked out of the meeting room and

ascended the elevator to the rooftop helipad where his dark blue EC155 sat with its blades turning slowly, ready to depart upon his arrival. Boucher was the only passenger. He was flying to Château Noir to meet with Visser. The urgency of the company's needs was better understood by Visser than it was by the straight-arrow Blackwell. He needed results or he would no longer be able to afford to fly in his beloved Eurocopter at the expense of Remilious. If a person could love a machine, Boucher loved this helicopter. He bought it a year ago because it held a dozen people. Which was sometimes required to transport staff or government officials. What had made him fall in love, besides its sleek appearance, was how quiet it was in the air and its incredible speed. It topped 300 kilometers per hour.

Boucher had always loved fast cars and had a stable of several in the Château Noire garage. But nothing compared to the speed and efficiency of this helicopter. The trip to the château would only take minutes. Going fast for this short distance was unnecessary, but it made him feel alive to be in it racing over the countryside.

*Blue Girl* sat down on the expansive manicured lawn at Château Noire. A golf cart waited to move Boucher to the front entrance. He walked by it, not acknowledging the driver. From long experience, the cart driver gave him plenty of space before he turned to follow him. The man did not want to incur Boucher's wrath, as had happened a month ago.

Boucher stopped, looking back to admire *Blue Girl.* Then he flicked a finger, and the driver quickly drove alongside him. At the door, he was met by Dominique, his female butleress. Boucher had no taste for being close to men.

'I'll have a small lunch with coffee. Have security sweep my study and get Visser there in forty minutes.'

* * *

'We are meeting shortly,' said Visser.

'Our venture?' said the Middle Eastern voice on the phone.

'We are nearly there,' answered Visser.

'Boucher's company project?'

'Closer with the modification of the virus than to developing the vaccine.'

'Your time frame for both?'

Visser knew he had to give his al-Qaeda representative an answer. They were his insurance policy; in case something went wrong with Boucher. It went against his science training. Exact timing could not be guessed, and they might never succeed. He sucked in air and said, 'Two months.'

'You're sure?'

'It's an optimistic probability estimate.'

'A guess?'

Visser didn't answer. Even if it was impossible to predict the results of his research, he felt he was close to success. Having the Somali would be his first human test. He worried Boucher would go broke before he could complete his pet project. If that happened, his work at

Château Noire and his experiments would be kaput. It would stop his childhood dream, leaving him with only his al-Qaeda "friends" for financing. He couldn't see anything good following that result, and he needed to do whatever he could to not end up under their control. It would likely be the end of him and his zombie dreams.

Visser was not directly involved in the non-egg-based vaccine development. But he invented the concept that would create the havoc and make the vaccine a necessity for the world. The script had then been hatched when Boucher suggested that the company had to have a survival plan if his Alzheimer's drug approval were not approved by the FDA, and because of the inept faking of the data, it had been rejected.

Boucher had prodded the FDA and paid the wrong people to tweak the data. Visser thought the approach they had taken was lame. He was not surprised that better minds had figured out they had tried to cheat the U.S. government approval system. Business types always seemed to underrate the intelligence of the scientific community.

Boucher knew little and had little interest in immunology. Business machinations were where he excelled and sometimes failed. Not understanding the intricacies of molecular biology, virology, and science in general had caused his misstep. *How could the man own a biotech company and have so little knowledge?* thought Visser.

The answer was simple: Boucher had stumbled into the biotech business from a tech company he founded. He envisioned biotech as the future, along with robotics and automation. He had been correct in that surmise. What he had never grasped was that ordering a result, shelling out large sums of money, would not guarantee the outcome. Scientific discoveries were often slow processes interrupted by serendipitous leaps forward. Researchers plodded along and sometimes got lucky with their results.

Visser's brilliance, combined with unscrupulous morals, found a partner in Boucher, a man who only cared about the prestige that money brought. Not how he earned it.

Boucher's biological ignorance had left Visser with an opportunity he could only have dreamed about. A monied supporter. A secret laboratory. He had thought about his masterpiece for years. To most, what fascinated Visser was ludicrous, if not reprehensible. Boucher had provided him with the means to bring his, as Heinrich called it, kooky zombie scheme to fruition.

# Chapter Seventeen

Brush had never thought about getting married. For most of his life, he had run from relationships. Not that he hadn't liked them or adored many of the women in his relationships. He enjoyed being with women. He liked them. In his own way, he had loved several. But when they got serious, an instant mental block formed. He knew deep down they were not the right one—the one he wanted to spend the rest of his life with.

Then he saw Glenda Rose Stuart at the Space Needle. He was immediately attracted to the shapely FBI undercover agent. Minutes later, she was shot by Najma in what turned out to be a diversion for the terrorist's group's primary goal—attacking the Seattle Convention Center.

Brush had rushed to Glenda, putting pressure on the three bullet holes in her abdomen. Scars that he now relished. Evidence that she was a warrior. He respected her, and as they lay together, he liked nothing better than feeling the healed wounds' bumpy ridges. *Well, almost nothing better,* he smiled to himself.

He freely admitted it was her double-D breasts and strawberry blond hair that had attracted him when he first saw her. Looking at her and seeing her still had the same effect on him that it had then. If anything, it had grown stronger with time. It amazed him. Deep down, he felt none of the resistance he had with the previous women in his life. As good and fun as many were, there was always a niggle. Something was always wrong, something missing that held him back.

The time they spent together as she recovered grew from attraction to like and enjoyment, an admiration, an easy companionship. A daily necessity to be together. An understanding that there was something much deeper between them. The best and most important part of their day became the time they talked, joked, and flirted. Her wounds, as she recovered, prevented them from physical activity. Brush had never been restrained from making love to a woman he had been attracted to for so long. It became apparent to both that it was a unique experience, getting to know each other while they fell in love.

Brush looked at Glenda as they lay in bed. The feeling was one of certainty. Then, for a moment, an anxiety penetrated his thoughts; that she really didn't feel the same as he did. He knew better, but the way he felt was so special, a way he had never felt before. He trusted her and her feelings. The moment of worry passed.

*Was it the right time?* He had planned to wait until

they had known each other for two years. From the beginning of their relationship, he had understood that she was the one for him. The one he had subconsciously been searching for. He became intrigued looking at engagement rings. The searching and finally the purchasing of the ring, a 2.78 carat diamond, flanked by four smaller oval diamonds on each side. He had picked gold for the setting after debating between it and rose gold for what seemed like ages. Then he wondered if the stone was too large. Was the ring too simple or too traditional?

He had been carrying it with him in his rucksack for over four months. It was a constant reminder of the questions that rattled through his thoughts about if it was the right ring. There were still another four months remaining before the two years he had decided to wait for were up. It would be spring and a nice time of year.

As he looked at her, she turned to him and said, 'You are the most special man in the world.'

His resistance crumbled. His emotions said no more waiting. The time was now. They were here together, and she would be leaving soon. With that realization, he became slightly nervous. Something that was totally out of character for him. He turned to his right and reached into the rucksack compartment where he kept the ring box. He put it next to him, out of sight from Glenda. *Why am I nervous?* Later, it would come to him that it was her importance to him, the knowing she was the right one. He never wanted to be without her. His desire to be with her, protect her, cherish her, and feel the same from her caused the momentary nervous jitters.

It was a big decision, and he knew it would be the same for her. He wasn't so much worried that she would say no, as it was about the stunning significance of what he was doing. How it would affect their lives. What it would mean to them both.

He turned his face to look at her. 'I have something I want to ask you, and I'm a little nervous.' She looked at him, slightly perplexed, wondering what he could be talking about. Earlier, they had joked about what he said he wanted for his birthday. 'You mean you want the twenty minutes of oral sex now?' Then the realization hit her. 'Are we on the same page?

While she talked, Brush had placed the ring box on her nightgown, just below her chin. She hadn't noticed as her mind wondered what he was getting at and sensed this was no normal request.

Her chin touched the box, and she reached up for it. She held it for a few seconds before opening it. Elation poured through her veins as she opened the red box. 'Oh my God, it's beautiful.'

Brush looked at her expectantly. 'What do you think?'

'Yes,' was all she could say as they looked into each other's eyes.

'But you didn't ask me anything. I want a do-over.'

He looked at her translucent skin, the light red hair skewed haphazardly across part of her face. 'I want to spend my life with you. I want us to be together always. From the moment I looked down at you bleeding in the Space Needle, I had a feeling that you were the one. The rare person who makes life worthwhile. We didn't know that, of course. I didn't know, but I remember the feeling. You are special, intelligent, beautiful both inside and out. Somehow, we met, which is a miracle. I don't ever want to lose you. I want to be with you always. Will you marry me?'

# Chapter Eighteen

Twilight grays gave way to red-orange skies, summoning a new Colombian day. Jim turned to the horizon, *perhaps the dawn of new and better memories,* he considered. Jim, Maria, and Cherry sat sipping strong coffee outside Maria's tent. An old man with a slight limp walked toward them.

'Buenos días, Doctora.'

'Buenos días, Señor Gonzáles.'

Maria nodded and smiled at the old man. 'Jim, this is my new friend and very special helper, mi amigo y ayudante muy especial; permítanme presentarles al señor Alfredo Gonzáles.'

Jim was remembering Duane. Alfredo was missing a tooth on one side as he smiled, just like Duane had on the ranch.

'Alfredo, conoce al Dr. Johnson.'

'Encantado de concerlo, señor Gonzales,' said Jim,

feeling pleased that with saying good morning and introductions, his Spanish was passable.

A small hand touched Jim's shoulder. As he turned, a sleepy-eyed Pedro said, 'Alfred is nice like my Grankin.'

Cherry stood. 'Young man, would you like a cup of my especial cremoso chocolate caliente?'

Pedro nodded as he rubbed his eyes.

Maria poured señor Gonzales a coffee and patted the chair next to her.

Golden orange replaced gray and pink as the sun rose into a steely blue universe. As the sun rose, the songs of katydids subsided, only to be replaced by the morning cicadas.

Cherry said, 'Thick hot-morning chocolate for you, señor.' Pedro smiled at both the hot chocolate and her calling him señor.

The morning's quiet dissolved with a distant woman's yelling as two men, each holding an arm, escorted her to the coffee drinkers.

Cherry rose and walked toward them, casually carrying her AK-47. The rifle was a natural part of her. The book *Extreme Places*, which she had left sitting on her chair when she picked up her AK, held new and fascinating places that were all new to her. Books were changing her view of the world every day.

Maria put a hand to her forehead and grimaced. 'Please don't shoot the WHO rep,' she whispered seriously. Jim conversely looked bemused. He understood Cherry was an experienced fighter and had killed before. That did not mean she would shoot the woman in cold blood in front of everyone, especially the children who were gathering after hearing the noise. He felt as though he knew her well enough to be certain of how she would react. She had been skilled and levelheaded, not subject to a temper or erratic behavior. Jim knew her manner was only intended as a visual intimidation.

The subdued Imala walked back, looking decidedly uncomfortable between the two rebels. Cherry walked in front with a small smile she was trying, without success, to hide. Imala Begay was no longer struggling and cursing at the two men.

'Let me go now.'

Cherry looked at Jim, and he gave a slight nod.

'I think that woman would kill me, given half a chance,' said Imala.

'Have a seat,' said Jim. 'Perhaps instead of shooting you for bad behavior, Cherry will pour you a cup of coffee.'

'I don't have time to be social. I have a problem and need it solved immediately.'

Maria had removed her hand from her head. With her eyes half closed, her head swayed almost imperceptibly back and forth. 'What problem?'

'These people won't let me help them. They won't talk to me or my people. We need to get them to assist us. You need to get up and go with me and make them,' said Imala in her rapid-fire way of talking.

'Ms. Begay,' said Jim.

'Who are you?'

'If I may,' said Maria. 'This is Colonel Johnson.'

'What's an American Army officer doing here?'

Jim didn't answer. He stood and said, 'Pleasure meeting you, if you'll excuse me,' as he walked away and removed his sat phone from it's carrying case attached to his belt.

'Will, Imala Begay just joined us.'

'Ahh. I see. Don't even ask. I'll have someone call her on your phone. Talk later.'

Jim returned just as his phone chirped. He held it out to Imala.

Jim said, 'Phone is for you, Ms. Begay.'

'Huh. Who?'

'How did you know it was for me?'

'A good guess?'

She grabbed the phone. 'Who is this?'

Then she went silent, made a few faces, twisted her lips, and narrowed her eyes. After twenty seconds, she handed the phone back to Jim.

'Sit and have a cup of coffee with us,' said Jim, sounding friendly but said as an order, not a request.

Imala's mouth opened to say something, but nothing came out. She sat, more of a plop, nonetheless sitting, as Jim had directed.

'How did you get the director of WHO to call?'

Jim ignored her and said, 'Now if you would explain what the problem is you're having, I'm sure that Dr. Dakinc will see what she can do to assist you.'

Cherry nodded; she was impressed. It wasn't as if she was not aware the Colonel and her new friend Maria had influence. It was that she had underestimated how much.

She poured a cup of coffee for the chagrined Imala and smirked as she passed it to her.

'Who are you two? Who do you really work for? You're not just any old colonel.'

Jim ignored her question again. 'How can we help?'

Imala Begay was thin, with a dark complexion and long, straight black hair. She slumped in her chair and threw her arms up, flexed her hands at the wrist in a submissive gesture, puffed out air, making a small vibrating noise, rolled her eyes, and said, 'Okay. Alright.'

# Chapter Nineteen

Sheilla started to open the door to the General's office. Before she could, Glenda tapped her on the shoulder, causing her to jump.

'I didn't mean to spook you, Sheilla.'

'I didn't hear you come up behind me is all,' said Sheilla as she looked down at Glenda's shoes.

'Nifty, comfy, and quiet. Nike Airs,' said Glenda as she followed Sheilla's gaze.

Over being startled, Sheilla asked, 'How are you?'

Before she could answer, a subdued voice emanated from inside the office. 'Are you two going to talk out there or come in?'

'Sorry, Will.'

'Don't be. Come in, sit down. A face-to-face is good after all this remote communication.'

'Nice to see you, face-to-face, General,' said Sheilla.

'I second that,' said Glenda Rose. 'So, what's up?'

Will summarized the most recent information from

the CIA, which he had received from Martin only minutes ago. Then he asked Sheilla to bring him up to date on BWC's end.

'The computer team is moving fast, but with some problems. I think Fred would be best to clarify where the techies are.'

Before Will Crystal could push a button on his phone, Sheilla said, 'He's waiting outside.'

Will looked at her appreciatively.

Sheilla stood. General Crystal motioned her down and, in a cringe-worthy voice, said, 'Fred, in here now.'

Fred opened the door and said, 'Roger that, sir.'

'Give us the latest,' said Sheilla.

'We're currently split into three groups: the first is investigating Remilious staff and contacts with the Middle Eastern terrorists; the second is coming at it from the opposite direction, looking into al-Qaeda and how they could be connected to Remilious; the third is tracing all connections with the Somali's sister and her boyfriend. Misa and Vidya are trying to penetrate Remilious' communication protocols.'

'That should be easy for them, correct?' asked the General.

'Apparently, it's not, and is very complicated, sir. They are talking about things I am only vaguely familiar with. The company's Peer-To-Peer Tunnelling protocol is a major problem to hack.' Fred looked at General Crystal to see if he had said the wrong thing. He wasn't sure if he should use the word "hack." 'Late last night, they borrowed one of my team members whose specialty is neural networks. They haven't come out of the "Cave" since then.'

'Explain.'

'They're looking for the communication information that the CIA has and that they need.'

The General remained quiet, thinking *his spy agency, one of the largest in the world, was being hacked again. If his BWC team could do it, who else could?*

Fred squirmed. 'The CIA and NSA have been working together to gain access to the type of encryption algorithm Remilious uses: the PPTP.'

'It's the first I've heard of that,' said the General. Surprising, our working relationship with the NSA is not always what I would like it to be. When this operation is over, I think it's time I come up to speed on some of these technical issues and see if I can improve our intergovernmental relations,' said Will.

'Oh yeah, Misa got Jason and Jake involved. They're working on breaking into phone communications between Remilious and the Middle East,' added Fred.

'What about having the CIA techs work with our team here?' asked Glenda.

'We've always benefited from keeping the agency and BWC separated. The CIA approaches issues in their own way. Multiple approaches might yield better information than teaming up, but best to work separately for now.'

'Okay, so how can I help? I'm not a tech expert,' said Glenda.

'And you're not a financial numbers pusher for a

hedge fund either. But starting now, you are,' said Will Crystal.

Glenda sat looking at him, wondering what that meant.

'Martin is standing by at Langley to explain to you and Sheilla what we have in mind. Another player is on her way here now. She will be your partner. In a few days, you will be in France.'

'My French is pretty awful, sir.'

'Abenaa, your new co-workers' French is excellent.'

'Hey, I like Abenaa, our "Born-On-Tuesday" Nigerian lady.'

'She should be here by noon. Let's have lunch in the conference room at 13:00. I want to flesh out weaknesses in Martin's plan after you hear it.'

'If you don't mind me saying this, sir, it seems there is a lot of effort going into this based on scant information?' said Glenda.

'Perhaps, but not where there is an al-Qaeda or EIF connection. It deserves our attention.'

* * *

Visser had always been an *odd duck*. As a child, he was not liked and considered a nerd. Possibly, it was his physical appearance and his decidedly non-athletic nature. More likely, it was because he had an exceptional mind, but one with distinctly strange thoughts. Visser would say it was his brainpower that had steered him to more important things than testing his body against others. He didn't have friends. He didn't need them. He didn't even like people. They were a hindrance. He had decided long ago that he would find a way to leave his mark on humanity. The plan he had concocted and felt he was close to executing would leave him remembered in the history books, the way he wanted—the opposite of a Mother Teresa. The plan was coming together with the Somali, and it excited him to his bone marrow. Boucher's plan, one also from Jelle's devious mind to keep his company afloat, was interesting, even diabolical, which made it worthwhile in Visser's eyes. Even so, it was nothing more than a sideshow for his idea of infecting humanity with an incurable wide-eyed personality disorder.

'You have three issues,' said Visser.

'No, I have one issue: saving my company.'

Visser ignored the comment. 'Number one is eliminating the U.S. egg production facilities.'

'We have the government's largest egg-laying suppliers identified,' said Boucher. 'And the dispersant mechanisms are ready.'

'Issue two,' continued Visser, 'We are in final testing of the modified avian virus.'

'You are certain it will infect humans?'

'Even if not, with the U.S. not being able to produce vaccines, it should have a positive effect on enriching your pockets when Remilious is the only one with non-egg-based vaccine manufacturing.'

'My company's coffers, not mine.'

'As you say,' added Visser, not minding how derisive he sounded.

Boucher tensed and almost snarled with an intensity surprising to Visser, 'That phase is important to me. I want to smash the arrogant American fucks.'

*They've hurt his pride with the Alzheimer's rejection*, thought Jelle. He was correct. Boucher's ego had been damaged. It was not the sole reason, only part of what caused his anger. It was that American bureaucrats could destroy the company he had built from scratch. Remilious was everything to him. Like a child, he would do whatever it took to protect her.

'Issue three, and the real problem is Remilious' ability to make vaccines fast enough that are non-egg based. When the virus is released, it will rapidly expand past borders. No one will be able to control it. Chickens and people will die worldwide. Your Marseille lab will be the only drug facility that will be able to save the planet, Château.

'Exactly what I want,' said Boucher as he made a fist and grinned.

Visser continued, 'Any other biotech companies experimenting in that area will jump in and some might be competitive. This is where Remilious could fall behind, and governments will throw billions at the problem looking for a solution. The lab needs to be either far ahead with a vaccine or the beneficiary of their research money when governments become desperate.'

'I am surprised you've thought of government funding.'

'Why? You think scientists are ignorant that the world turns on money?'

Now it was Boucher's turn to ignore Visser.

'What I want are results. After the chicken and the egg work is resolved, I want you in Marseille.' *Especially after I follow up killing a big part of the U.S. chickens and people start dying with the new genetically altered bird flu,* Boucher smugly said to himself. *What will Visser think when he realises I already infected the U.S. bastards with his modified virus?*

*Kak,* said Visser under his breath. *You're so full of kak,* remembering a South African school friend's favorite saying.

'Ja,' answered Visser, 'I am holding up my end. It's the Marseille lad that needs to up its game, and I can do my job better from here both now and in the future.'

*You'll work where I want,* Boucher said to himself. He decided it was not important to aggravate Visser anymore at this juncture. He needed him to get what he wanted, so he changed the subject, 'Up their game, an American expression?'

'My educated opinion is that you have the best vaccine shot—Visser chuckled at his pun—with the safest and quickest response being, as I said, DNA plasmid. The problems with it in its current state, in my opinion, can be fixed. You've got a lot of intelligent people. They should be able to solve the problem. *But if it were me, I would spend my money on the VLP approach.*'

Boucher sighed, wondering why smart, expensive people couldn't solve problems.

Visser continued, 'Maybe your lab director, François, should start working on a backup to the vaccines, monoclonal antibodies. It makes sense to have your pan-vaccine research group see how they could generate substantial quantities. It would put you ahead of any competitors.'

'What are you talking about? You never mentioned this before?'

'It's not a vaccine, so no, I haven't, but I am mentioning it now.' Visser stood. 'I've discussed it several times with François and others in Marseille. I need to get back to my lab.'

'Sit. I want you to explain what you just said.'

Visser wished he had kept his mouth shut.

*Kak.* 'It's a way of producing antibodies in the lab that recognize a specific virus. Give your approval to François for the researchers working on the pan-vaccine to start researching monoclonal antibodies or convalescent plasma. After you talk to them, I'll put something in writing for you.' Visser almost added, one your simpleton mind can understand.

'You'll put it in writing immediately and before I say anything to anybody. And don't throw any more surprises at me like this.'

Neither of them said a word. The contempt each felt for the other permeated the room.

*I need this man, but damn, I hate him,* Boucher said to himself. *I am going to enjoy the day I can give Moriac the order to terminate this arrogant prick.*

While Visser was thinking, *the labs should focus on VLP, not Plasma. But I want to stall them so I have time for my rabies development.* Boucher would want to cause worldwide havoc infecting people after he successfully developed a virus that would jump from chickens to humans. But that day would have to wait until they had a cure and Visser thought, *and until I can cause my havoc for which there will be no cure.*

General Crystal walked into the conference room.

'Help yourself to sandwiches,' said Sheilla.

Will selected a chicken and coriander baguette from the tray.

'I haven't had one of these since I went east.'

'You mentioned you liked them once,' said Sheilla.

Will smiled at Sheilla and said, 'Glenda, your comments on Martin's plan.'

'The cover story fits. The weakest part is me and the finances—coming up to speed on interacting with their people. I expect they will be très sharp, which is about all I remember in French, other than Bonjour.'

'As many years as you studied it, I'll bet it will come back to you,' said Sheilla.

'You'll have training. Language skills for you are not important. You have accounting experience, and you will have backup support from both the CIA and your team here. And you're smart enough to adjust and think on your feet,' said Martin, as he looked at the group in the conference room on his monitor. 'I don't see it as an issue; you'll know enough of the finance details to get by.'

'Sheilla, your thoughts?'

'Her credentials are perfect. Just the sort of person a

hedge fund would recruit, and Glenda probably knows more than most with a JD and master's in legal accounting. Abenaa's degrees are less convincing.'

'It works,' said Martin. 'She's an engineering electronic tech analyst. She is there mostly because of her fluency in French.' *This is hard seeing Sheilla,* he thought. He had to focus, for the last several hours, to prevent telecasting his feelings to everyone when he looked at Sheilla. *Okay.* Then he continued, 'I want to send an assistant along who is fluent in French with good hearing that does not acknowledge his or her French language skills.'

'An eavesdropper,' said Sheilla.

'How long to prepare and get this on the road?' asked the General.

'I'd like a week,' answered Martin. 'But I'm pretty certain that long is not in the cards. Two days minimum; three would be better.'

'Two days here. You'll get the third day en route.'

'How certain are we that your hedge fund will back us properly?' asked Abenaa.

'Let's just say we have a lot of leverage with Brightwater's founder,' said Martin. 'Also, we have an asset in their company.'

'Why not use the asset to work with Glenda?' asked Abenaa.

'The finances are not the mission,' answered the General. 'We're investigating terrorist connections, not finances. Civilians are unreliable if the situation gets tense.'

'Understood, sir.'

'Our hedge fund expert will be on the plane to coach you and be available twenty-four seven in France along with a support team you'll have there and here.'

'Abenaa,' queried Martin. 'What is your petroleum engineering knowledge level?'

'It's almost like a second language. All I heard about growing up,' she said, thinking back to her childhood. 'I used to visit sites with my dad in Nigeria and Niger.'

'Your cover then will be that you are switching from an oil industry analyst to tech and biotech.'

'Glenda, your finance expert, Glen Adams, is here from Brightwater,' said Martin. He'll start you out. Abenaa, Fred will introduce you to the newest members of the computer group and then talk to Sergeant Williston about any gear you want to take with you. We meet back here at 0800.'

'How are things with my favorite cowboy?' asked Glenda.

'First time I've buried my whole arm up the personal parts of a cow,' answered Brush.

'Roy is bringing you up to speed with calf deliveries, huh?'

'More than I ever thought I wanted to know. So, what did the General want, eh?'

'He's sending me on a little trip to France.'

'He's not going to partner you up with some swanky French guy, is he?'

'Very swanky partner who speaks French, dark-skinned, muscular, smart.'

'So, I get to see the rear ends of Angus cows' day and night, and you get some tall, dark, and handsome French dude, eh?

'The "dude" has been here all afternoon, and you know her: Abenaa.'

'Ah, beautiful, you had me going for a second. I was about ready to tell Roy that I needed a vacation and head to France. So, what's the mission?'

'We're in business,' said Visser. Cigalle has developed a temperature. I allowed the sedative to wear off. He complained that he had a headache, muscle soreness, and was uncomfortable.

'You are certain he is symptomatic from the virus? That was fast since it normally takes weeks, and sometimes longer, in wild populations.'

'Considering the large dose I injected, and that it has been known to manifest itself in days. It's plausible. I think probable.'

'Maybe it makes sense,' allowed Heinrich.

'Let's consider ourselves lucky. Page the team and have them meet us here in one hour,' said Visser.

Visser, Heinrich, and nine others crowded around Cigalle's bed, where he lay sedated.

'The patient arrived last night,' Visser smoothly lied to the group. He might have told them the truth about

Cigalle, as everyone present was involved in some manner in his secret side project. It was Visser's basic distrust of people that prevented him from trusting unnecessary details with his co-researchers. Each of them, thanks to Boucher's money, was receiving double their normal pay. They turned a blind eye, so far, to what would be perceived as unethical research, such as using the human Cigalle as a virus reservoir. The researchers were well bribed, but as far as anyone knew, besides Heinrich and their al-Qaeda contacts, their research was to thwart terrorists using the virus against humanity, just as the BWC's primary mission was. The group convinced themselves that the unethical means balanced against the future positives for humanity made it acceptable. The idea had been pitched that they needed to modify the rabies virus to shorten the latency period. That was what a terrorist group would do and then find a vaccine to prevent it. They had no idea of what Visser's real plan was. Nor that Cigalle had been purposely infected.

'The patient was delivered to us with a 38.2 C temperature. While out of sedation, he complained of general discomfort and uneasiness. In short, flu-like symptoms. Since there is nothing, we can do to treat the disease after symptoms appear, I sedated him so he would be more comfortable. We, of course, will continually extract blood, spinal, and cerebral fluids for our research.'

'If he is sedated, how will you know when the symptoms have progressed past the initial phase?' asked one member of the group.

'This is precisely the question we must answer and

agree on. The patient is beyond hope. We cannot cure him. He's a lost soul. For our research to see the best benefit of preventing this awful disease from killing the 50,000 plus every year, we should correlate biological samples when his symptoms develop. The only way to do that is to have him conscious, or perhaps only partially sedated. It is the only way we will be able to monitor as the symptoms further manifest themselves. We have to decide.'

'In other words,' said the man who had asked the question, 'this is highly unethical research. Instead of following our oaths to do the best we can for the patients, to help and cure people. We're going to watch him go insane.'

'Perhaps, one man who is doomed to die to save thousands,' Heinrich countered.

Visser wanted to elicit the group's approval for one reason only. Three of his researchers were necessary for the completion of the genetic phase of the project. He would keep them only as long as he needed them and not a second more. After they had served their purpose, he had a plan to deal with them.

One of them added, 'As doctors, it will not be ethical to put this man through that kind of torture.'

'On top of that, not only do we not try to save him, but we do nothing to alleviate his pain and blithely collect samples,' said another member of the group, and one that Visser thought would eventually cause problems.

'It will be almost too terrible to bear, for me,' said Heinrich. 'But we must decide what's best, and I know of no other way to get the data we need. Does everyone agree?' While he waited for their answer, he wondered *how they would feel if they knew he and Visser never had any intention of sedating the Somali*. Visser wouldn't miss seeing the physical symptoms manifest themselves. All eventually, if unenthusiastically, nodded in the affirmative, including the complainer.

When the others had left, Heinrich said, 'You know that both Dr. Benthal and Dr. Krasner are going to be a problem?'

'Yes, and likely Christensen, too. We need them for the present. They're the experts we need for genetically modifying the avian and rabies viruses.'

'Are you sure we couldn't find different researchers for each? Our sponsors would pay. It is not effective to have them spread thin working on two projects at the same time. Most of us are working day and much of the night. I'm surviving on two to three hours of sleep. I can't keep it up much longer.'

'The modification of the $H_5N_1$ virus is proved easier than developing a vaccine. I think that is done except for double checking. I sense we're close with the vaccine. But, and it's a big but, who knows. We're going to have to give Boucher the transmissible virus soon. Only a small quantity. But I want a vaccine first, at least for me ...

Jelle paused mid-sentence while he focused on a thought. His mind was always racing around multiple problems. 'I know there's a vaccine solution.'

'What solution?' asked Heinrich.

'There's a solution to the receptor preference on the respiratory cells. I just can't figure out exactly what it is, but I know the answer is just sitting there waiting to be discovered. Kak, why can't those idiots in Marseille figure this out? Find a solution.'

'Good question,' said Heinrich. They have dozens more people than we do. Here it's almost impossible to find the time to deal with both projects at the same time,' said Heinrich. *What was Visser smiling for? I'm scared and tired, and he looks happy.*

'I understand, Heinrich. But if, after all final checks, we are successful with the modification of the bird flu, we will have time and money to focus on our other project, but if we can't deliver the modified avian flu ...'

*Your special zombie nutso project, not ours,* he grumbled to himself. 'Boucher will shut down our lab when he gets what he wants,' said Heinrich, finishing Visser's sentence.

'We have a contingency plan to move to Egypt,' said Visser.

'I don't trust those radicals,' said Heinrich.

'And you shouldn't trust zealots of any stripe,' added Visser. 'It was a trick getting them to provide additional money and getting them to agree to get the Somali here where they couldn't directly control us.

'I'm still not sure how you pulled that one off.'

'Partly money. We're using Boucher's, not only al-Qaeda's. The other was luck with Boucher's problems and the solution we offered with the avian flu. Both projects meet the goal of disruption that the backers are after. If we succeed, we can cause more damage than they ever prayed for,' said Visser.

'If we move the lab work to one of those dust bowl countries, they'll steal our data. We'll become expendable at some point. I don't want to die there,' added Heinrich as he looked at the Somali.

'We have plenty to accomplish here first, and not much time,' said Jelle. He tipped his head back and looked at the ceiling while he calculated and guessed the days needed to complete both projects.

Heinrich said, 'Those doctors will never keep their mouths shut after we finish.'

'I'm working on something to ensure that.'

Heinrich looked at Visser, knowing that if he wanted to have a life after Remilious, he needed his escape plan.

Visser smiled. Cigalle would provide him with hours of enjoyment. He would gladly sacrifice all his sleep time to see every aspect of the symptoms as they appeared. He would continuously film and have many hours of enjoyment watching Cigalle act out in his very own movie.

'Okay, Heinrich, I think it's best to keep our esteemed researchers away from the Somali. Tell them we decided after careful thought that it was not moral, and we will keep him sedated. I'll collect the samples. You make sure they focus on the gene alterations for both projects,' thinking now that he should never have allowed all the self-righteous scientists into his pet research project. *How is it possible for anyone not to want to turn the ignorant human race into zombies? Yah, because they already are.*

# Chapter Twenty

'Reminiscent of your days with the FBI?' asked Abenaa.

'With one exception, I had a little more time to prepare for undercover work,' answered Glenda.

'Martin has been grilling me,' said Abenaa, 'on our cover background. They are making our cover story the real us, as much as possible, but we'll use different names that they are inserting in the college and school records. It's easier to remember our new identity when most of it is true, like where I went to uni at the University of Miami,' said Abenaa, looking at Glenda directly with a small smile.

Glenda jumped forward in her chair. 'You went there too?'

'Yep, amazing, isn't it! They told me you did, too, on my flight out here. Cool, isn't it!'

'What did you major in? When were you there?'

'I'm excited to tell you, and it's also exactly what Martin wants us to do for the next couple of hours—reminisce. Get it fresh in our minds. He figures since we both went to U of M, we'd have an easy time with that part. Let's discuss our college days and then we can read our post-college cover stories, and I'll quiz you, and after, you grill me.'

'Okay. When were you there? From what year?' asked Glenda.

'Eleven years after you, I started in 1992. Did a joint degree in EE engineering.'

'Electrical engineering?'

'Close, electrical and electronics? Is that the joint degree?'

'No, just one, but I did a BA in Romance languages. Then I started a Ph.D. in French lit, but I dropped out. An M.A. was my consolation prize.'

'Why'd you drop?

'Some Special Forces recruiters took me up to Benning. They gave me a couple hours training and we did a static line jump. I loved it and they were serious about wanting me. So, I joined the army instead. Fort Gordon, Benning, and then Fort Bragg. I was part of an A-team for a year and then Neilly asked me to go to Rio and Colombia.'

'That was your first mission with them?'

'Yes,' she paused, 'I like that group. And it's like a big deal if I get to stay with Neilly's SF Special Activities Division. That first mission was just a checkout. What about you? I already know you did a JD with a master's in accounting. Sounds like you are perfect for dealing with the finance types at Remilious.'

'Let's hope that's true.'

'What sort of accounting?'

'There are several add-ons you can do with a law degree. I specialized in tax accounting. The FBI recruited me in my last year. I loved the training and the work at first … later, let's say I didn't like the male culture.'

'Understood. I expected it in the army, but it never happened. I always felt like an equal except for a couple of dumbasses here and there. I was accepted for who I am in Special Forces and especially with Neilly and the SAD guys.'

'I had some FBI supervisors who were gold star misogynists. One told me he picked me because of my boobs for undercover.'

'Did you straighten him out?'

'Waste of time. That was the accepted attitude.'

'What did the schmuck mean by the boob comment?'

'Said something like, with two missiles like those, you are way too obvious for undercover. You're such a standout with your bod and copper hair that no one in their right mind would think law enforcement would pick you to be incognito. My guy, Brush, admitted he sort of mumbled the same thing when he first saw me.'

'Did you forgive the Major for that?'

'Eventually, and it's nice to know he has always been attracted to me, and not only as a sex symbol. I found out what he really thought when I was recovering in the hospital, and we talked for hours.'

'I want to hear all about when and how you two first met.'

'Sure, when we can relax sometime. One thing I learned doing undercover: It's hard enough to live in your adopted ID. So, let's not confuse each other now with anything more outside our cover story. When it's over, hopefully, we can spend some downtime and get to know the real us.'

Boucher sat in his study looking at reports from the lab. 'Merde,' he grumbled. 'This is nothing but acronyms, mumbo-jumbo.' *How does anyone comprehend this crap?*

He picked up his pager. Heinrich called back a few seconds later as he rolled his eyes at Krasner.

'You have any lab junkies who speak good French? Someone you can send to my office? I need a clear summary of your reports. C'est n'importe quoi ! Immédiatement.'

'Oui, monsieur.'

'Not me,' said Krasner. 'I'm not going to get humiliated by him.'

'Suggest someone then. I've got to send a body tout de suite.'

'Forget your French. It's ridiculous.'

'That saying's universal. Come on, find me a person to explain the science to the boss, rapido.'

'At least you can pronounce German. Down by the third lab bench, see the guy with an earring and the multi-colored handkerchief on his head.'

'He'd better be good,' mumbled Heinrich as he zeroed

in on the man with the colored bandana who had his wrist bent and fingers down, doing a little dance as he worked.

'Enter.'

Boucher's PA opened the door and ushered Dr. Josh Ingram, minus his yellow and blue headscarf.

'Yes, sir. I was told you would like some explanations.'

'You have ten minutes to explain some of this in simple terms.'

Ingram studied the report that Boucher passed to him. 'What do you want to know?'

'I want to know what the fuck you are doing in your lab, using clear, simple words so I can explain to members of the board. None of these abbreviations.'

*They sent me as a sacrifice,* thought Josh.

'Are you just going to sit there? You're wasting my time,' said Boucher.

*Okay. If I can explain it to my partner at home and he says he understands it, I should be able to explain it to Boucher.* Josh took a deep breath.

'I'll throw out some basics to set the stage. The immune system is made up of two parts. The innate and adaptive. The innate kills invasive microbes as soon as it detects them. There are several types. The adaptive takes longer for the body to produce but is very specific to the particular bug it is being created for. I know this is far too simple for you?' said Josh, not wanting to insult Boucher and wondering what the correct level should be.

'Go on. This is what I want.'

'Let's stay with viruses. They have antigens the body uses to detect them and eventually destroy them with antibodies. It takes several days, up to a dozen, to produce enough antibodies to kill invading living entities.'

'Are you saying a virus is alive?'

'Some say that. Nobody agrees.'

'Keep going, rapidement.'

Upping his pace, Josh said, 'The virus we are working on is composed of RNA. Others are DNA. It's an obligatory parasite that uses a cell to survive and replicate. *He's got to know all this.* It can't live for long outside a cell, and it can't reproduce unless it's inside a cell. The answer to whether it is alive depends on your definition of life.'

'A human parasite. I like that. Proceed.'

*Amazing, he doesn't seem to know something so basic.* 'Some viruses live in human cells and some in other living things. The one we are interested in is an avian flu virus that has its reservoir almost entirely in birds. The three main types of viruses are: A, B, and C. We are concerned only with A, which infects humans and birds. *And other critters,* he thought. *Keep it simple stupid.* Viruses are divided into high pathogenicity and low pathogenicity. We are interested in HP viruses and their preventative vaccine.'

'This is going to take longer than ten minutes,' said Boucher, 'but I'll let you go on for a couple more. I'm looking for ways to present this simply to the board and our uneducated bankers. Will you write this out for me and go beyond the basics while keeping it simple?'

*Gardez les choses simples,* Josh repeated to himself. *The more I say, the more he'll expect in writing.*

'Of course, sir.'

'Continue.'

*No choice,* 'High pathogenicity avian influenza, HPAI, with the most well-known being the 1996 H5N1 bird flu that appeared in China and later in North America, but as an LP low-pathogenicity variety.'

'One more minute is all the time I can spare. What does H5N1 stand for?'

'It is just a simple designation for the seventeen or so viruses we know of. The "H" stands for hemagglutinin and "N" for neuraminidase.'

'Write it, but in simple words, for Christ's sake. Names like those two you just used will only confuse people. I know them and everything you are saying, of course.'

*He's the big boss, and it's obvious he doesn't know this stuff.*

'I'm just looking for simpler ways to explain to people with no training.'

*Un-huh,* thought Josh. 'Sorry, I'll put it in the written report in as simple of language as I can. *Dumbass. How do I simplify a science word?* Instead, he continued, 'Okay, if chickens get bird flu H5N1, they die, but so far it is only very low transmissibility to people, and we want to develop a vaccine for that because it's inevitable that it will eventually evolve into high transmissibility and kill humans. Once we have modified it, then a vaccine can be found.'

*Oui. Il ne sait pas,* thought Boucher. *He isn't part of*

*the plan. He doesn't know that we are going to release the modified virus.* Boucher smiled as he said to himself, *we'll kill a few million Americans before they get our vaccine.*

Joshua wondered what he was smiling about. Then he continued, 'But creating a bird flu that infects humans, one that is highly transmissible and lethal, has been difficult. This can happen naturally through reassortment. Two viruses come into contact with each other, and their RNA gets mixed up. In the lab, inserting RNA sequences into another virus's RNA is called recombination. What worries all of us is that we contain it while we develop a vaccine.'

'How close are you?'

Josh bit his upper lip and said, 'Very, I think.'

'Anything to add? Time for one more comment.'

Josh thought, *phew,* to himself. 'We have been recombining the H5N1 with the 1918 flu. It's our model.'

'Schedule another session on your way out. Get me a written report.'

'Of course, sir.'

'Send it to my secretary when you are finished. Before you leave today.'

Josh closed his eyes, relieved to be away from Boucher and peeved that Heinrich had gotten him into this. He knocked on Heinrich's door.

'How did you do? Survived, it seems?'

'Yes, I guess. He wants me to write up something and give it to his PA today.'

'You must have done well. Still employed. Better get to writing then. I want to see it before you give it to Boucher.

Give me the recording device I gave you. Krasner is looking after your lab chores.'

* * *

Maria slumped into a chair near the front of her tent. She closed her eyes for a minute. 'I'm going to have a glass of wine. Do you want to join me?' she asked Jim.

'Sure. You look exhausted.'

'Imala Begay has that effect on me. She talks fast, moves fast, and jumps from one topic to another. It's like being scooped up in a tornado.'

'Yep, I read her profile. A classic narcissist.'

'What mostly bugs me, though, is how good she is at her job. It's like she has some special insight. She proposed a solution to our pox tracing and inoculation problem. Blatantly simple idea. WHO is now doing random testing in each village or neighborhood in larger cities. It takes far less time than testing the entire population. If they get a positive, they vaccinate everyone in that group or village. She's calling it group random testing. Her theory is they will catch more cases way before they're symptomatic. They can test many more villages. Eventually, everyone will get inoculated, but it will take some time. This just focuses the process and will save lives.'

'Sounds efficient,' nodded Jim. 'What about the people who have traveled farther afield and to different countries?'

'Basically, the world's med community is alerted to watch for symptoms. Some countries are inoculating people who have flown in since the exposure. Others seem to be taking the wait-and-see approach if anyone becomes symptomatic. WHO is pushing a different strategy to the countries to get everyone they can inoculated. It will be several months before it can be completely stopped like when it was initially eradicated. It's a matter for WHO now. I don't need to be here or dealing with Imala.'

'As I see it, you have a problem. You can leave, but you don't want to?'

'You got that right. And are you here for a while longer or heading off?'

'I'm ready to leave for Ecuador,' said Jim.

'I had a feeling you might be.'

'It's been nice for Pedro and me to be here. Having coffee, sitting around the fire with you and the others. I hope to see Jago, Lobo, and the rest before leaving. All in all, a nice time. I've never seen Pedro have so much fun. Making friends, speaking Spanish. It turned out to be a perfect way to take his mind off what happened.'

'You can stay closer to him in this small community environment than you can by popping in and out of his life back home. *And nicer for me staying closer to you*, she thought, but instead said, 'Pedro's come alive, blossomed here.'

'I hope it will be the same in the Amazon. Not having Jean-Paul interpreting will change the dynamic. We'll have to find a way to communicate with the Shuar,' said Jim. 'Talking is out unless we can get an interpreter who is as good as JP. Angel might be able to provide us with one. She's busy, I hear, being an up-and-coming public official in Quito. Following in her father's footsteps, but her passion is still with the indigenous groups, especially the Shuar.'

'I have very fond memories there, too,' said Maria. 'Not the least of which was learning about the ancient head-shrinking methods. That was unique. And I sensed a lot of what I feel here. Small communities without freeways and TV have a different feel. Do you plan to contact Angelica?'

'I don't know. I haven't given it much thought. Maybe if she could provide an interpreter.'

'Angelica Noboa is attracted to you, Jim. I could see it every time she looked at you. There's another one too, our Rio professor, Zarita.' Maria looked at Jim, thinking, *does that make three of us?*

Jim gazed into the fire. 'They're both fine women for somebody, but it takes two for a relationship. Even if they were interested, I don't have any interest in another relationship, and I'm not sure I ever will.'

'We both miss her. It will take time.' Maria reached over and took his hand. 'You will be okay, and you have lots to take care of—the ranch, the lab, and especially Pedro. Heather never would have doubted, Jim, that you would watch over everything she cared about.'

'I guess it is her legacy.'

'I often think about the four crazy years we spent together at uni. Ben got an earful about some of our adventures when we were on my sailboat. I think more stories than Heather wanted him to hear,' she said, smiling as she picked up her wineglass.

'I don't suppose I've heard them all, either. But she talked quite a bit about those days and you, as her best friend.'

'I felt the same.'

'Jim, I'm a little worried about my new best friend. I'm pleased that Cherry has a passport and can potentially see some of the places she is reading about and incessantly talking about. I'm wondering, however, what is being unleashed on the world?'

Jim laughed and said, 'Cherry deserves, for the first time in her life, to be able to follow her dreams.' And then added, 'I think she understands there are two different worlds with different sets of rules. I'll try to discuss it with her if I can find a tactful way. She's not stupid.'

Maria looked at Jim, thinking she had always found him attractive. Going further with that thought had not been an option. She had dismissed it a long time ago because of Heather. Now, with Heather gone, should she explore her attraction? Then she shook her head. *Nope. Heather is still very much here for both of us.*

Jim wondered what the head shake was about. 'What happened to Professor Zarita Iglesias?' asked Jim. 'I thought you said she wanted to visit here and learn something about the smallpox virus?'

'She did, but she wrote, apologized, and said she couldn't break away from work on some big new project.'

The camp was becoming still under a star-filled sky. They sat sipping their dark red wine. Maria drained the last droplet and set her glass down.

'I think you've done an exceptional job here, Maria,' said Jim.

'Thank you, sir. I appreciate you saying so. A trying day today, to say the least. My eyes are drooping. Our narcissist whiz-brain has me yearning for sleep.' Maria stood, holding onto Jim's shoulder with one hand. 'Night, night. See you mañana.'

* * *

'I could get used to flying this way,' said Glen Adams. 'We travel in first class with the hedge fund's money, but nothing like this.'

'The General sent us in style, and we needed privacy,' said Glenda.

'He looked less than happy when we dropped him off in D.C.,' said Glen. 'Seems like the head of the CIA is a pretty plum job.'

'Some would say so, but he's a med doc and his heart lies elsewhere.'

'I didn't see anything medical about the offices we met in at Lewis-McChord.'

Neither Abenaa nor Glenda responded or gave Glen any indication that the BWC offices above the lab's underground facilities, where Glen had been coaching them, were anything other than camouflage for the lab workers coming and descending into their below-ground lair.

'Government facilities tend to be rather dull,' said Glenda.

Glen looked back at the four oversized executive

lounge chairs toward the rear, thinking the offices might have been drab, but this plane looked the opposite. The chairs were filled with three new arrivals from D.C., all sleeping. One that he had not met who boarded with them at Fort Lewis was busy looking at a large monitor.

'Interesting bunch we picked up in D.C.'

'If that's a question? They're CIA technicians. Part of our backup.'

'What about that guy?' asked Glen, pointing his finger.

'Tom pushed his hat up. My nickname is Techie.'

'How did you know I was pointing at you? Do you have a peephole in your hat?'

'Sixth sense,' said Tom as he looked at Glen.

Who thought for a second and said, 'You look more military to me than you do a technician. So do you, Abenaa, for that matter.'

'How does a military person look?' asked Abenaa.

'Um, ah, you look pretty fit. Maybe it's the way you walk. You walked up the steps in front of me, floated up them like you were hovering over them.'

'I work out,' said Abenaa, smiling.

'Me too,' said Techie.

'Let's get down to business,' said Glenda. 'What's next on your teaching us finance agenda?'

'We go over jargon again. You must have all those nasty words and acronyms down cold, or you'll get caught out. This is a big company with high-end people. Your cover is to grill them and see if they have a future worth putting millions of dollars behind for our hedge fund. They'll be a lot more interested in grilling you about

Brightwater. If their company goes down, they'll be looking for jobs and we are the top of the desirable list. Truthfully, while I'm going to be trying to keep you two out of trouble, I'll be scouting them for standouts. I have bios on several of them.'

'I wouldn't mention your side project to the CIA, Glen. Everyone will be expecting 100 percent involvement in our mission, including me.'

'Point taken, and you'll have it, but I can still keep my eyes open.'

Tom tipped his hat down, shifted his chair to face the front, stretched out his legs, and said, 'Sleep when you can.'

'You ready, Abenaa?' asked Glen.

'Twenty questions again. Yeah, I'm ready. Fire away.'

'It's more like 220,' said Glen. 'Let's start with simple derivatives and move into some more exotic swaps later.'

Before they could begin, the steward said there was a call for Glenda.

'Heh, Martin. You're already back at work?'

'You joke, of course.'

'Martin, let's have Abenaa join the call.' She motioned to Abenaa.

'Sure, I'm not back in D.C., still at the labs. We have new information from my group and from the BWC. You should be getting a fax with full details. I'll summarize for you. The Somali family was found dead. Executed at their home. Unfortunately, our informer was also found dead. His last report said the trail led to the Egyptian Islamic Jihad or EIJ and probably all the way to the top man Ayman Mohammed Rabie al-Zawahiri.'

'Apparently, your informer was getting too close to something, or someone is covering their tracks, or both,' said Abenaa.

'Exactly. The Somali and Remilious now look possibly connected to EIJ. The second thing is much more detailed. The computer team intercepted an unencrypted message from a Remilious employee's email. The full text is in the fax. The man said he would be late getting home because he had to write up a report for the big boss on the project. It goes on to say the boss is ignorant and this employee, Josh Ingram, was given the duty of explaining some basic virology along with some of their top-secret genetic modification research.'

'Any idea what he was talking about?'

'No clue yet.'

'Alrighty, thanks. Later, Martin.'

* * *

'Moriac, assure me everything is in place for this phase?'

'It is. I'm ready to depart.'

'Leave tomorrow. The plane is waiting. I want you on-site the day after.'

Marcel nodded, signifying "yes" to Boucher.

'There won't be anything that can come back and bite me, will there?' asked Boucher.

'You hired me because I don't fuck up,' as he bore into Boucher's eyes until the CEO dropped his gaze.

'The chicken facilities are all similar and their security systems are nonexistent. We release it first in Mississippi. Then I'll drive to the northern states. The plane will pick me up and I fly back to France from there.' Moriac, however, trusted no one. He had no intention of releasing in Mississippi or any southern state. The largest producers were in the north. He wasn't going to give Boucher or anyone else his true plan. He wanted in and out of the country as fast as possible, not driving a thousand miles exposing himself.

Boucher hesitated while contemplating Moriac's stocky body, large, scarred hands, and his reputation as a bad guy before Boucher's "I'm your boss" nature took over. 'Why is it going to take you three-plus days? It's a one-day drive.'

Marcel thought that this man would last two minutes in the field. 'Caution, so it does not come back and bite you,' he answered with an unsmiling look that ended the questions.

# Chapter Twenty-One

J im's and Pedro's plane ride to Cuenca was not as plush as Glenda's and Abenaa's had been to France. In an unexpected decision, Maria had asked if she could go with them to the Amazon. Then her new friend Cherry, who had gotten a travel bug, wanted to go too. In the end, thanks to Angelica's newfound authority in Ecuador, Cherry, a known, however *retired* guerrilla fighter, was allowed to enter the country officially. After Colombia had been persuaded to issue her a passport. For the Colombian government, it was an acknowledgment that she had been instrumental in ridding Colombia of its rogue army general. Combined with a small amount of prodding by the U.S. government.

The Colombian authorities provided an Airmada de Colombia navy-gray Beechcraft King Air to transport them to Ecuador. Three seats had been removed to make room for extra cargo Sergeant Williston had packed for them at the BWC. Jim always felt naked without ways to defend himself and the group, especially with Pedro and Maria along. He was glad to have Cherry with her skill set. Jim knew the risks were small, nevertheless, he had no illusions about the dangers posed by pockets of guerrillas, army deserters, rogue miners, and those opposed to Angelica Pérez's desire to protect the tribes and their lands. He had no worries about the indigenous Amazonians or the Shuar. It was the "civilized" people he worried about.

The Citation X landed in France. It was immediately hooked up to a tow truck and pulled into a large hangar. The cabin crew was ordered to keep the door closed until they were given permission to open it. After several minutes of waiting, the door opened, and the steps were lowered. Three men and two women stood near three vans. One came toward the steps as Glenda descended.

'Bonjour.'

'Mon français est très mauvais,' answered Glenda.

'I am Liam Allard. Pleased to meet you, Ms. Stuart. And you, Ms. Bissong,' Liam said as Abenaa walked up.

'You know who we are?'

'But of course. The agency sent your information ahead.'

'You work for the company?' asked Glenda.

'In a manner of speaking, yes. The five of us are here to assist you. Please let's talk in the car. It's only twenty minutes to our command post on the outskirts of Aix-en-

Provence. Remilious has someone watching our building out on the street. That is one person we have spotted—there may be others. Which is why we directed the plane to park inside the hangar before letting everyone disembark. If you please, let's get in the cars.'

'Remilious is expecting us. So, why the secrecy?'

'You have several more people than would be normal. Your cover story would dictate that you would only need you two and perhaps one assistant. It might have been better to have them travel separately. Not to mention they might try to find my team's affiliation.'

'C'est vrai,' answered Glenda. 'You have three cars with blacked-out windows. They won't know how many there are of us.'

'Precisely,' said Liam.

'What make of vans are these?' asked Abenaa as they walked toward them.

'You are interested in cars, or in this case, vans?'

'Weird passion. Surprising to see one I don't know.'

'Nine-seater Peugeot Expert Tepee or cargo van.'

'Interesting name.'

'Oui. Whoever was responsible for that bit of creativity needs their head examined.'

'Je ne pourrais pas être plus d'accord,' said Abenaa.

'You agree the name stinks. My briefing mentioned you were fluent in French and Ms. Stuart had studied some French in school,' said Liam as he closed the door to the second car.

* * *

'Tom, I want to ask you again—do you mind if I call you Shuskin instead of Tom? If it bothers you, I won't, eh?'

The ex-old man of the woods shook his grizzled head. Tom Shuskin looked at Brush as they stamped off snow on the cabin's porch.

'It's an oven in here,' said Brush.

'I could feel the heat seeping through the walls on the porch,' said Ben.

'Is it okay for Ben and Roy to come in?'

Shuskin didn't answer. 'It's up to you,' prodded Brush.

'Uh huh,' Shuskin answered, looking down at the floor.

'Ben, Roy, come on in and get toasted,' said Brush.

'You like it this warm?' asked Roy.

Shuskin stared but didn't answer.

'Well, that there means this iced beer is going to taste mighty good,' said Roy. 'Yep, Ben, one for you too.'

'Sounds like a winner,' said Brush.

Roy passed a beer over to a confused-looking Tom Shuskin. 'One for you too iffin you want it.'

'It's plenty cold out there except for when my arm is stuck inside a cow,' said Brush. 'How many more calves are still due?' he asked Roy as he pulled out a bottle opener and flipped the lid off his and Shuskin's beer.

'You'll be happy to know we's about half done.'

'Half!' exclaimed Brush. 'How many winters have you been doing this?'

'Most ah my life.'

'I still think you could find a way to have them when it's warm. And I know, I remember you saying that you have to feed the yearlings all the next winter if you had them in the summer.'

'Best to have them now and sell them in the fall, like we've always done. You know we can handle the rest of the birthing, Ben and me.'

'Ah sure, I know. But it's a new experience for me. It's a surprise learning just how hard you rancher types work. Besides, you think I could sleep peacefully knowing you two were dealing with the calving all night while I was getting my z's.'

'That's right nice of you,' said Roy. 'You and Jim are cut from the same mold.'

'Shuskin,' said Brush, changing to a new topic. I'll bet you wonder what we're doing here in your home.'

Shuskin stood with his mouth wide open. *Home, Brush had said, my home.*

'It's a social call. If you want us to go, just say so. It's your place.'

Shuskin didn't move, staring at them for a minute before nodding to the chairs at the table.

Ben said, 'Here's to warm cabins and good friends.'

'I'll drink to that,' said Brush.

Shuskin was still having a hard time figuring out why they were in his cabin. Social calls had not played a part in his past life. Ben had become his ranch pal, and he remembered his first encounter with Roy up in the mountains. Roy had treated him like everyone else, just as they were doing now. He slowly raised the Budweiser bottle to his lips and took a sip.

Brush looked at Roy and Ben. 'We can't stay long. We

only wanted to stop by, say hello, and warm up. Roy and Ben got the message.'

'Stay,' said Shuskin through a mouth surrounded by several days' gray stubble. He gave them a lip-pinched-together smile that obscured his new dental work and sat on his bed. The cabin was small, twelve by twelve feet. The table was in the center. The room felt full with three visitors occupying rickety light, blue-painted chairs. The paint was peeling and smudged. One chair had a wire barely holding it together. Shuskin's bed was against one wall and the pellet stove Jim had installed for him on the opposite side, throwing off a near-suffocating heat that blended with the ice-cold air seeping through the cabin's cracks. There was a window over the bed, one on the back wall opposite the door, and over the sink. Adjacent to the sink, a weathered wood board with a four-burner propane cooker sat perched on top of a none-too-stable wood stand. The sink stand had a hole cut out to hold an old white porcelain sink. The drain went straight down through the floor, three feet into the ground, and then angled down another two feet to a buried plastic drum with holes drilled halfway up to the lid. A miniature septic tank. There was no running water inside. Outside, just past the porch, was a red frost-free hydrant with tape wrapped around the handle to keep moist hands from sticking to the metal.

The frost-free hydrant was supplied with water via gravity through pipes from the artesian well near the house. The same gravity system fed the barn and the lower fields. Pipes buried five feet below the surface might have been deeper than necessary to keep the water pipes from freezing. Jim had reasoned when he dug the trenches that the extra couple of feet only took a little more effort and provided extra insurance against freezing winters that were often long and cold.

Shuskin withdrew water from the frost-free and filled a plastic container inside his cabin that sat next to the silver metal propane stove. The five-gallon jug had a valve near the bottom to let water out.

As primitive as it sounded, Shuskin thought he was a sheik living in a Hilton penthouse suite. That is, if he had the slightest concept of rich Arabs or penthouses. As he sipped his beer, he didn't say anything but nodded a few times. All of them were starting to feel certain he liked that they had stopped by.

'Well, guys. It's dinnertime,' said Brush. 'I'm thinking I'll go up to the house and then check the cows six, eight, and ten. Ben, you're up for the middle-of-the-night shift?'

'Yep.'

'Shuskin, you want to ride up with us for a Lola special?'

'Not me,' said Roy. 'I'm a go'n' down and sack out if I gotta be up here at six to spell Ben.'

'You could sleep in and come up at eight,' said Ben.

'Nah, I'll meet you at the upper barn at six. Kinda like it thata way.'

'Shuskin, how about you ride up with Ben and me?'

As was normal for the old man, he never really knew what to say. When new things happened to him, it befuddled his brain. He was still a little uncertain about the social call and exactly what it was, but for some reason, he kind of did like it. The old man of the woods however understood a dinner invitation of Lola's cooking. He stood up and followed them out the door.

*** * ***

'Vidya says he has an idea for breaking the encryption on the tunnelling protocol. Something to do with the developers using only a few prime numbers,' said Fred.

'Amazing, at least I suppose it would be if I knew what you were talking about. I think I understand how difficult the project is, though,' said Sheilla. 'What else?'

'Communication is set up at the French operations center. Glenda, Abenaa, and Glen Adams are still prepping for their cover. Doug Perri has a secure tunnelling protocol communication back to us.'

Sheilla looked at Fred with raised eyebrows.

'Yeah, I know if Vidya can hack Remilious' encryption, it means someone could hack ours. Maybe, but the Wolfy's say ours is the best.'

'Hmm ... there's always someone better,' said Sheilla. 'Let's keep that in mind and talk about it when this mission is over. I'll be back in an hour. Page me ...

'If we need you, I will,' said Fred.

Sheilla turned to leave. Before she could, Vidya shouted from the far side of the cave door entrance.

'We cracked their email encryption. We're going to need a smart program to find the stuff we're interested in, however. There's an immense quantity of emails.'

Vidya turned as Misa pushed up against him. 'Mikey.' He was rewarded with a sharp elbow to his side. 'Oops,' he laughed, knowing she hated it when he called her that. 'I meant to say, Misa has found something that might even be more important.'

'Actually,' said Misa, 'not just me, but with the help of the NSA and CIA. It was a trick because the encrypted Wi-Fi at Remilious has a kill switch. If we try too many times with the wrong password, alarms go off and unless someone intervenes, the data gets erased.'

'Pretty aggressive,' said Sheilla.

Vidya said, 'The cool part is Mik ...,' he looked at her ... 'Misa hacked the kill switch. So, we're monitoring both the Egyptian professor's email and phone. Nothing suspicious yet.'

'We still aren't able to find the exact location of the phones within Remilious,' said Misa. 'We might not be able to. And the general area the calls go to is in Egypt's northern Sinai Peninsula. Gloria, Peter, I sent you some tech problems we need to work out solutions for before we can trace them more precisely.'

'We'll do our best,' said Peter.

# Chapter Twenty-Two

Pedro lay asleep on a tattered old sofa in the mess hall shack that used to be a CIA Toucan training headquarters east of Cuenca and west above the jungles of Ecuador. His head was nestled on Maria's lap. Cherry lounged in a matching chair, reading a DK travel guide Jim had brought. She had been in the Amazonian jungle several months ago when the Special Forces team, along with Jim and Brush, had captured her and Jago's FARC band.

Cherry was excited. Her eyes stayed open as though held by an invisible force. The pages captivating her. This was the closest she had been to a city, and she couldn't get enough reading about it. Her life had been in the mountains and the Amazon, which was all the same green jungle whether in Colombia or Ecuador. What fascinated her were the places she had never seen, cities and ocean: Cuenca, Quito, and the Galapagos Islands. She had never been to a large city or seen an ocean. The unique animals and reptiles of the Galápagos enthralled her, but not as much as the sea.

Jim sat on a dining room chair facing Maria. Its pitted chrome and vinyl was straight out of a '50s kitchen. His left elbow was resting on an old Formica-topped table. Someone years back had ferried in the furniture for Toucan's CIA and SF training soldiers.

Jim looked at Cherry and back to Maria. The two women radiated confidence and strength of character in different ways: Maria with tousled brown hair with light-blond highlights, Cherry with her jet-black hair and darker complexion. Jim chuckled to himself at her fitting nickname, "Cherry Bomb." Both women were average size. Cherry was the voluptuous one while Maria lacked Cherry's physical attributes; she had alluring puppy dog eyes and a comely lopsided smile. Even though their looks contrasted sharply, their character, is what drew them together. They couldn't be more alike; they both knew who they were and radiated confidence, were quick, proud, and determined.

Maria softly stroked Pedro's hair. She closed her eyes for a few seconds. 'I understand why he's tired. The flight and the drive wore me out too.'

'You've been busy working in Colombia. You have a right to be exhausted and sleepy. It's always been the opposite for me—not having any work responsibilities almost always leaves me feeling relaxed but not tired.'

'You might be right. I have had little time off since that day on the boat with Ben. I'm looking forward to getting back to the Shuar village and seeing Pwanchir and

Pempeyo. I can't wait to see how the shrunken heads turned out.'

'Your curiosity about those heads will continue to make you a hit with the Shuar.'

'You think it's odd?'

'Not a bit. I understand it.'

'You don't think I'm morbid?'

Jim shook his head.

'Maria smiled at him, thinking, *we've both seen a lot of death and suffering. Maybe it leaves us having a similar view of the world.*

'J-P said the Shuar didn't have the same conception of time that we do. He said he did his best to say I wouldn't return for some time. I'm glad it won't be long now. He was worried that Tshui would be disappointed.'

'She became very attached to you. Won't it just make it worse if you show up and leave again?'

'Don't know. It's a conundrum. One step at a time, and hopefully something will happen to help resolve it.'

'I seem to remember Heather telling me that was often your attitudeif no good solution to a problem can be found, then you set it aside and wait, not forcing it, assuming an answer will emerge.'

'True. I don't know what else to do about Tshui, Maria.'

'You mentioned the shaman said they had to move their village after the snake bite. Do you think they have?'

'I checked satellite at the labs. It hadn't moved, it was still in the same place as when we left.'

'As soon as Pedro wakes up, I'm going to hit the hay,' said Maria.

'Go now if you want. I'll carry him. He won't wake up.'

'It's a nice feeling having him lying here. It makes me wonder if my career ahead of all else was worth missing this. Having my own children.'

'Maria, you would have made a great mom, but there are lots of parentless children in the world. Ones that desperately need a family and a place to call home. I always thought I wouldn't seek one out to adopt. But if one fell into my lap, I would. I got lucky with Pedro. Maybe the same will happen to you.'

*Pretty slim possibility*, thought Maria.

'Heather was still undecided about kids. Finding Pedro made her realize that what you are feeling, being close to him and him to you, is more important than passing genes along. It's the caring and love that counts.'

'I want to hear the story again about your first meeting with Pedro in Mexico. Not now, but when we have time.'

'Instead of mine, maybe we could get Pedro's version.'

'I'm not sure that is a good idea yet?'

'I don't think it would bother him.'

'You're probably right. Heather wasn't there.'

'It was Najma shooting at us that might upset him and remind him of her.'

'Possibly, but I doubt it.'

'It's hard to know how protective to be. It's not something I've had much practice with.'

'Me neither. Here's another question: How did you and Brush meet?'

'I thought you were tired?'

'I am, but I've wondered for a long time. Just start, and if I fall asleep, it's not because I'm bored.'

'An abbreviated version for now. Okay?'

Maria smiled. 'Sure.'

'I was recruited by the CIA. My first mission with them was to go into Cambodia and do a firsthand recon of the NVA coming down the Ho Chi Minh trail.'

'You went there in the army first, not as a super sleuth?'

'I never was that, but yes, I went there as a lieutenant. I penetrated the border southeast of Tây Ninh near Trâng Bang.'

'You were alone?'

'Easiest way to stay incognito. So, I had been there for several days when a firefight erupted. I got in close enough to see that a small group of American soldiers were over-whelmed by a North Vietnamese Army force about four times their size. And more NVA likely on their way. Both sides were getting reduced to half their original. The Americans were better trained, taking out three or four for every one the NVA killed. I didn't know at the time that it was a six-man recon patrol. The army wasn't supposed to cross the border, but somebody wanted the same intel I was sent across to find for the agency.'

Jim smiled as he watched Maria's eyes close and her head tilt to the side. Then her head popped up. 'And you did what?'

'I worked my way around to the NVA's flank. I didn't know it, but by then the Americans had lost four of their six. Caught in our crossfire, the NVA that didn't die retreated. Everything went quiet. I moved to the American position. There was only one left.'

'Brush,' said Maria.

'He said he was part of an army LURP patrol that was doing the same thing I was.'

'A "LURP" patrol?'

'It's a long-range reconnaissance patrol, LLRP. We pronounced it like "slurp" minus the S.'

Maria's head tilted back, and her lips parted. Jim just sat and watched her sleep for a few minutes. Then he looked over at Cherry, whose head was drooped over with her book lying open on her lap. The air was still, with only a faint sound of katydids. Maria's head fell further back, which woke her. She opened her eyes and smiled drowsily.

Jim didn't say anything. He walked over and scooped up Pedro, balancing him on his shoulder with his left hand. Jim reached down with his right hand and guided her to her cot. He decided to leave Pedro with her. Maria half-closed her eyes and held onto the still-sleeping Pedro. Jim turned back at the door and looked at them. Maria was already asleep with her arm over Pedro. She had never really woken. More of a dazed zombie walk to get to her cot. She was still dressed. Jim was glad he had put one blanket over them as the night chill descended on Toucan.

* * *

'This isn't what I imagined,' said Glenda. 'I thought we were going to be squeezed into a tiny, shabby room or warehouse. This place is huge, like a palace.'

'It's a pretty impressive château. A friend of your employers.'

'A Brightwater Management friend, you mean?'

'I do,' said Liam. 'We set up our little ops room and stocked up on food for a few days ago. Our plan is that most of us won't venture out until we wrap this up. You and Abenaa—interesting name—and your assistant French-speaking spy slash eavesdropper, tech nerd, Douglas will go out obviously. It was a good move choosing a computer guy fluent in French. We have some key loggers for him to insert when all of you are at Remilious. It's a good cover.'

'We might get lucky, and he'll overhear something useful,' said Glenda. 'Good grief, this place is huge,' as she looked at the tall ceilings, massive doors, and ornate stone carvings.

'Yes, true. Thousands of square feet. It's still quite a bit smaller than Boucher's Château Noire. We're in a wing here where no staff members are allowed. Plenty of places for everyone to sleep.

'How did you sneak all this equipment in?'

'I don't think the staff pays much attention to possessions coming and going. With the super-rich, there is always something going on.'

'Bring me up to speed with what we have here. The comm protocols and so on.'

'We have comm links to the CIA and BWC, sat coverage for about half the day.'

'You know about BWC?' asked Glenda, astonished that the French knew about the labs.

'Yes, we are not unsophisticated as an intelligence group,' said Liam, *standing just a little taller and sounding a bit proud,* thought Glenda.

'A drone if we need it. Glen Adams has links back to Brightwater. Two of my team will track phone calls at Remilious. We want to know immediately if your cover is blown. We have no idea how deep the terrorist groups have penetrated Remilious.'

'So, if Abenaa and I are dinking around with their financial guys. How are we going to investigate the Somali?'

'That's a problem. Someone is going to have to get inside the château and find him. It's the only way unless we intercept something on their comms. The CIA has been getting site plans for Château Noire. We're also digging into shipping records and invoices for anything delivered here in the last five years. Maybe it will give us a clue as to what they are up to.'

'What's their security?'

'Lots of cameras. They appear to have one weakness; most of the doors are lock and key, not electronic. Let's assume that wherever there are electronic entrances, are the places they don't want anyone to see.'

'Makes sense. Any contacts inside their organization?'

'Unfortunately, none. We're trying to get people in, a cook or a cleaner, and especially a tech even if only low-end type. Getting anyone hired, however, and inside is not likely to happen in the next two days.'

'Even if my cover works,' said Glenda, 'I'm not going to find much worthwhile with the finance guys about why the Somali ended up here. It seems highly unlikely they would be clued into something like that.'

'We have to play it by ear. We've got several gizmos for you: an electronic scanner. If you manage to get into the depths of the Château, the scanner should open the electronic doors. I'm trying to get a tech repair team in. We're planning to take down their internet, and then our guys can fix it.'

'And insert a worm?'

'In some ways, similar. It spreads within their system, giving us a mirror image of their screens.'

'Don't they have in-house tech repairman?'

'Yes, they do. We'll find a workaround,' said Liam, a little more confidently than he felt.

Glenda wondered how Liam would find a way to let outsiders mess with Remilious' internet systems.

'You've got about ninety minutes before you meet up with Remilious' finance guys for dinner.'

* * *

'Everybody ready and up to speed?' asked Sheilla.

'Our guys are at their new home in the Château. Everyone has comms. Our job is to coordinate and protect Glenda, Abenaa, and Douglas. This shouldn't take more than a couple of days. Nobody goes off-site here until the mission's over. Kramer, you, and Mark will alternate as our mission control. One of you is here at all times. Any questions?' asked Sheilla.

'This seems to be a big operation when we don't even know what we are investigating,' prodded Kramer.

Sheilla didn't answer Kramer, assuming rightly that it was more of a statement than a question. 'Fred, summarize what we know.'

'Mega biotech company with financial problems. Partly caused by the U.S. authorities' rejection of their requested drug approval. An unknown connection to Egyptian Islamic Jihad and al-Qaeda. Looks like someone is covering their tracks by killing the Somali family and an informer. That should be enough to elevate everyone's concerns.'

'And Remilious thinks it's important to hide the Somali,' interjected Sheilla. 'Go on, Fred.'

'Satellite shows dozens of people coming and going from Boucher's Château. Something is going on inside. We have identified enough of them to know they are mostly biotech types.'

'Okay. I didn't know all that,' said Kramer.

'No one did until a few minutes ago.'

'But, so what? Remilious is a biotech company.'

Fred looked happy as he said, 'We've identified a known Syrian molecular biologist standing outside, having a smoke.'

'Explain?' asked Kramer.

'We have watchers on the grounds of the Château. Two someones. This part is restricted to just us and

Martin at the CIA. We have two of Neilly's watchers on-site.'

'Shouldn't Glenda know?' asked Katarina.

'Not now,' said Sheilla. 'It's not that we don't want her to know. It just isn't necessary at this point. She's got enough on her plate. As Kramer pointed out. Lots of moving pieces and people. We compartmentalize as much as we can.'

'This is the first time we've shared a mission with the CIA,' added Mark.

'Why the change in procedure?' asked Katarina.

'We wouldn't even be involved if it weren't for General Crystal. This is the CIA's mandate. And they tumbled to the problem first.'

'Because of the General,' agreed Kramer.

'Besides, I think,' continued Sheilla, 'with the General at the CIA, he's developed more trust for them. At least for some people there. Don't get me wrong, we're a smaller, tighter group with a smaller chance for leaks. CIA is unaware of Neilly's watchers, except for Martin, Bertrand, and the General, for instance, at least so far.'

'First contact in less than thirty minutes,' said Mark. 'Glenda has bios on who she's meeting. Katarina will be assessing and profiling them continuously.'

'Katarina nodded at Fred, who clicked a few keys and brought up a screen with the Syrian molecular biologist's profile. I am going to run these short profiles pretty much in real time on that screen. For everyone we know or encounter, I put up a short profile, such as the finance types, at the welcome dinner. You will be able to scroll through them anytime you like.'

'This profiling biz, having it on the screen, is new. I like it,' said Kramer, who was thinking he also liked the color mix in the room. Sheilla with her long auburn hair, Katrina's light-blond hair, Fred the ordinary white guy, and dark brown skin for Mark, and toward black for me. *More than the ethnic diversity,* he thought, *I like the intelligence and street smarts in this room. It's why I like it here. I wonder what they would think if they knew I was the General's undercover security mole. Probably they wouldn't like it. No doubt surprised. But since there has never been a security problem. They might accept that it was a prudent measure.*

# Chapter Twenty-Three

Dr. Jelle Visser could hardly contain his excitement. He flicked a finger at the vial of blood he had just drawn from Cigalle.

'How much do we have now?' asked Octavia Mustafa.

'Enough for our work.'

Visser checked the restraining straps on Cigalle. Then he twisted a valve below a litter bag. 'He should regain consciousness in a few minutes. He was displaying symptoms the last time Heinrich and I did this.'

'Is it wise?' asked Octavia.

Jelle didn't know if it was or not. He didn't care. Watching the man lying before him, nearing a full display of symptoms of his virus, was his life's dream.

'We have collected enough of the virus. With symptoms developing, he will die soon. I don't see that it will harm anything to how he acts.' Then Visser added a little lie for his Jihad representative. 'Verification is necessary that this virus strain causes the symptoms we are after. It is imperative to determine how long the patient survives. The strain he was infected with was obtained in Rwanda because people infected with it live longer than with other strains.'

'If they live longer there is time to treat them. Isn't there?'

'If the people die too soon after they display symptoms,' added Visser, 'their negative effect on society will be diminished.'

'Yes, I understood this from your earlier talks with our sponsors,' said Octavia. 'Because I am not one of your nerdy scientists. It does not mean that I don't understand the project well. You would do well to remember that. I have to report. Your man looks as though he is reviving.'

Jelle was distracted from the Somali, thinking about what Octavia had said. *Did she know more about the science than he thought?* He observed her plain appearance without makeup before she turned to walk away. She was slender, with dark brown hair and matching eyes. It occurred to him she might be pretty, perhaps even beautiful if she didn't take great pains to make herself appear unattractive. She always wore simple, high-necked, almost dowdy, baggy clothes. Never tight pants or low-cut blouses to show off her slender figure. *Could she be a Cleopatra in hiding, an Egyptian beauty,* he wondered? *No, she was born in Syria.* He blinked back to the present as the door closed behind her.

'Observe his eyes. Ask him in French how he feels. Offer him water, Heinrich.' Henrich was seriously wondering how he got involved in Jelle's side project. *But here I am fully mired in it.*

They watched as his head started moving in circles. He didn't respond when asked how he felt. Heinrich held out a glass of water to the Somali. Cilgalle's eyes opened in panic, and he violently shook his restraints.

'Ya. Ya,' said Visser, while he clenched his fist excitedly. He turned the valve, allowing the sedative to flow to Cigalle. His head rolling slowed. He quit opening and closing his mouth. His eyes, still open wide and wild, slowly closed. 'We have enough of the virus. But I still don't want him dying before we revive him and get to observe more. Tomorrow, I think, he will mostly be brain dead.'

'I want to talk to you,' said Octavia.

'Yes, okay. We will go to my office and speak.'

Visser looked at the vial with Cigalle's blood and passed it to Heinrich. I'll be along shortly after Octavia, and I have a chat.'

As they silently walked to his office, Visser once again noticed the two were the same height, except because of his lifter shoes,in bare feet she would be taller. He didn't like women who were taller than he was. They made him feel uncomfortable, maybe even slightly inferior.

At Remilious, Octavia acted as an assistant to Jelle. Most of the lab staff paid little attention to her. Only Visser and Heinrich knew her connection as the go-between for the Islamic nuts, as he thought of them. She was the tip of the spear. The connection to the backing for Visser personal project. The representative of a vast and dangerous network in the Middle East. One with money and resources to support his fanciful endeavour.

As they sipped dark sweet coffee, a new thought occurred to Visser: *Perhaps I have underestimated her? Is she more intelligent and knowledgeable than he had given her credit for?* If she was, his dislike for her would be supplanted with more respect. *Ya, I think I need to be careful. If she is concealing her beauty, it stands to reason she is also hiding her knowledge and authority with the terrorists.*

'You can report that we are making excellent progress with combining Cigalle's virus,' said Visser, breaking out of his daydream.

'I report what I see. The question is, how long before you're done?'

'It is uncertain, of course. Sooner than I projected. If the results show what I hope they will tomorrow with the young would-be jihadists you so kindly kidnapped for our experiments.'

'A time frame, please?'

Jelle wondered if her sometimes courteous use of words concealed a cruel killer. Was it all an act, a carefully planned staging of both her true personality and appearance?

'It is only an estimate. Only a few days to finish the genetic work. You can pass along to your contact that we only require a little more evidence before we can proceed. And it will take longer to manufacture sufficient quantities to begin infecting people.'

'This is sooner than expected?'

'We have had good fortune with our latest lab experiments.'

Dr. Jelle Visser didn't care about anything other than seeing the symptoms manifest themselves in a town or village outside of a lab. Watching the effects on humans in the lab was the culmination of his life's desires. But that paled in comparison to watching a larger group symptomatic in a natural setting. Just like a movie. *My very own movie production.* He smiled as he thought about it.

They had made a breakthrough in combining the two viruses. In other, more normal circumstances, he would want to spend months to years testing and verifying the results. He had a nagging feeling that wouldn't happen as there were too many problems for him to spend much longer here. Too many dangers that could stop his plan. The Remilious project could be unsuccessful. Boucher was unreliable. While he distrusted Octavia and his Middle backers, he was willing to risk anything to see his experiment live on the human stage. He had no choice. He had to chance it.

Octavia set her small Egyptian coffee cup down. What shall I say about Remilious' second-phase project?'

'I will know better after I sit with Blackwell this afternoon. We are on track with the genetic part of that virus, too. The procedures and the results we want are similar to our project.'

'How do you mean?'

'Combine RNA so we can achieve the transmissibility we desire.'

'So, you are close to successfully engineering the virus

for our project? *My project,* Jelle said to himself. 'However, we need certain verifications.'

'What verifications?'

'Bigger tests in humans would be preferred.'

'You have the six that we provided to you.'

'I am glad your organization supplied them, as you agreed you would. My concern for testing is that there are five females and one male, and all are under twenty-six years old. I would like a larger group with mixed ages and more males for testing.'

'You did not request this before. Why didn't you say so before we diverted the six kids here? They were potentially valuable soldiers to our cause in Iraq. They are almost always young, and many are female. It is the usual case.' Olivia could not have cared less about the recruits. They were expendable. She wondered what Visser was up to. 'My leaders do not like these kinds of surprises.'

'My data suggests that it would be advisable to have a wider age range and more males. I didn't consider this previously,' Jelle lied, thinking that it was prudent to do so rather than admit it was his wish. What he was asking for was not needed for the success of the experiments. Neither the modified bird flu virus nor the African rabies would be affected by age or sex. Especially Cigalle's virus project, which affected the brain regardless of gender or age. What he wanted was to see his dream with hundreds, with as many humans as possible, a cross-section of humanity, but on a scale where he could observe them in person, such as in a village with 100 to 200 people. Not remotely through reports and perhaps some video. He wanted to be part of the movie, his movie. He would like to see the spread of Boucher's bird flu to human populations too. Interesting watching humanity get what it deserved, but nothing like his hydrophobia scheme for which there would be no cure, no vaccine. If Boucher's grand plan failed, so what? He would still have his project. He was getting excited. If Octavia could convince her organization to provide a larger group to infect, he would get to observe them firsthand. Everything he had always wanted. Even better if he could see many more people infected. *Damn the risks of going to their shit country,* he rationalized.

'I'll make another call and return in a few minutes,' said Octavia.

As she walked out, she smiled to herself. This had been hers and her boss's plan all along, a visual demonstration at home for the leadership before they released the virus in Paris or Tel Aviv. The only problem she had envisaged was coaching the doctor to their country, where they would control him.

Visser busied himself while he waited, looking over the latest analysis of their RNA sequencing. Suddenly, he had an inspiration. An epiphany about their avian virus. He would discuss this with Blackwell this afternoon.

Octavia walked back in and closed the door. Visser turned on the tape recorder. The tip of the microphone penetrated a small box on the front of his desk. The box was designed with decorations to obscure the tiny mic. He would have been shocked to know that Octavia carried a scanner and long ago detected its presence. She smiled thinking about Visser's stupidity and arrogance. She would be gone from this ridiculous, amoral country soon. When she reported the tapes to the leadership, they were adamant. The tapes were never to be heard by the infidels. She had entered his office late one night and found where he had carefully dated and categorized the recordings. When she reported this information, she had been provided with a device to erase the tapes. She smiled at destroying his secret evidence. She had never liked this poor specimen of a man and his gross, fatty paunch. One day soon, he would no longer be needed.

EIJ had promised Visser that they would give him a well-funded laboratory. But he had no wish to go to their dust bowl country, as Heinrich had called it. But, and a big but it was, the thought of watching in person a Day of the Dead of his making would be worth the risk. *They will let me return here. They must, for me to finish working on the avian virus.* Deep down Visser knew he was being irrational. He would be expendable when the jihadists' scientists could duplicate his work. *No, I have to get what I can here in the lab if I want to live,* he thought. *I have my escape plan.*

He had arranged for minor facial surgery, and happily, he would have his trademark stomach fat liposuctioned. Unbeknownst to anyone, even Heinrich, he had special shoes that raised his height nearly two inches. He would again walk in comfort with his normal, shorter height, a trim midriff, a slightly altered face, dyed hair cut radically differently, or *should I shave my head,* he wondered. And with a lot of money in the bank along with his films of the

Somali, *he would have a wonderful life*, and stay amused. It would have to be enough. If he was lucky, he could observe on the news the terrorist's results infecting a broader swath of a population somewhere in the world. *Zombies marching in Paris*, he chuckled to himself.

He wasn't certain yet where he should go. He was still toying with ideas: Central or South America, or possibly Cuba. His journey getting there would not be first class, but rather aboard a rust bucket of a transport ship based in Tenerife that stopped in Cuba and Panama.

'This will be no problem,' said Octavia. 'We can arrange for a village to act as a trial for the H5N1 virus and another for your modified rabies virus. Does that make you happy?'

*Fantastisch*, thought Visser. *I could see an entire group transformed, but—and a big but*, he thought—*can I risk putting myself under their control? A pity, maybe*, his mind flip-floppingdeliberatingweighing. Surely, they will let me return here. *I'm too important here.*

He wanted to leave the option open; 'Indeed, it does,' he responded. Visser was deluding himself about having free will. He would never be free if he went to Octavia's country.

Octavia's sister in Cairo, Ayesha, did not need to confirm with EIJ or al-Qaeda. It was exactly what she had been presented as a plan to be executed when the viruses had been developed. How convenient that the doctor would need no convincing to do what they desired of him.

'Where will this be?' asked Jelle. Visser said will rather than would. He wanted her to think he would follow her plan. His back and forth had left him with the desire to live rather than see a village of Zombies. His final decision, and not an easy one was to "Get out of Dodge," a phrase he had learned in an American movie.

'We will be informed. My contact said either Sudan or Somalia.'

'Turn your earpiece off when you arrive. Don't turn it back on until you've scanned them for listening devices,' said Liam. Douglas is going to stay in your van on his computer, coordinate with us, and see if there are any other snoops or communication devices we can find at the meeting. You'll take the van that only has one row of seats in the back. Behind those, Douglas will have a small blackout working area with surveillance cameras, various monitoring, comms, etc.'

'This part is trickier. Before you get to the drop-off point for your man, Techie Tom. Cute name. I'll give you specific instructions as to speed and distance. You'll slow as we discussed when we give you a signal. He'll exit the side door while you're moving. I've been through it several times with Douglas and Techie. We are assuming you will be followed, so timing is critical. Good luck.'

'We're off then,' said Glenda.

'Hey, Douglas,' said Liam as they were leaving. Watch your back. They could have someone outside, possibly checking vehicles. They could be doing what you are. We won't have sat coverage, so keep an eye on your surroundings.'

'Got it.'

Glenda was thinking that Liam was quite thorough. Having three identical transport vans with one a dual-purpose transporter snoop mobile with a hidden work area. She turned to her partner, 'Abenaa, how are you feeling?

'Good, I think. We'll have to be careful not to get too caught up in tech jargon until we have comm support. I think we'll do okay. It is a social get-to-know-each-other meeting, not so much finance talk.'

Techie Tom's exit had gone flawlessly. After the van and had turned a tight corner, Tom jumped out and moved to his observation point. Liam knew there were risks, but, in the end, decided it was safer than being observed leaving their Château.

The van pulled up to the main entrance of Château Noire. The outside walls were lit with floodlights. 'Are you kidding me!' exclaimed Glenda. 'This is more immense in person than in the photos. It's bigger than ours. Who can afford this kind of place?'

A man opened the van door. Glenda and Abenaa climbed out. They were escorted up the front steps into what they recognized from the diagrams as the main reception hall.

'It's even more,' she struggled for the right word, 'ahh, opulent in person,' whispered Abenaa.

They were ushered into a smaller side room. Equally ornate; however, not so large as to become impersonal. A fire blazed in an oversized fireplace. A table was set for three. Two large chairs faced the warm flames. As they walked into the empty room, a woman rose from one of the chairs.

The woman smiled and strode toward them. Held out her hand. 'I'm pleased to meet you, Ms. Stuart and Ms. Bissong. I'm Gabrielle Albrecht.'

# Chapter Twenty-Four

'I have never understood why we have two separate labs,' said Murray Blackwell.

'You have limited space in Marseille, and we approach projects differently,' answered Jelle.

Murray shook his head, 'That's about as much detail as I ever get.'

'Explain what you mean.'

'General research. Your goal is to develop vaccines: both a pan vaccine and a quick response vaccine. Ours is basic research, such as gene insertion.'

'Yes, alright. Let's get on with it. Boucher is pushing us. He wanted me to have this meeting with you. I don't want to spend any more time than necessary. What is this rush all about, anyway? It took fifty years to develop a polio vaccine. We're supposed to do this in months?'

'Money is the reason, Murray. And we've come a long way since polio. Better lab techniques.'

'Okay, Okay. Let's move on.'

Fair enough. I have no more time than you. Your latest thoughts on developing vaccines?

'Boucher and you seem to be pushing the DNA plasmid approach. I disagree. Viral Like Particles is the way to proceed.'

'VLP might be worthwhile; if there were time, I would suggest exploring both and you have the staff capacity to do that. The problem is time. You have none. Boucher needs a breakthrough. You have to take your best shot and focus.'

'We're scientists, Visser. Not gamblers.'

'True, but you are not in an academic research facility. You are in a commercial one and you will have to have a leap of faith and choose a direction. If you are wrong, you lose your job. If you are correct, you will be a superstar, given a pat on the back and a raise.'

'Enough business psychology. Convince me why you think DNA plasmid is the approach.'

'I don't think it is any longer.'

'You mean you agree with me?' he exclaimed, astonished.

'I now believe there is a better approach.'

'That's crazy. A third method.'

'Listen. This is close to what you like with VLPs. You are trying to find ways, more efficient ways, to activate the immune system. One problem is the survivability of the particles.'

'Yes, that is correct. However, we have discovered superior methods to encapsulate the VLPs to prevent their degradation, but still, the antibody response lasts only for a short time.'

This was exactly what Visser was hoping he would say. 'The goal, of course, is to stimulate the passive immune system. Create immunogenicity.'

Murray sighed, wondering what he was doing here listening to Visser talk about immunology 101 principles.

Visser continued, undeterred. 'I now think that a section of RNA injected would stimulate passive immunity, but ...'

Murray shook his head, 'Probably true if it weren't for the active immune system destroying them before the passive has a chance to build an antibody response. That was the result of all the early mRNA experiments, too. Even after some limited success in encapsulating them in lipids.'

'Exactly, however, I am going to suggest a way to produce H5N1 VLP's from the co-expression of plasmids, or even better, NP's assembled ... '

'No, no, not possible. Nanoparticles have less immunogenicity than VLPs.' Blackwell shook his head. Jelle would not have anything new to say, but for some reason, he kept listening, asking an occasional question. Visser had not wanted to spend this much time, but the excitement of his idea prevented him from stopping. When Murray realized Visser's idea was viable, he forgot all about the time.

Boucher burst into the room. Visser had moved up their meeting. He had been certain he could convince Blackwell of the RNA approach and wanted Boucher's endorsement.

'What's it going to be? Tell me you can deliver a vaccine,' demanded Boucher. His impatience and arrogance permeated the room. He usually displayed a civil attitude with Maury. He rarely let anything other than his true feelings show through with Visser, as he knew Visser wouldn't leave and Visser had him by the balls knowing his unscrupulous plan. There was no compelling reason he needed to pretend to be nice, especially since they both knew they detested each other. If he was caught, he planned to move all blame to Visser or maybe discuss his fate with Moriac. In his arrogance, he never assumed that Visser would be recording all their conversations, nor that Dr. Jelle Visser would be equal to him in having a self-protection plan. Some of the recordings would cast proportionate blame, but Visser wasn't sure it mattered. He had an escape plan, and he had decided to use it.

As he often thought, if his special virus scheme and the company's devious plan were executed, he would be notoriously recorded in history. Probably as a diabolical genius. A genius, nevertheless.

'Have a seat, sir, and we'll explain,' said Visser pleasantly.

'We've had a bit of luck,' said Bertrand, as he sipped his favorite tea.

Drinking Earl Grey tea was something he learned from his mother, an Indian immigrant. She tried to do things the British way. Including when she stumbled onto his name. She had been waiting for a job interview as a cleaner at the British Library. Sitting on a table was *A History of Western Philosophy,* authored by Bertrand Russell. A passerby tapped the book and remarked that he was one of the smartest Englishmen ever. Nahla had named her six-month-old son, at birth, Shambulinga and promptly decided to rename him Bertrand. He would grow up now to be the perfect British gentleman, she had reasoned.

Bertrand had fulfilled his mother's wish for him of attending the University of Oxford. He was intelligent, passed the interviews, and it was where the CIA had recruited him. The dark-skinned, five-feet-eight-inch-tall Indian rose through the ranks to become the Director of Intelligence, and therefore one of the most powerful people in the CIA behind the Director of Intelligence. While General Crystal thought Bertrand was the best person to succeed him as the director of the CIA, Bertrand had no wish to do so. He liked doing exactly what he was doing: solving the riddles that were frequently part of his job. Which is how he had spent his morning with the latest intelligence from Martin and Sheilla about Remilious and the Somali. As was nearly always the case for him, he inserted a few pieces into the puzzle, confident a complete picture would soon emerge.

Bertrand set his white china cup down on the table that separated him from the General. 'A Remilious employee sent an unsecured email to whom we assume is his live-in partner. He said he would be late getting home as he had to write up a full report in simple language for

Boucher. Then, to our good fortune, he proceeded to brag about his earlier meeting with the big boss. We learned there are research facilities at Boucher's château. Unfortunately, he did not state many details, nevertheless, some important information. From the email, it appears he has probably already told his partner about what they are researching. He went on to say he was instructing Boucher on basic, very basic immunology, in his words. It's all in your summary report. Here are the interesting points: RNA viruses that infect humans and birds; reassortment versus recombination, using the 1918 virus as a model.'

'Yes. Among other things,' said Will, 'they're an immunology lab. It stands to reason they would investigate RNA viruses. Especially ones that infect people. What's interesting and something I would not expect is using the 1918 H1N1 virus as a model. Of course, there has been a lot of interest in its proteins lately after the sequencing of the virus's hemagglutinin HA gene.'

'I think I am going to have to do some research myself if I'm going to understand what you are talking about,' said Bertrand. 'I'll look at the report. If it is in introductory language, it might help me learn something about what they are doing.'

'Yes,' agreed the General. 'It might tell us what we need to know. To satiate your curiosity, the HA gene determines the properties of the virus's surface proteins, which is what allows the virus to enter respiratory cells. I can see a lot of reasons for them to investigate this.'

'That still leaves me perplexed,' said Bertrand. He changed the subject. 'Another interesting piece of intel.

There was a call made to the postdoc at Scripps Institute from the professor in Cairo. Not surprising either since they tried to get a State Department grant, and even though they didn't receive one, they still might intend to collaborate. What isn't normal is the encryption used for the phone call.'

'Could it be that they want to keep their research ideas hidden?'

'Maybe. The next intercept is more interesting, but with no more substantive information. It was another encrypted call, this time to Afghanistan. It's the same encryption method al-Qaeda uses.'

The General pondered the al-Qaeda significance and then switched back to Boucher's employee, he said, 'We need the full report from Boucher's employee.'

'This is what I am thinking; you may have already guessed this, Director, but from what we have found, it's unlikely the employee or his partner are terrorists or al-Qaeda.'

'Meaning one of the two might easily spill the entire story with a little convincing.'

'Exactly.'

'What about the Somali?'

'With the family deaths, we're at a dead end. Nevertheless, their sudden demise tells us someone is tying up loose ends. And that indicates it's important to that someone.'

'The ground team in France is attempting to replace Boucher's PA or get some other lower-level people installed at the château. Now that we know there the virus research is being done, we'll try to get someone hired at the château. In your update, we installed a technician at their Marseille laboratory. We've found nothing out of line so far. Only research that would be expected.'

'In summary,' said General Crystal. 'The report made to Boucher could be helpful. And we need to break their encryption, both phone and computer. Dinner later here?'

* * *

'Ladies, I have never been able to shake a bad habit of an after-dinner smoke. I would also like some fresh night air,' said Gabrielle.

Glenda thought she had not reacted or passed any negative facial cues about Gabrielle smoking.

But Gabrielle responded by pulling on a long green wool coat, 'Yes, I know—fresh air and smoke—a contradiction in terms.'

Gabrielle waved the doorman away and opened the heavy oak door, motioning Glenda through, and then Abenaa. Just before the steps, she squeezed Abenaa's muscular arm and said softly, 'Please wait here.'

Gabrielle then took Glenda's arm and walked several meters past the drive onto the lawn. With the illumination now dim from the château, the perfectly straight mowing lines on the flawless lawn disappeared into the night.

Glenda waited for Gabrielle Albrecht to start the conversation. When they stopped walking, Glenda put her hand in her pocket and switched on the signal scanner. When Gabrielle turned to look back at the château,

Glenda glanced at the scanner. Nothing detected. She had been concerned that the coat might contain a listening device or detection scanner like she had. She then flicked the comm on with a remote switch in her pocket.

Gabrielle extracted a cigarette from a pack labeled HB and flicked a lighter before inhaling deeply. She looked up at the stars mixed with low winter clouds and exhaled. 'Very pleasant out. I like the biting chill this time of year. A reminder of my childhood in Bremen. I did my first degree at Oldenburg University near there.'

Glenda didn't answer. Gabrielle ventured, 'So close to Germany's North Sea. It gets quite cold.'

Glenda smiled, thinking just how tactful this woman was. Glenda had been unfamiliar with where either Bremen or Oldenburg was. 'Thank you,' she responded.

'Tomorrow we will be flown to Marseille in what I gather is a special helicopter. At least that is what I discerned when Boucher mentioned it. Bluebird, he called it.'

'The financial information is more easily accessed there, and you can question whoever you like.'

'I expected we would work here.'

'I understand, but it will only be a short ride and for a few hours. That is, unless you feel you need more time,' turning her face directly toward Glenda. 'We will meet here at 8:oo a.m. if the time agrees with you. I know it's early after your long journey from North America.'

'The time will be fine,' answered Glenda.

Dropping her cigarette on the lawn, Gabrielle said, 'Let's walk back, shall we? I intend to work a little before I retire. It is a shame you are not staying here, as we could have a nightcap. Perhaps tomorrow evening we will be able to.'

As they neared the driveway, Glenda nodded to the driver, who moved the car alongside them. Gabrielle gave Glenda a peck on the cheek. As she did, she whispered, 'I know who you are.' Then she shifted to Glenda's left cheek in the French fashion and said, 'I am here to save a company. If there are problems, I'm not aware of, I want to know them.' She turned before reaching the château's steps and said, 'Safe drive and I'm looking forward to seeing you here in the morning.'

'Liam, I have good visibility. I'm up a tree outside the château's wall. As soon as Glenda, Abenaa, and Gabrielle walked out the front door, Teckie toggled his radio and reported to Liam and Douglas. 'I have the three women in sight. It's easy to keep track of them. They're each so distinctive.

Then he saw a movement from an upper story of the château. Standing back a few feet from an open window, a dark figure moved. Tom, peering through his scope, was able to see a person holding a parabolic microphone. 'Château personnel are listening in on the women's conversation,' he reported. A second later Glenda said, 'Liam. Can you hear me?'

'Oui.'

'I thought the new finance chief was wearing a transmitter or recorder inside. Outside, I didn't pick up anything.'

'It means the room was bugged; she wasn't.'

'We heard you talking to her on the lawn after you switched it on.'

'There's a part I'll bet you didn't hear when she whispered to me as we were leaving.'

'No. What?'

She said, 'I know who we are.'

# Chapter Twenty-Five

'We were caught off guard,' said Bertrand. 'Our ground team expected the dinner to be with some financial types, not the new CFO.'

'Yes, Sheilla and Martin discussed it with me two hours ago, just after it happened.'

Bertrand nodded.

It shouldn't be a surprise that Ms. Albrecht had Glenda investigated. She would still have deep contacts with Interpol or perhaps German Intelligence. Our cover wasn't good enough for that sort of scrutiny,' said Will. 'Your PA will bring your dinner request. It should arrive shortly. I hope you don't mind eating in?'

'My favorite,' said Bertrand.

'How does Gabrielle Albrecht change things?'

'Martin and I concluded there isn't much we can do. We have to take her at her word. This is a commercial company. Their security can't be all that good. They aren't pros, I think. We shouldn't have to worry about the safety of Ms. Stuart and Ms. Bissong.'

'But the early brief suggested that they had extensive security.'

'If they do, it's more likely geared to protecting their data than to their physical security. I've asked Martin to take a closer look. He said he would have a report for us in the morning.'

'Very good,' said General Crystal. 'How do we adapt?'

'I'd like to give Liam permission to bring the emailing doctor and his partner in for a chat. Everything suggests they would be compliant.'

'Your call.'

'Alright, excuse me for a few minutes and I'll arrange it.'

When Bertrand got off the phone to France he said, 'It's being set up.'

'Let's go over tomorrow,' said Will. 'Glenda goes, as Ms. Albrecht said to Marseille. We arrange for a secure phone. Glenda will pass it to her. She'll also try to have a private conversation. As Martin told you earlier, the Special Forces technician spotted a window open with a parabolic microphone aimed at Glenda and Albrecht. The room where they had dinner was bugged at least at the table when Glenda scanned it. Despite being a commercial company, we have to assume their internal security is not completely unsophisticated.'

'It's the one thing that gives me pause,' said Will. 'Is the honorable Ms. Albrecht involved?'

'We don't know. After reviewing her past, my guess is she would not risk anything that was not above board.'

'Let's chow down while we discuss this.'

Bertrand picked up his phone, 'Liam and his crew are going to pay a visit to Josh Ingram's residence at 0100. The doctor and his partner are home. Liam has two men on-site outside their apartment.'

'We have ninety minutes before they go in. I missed lunch. Let's eat and then meet in the operations room at 1900,' said Will.

* * *

By the time Glenda, Abenaa, and Douglas returned to their château-operations center, Liam had been given the okay and had formulated the plan with his bosses and the CIA's assistance.

'The upside,' said Liam, 'is that you've learned something about high finance.'

'Uh-huh,' said Glenda, giving Liam a light punch on his arm.

'What's your take on Albrecht?'

'My gut tells me she is a straight shooter. What's the plan?'

'We've got a mission on for 0100. I've put two people outside their residence. One followed our primary target from Remilious to his apartment. Both he and the boyfriend are there now.'

'I guess you don't have to stay cooped up here if you want to come along?'

'You're joking. Do you even think it would be a possibility that I would sit here while you have all the fun? What about the Remilious snoops? They're only watching during the daytime. Pretty unsophisticated.'

'Hard to believe.'

'I thought so too, but it seems to be true. It appears that finance types don't merit round-the-clock surveillance.'

'Hope that's correct. Tonight's a snatch-and-grab, eh? As my partner back home would say.'

'You mean Major Brush McGuire.'

'Liam. I guess we're even. I've read your file too. Yes, Major McGuire,' *but he doesn't know the full story*, she smiled and asked, 'We're going to bring this Josh and his partner here?'

'That's the plan.'

'Okay, spell out the evening's events, in detail for me?'

'We leave your Techie Tom at the château. You and Abenaa join us for the night's activities. Their apartment isn't far, outside Aix-en-Provence. We attempt a quiet entry. Five of us go in. We search for any documents and bring their computers and phones back here.'

'Does their building have any security?'

'The building is three stories with six apartments. No doorman. Simple key lock. We have diagrams. We checked their phones, security companies, and found no evidence of any alarm systems. It should be straight-forward.'

'As if anything ever is.'

* * *

There was a soft glow from six computer screens. One of the station's screens was dark. Perri's screen sat idle. Sheilla was looking over the shoulder of Ilana, the only female IT tech other than Misa. That is if you put Misa as an elite in the same category of the other techs.

There was no jealousy among the IT staff. While Fred and everyone under him were the best BWC could recruitMisa, Vidya, Jake, and Jasonwere 'Elite'. Instead of envy, the techs aspired to achieve the same status. Most knew they never would be. It wasn't an official title. It was conferred on the best at what they did by their peers. All the techs had great admiration for anyone accorded the 'Elite' status.

Ilana sat in her chair with white jeans, a green and rose-flowered shirt, and her sandy brown hair tied in a short ponytail. She was searching through the millions of emails that were now available to them since Vidya and Misa had found a way to break Remilious' encryption and hack their systems. Martin had arranged for one of the CIA's best computer specialists to work with Ilana. His nickname was B, since he looked almost identical to Jack Black, the actor, with his stout body and dark hair accompanied by an acerbic wit. The B stood for Bruce. He had come to the CIA from the NSA, where he specialised on machine language applied to keyword searches.

A BWC's mainframe was churning through Remilious' emails and filling them into groups according to the search keywords and phrases the two techs had prescribed. The protocol B had suggested required more than one cycle for some words and phrases. Eventually, they were filtered into categories that could be reviewed.

'Jeez, Sheilla. This automatic search protocol is nothing short of amazing,' said Ilana. 'Us techs are becoming superfluous.'

'Somebody has to design the whole thing. Once you have the computer data, you're still needed for the evaluation. For using your intuition to solve riddles.'

'I'm not at all sure what our future will bring. Robotics, neural networks, and automation are on the horizon.' Ilana paused and focused on her monitor. 'We're getting close. My bar timer is fluctuating around eighteen minutes for the keyword search to complete. It's currently building connections for al-Qaeda, Bin Laden, Somalia, "et cetera, et cetera, et cetera,"' said the King of Siam.

'Huh?'

'*The King and I*, King Monghut's favorite phrase.'

'You're a movie buff?' asked Sheilla.

'Naw, but I loved that one when I was a kid.'

'If I ever have time, maybe I'll watch it,' said Sheilla.

Ilana kept her eyes on the monitor.

'We ended up with about forty parameters for the Egyptian scientist and the other players.'

'With machine learning, what do you think is in our future?' asked Sheilla.

'In my opinion, a bleak one, I'm afraid. AI seems stalled right now—no quantum leap advances, rather, tiny little creeps forward. Research has flatlined. Someday there will be a breakthrough. When that happens, machines will be able to teach machines. When they start reasoning like us, they will have the ability to replace humans.'

'Really.'

'We won't need warm bodies cooking burgers at fast-food joints when a machine can do it or sitting here thinking up protocols.'

'Hum, do you think machines will be smarter than people?'

'Most everyone disagrees with me, but yes I do, and I think if Alan Turing were here, he would agree. That's my posit. Back to our project,' said Ilana. 'B is very smart. And while we are cooperating and working with the CIA, I'll keep in mind what you said—they are still not our friends.'

Sheilla's vision lost focus as she thought about Martin, wondering, hoping their relationship was what she thought it was, or could he be ingratiating himself with her? *Is he a spy?* Could she really trust him? *Is what I feel —me deluding myself.*

Ilana's voice broke through her thoughts, 'Misa and Vidya didn't trust uploading the CIA program we're using. So, the mainframe that is crunching the data was scrubbed and is not connected to the BWC net. The problem is if anything is embedded. Whatever we share from this computer could have a worm, or virus, or maybe a back-door for the CIA to our computers.'

'So, it's isolated but we can't share it.'

'Yep. Vidya is looking at the code. I think until we know, to be safe, we should hard-copy the files and fax them to whoever gets the info.'

'That's over my head, Ilana. It's up to you, Fred, and

the *Cave Dwellers*. I trust you all to make the appropriate choices, but can't a fax be hacked?'

'Sure, but it's so outdated that no one much looks at it anymore. And the point is, any pesky little bits of code would be lost in the fax. Totally cumbersome, though.'

'Hmm.'

'The results will be available in a couple of more minutes.'

'While we wait, can I bring you a coffee or tea, Ilana?'

* * *

Henri carried an oversized duffle for the items they expected to remove from the flat. Colette would collect any electronic devices in a canvas rucksack she carried on her back.

Colette picked the apartment lock. They stood to the side as she slowly swung the door open. Liam peered in and saw no one. There was a soft glow and sounds coming from the bedroom. All carefully moved into the empty room. The floors didn't squeak as they crept toward the sounds. Liam motioned to Henri and Colette to the other two doors. Liam, Glenda, and Abenaa moved toward the door with the light.

As the sounds became more pronounced, Glenda whispered into her mic, 'Naughty boys.'

Liam nudged the door enough so they could see Joshua face down on the bed with Renard pumping up and down on top. The three moved into the room without being noticed. Liam nodded to Abenaa to turn on the room light. Henri had a small video camera and was recording the scene.

Renard froze. Their murmurs ceased. Suddenly, Renard jumped off Josh, and Josh rolled over and sat up, shielding his eyes. Renard said, 'C'est quoi ce bordel!'

Abenaa had moved to the side of the bed that Renard had rolled onto, while Liam went to the opposite side, closest to Josh. Glenda stood at the foot of the bed with her Glock trained on Renard. Liam said, 'Désolé d'interrompre.' And in some ways, he was sorry to interrupt them. More and more, he had moved from being bisexual to preferring men. Something he had been able to keep a secret from his team and bosses.

'Stand up,' said Abenaa in her perfect French. Her tone was authoritative. Liam noted that she spoke more assertively than was necessary. He would find out later what the reason was. It would have a bearing on how they interrogated these two, who were soon to be houseguests at the château.

'You two have suitcases?' asked Liam.

'You have no right to be here!' Renard shrieked. 'Are you the police?' And then, 'What do you want?'

Liam stood. 'Tell me where your suitcases are, so we can pack some personal items for you. You won't be back for some time. Your choice if you want to stay naked.'

Josh looked toward the multiple closets behind Liam, who proceeded to open one door after another, keeping his eyes on the two men. Then he nodded at Glenda. She acknowledged that she understood he wanted her to cover the two men. Liam looked in the closets. Some held shelves and others neat rows of shirts, suits, and pants. In one were two large suitcases and two smaller carry-ons.

Liam went to a side chair and grabbed the clothes that were lying on it. 'Get dressed. Move it.'

Josh tilted his head a little while looking at Liam. The terror of the intrusion dissipated a little as he recognized Liam as gay. He winked at Liam and then stood.

Abenaa moved in a little closer, with her Beretta pointed at Renard's head. 'Maintenant! I'm tired of looking at your dick. Move it, now.'

Liam opened the two larger suitcases on the bed while the two captives dressed. 'Anything interesting, Colette, Henri?'

'We've packed their computers and bathroom supplies. We're gathering papers now. These two are neat freaks.'

The two men didn't know what was going on. Liam refused to tell them anything other than that they worked for the government and if they did what they were told, they would not be harmed.

'Henri, you're done?'

'Ready.'

'Henri, you and Colette, leave first. Bring the vans around in front.'

Liam ordered the men to hold their hands out. He cinched snap ties around their wrists.

Joshua and Renard realized the futility of complaining. Under Liam's supervision, they had packed their suitcases. They walked compliantly behind Liam and Glenda, with Abenaa following several feet behind. The three vans were lined up in front as they strode through the lobby. Liam pointed at the middle van and motioned Renard into it. 'Take Dr. Josh Ingram to the rear van.'

As soon as Renard got into the van, Liam moved in beside him and pulled a black bag over his head. Abenaa did the same with Josh before the convoy left. Glenda rode silently, wondering why Abenaa's usually congenial attitude seemed so hostile.

'Smooth execution,' said General Crystal.

'Liam is experienced,' said Bertrand. We didn't have enough time to get an in-depth profile on Ingram and Blake. It's a surprise they are gay. Liam Allard is too, or perhaps more appropriately, bisexual. Something he thought no one knew until recently. Your SF lady looked a little ferocious. With Glenda's and Liam's experience, that should play well if they use Ms. Bissong as a bad cop. Liam comes in to befriend them. It's a nice setup.

'I don't think it will be long before they get information from these two,' said Will. 'I'll be in my office.'

'I'll stay and watch the interrogation,' said Bertrand.

# Chapter Twenty-Six

'I read the report from Ingram,' said Boucher. 'I want to discuss it with him at three this afternoon.'

Heinrich took a deep breath. 'He didn't come into work today.'

'Why? You called him, right?'

'There was no answer.'

'Send someone to his house. No, don't. I'll send someone from security.'

'Yes, sir.'

'What I want from you,' continued Boucher, 'is a firm deadline for the modified human-avian virus.'

Heinrich clenched his jaw. 'Mr. Boucher. I can't, science doesn't...'

Boucher cut in. 'We're stepping up the release of the bird flu at the egg farms in America. I want it followed up near those sites with the human-modified virus. I want it now. Do it.'

Boucher didn't mention that the viral release to infect chickens was already in motion.

Henrich felt trapped between Visser and Boucher. Visser had forced Henrich to hold back telling Boucher they had modified the H5N1 to infect people.

'No excuses. I'm not giving you more time. Solve it. I want it now.'

Boucher stood and walked out of his office, leaving Heinrich feeling cornered. *This is, this is ... Scheib.* He sat for several minutes. Eventually, he went back to his lab, thinking that living in a dust bowl country might not be so bad. 'Fick dich,' he said out loud when he was sure no one would hear him. *I must call Visser.*

A powerful hand grabbed Joshua's arms and handcuffed him to the chair he was sitting in. He squinted as the hood was jerked off. The room was brightly lit. The only furniture in the room was a bare table and another chair. A video camera perched on top of a tripod was pointed directly at him.

The black woman gave him a stare that made him hold his breath. *Who are these people? What do they want? This woman is going to torture me. I can't take pain.* Then he started to cry. *What have they done with Renard?*

Joshua's eyes looked down at the table, away from Abenaa. She turned to the door and walked out.

'This puppy is going to be easy to break,' said Abenaa.

Liam and Glenda stood watching Joshua sitting alone

in the room. 'Let's do the usual,' said Glenda. Let him sit. Same for Renard, and then Liam and I alternate as friendlies. If they give us a good story, and the CIA buys it, we're done. If not, Abenaa goes in heavy-handed.'

'We promise them safe conduct somewhere. I think they will jump at it,' said Liam.

'First things first. I want a conference with both the CIA and the BWC and see where we are. After, Douglas, you fill me in on what you have from their computers. One question.' Glenda looked at Abenaa. 'What's with you today? It wasn't an act. You were angry.'

'I'm over it now. It's not that big a deal.'

'Doesn't cut it,' said Glenda. 'I want the story. I felt like I knew who you were, and now I'm feeling I don't.'

* * *

Visser stood next to Cigalle, who was starting to twitch and drool. 'He's ready, Heinrich.'

'Well, what are you going to do?'

'I decided not to have our other researchers observe him. I don't trust their involvement after thinking about it and listening to their gripes. I'm going to inform them that we tried everything we could to save him. He died despite our efforts, and they need to keep up the research.'

'What are you going to do with the young women and the guy?'

'Maybe nothing. If our Middle Eastern sponsors are willing to inject an entire village of a hundred or more people and then move another group to the village to test transmissibility.' *I want to be there,* thought Visser. *I want to but it would be stupid.*

'It will take some time for them to become symptomatic.'

'I'm optimistic that as with our Somali's blood, a high dose will cause rapid onset and they will just as rapidly infect the test group.'

'Children too?'

'Can't be helped, can it?'

While Heinrich didn't possess many scruples, killing children, old people, and helpless people was a line he was not happy to cross. Deep down, he knew all Visser cared about was seeing people turn into zombies. It was his love since childhood. An insane pleasure bolstered by his equally insane dislike of humanity. *Could I get away with driving off into the night and disappearing?* he wondered.

'I'm trying to figure out how I can spend time away from here with Boucher pushing us for avian flu answers,' said Jelle. But I'm not going to miss being on-site with a whole village manifesting symptoms. Think of it, Heinrich. It will be grand. I want the movie footage. Ayesha is getting a phone meeting arranged with Professor Mustafa tonight.'

Heinrich stared at Visser and after a moment of silence decided to placate Visser and said, 'I will be happy to wait and see the film. I don't want anything to do with those zealots or their dried-up country. Do you trust them? I think you'd be crazy to go there. They'll never let you leave.'

Jelle decided he had been right not to tell Heinrich

that he would be going to Syria. Heinrich didn't want to go willingly to a dust bowl country, as he called them. *Easier to give him no choice,* Visser thought. Besides, his sponsors would not allow Heinrich to be interrogated. He knew too much. It was either take him or Ayesha would

terminate him. *They probably would, in any event,* he thought. *I have to see this no matter what.* Then a slight depression overcame him as he considered all the risks. His secret disappearing plan. 'Schijt,' he exclaimed while he walked down the hall. *Going with Octavia is suicide. I can't do it no matter how much I want to.*

In Visser's original plan, if he had to escape the lab, he would mail a letter to the authorities and press, saying he was disgusted when he heard about Boucher's intentions, and he was afraid that Boucher would have him killed if he knew he was leaving. A letter to the authorities might not sway anyone or exonerate him, but it might have some effect, at least he hoped.

He closed the door to his office none too softly and swore and kicked his desk still debating with himself. *I'm so close to realizing my dream. Even if I died in the flea-bitten desert* and then he smirked, I might get to see my private *Day of the Desert Dead* movie in real life. Survival versus watching the beginnings of the destruction of humanity. Deep down Jelle knew he had to give up the debate.

* * *

Abenaa sat down in the desk chair facing Glenda Rose. She remained silent for a minute before saying, 'Liam, would you leave us?'

Liam turned and walked out of the room.

Glenda kept eye contact with Abenaa, waiting for what she had to say.

Abenaa sat looking back at Glenda. 'I've never confided this to anyone. Outside of my family, that is. It was a long time ago. I had two older brothers and one younger brother. Jimi, the youngest, was my pal. We were very close and always together. Our oldest brother Chindindu was eight years older. I was nine.' She paused again, and Glenda could see her struggling.

'Abenaa. I don't know what you are going to say. I have an inkling it might be something, ah, quite personal. If it is and it won't affect the mission, you don't need to share. My concern is that there is nothing that will have any impact on your judgment when we are working together. The way you looked the other day, my first thought was, she is going to kill these guys.'

'I am sorry. I've been told that when I'm angry or upset I can look, ah ... severe.'

Glenda laughed. 'More like a warrior from hell.'

'That bad, huh? Thank you for letting me off the hook. But it's time I confided in someone, and I guess I'd like it to be you.'

Glenda's eyes crinkled. She didn't smile, but with her lips together and an imperceptible nod, she let Abenaa know she appreciated her confidence in both their professional relationship and their friendship.

'I'll try to make it short. I heard Jimi cry out and walked into his room. Chindindu was on top of him. The scene in the apartment was nearly identical to the one in my memory.'

Glenda nodded, visualizing the replay of old events that had set Abenaa off.

'Chindindu was quite big, and Jimi was a small boy even for a seven-year-old. Jimi collected rocks. I was so angry that picked one up and bashed Chin on the head. He rolled onto the floor. I didn't know much about the sexes. I had seen, however, what pain boys had when they were hit in the groin. I wanted to cause pain. I then kicked him hard in his crotch, really hard. I think it did permanent damage. Jimi was crying and bleeding. After that, he was never the same. He needed stitches as his rectum was torn. He became infected. Anyway, it took months before he was normal physically. He never recovered mentally. Six years later he committed suicide.'

'That must have been awful for you and your family. It's as disgusting as it is a tragedy. Something that never should have happened. Abenaa, we have a professional relationship, but I have started to think of you more as a friend. You can always talk to me.'

They stood and hugged. Glenda said, 'I'm not sorry to say that if Liam and I don't get what we need from these two by morning, your warrior's face is just what will be needed.'

Abenaa smiled, her teeth white against her dark skin. 'I might be able to manage that.'

* * *

Marcel was pleased. His already healthy bank account was growing rapidly. He would receive the large payment that would set him up for life after this, the final trip. The first trip had been to infect the chickens. This one to infect Americans. A culture he had no liking for. Arrogant and they think they are better than us French. After the mission he planned to disappear to Belgrade. He had thought long and hard about this decision. Belgrade had surprised him. His first choice had been Vietnam. After much thought, however, it would be safer to go to a non-French-speaking country. And one where his looks would fit in. If Boucher's plot was discovered, Boucher would disavow any knowledge, and of course, implicate him and the lab jockeys. If he left no trail, his pursuers would first try to track him to countries where his native French language was spoken. Reluctantly, he determined it would be safest to stay away from French-speaking countries.

The atomizers had worked perfectly when he infected the chicken breeders. Hundreds of thousands of chickens in the U.S. government's egg-laying facilities would already be infected and would soon start dying and passing the virus on to other birds. When the virus was discovered, which would be very soon, they would have to euthanize millions of chickens to halt the virus's spread.

While the U.S. stockpiled millions of eggs, with the replacement supplies stopped, they would be unable to manufacture large quantities of vaccine for the flu season. Remilious' stock would rise as investors learned Remilious was the only company capable of manufacturing vaccines for the next winter's flu. And after he dispersed the human H5N, millions of Americans would start to die.

Marcel stood and looked in the mirror. He had retained his physique. He was stocky, five feet eleven inches, thick bulging muscles with short brown hair and brown eyes. He stretched as the company jet pulled to a stop at the Marseille airport on his fiftieth birthday. *A nice present. Another three million into my retirement fund,* he thought. *A few more days. Eliminate loose ends and execute my disappearance. Voila.* The original plan called for him to return to the same egg-laying facilities and then move on to ones farther north. He considered it too dangerous. While Boucher had assured him that the virus would not be detected in the chickens this soon, he knew nothing about viruses, but he did not trust what Boucher told him. He had a new plan—Marcel gave Boucher false details about the locations except for one. He had survived all these years because he distrusted his commanders, and in this case, his boss.

Sheilla sat back in her chair, pushed it back, and swiveled twice, not allowing her mind to think, stopped, brushed her long auburn hair back from her left ear, and dialed Martin.

'Hi,' he said.

'Hi,' she said. 'I want to see you. I want to know if what I am feeling is real?'

'Me too.'

'I have no reason to go to DC. That leaves you coming here.'

'When was the last time you took a vacation?' asked Martin.

'A what! I can't even remember,' said Sheilla.

'That's our answer. We finish the Remilious issue. Put a period on our reports, pick a place, and make a reservation. Where would you like to go?'

'Ah. Go on a trip together. Somewhere safe, I guess, where it's warm and sunny...'

'Have you been to Mexico?'

'Are you kidding? Too many awful memories from there.'

'Some for me too.'

'Why go there, then?'

'I think sometimes the best way to get rid of bad memories,' said Martin, 'is to face them head-on. I wasn't thinking about Tubutama or anywhere close to Guillermo's cartel. I've heard of a great small hotel on the beach right at the tip of Cabo San Lucas. My friend Tom said you could walk into town. He said it was one of the nicest places he has ever stayed.'

Sheilla grimaced, even considering *Oh Mexico*.

'What about Hawaii? It's a long way from DC to travel,' said Martin. 'Just like the Caribbean is for you. Cabo is even pretty far for me, but it's doable. Mexico makes the most sense. Another place might be Belize.'

'You're right,' she said, 'Let's replace our Mexican

memories with new ones, as long as they're far away from Tubutama and the cartel.'

'I'll get links to a hotel and send them to you.'

'Martin, we hardly know each other. And we're going to go on a trip together.'

'We can get separate rooms. Let's think about it and talk later.'

'The reason I called, besides wanting to hear your voice,' Sheilla blushed as soon as she said it. She closed her green eyes and stopped talking.

'Sheilla, I want to hear your voice too. I'm really glad you phoned.'

'Thanks for saying that. It just sort of slipped out. Okay, deep breath. Why I phoned is, we've made progress with the Remilious emails. I'm going to send you a summary of them in categories. We're starting to analyze them. There are a lot. And it's a slow go. You have more people than we do, so both of us working together perhaps will be more productive.'

'From what I know, you have some highly skilled personnel. So, we are even. A new era for BWC and CIA.'

'Can't be helped with the General at both.'

'Good idea,' said Martin. 'Not to mention that I trust you and probably wouldn't have previously.'

'We wouldn't have even talked before,' said Sheilla. 'I'm glad we are.'

'Me too. How are you doing breaking the phone encryption?'

'Nowhere yet. Several issues.'

'If we can do anything?'

'I'll let you know,' said Sheilla.

'You're probably right. I doubt any of ours are any better. Still, multiple minds might find a solution sooner. Keep me posted.'

'I will. Take care.'

*Am I being silly? What's my reluctance?* Sheilla spun once in her chair. She stopped the turn with her foot. *Could we ever have a long-distance relationship with our jobs on opposite coasts?*

# Chapter Twenty-Seven

'I'll start with Dr. Joshua Ingram. Are you comfortable with that?' asked Glenda.

'Oui, Renard pour moi. Ingram looks like the weak one. So, an escalation from you to me to Abenaa, if needed.'

'Hey, ah ... Liam. That sounds like you think you're a better tough guy than me. A bit misogynistic, don't you think?'

'Definitely not. That's what makes sense to me. Let's get started.'

'Okay, but we'll see how it goes after I question him,' added Glenda Rose.

It was four in the morning. The two captives sat shivering. The room's windows were open, with cold air spilling in. Glenda put on her coat and walked into Joshua's room.

As soon as she entered, she was greeted by, 'Please close the window. I'm freezing.'

'Sure. I wish I had known earlier. Poor thing, you're shaking.'

'Can I have a coat, and is there heat?'

'Let me get the window closed. That should help.' Glenda knew it wouldn't. He was cold, and he was going to stay that way for a while at least. 'I want to ask you a couple of questions first. You help me, and my boss outside will let me bring you a coat. Okay?'

His hands shook, and he uncontrollably shivered. He nodded his head up and down.

'We know what you are doing at Remilious. Tell me how you got involved?'

'What's going to happen to us? Are we going to prison?' which made him shake even more.

'You cooperate with me, and I'll see you don't. The full story. No holding anything back, or I guarantee you will be in jail for the rest of your life.'

'Please, a coat, and I'll tell you everything. Can we speak French?'

Glenda pushed her chair back and walked out.

'I told you he would be a pushover,' said Abenaa.

'Not a huge surprise,' answered Glenda.

'Yeah. Pretty obvious, I guess.'

Glenda pushed the comm switch for the CIA.

'General, Bertrand. What can I offer him?'

'Depends on what he has to say and if he holds back,' answered Will Crystal.

'I don't think he is going to hold back. I'll push him until we're convinced we have everything.'

'If he is fully cooperating, we'll get an agreement worked up by legal.'

'Good. He's scared and doesn't know the game.'

'I don't want to give him my word and not have it backed up.'

'Let him talk. Use your judgment. If he is cooperating and has something worthwhile to say, you can offer him a plea deal. I'll support you.'

'Thank you, General.'

'He wants to do this in French. I think it's a good sign,' said Glenda. 'I'll take him a coat. Abenaa, you follow me in and stand there giving him the death stare and interpret for me.'

Joshua looked terrified at Abenaa. 'What's she doing here?'

'You have two ways to go,' said Glenda. 'The full story to me. Answer all my questions. If you don't, I can't help you, and she will take over for me. I won't be able to stay.' Glenda Rose grimaced for effect.

Abenaa said, 'Pas une putain de chose. You don't miss one fucking detail. Comprendre?'

Abenaa, looking impervious to the cold, flexed her arm muscles as she glared at him.

'Start from the beginning,' commanded Abenaa in perfect French.

Two hours later, the General said, 'Bertrand. Give me a synopsis before we have the conference call with BWC and Martin's group. We cross-check his story with everything we know, including the emails.'

'Ms. Stuart and Bissong did well with Ingram,' said Bertrand. 'The other one hasn't given us anything yet. Here's what we think we know: they are going to infect the U.S.' egg-laying chickens, limiting our ability to make H5N1 vaccines.'

'Or any vaccines.'

'My first surmise is that with the U.S. egg stockpile reduced, Remilious is in the forefront for developing vaccines,' said Bertrand. 'That seems obvious.'

'As far as I know, they use the same egg-based techniques we do. So, how do they manufacture them?'

'The experimentation with combining genes with human viruses: I'm not sure how that fits in either.'

'Ingram is guessing,' said Will Crystal, 'that Boucher is expecting, or is assuming the avian flu will jump species to humans.'

'Is it possible?'

'It is. There have been only a few cases of that happening. It hasn't been a threat so far. If the virus recombined and became transmissible, it would be a serious and possibly deadly issue.'

'That fricking idiot is going to try to infect people,' added Martin. 'His goal is to save his company at any cost. Zero scruples.'

'Causing havoc for a profit,' added the General.

'Let's step back,' mulled Bertrand. 'Does he think that the sheer quantity of infected birds will then make it more likely that it will mutate and jump species to humans?

And he saves the day by being ahead of every other company with a vaccine? Or is he going one step further?'

'Good question,' answered Will. 'It would make sense for him to understand how the H5N1 could recombine, just like what we do at BWC. Develop a prophylaxis.'

'Having a prophylactic vaccine in development would give him a head start on every other company if the virus did jump to humans.'

'Would it leave him looking suspect?'

'I don't see why it would,' said Bertrand.

'It would,' said Martin, 'if people became infected near his labs. Otherwise probably not.'

Let's nail this down beyond speculation,' said Will.

'How does the Somali fit with any of this?' asked Bertrand. 'I need a psych profile on Boucher. We verify Dr. Ingram's story and put it together with the other data. I might have some further questions for our Dr. Ingram.'

'You're the magician with mysteries. Katarina has a profile that Sheilla can send you. Call her.'

'I'll get it for you,' said Martin. 'How do we handle the encryption issue?'

'I have little doubt that Vidya and Misa could eventually breach their encryption. I don't want to waste any more of their time. Go ahead and tell them about Cryptocon. They have proper clearance.' *I'm surprised that Vidya hasn't already discovered our big secret.*

'Eric is waiting outside to go over the morning brief. I'd like to skip it,' said Bertrand. 'I'll phone Sheilla, Martin, and then I want to see if Ingram's story cross-checks with his partners before the conference call.'

'Depending on what Eric has,' said Will, 'I might be a few minutes late. Start without me.'

'I feel like we are chasing a ghost. Perhaps one that doesn't exist,' said Sheilla.

'No. There's something going on,' said Misa. 'The connections to the Middle East tell us that.'

'It might just be research,' said Sheilla.

'So far, all we have with Remilious is the chicken plot. I've never thought about chickens and eggs before in making flu vaccines. I guess it's a big deal.'

'You've become used to missions with people in direct danger. Chickens don't fit that mold. Their danger is secondary. Except I am not sure we are anywhere close to the full story. Vidya says he and Jason will keep trying to crack the encryption being used between Egypt and Remilious. They aren't switching phones on either end. If they are working on a terrorist scheme, it's a mistake to keep the same phones.'

'It's the one thing that gives me pause,' said Sheilla. 'They aren't using throwaway phones. So maybe there is nothing to hide.'

'Could be either. I think we'll know soon,' said Misa.

'Conference call with CIA in an hour.'

'Will Martin be there?'

'Yeah, I expect so.'

'It's your business, Sheilla, but we're friends, so I feel okay saying this.'

Sheilla held her breath, wondering what Misa would say. *Should I stay away from Martin because he's CIA?*

Sheilla let out her breath when Misa said, 'Don't hold back. We don't have many chances in life. You won't meet anyone new here. You'll be stuck with the likes of Nusmen.'

'Oh God, no. What a thought.' She jumped up and hugged Misa. 'You're a good friend. I'm lucky.'

The Blackhawk descended toward the Shuar village. This was the first time they had announced their arrival rather than surreptitiously landing far away. Below, trails of smoke drifted lazily, mixing with the morning haze. They could see people scattered about, mostly sitting. When the sound of the helicopter reached the village, people walked out of huts and stood staring up.

They didn't fly directly over, but over the end, where Pempeyo and Pwanchir lived. Maria shook her head and closed her eyes when Jim sat on the floor and swung his legs out, resting his feet on the skids. Jim instructed the pilot to slow. He scanned the area, searching for Tshui. A small group of children ran out of a hut, jumping and waving. Jim waved back. Maria forced herself against her fear of heights to move closer to the edge and wave, too.

Pedro was in the co-pilot's seat wearing a large helmet that dwarfed him.

'You see them, Pedro?' Jim said into his mic.

'Si.'

'LZ, chief.'

'Roger that, sir.'

A few seconds later, they descended to the same meadow they had landed in before Christmas, where Glenda had been in her first jungle firefight. Memories flashed randomly through his mind: Angelica's father was bitten by the bushmaster; their fight with the miners; Brush nearly dying from the Shuar poison dart; the tribe marching off carrying heads severed from miners and soldiers; Maria's intense interest in the shrinking process; Gaston, Neilly's second in command, dying during the fighting.

Jim jumped to the ground. Followed by Cherry, holding her AK-47. The pilot climbed out after shutting the helicopter down and came around to help Jim with the vinyl case holding the weapons from BWC. They concealed it just outside the clearing.

'Cherry, could you leave your rifle and take a pistol?'

Jim picked up his Beretta and the small Browning .25 caliber auto. He strapped the .25 to his ankle. He fastened the snap on the nylon belt holster holding the Beretta under his shirt.

'If you think best,' she said reluctantly.

'Your choice, but I think it would look better if you left it. Less aggressive.'

Cherry put her AK into the case and lifted out a Glock 19, hefted it. 'Feels full.' She pushed the release and inspected the magazine, inserted it, and pulled the slide back to glimpse the bullet in the chamber. Fifteen in the magazine and one in the chamber. 'Dieciséis. Sixteen bullets. Why call it nineteen?'

'It's just the series number. There's a 33-round magazine in there too.'

Cherry brushed her black hair back as she bent over the case. 'Many magazines. Good. I take one.'

Pedro jumped, excited and shouting. 'Let's go.'

'Everyone ready?' said Jim.

Maria had on a large red backpack. Jim picked up a rucksack and slung it over his shoulder. Cherry did the same and looked at Maria with raised eyebrows. 'Por qué la mochila roja tan grande?'

'Mostly for medical supplies and a few presents.'

'Okay bien.'

They walked down the familiar trail, no more than 100 yards when they heard screams as the children rushed toward them. Tshui was in the lead and ran straight for Jim. She leaped into his arms; he caught her and swung her around once. He held her out and looked into her eyes before holding her against his chest. After a moment, he set her on the ground.

'Tshui, this is Pedro, my son,' not knowing if she understood what he said or meant.

Tshui beamed, showing the small gap between her front teeth. Jim smiled. It made him happy to see her smiling, round face. She was wearing the same azure blue dress. This time she had a matching bright blue feather in her headband, holding back sleek black hair from her round face, which bore the same red Chiote plant face markings as Nusmen had after his psychedelic night with the Shuar's medicine man.

Pedro stared at Tshui's face. 'Markings on her face?'

'Every culture has its way and adornments.'

Pedro shyly reached out a finger and touched her cheek. Tshui giggled, reaching up and took his hand.

'Life is precious,' said Maria. Tshui and Pedro skipped ahead. Maria, Cherry, and Jim were all holding hands with the other children. A small boy held Jim's left hand before Jim lifted him, perching the young boy on his left shoulder. As they strolled toward the village on the shaded dirt trail surrounded by jungle vines, tree trunks, and overhead leaves, Pwanchir and Pempeyo appeared.

Jim thought about what had transpired since the last time he, Cherry, and Maria had been here. He wished Heather could be here. He knew she would approve of them being here now. It was the right choice to come.

# Chapter Twenty-Eight

'Sheilla. This is Bertrand Gupta. How are you?'

'Good. And you?'

'I'm fine, thank you.'

'Nice to hear from you. What can I help you with?'

'General Crystal and I just had a meeting. He said you had a psychological profile on Boucher.'

'We do.'

'Would you send it to me?'

'Certainly.'

'Also, we have a secure video meeting in twenty-five minutes. General Crystal wants your two computer experts in that meeting, along with me, Martin, and you.'

'Misa and Vidya?'

'Yes, correct, and no one else.'

'I'll see to it.'

'I appreciate your help.'

Sheilla sat mystified for a few seconds before calling

Katarina to send her most current profile to Bertrand. *Ilana, Fred, Kramer, Jake, and Jason were not invited. Why?*

'Your playmate told us everything,' said Liam.

'I don't believe you,' guffawed Renard.

'I'll be totally honest with you...'

Renard interrupted him, 'You are so full of shit. But if you don't close the window and give me a coat, I'm probably not going to survive.'

'Here's a little pearl of wisdom for your condition—Life is a sexually transmitted condition with a 100% mortality rate.'

'You're a stupid fuck.'

'Look,' said Liam. 'I waited to hear your story until after your partner finished. I'll close the window when you start talking to me.'

'Screw you.'

Liam picked up a glass of water and threw it at Renard.

'Chill asshole.'

'Screw you.' Renard, naked except for his boxer shorts, felt the icy wind hit his damp flesh.

'Give me a shout when you want to talk.' Liam walked out of the room, slamming the door behind him.

'The doctor is signing his statement,' said Glenda. 'A total pussycat. Not so with your guy?'

'He's playing at being a hard case.'

'Let's change tactics,' said Glenda. 'I go in and play

nice, tell him bits of Ingram's statement. He has no incentive not to talk.'

'Take Abenaa in with you. He doesn't speak English.'

'You ready, Abenaa?'

Glenda grabbed a coat and opened the door.

'Team two?' said Renard through chattering teeth. He was shaking so hard that his wood chair was dancing on the stone floor.

Glenda walked to the window and closed it. She cut Renard's restraints and handed him the heavy brown coat.

'A new tactic,' said Renard. 'The bad guy and now the amiable woman.' He looked over at Abenaa, who had her face on, thinking, *at least one nice woman.*

Glenda said, 'I'm not going to bullshit you.' She paused while Abenaa translated.

'We don't need you for anything. We got what we need from your partner. He will be free or in jail with you. It depends on what you have to say. We're investigating Remilious, which, other than your relationship with your partner, you have nothing to do with our investigation. Is it worth being a tough guy and going to jail?'

'What reason do I have for talking to you?'

'Renard, you need to understand this. You're a probable accomplice to violating several terrorist laws. Neither Joshua nor you will likely ever see sunshine outside a prison yard. The French will allow extradition of him to the U.S. You seem smart enough to have realized this. Is this registering yet? You tell the truth. Confirm his story and you both get a deal.'

'What do you need me for?'

'Simple corroboration. A few words in exchange for sitting in a cold cell thousands of miles apart for the rest of your life.'

For the first time, Renard didn't respond with a smart-ass comment.

'Abenaa, I'm going to step out for a minute. Let him know their situation. They're not arrested, but at the moment they're amongst the missing and have no rights. Embellish it however you want.'

'We're about to tell you something that has been held in the highest secrecy for years. Few people in the agency or anywhere for that matter know what I am about to tell you,' said Bertrand. 'There have been a few minor leaks over the years that the press has gotten wind of, however without evidence, they dropped it.'

No one said anything, but it was apparent that Bertrand had set the stage for a premier event. Sheilla, Misa, and Vidya's curiosity could not have been more intense. Vidya wondered if this was something that he had missed when he hacked the company's computers.

'I see I have your attention and rightfully so,' said Bertrand. 'When and if it is exposed, it will decidedly be thought of as the intelligence community's coup d'état of the century. I can't overemphasize the secret nature of the information we will relate to you.'

'If you had my attention before,' said Misa. 'You really have me hooked now.'

'We all understand,' said Sheilla, 'that this goes above and beyond, and I think I can speak for all of us in saying we will treat what you say with the highest confidentiality.'

'Simply put, we have backdoors into over 100 of the world's government crypto-security ciphering machines.'

'Even more simply put,' said General Crystal. 'We know almost every government's secrets as they are communicated, except those of China and Russia. They didn't purchase the software.'

'You hacked them?' asked Vidya, astounded.

'In a sense. In the early days, all the governments controlled their encryption,' continued Bertrand, 'then Germany and the U.S. formed a private company, Cryptocon GmbH, that invented an encrypting method and sold its "secure" encryption to the world's governments. The employees of Cryptocon, bar a select few, were unaware of the CIA's involvement.'

'Vidya,' said the General. 'Since the CIA is taking you into their confidence. You have my permission to reciprocate with Bertrand and Martin.'

Vidya felt as though General Crystal had just hit him over the head with a sledgehammer. *He's right. But I still don't want to tell anyone, but what choice do I have? Hacking the CIA is my special thing,* he thought to himself.

'As Sheilla said, I can speak for all of us that what you say will also be treated with the highest confidence,' confirmed General Crystal.

'Wow, tit for tat,' said Martin. 'Now you have us sitting on the edge of our chairs.'

Vidya couldn't say anything but nodded his consent to the General.

'Remember the exercise we had to see if the CIA techs and/or BWC techs could break into each other's systems? Vidya succeeded in hacking us.'

'Jesus Christ!' said Martin.

Renard's face turned crimson after hearing what his lover had confessed. *Merde. Then how do I know he did? They're making it up. But they aren't, are they?*

Glenda sensed his thoughts. 'We don't need you. Keep that in mind. You're nothing more than extra baggage. And throwing you in jail would appease several people. You've got one opportunity. Take it now or I won't give you a second chance. You tell us what you know. I've shared enough of Joshua's statement with you so you know I am not BSing you.'

'I rather like translating this,' said Abenaa.

'Add this to our reluctant Renard. If he does, we'll guarantee a new identity and funds to start a new life.'

After Abenaa translated, she could not help adding an extra sentence. 'Simple choice: hump Joshua in your private digs or he gets humped in prison. The lady is not kidding.'

'How do I know you will do what you say?'

Abenaa translated.

Glenda slid a sheaf of papers toward Renard. 'Signed statement by the assistant secretary of state.'

'You owe us an apology for busting into our home.'

'You'll survive,' said Glenda.

'Merde,' said Renard. His features tightened. He hit the table with his fist. Spitting out the words, he proceeded to tell what he knew, which was only what his partner had confided in him.

'Glenda's good,' said Bertrand. 'These two have put a whole new light on this story. We are still missing something, but we have several pieces of the puzzle. It's a start. And I like our new code name for this operation. Distinct, and it slips right off one's tongue: Suoilimer.'

# Chapter Twenty-Nine

Marcel Moriac was raised by his mother, Monique, in Nîmes. He knew his father only by his name: Paul Moriac. There was nothing extraordinary in his childhood. He was bored in classes and at school but graduated from le lycée. He was never certain why they had graduated him. Perhaps it was fear of keeping him, or possibly simply to get rid of him. With his stocky physique, he excelled at sports. Rugby had been his first love. He was broad, not tall when a schoolboy. As a teenager, he gained height, eventually reaching just shy of six feet. He had a wide face and close-set eyes underneath a broad forehead. The edges of his hair were touched with gray. He was rarely without a three-day dark stubble. The face of a man who knew his strength.

He joined the French army where he excelled and was awarded a single red chevron: soldat de premièr classe. His physical ability attracted the attention of a sergeant after seeing Marcel defend two drunk buddies in a bar. The sergeant watched enthralled as Marcel, without emotion, took the three men apart who had mistakenly thought the inebriated buddies were easy targets. To the sergeant's eyes, this was someone he felt he would trust in tough situations. The stout man was an efficient, unhurried, fearless fighter who used his strength to his advantage. He used no fighting techniques. It was obvious he was not trained. He was simply a young man who intuitively knew how to fight.

The brawl ended with the three attackers hobbling out, no doubt going straight to the hospital to repair a broken jaw and wrist. Chief Sergeant Dion Côté of the $13^e$ Régiment de Dragons Parachutistes, approached Marcel and offered to buy him a drink. The night ended with Sergeant Côté, inviting Marcel Moriac to a small airfield where several friends planned to spend Sunday skydiving. The next day ended after Marcel made his first parachute jump, followed by a second and then a third without a static line. At the end of the day, Dion Côté knew he wanted Marcel for his unit.

Months later, as Marcel neared the end of his Foreign Legion training at the "Farm" near Castelnaudary, he completed the mountain training segment and the final seventy-five-mile three-day hike. After graduation, he received orders to report to the Legion's special forces element for further training. Where he excelled with the Groupement Commando Parachutiste. He loved the life, the men, and the rigor. The training was special, and he left feeling that he had found his calling. When he finished, he was ordered to Martignas-sur-

Jalle, west of Bordeaux, where he was reunited with Sergeant Côté.

'You've done well in your training. I expected nothing less.' Dion slapped Marcel on the shoulder. When Marcel looked, he saw that Sergeant Côté had stuck a red two-chevron patch over his single stripe. 'Pull off the Velcro and sew it on proper. But first, we drink.'

'We met in a bar, we spent a day together and I feel we have known each other all our lives. Welcome to the dragoons, Corporal Moriac. The rest of the team is in the bar waiting to meet you.'

'Jeez,' said Brush as he stepped outside the back door of the ranch house at 0200. The stars shone brilliantly. The air was biting cold. Between the starlight and the nearly full moon illuminating the crusty snow, *I almost need to wear my sunglasses,* he mused. A great-horned owl hoot echoed up from the aspen grove. *The night has its charms, but I'll think twice before I volunteer for the night shift again.* Other than the one evening Brush had always had Roy or Ben if something happened.

Roy had assured him that he would be okay alone taking care of the birthing. 'Mama will lick 'em off. Get 'em up under mama's teats, and they'll know what to do.'

'Hmm,' was all Brush could say. *I hope he's right. Maybe I'll be lucky, and there will be no calves born tonight like the other evening.*

Brush's midnight watch was not destined to be like he had hoped. When he arrived at the upper barn, one cow was bawling as it lay on its side. Another cow was kicking a newborn away when it tried to get up under her to suckle. Brush tried to put it under the mother like Roy said and got the same treatment. Brush knew he was in over his head. Just when he thought nothing else could go wrong, he looked at another cow that had one hoof protruding from her backside.

He took a deep breath and dialed Shirley, the new vet in Twisp. He felt guilty about calling. 'Sorry to call this time of night.'

'Don't be. You're lucky to even catch me. It's pretty rare this time of year for me to get any sleep. What's the problem?'

'I drew the night shift and I think a cow is in trouble and she can't get a calf out. Another won't let the little one nurse, and the one I'm looking at is pushing hard, but there is only one foot sticking out.'

'I'll get right up there. Stay on the phone. Upper barn?'

'Yup.'

'I'm on my way.' Brush heard a car starting in the background. 'I'll talk you through a couple of things while I'm driving. Okay?'

'Shoot, Doc, but I don't know much.'

'I know. You're the Canuck that Roy told me about.'

'Guilty,' said Brush.

'I'm about twenty-five minutes away. First, go over and pick up the calf. Separate it from the mother. She might not want to feed it, but she could be protective and push you around some.'

'I like this job. Mad cows, eh?'

'You get her out yet?' The phone was silent while Shirley listened to the banging in the background.

'Okay,' said Brush, breathing heavily. 'What's next?'

'Good start. The mama made you work, huh? You ever delivered a dystocia?'

'A what?'

'Abnormal presentation. It can't wait. I'll talk you through it.'

'If you think I can do this.'

'She's standing, right?'

'Yep.'

'Still one leg out?'

'Roger that.'

'Get your coat and shirt off.'

'I'm spoken for, Doc, eh?'

'Levity is not appreciated in emergencies. Work your hand in along the leg and tell me if you can feel the other leg, hoof, or head.'

A few seconds went by. 'Here goes. It's a tight squeeze.'

'Do you feel anything?'

'I think a head, eh? Is that good?'

'That it is, yes. Work down the head to the neck and then to the shoulder. You should find the other leg. You need to get hold of the hoof. Tell me when you have it.'

'I think I have it.'

'Legs only bend one way. Finesse the foot toward the body. Don't bend it backward and break it.'

'It's moving okay. She's squeezing the blood out of my arm.'

'Relax. She'll stop contracting after a few seconds. Easy now. Pull the hoof and leg forward and get it out next to the other one.'

'I got it. Now what?'

'Start pulling. Not too much, but firm. Tell me when you see a nose or the head.'

'I see it. Sliding right out.'

'Make sure its nose isn't covered so it can breathe. Same for its mouth. Run your fingers around and scoop out any gunk.'

'Jeez. It hit the ground hard.'

'No worries. It happens when a ninety-pound calf falls out of a standing mother. Are you certain the nose is clear?'

'Got it and it's breathing, okay. The mother's licking it.'

'Good job. Take a breather and wait for me. The third cow. What is it doing?'

'It's alive. Looks like it's in bad shape. Not moving much.'

'Driving by the homesteader's cabin, I saw a head poke out of the door.'

'It's the old man, Shuskin, I've heard about. He lives there.'

'One and the same.'

'I've never seen him before.'

'He's pretty shy.'

'Coming up the road to the barn. I'll be there in a minute.'

Brush didn't know what to expect of the new vet that had taken over Murray's practice. He turned as she slid the big barn door open. A cloud of vapor enveloped her head as she exhaled. She was tall, almost Brush's five-foot-eleven inches, with long dark hair. A thin face. Nice looking with stout legs and wide hips, but thinner on top. She smiled at Brush. 'The dystocia delivery looks good. No bleeding. She'll pass her afterbirth shortly. Take it outside when she does.'

'Roy mentioned that.'

'Calf is trying to stand,' said Shirley. 'We'll try to take care of the down cow first and then worry about this one and the other.'

Shirley pulled her coat off her left arm, rubbed on some gel, and reached up into the cow. Brush noted that her arms were covered with golden-red hair over taut muscles. *Must work out,* he thought.

'We're going to have to move fast. She's alive. It's a breech.'

Brush thought back to what Roy said, 'He'll plop out and just get him up nursing.' *Not much right in what he said so far. The calf I pulled out is a little girl, and this mama is dead or close to it.*

'Get down here with me. She quickly used a battery-powered shear before shaving the rest of the hair in a large arc down its side. She handled Brush a bottle. Pour this iodine where I shave, be generous with it. Shirley poured another liquid on her hands and scrubbed them before spraying the red-orange area with a bottle labeled seventy percent alcohol. That stain will come off in a few days. Brush looked at his hand stained with the seven percent iodine. 'Who wouldn't want orange hands?'

'With those, you're real ranchy now.'

'Ranchy or raunchy?'

'Enough already. This lady's about done for, but I'm still going to give her an anesthetic. She inserted a long needle into her spine. Shirley drew an imaginary line across the shaved area with her finger. She took a scalpel and made a neat incision a foot and a half long. Then she retraced the cut, opening the cow's abdominal cavity, and then fussed with the scalpel more. Brush couldn't see what she was cutting. She reached inside and pulled a leg out of the opening and then the other leg. 'Help me out here. Grab ahold. This will take some muscle power as we're lifting it up. She's a big one. I expect she weighs north of 100 pounds. Don't let it slip and try not to touch anything but the legs.'

They lifted the calf out, put it on the straw, and cleared the nose of afterbirth. It didn't move. 'Push on the heart.' Shirley bent down and breathed into the calf's nostrils several times. 'Alright, good. Watch it. Make sure it keeps breathing. And towel it off.' She threw a towel at Brush. 'I'm going to suture her up. Probably not much use, but she is still breathing, so we'll try to get her up. Oh, oh, I take that back. She's dead. Not your fault. She would have looked normal and started a couple of hours before you came out on your rounds. You probably wouldn't have noticed she was in trouble if she hadn't been down on her side. Hard to tell with a breach. You got any colostrum up here?'

'Not that I know of. Especially since I don't know what it is.'

'It's the first milk the little one needs. Helps impart immunity. There's some in a freezer at the lower ranch house,' said Shirley. 'Roy told me where. I'll get it after we get this other little guy nursing. She opened the gate into where the calf's mother stood. Bring the calf in. Shirley reached under the cow, who kicked at her. Shirley didn't move away. Instead, she leaned into the cow, holding its leg with one hand, and pulled on each teat with the other. The mother stopped kicking. Hold her up and put her mouth near a teat. Shirley squirted a little of the golden cream out. The calf wiggled its nose and in a few minutes was sucking for all it was worth. The newborn fell over twice and managed to get herself back up to suck some more.

'That one was easy. Sometimes they're a touch tender at first.'

'Amazing, she's getting stronger by the minute,' said Brush.

'The one you pulled out looks fine. It'll be okay on its own. You want to carry our cesarean baby down to the house and keep it warm. It's none too strong.'

It was nearing 0400 when Shirley's pickup pulled up to the house. Shirley had driven to the lower ranch house and taken a quart of colostrum and two gallons of milk from a freezer.

'You want some coffee?' asked Brush.

'Good idea. No sleep tonight as more calls come in just before sunrise.'

The all-black calf lay on a blanket near the woodstove with its head up quizzically, looking at them with large brown eyes.

'Suppose it realizes something is missing but doesn't know what.'

'Yep. The little squirt is hungry. We'll get the colostrum thawed out and I think she'll be fine.'

'Two girls and a boy. And I'm starting to feel like a rancher. But I didn't expect a death on my first night. Guess Ray will help me with what to do with the mother.'

'He'll have a place to pull her out with the tractor. Life is full circle on ranches. Birthing and dying.'

Shirley's cell phone rang. 'Be there in forty to forty-five minutes. I'm going to stay for another ten minutes until we make sure your new child is nursing. And I get a slug of that coffee you promised.'

'It's starting to perk, so the coffee's almost ready. And the water in the pots is getting warm.'

'Take the water off the stove and put the colostrum bottle in it. Not too hot. Like a warm bath temp.'

'What you do in my kitchen? Making noise in the middle of the night,' said Lola.

'We're having coffee,' said Brush, smiling.

'You brought animal in. No good,' said Lola.

'Lola, meet the new vet, Shirley. This little girl's mother died, so we have to take care of it.'

'No good. No have animal in house.'

'Go give her a little pet,' said Brush.

Shirley laughed, wondering how this would come out. 'While the colostrum is thawing, let's start her out with what I was able to milk out of her mother. I milked a little out before we left. Shirley pulled a baby bottle out of her pocket and partially filled it using all the colostrum she had obtained from the dead mother. You take the bottle, papasan. I'm going to stand her up,' said Shirley.

'Now I know where you got your muscles, Doctor, I thought you trained.'

'No siree. Not needed when you do what I do day in and day out wrestling big animals. And I was just born with muscles. It turns a lot of guys off.'

*A lot of guys ain't too bright*, thought Brush. *This woman is a keeper for somebody.*

'Understand about some guy's attitudes, but clue me in on where the word papasan got into your vocabulary?'

'Long story. Maybe later, sometime.'

Shirley stood the little girl up. 'She's pretty big, near 100 pounds. Put a little colostrum on your finger and let her get a sniff. Rub it on her lips. Feed her every two hours today, but not between midnight and six.'

'Look at that. She's licking her lips,' said Brush.

'Well, put the bottle upside down and the nipple touching her lips.'

The girl started hesitantly at first, and then, after a few seconds, sucked like she had been nursing all her life. Lola knelt and stroked the calf with a motherly look. Brush was holding the bottle, grinning. Shirley stood and walked toward the door smiling, raised her hand goodbye without looking back, and thought, *they're hooked, alright.*

'The vials have been secured in the plane,' said Visser.

'How many?' asked Marcel.

'Fourteen.'

'Not much,' said Marcel.

'Tens of millions of the virus are more than enough for this job and then some. When the processing lab guys get them into the right media, they'll multiply exponentially.'

'I don't like being there longer than I have to. How do you know the Americans haven't found out about the lab?'

'It's not much of a lab. They don't need much to get the job done. Security and delivery are your concerns, not mine. I created the virus.'

'Exactly how long will it take for there to be enough virus for the atomizers after I get there?' asked Marcel.

'Two days, more or less.'

Moriac's years in the Dragoons took over his thinking. *Caution buddy, this is close to being home safe.* He called the pilot, 'We leave at ten hundred tomorrow'.

Marcel had everything he needed to return to America packed and sitting next to the door of the room he had been assigned for his use in the château. It was two hours before sunset. After dark, he would do what he had done for the past twenty years in the army: recon the plane and airfield. It was probably an unnecessary step, but it was the first measure he would employ to ensure he controlled the mission. He went to a room he'd been assigned, leaned back in the recliner, and turned on the stereo. He plugged in the headphones. Soothing sounds of Léo Marjane entered his ears and his mind. His mother had often played her music in his teenage years. He closed his eyes as the singer's voice took over his thoughts.

Visser peeked into Marcel's room through the partially opened door. He wanted to have Marcel pass on a message to the makeshift virus lab in America. He studied the man. His eyes were closed, black headphones over his ears. *I wonder what he is listening to.* Short hair, slightly graying, a square face. He looked like a fighter. Jelle knew he had special military training. He started to back away when Marcel's eyes opened, looking directly into his eyes.

Jelle wanted to retreat. Instead, he opened the door. It made a screeching noise that startled him. 'I, ah, forgot to tell you and wondered if you would pass a message to the lab techs when you get there?'

Moriac made no sign that he heard. He continued to stare with close-set brown eyes framed in his blunt forehead. Visser swallowed. 'If you would please ask them to make sure he or they are using HeLa. I've not been involved in setting up the lab, but I want it to be successful.'

'Marcel continued to bore in Jelle's eyes. Jelle looked down and started to turn.

'Is that code?' asked Marcel, finally speaking.

'No. It's what this virus seems to replicate best in. It's named after a young American woman, Henrietta Lacks. They took her tumor cells when she died.' Marcel continued to stare. Visser stammered, wondering why this man made him nervous. 'She was from Baltimore. Through a process of transformation, her tumor cells had the unique ability to divide continuously. A doctor from Johns Hopkins took her cells without her or her family's permission.' Marcel held up a finger. Visser stopped talking. Then Marcel motioned him away with the same finger as he closed his eyes. Jelle was relieved to back away from the door.

'Put the door back as you found it, Visser,' said Marcel without opening his eyes.

# Chapter Thirty

'Ms. Albrecht,' said Glenda as she stopped next to the new chief financial officer of Remilious.

Gabrielle turned to Glenda Rose. 'Ms. Stuart, if we are going to be working together,' she said before a long pause. Glenda nodded, understanding what the short, frizzy, dark-haired woman was asking. 'You must call me Gabrielle. It will be more comfortable, wouldn't you say?'

'So be it, Glenda and Gabrielle. Shall we board?'

'After you.'

The pilot pulled in power, raised straight up, and dipped the nose.

'This is the quietest helicopter I have ever been in,' said Glenda.

'I understand it is Boucher's favorite toy. He even has a name for it, as I mentioned yesterday: *Blue Bird*.'

'This is a fast chopper, moving fast,' as she looked unwaveringly into Gabrielle's eyes.

It was as much or more Gabrielle Albrecht's word game that they had been playing than Glenda's. However, Glenda's underlying meaning left Gabrielle flailing blindly to understand what she meant by *moving fast*. Hoping to elicit clarification without showing her ignorance, she said, 'I would be curious to know the answer too. Precision is an important part of my life.'

The pilot, accustomed to being silent with Boucher, toggled his comm switch to the cabin, cutting out air traffic control, and said, 'Our top speed is just under 300 kilometers per hour.'

Gabrielle smiled broadly at Glenda, pleased that the pilot had interrupted the wordplay. 'Thank you. I would think having more power for speed would make it louder. That does not appear to be the case. It is quite quiet.'

'Only about seventy dB, ma'am. Besides retractable gear and an aerodynamic design, what allows it to be fast are five rotor blades and an encased ten-blade tail rotor.'

'Thank you, sir,' said Gabrielle, smiling as she looked at Glenda.

The pilot hesitated, knowing he had talked more than he should have. Boucher did not allow the pilots to engage in chats with passengers. 'ETA approximately four minutes.'

Three men stood near the edge of the helicopter pad on the roof of Remilious' Marseille laboratory. 'Do you think those three are meant to equalize three women?' asked Gabrielle with a wry smile.

Glenda could not help but smile, looking into Gabrielle's round brown eyes. She wondered if they were going to continue their veiled communication. 'Abenaa sends her regrets and hopes she will feel better for our lunch. That leaves us outnumbered, at least physically,' as they stepped into the crisp morning air.

'Physical has never been my strong suit,' responded Gabriel.

The three men simultaneously nodded their heads. Word had spread fast through the financial department. A new top financial boss was intimidating enough without the addition of her also being the famous Gabrielle Albrecht. The next several hours was now destined to be a dual-purpose briefing split between the new CFO and the financial analyst from America.

The financial team was eager to please. They fawned and presented pages of documents after a brief slide presentation. *Lucky me,* thought Glenda. *Gabrielle has taken their focus away from me.*

'Gabrielle, would you like to have lunch with us? It's not far; we could ride back together from Château Noir.'

'It is a little early still. Perhaps we could take some time to discuss the Remilious finance issues first?'

'Miss Albrecht and Miss Stuart, 'Excuse me for interrupting, but the Blue Bird is at your disposal until 0200 this afternoon. I could fly you.'

Glenda looked at Gabrielle, who gave a slight nod. 'Splendid. Do you know where we are staying?'

'Yes, ma'am. I was informed.'

As they flew toward their Château Glenda reminisced about Brush and wondering how long she would be a Miss. That hadn't discussed dates. She wasn't anxious as she trusted their relationship whether they had a church or government sanction or not. Nevertheless, the idea of them being secretly engaged pleased her.

Gabrielle patted Glenda's leg. 'You look happy in your thoughts, young lady.'

Douglas rushed out of the front entrance moments after Gabrielle and Glenda stepped from their helicopter.

'They should have taken me with them,' said Douglas into his mic while approaching the deep blue chopper. 'She's pretty smart, but she doesn't have the deep understanding of the investment business needed. I'm afraid the Remilious people will be able to pick up on her lack of depth. Wow, what a pleasure, Miss Albrecht.'

'We want to discuss what we heard this morning in Marseille,' said Glenda. 'Perhaps Abenaa, Douglas, and Liam would join us, and afterwards we could have lunch?'

'Francine, could you make sure the lounge is suitable for a discussion with Miss Albrecht?' said Liam as the visitors moved through the château's oversized door. They walked up one flight of stairs and turned left, avoiding their comm center. As they entered the lounge, Francine held a small bug detector that she was passing over a wall receptacle. Techie Tom caught Liam's eye as they passed into the room and looked toward the windows before saying, 'I'll be up top if you need me.' Liam understood his concern about someone positioned with a listening device aimed at the windows.

'It's a bit cool in the room. Tom, could you pull the drapes before you leave?'

'Sure thing.'

Techie went into the comm room and grabbed his binoculars and sniper rifle. 'I'll be up top. Is anyone up to fixing lunch for the guests?'

'I'll do it,' said Colette. 'It won't be very fancy.'

'They ain't gonna starve,' said Techie. 'What more could a body want?'

'Americans … no sense of the pleasures of gastronomy,' as Colette shook her head.

Tom nodded, 'Burgers and fries, all a person could desire.'

Colette turned away singing, 'Ooh La La Dis-moi étranger, tu te rappelles le goût de mes lèvres,' and then she looked back and winked at Techie.

Tom looked at Francine translating what Colette had said into English, 'Ooh La La. Tell me, stranger. You remember the taste of my lips.'

'Hmm. An extra pair of eyes up top would be good, Francine. I gotta hustle. You want to come up and help me?'

As they climbed the steps, Techie said, 'I'll look for directional mics on the window side. You do a wider scan for anyone else hanging about.'

* * *

'It's a pleasure to meet you, Miss Albrecht,' said Douglas.

'I've seen you so many times in the news and newspapers. I almost feel like I know you.'

Gabrielle dipped her head in response. She turned to Glenda. 'It's time you took me into your confidence.'

Liam smiled, watching her closely, and said, 'Remilious is engaged in terrorist acts.'

Gabrielle sat speechless. This was not what she expected to hear. After seconds of silence, she said, 'Tell me who you are and who you represent.'

'From what you said to Glenda, I thought you knew.'

'Only that Miss Stuart and Bissong were not financial employees. I assumed they were investigating the misrepresentation made to the U.S. Federal Drug Administration.'

Liam picked up a phone and said, 'See if the General is up for a video discussion. Yes, I know it is early in Washington.'

'Miss Albrecht, this is much more serious. It involves a possible threat against the U.S.' Liam picked up the phone and said, 'Thank you. We can continue in the communication room. Please follow me.'

'On screen,' said Liam.

'General, sorry to call ...'

'Pleasure to meet you Miss Albrecht. I'm Will Crystal, the director of the CIA.'

'Yes, Director, I recognize you and I'm pleased to meet you as well. At least I hope I am after learning exactly what your organization's involvement is.'

'It is also your government. They will explain.' The

screen went dark. Static and slashes pulsed before another image appeared.

Another man, one that Gabrielle knew all too well from her years as the head of the Bundesbank.

'Gabrielle. It is always nice to see you.'

'Gerhard.'

'Please cooperate in all ways with these gentlemen and ladies. This is a serious matter for both the French, our government, and the U.S. The effects could possibly extend farther and into many countries. The French intelligence will fill you in.'

'As always, a pleasure, Gerhard.'

'When you next return, perhaps a quiet dinner.'

'Yes, Chancellor. It would be my pleasure.'

The screen went blank.

'Phew,' said Gabrielle as she exhaled, her eyes wide. 'I thought I had seen everything. This, I think, is something entirely different. Something insidious,' as she looked first at Glenda and then at Liam.

'The General wants you back at the BWC pronto,' said Sheilla.

'What's up?' asked Brush.

'Tell you when you get here.'

'Whatever it is, it won't be any harder than being up all night delivering four-legged babies, eh,' replied Brush.

'You mean calves?'

'Everyone here calls them babies. I'm getting the idea

of what it feels like to be a father: bottle-feeding my favorite little girl, and the little deer fawn when Ben and Roy's away, and now there's a camel baby, but she's nursing fine on her own, born yesterday. Talk about a gangly, not-so-little either, but a real sweetie.'

'What or who are you bottle-feeding?' asked Sheilla, her voice rising slightly.

'An all-black girl calf. Its mother died in childbirth. It's nuzzling and pushing my leg as we speak. Which means she's hungry.

'Sounds like you're smitten, Major.'

'It's hard work, it's blighty cold, blood and afterbirth, cow muck everywhere, but the babies quoting Roy are "dern cute." When do you need me back?'

'General wants you back like now. Chopper's on the way and arrives in about thirty minutes.'

Jim watched an oversized orange caterpillar inch across his path. A prismatic drop caught between stiff bristles refracted a miniature rainbow. Warm rain dripped from the foliage, monkey howls echoed, large and small winged insects did buzz-bys, cicadas brashly rubbed their song, frogs burbled, and frequent bird calls sliced the air, with their vibrant colors obscured in the damp foliage. The discordance was infrequently punctuated by moments of complete silence. The temperature was a low-bake oven, and the heat hung heavy even though masked temporarily by rain. To some, it would be stifling. Jim's T-shirt and pants were soaked by the warm droplets. The cloth clung to his skin, which he had learned through years of experience to embrace. An unnatural chirping added to the cacophony. Jim unsnapped the cover to his satellite phone.

'Colonel. You there?' asked Sheilla.

'I am.'

'I don't need to ask you where you are. With all those noises, it could only be the jungle.'

'The rainforest is never quiet. It's soothing and peaceful in its way. What's up?'

'The General wants Dr. Dakine back here as soon as. There's a possible problem with a bird flu jumping species in Mississippi.'

'Natural causes?'

'General thinks not. Possibly the work of a French lab having financial issues. We don't know the whole story yet. It's a precaution. And direct orders are for you to stay put. I quote, "No ifs or ands about it. The Colonel stays where he is." He means it.'

'What's the plan?'

'You fly her to Cuenca, and we'll get her back to the BWC from there.'

'When do you want her there?'

'Her transport will be there in three hours.'

'How serious is this?'

'We don't know yet. If it is, I'll let you know.'

'Okay. We'll get her bundled up.'

'Thanks. How are you and Pedro doing?'

'I'm fine. Pedro's settled in like he's been here all his

life. Picking up Shuar words left and right from Tshui. I'll call when we get to Cuenca.'

'Do you understand what Tshui said?' asked Jim.

'Something about the spirit would keep her. No sé,' said Pedro.

'She thinks planes are spirits or gods. What did you tell her?' asked Jim.

'I tried to say it was fun, and she would be safe.'

'Are you sure she wants to go with us?'

'She here. I guess so.'

'You've picked up a lot of Shuar vocabulary,' said Maria.

'I learned the word for "safe" from Tshui. The word for fun, I don't know, so I tried to smile and laugh.'

'Let's move,' said Jim.

Jim turned around and looked at Pedro and Tshui. He smiled as the kids giggled. 'I think maybe it was the right thing bringing Pedro to Colombia and here.'

'He seems to be doing wonderfully, but I wonder how much pain he is holding in and when it will break out,' she said as she looked up at Jim, wondering how they both would be.

'I've often wondered the same,' said Jim. I'm not worried about myself.

Maria touched Jim's arm with her palm and fingers. 'I hope that's a correct assessment, Jim,' she said, looking at his gaunt face with her clinical eyes. 'You have Pedro to look after.' She paused, casting her eyes up toward the tangled branches and vines before she changed the subject. 'I can't make up my mind whether Cherry should or shouldn't go back with me.'

'Tough call. She won't like it if you refuse her.' Jim waited to see what Maria would say.

'Damn it. She doesn't know what we do. The FARC are completely open with us. Upfront and honest, and here we are secretive and can't share even with our friends what we do. It's no wonder she wouldn't understand.'

Now it was Jim's turn. He stopped and put his hand on her shoulder. 'Don't make it too hard on yourself. You know you can't take her with you.'

'It's not only that; I wish we could all go back and stay in Colombia. It's real ... real ... life there. My heart feels whole there.'

Maria and Jim walked silently, each in their thoughts surrounded by the sounds, the heavy green, and the laughter of children. Like a light at the end of a tunnel, the meadow shone golden. The helicopter came into view. Cherry waved. Maria knew she would leave for the U.S. without her friend, but her new friend would be a big part of her thoughts, new thoughts about what they each wanted from life. Cherry hugged Maria and casually saluted the Colonel with her beaming brown face and hair as black as Tshui's. Her countenance was anything but the bandoliered guerrilla fighter she had been when they had first met.

'I now am going to see places I have seen from the books. Very exciting to me.'

Maria looked down, thinking about split infinitives, and knowing Cherry's hopes for traveling with her would soon be dashed.

'It will be my first time in a big city. It is the third largest in Ecuador, no?' said Cherry, enjoying her newfound knowledge and smiling broadly.

Maria looked up at her, stunned that Cherry did not want to go to the U.S. with her. 'Yes, Cuenca is a good-sized town.'

Even though Maria assumed Cherry must be disappointed, her smile was contagious, and despite her concern, Maria joined her with her own broad smile. 'Jim, will you be able to show her Cuenca?'

It hadn't occurred to him that they would stay in Cuenca. He had only assumed they would drop Maria off, fuel the chopper, and head back. He shook his head as a small smile came across his lips. He looked at Tshui's round face framed with short ink-black hair. She stood, her opaque pupils staring at the helicopter. Jim knelt. He reached up to her with two index fingers and gently pushed the corners of her lips into a smile. *Would it be a good for Tshui, or not, to see a city?*

Maria sat in the back of the helicopter alone, knowing she did not want to leave this place anymore than she did Colombia. *I won't. I promise to follow my heart. Something I've never done,* she promised herself with a strength that surprised her as the helicopter lifted above the placid green jungle sea and turned west.

Jim said, 'You have the controls.'

'I have the controls,' said Cherry dutifully. 'Easy, no. Maybe hover next time I try.'

'My turn,' shouted Pedro. He was anxious not only to fly, but he also wanted to show off to Tshui, who sat scrunched up to Jim, holding him so close that she melted into him.

'Tshui, watch me.'

'She turned her head hesitatingly toward Pedro, not relinquishing her tight hold on Jim. Her familiar world slipped away underneath them as they rose toward the sun. A god's-eye view of her rivers and jungle. Soaring, the helicopter rose above the greenery into the blue and climbed the lush hill to the west.

'Me now. Controls por favor.'

'Sí, sí, chiquito.'

'I'm no little.'

'It means I like you, at least most of the time,' Cherry said, laughing. 'You have the controls.'

'Sí, I have the controls.' Pedro grinned at Tshui as he held the cyclic. He lightly pushed left, then right as Tshui realized he was telling it which way to go. Mesmerized, she relaxed her hold on Jim a little. Jim gently took her hand and placed it on the stick under his. 'I have the controls.' Pedro frowned, mumbling, 'You have the controls,' and he realized what his dad was doing. He was pleased watching his new best friend, but also a little jealous. Jim nudged Tshui's hands on the cyclic, left, right, and then back. Her mouth hung open. Fear dissipated a little as she realized they were talking to the spirit thing.

Just as quickly, her illusion of control vanished as they approached the field near Cuenca. Jim could feel her body go rigid as he settled the helicopter on the dirt tarmac. Both Cherry and Pedro lightly held the cyclic, each living their own fantasy.

Tshui's eyes roved outside as the helicopter blades slowed. Panic consumed her for seconds and then slowly turned to awe as she felt Jim's relaxed manner. Another of the sky spirits, a huge one, sat a short distance away. The Gulf Stream had its steps down waiting for its passengers. Jim stepped out of the chopper carrying Tshui, as she clung to him. They walked from jungle dirt to asphalt toward the air force crew member, standing by the steps, who snapped a salute. 'We're prepared to depart as soon as you are ready, sir.'

Maria looked at Cherry, who surprised her with a grin. 'I no go with you, Doctor, as I said.' Maria stood, waiting for an explanation. 'I thought you would want to go.'

'The Colonel said you have work, and we will spend the day in Cuenca. Very exciting for me as I said to you, to see a place from the books. Maybe later we go to your home together when you back.'

Relieved, Maria gave Cherry a long hug. 'I will be back. I want to be back. Thank you for being my friend. Nos vemos.'

Cuidate, mi amiga,' said Cherry as she squeezed Maria's arm.

'Pedro, you want to have a look inside Maria's transport?' asked Jim.

'Yes, please.'

'Not without me,' said Cherry, looking first at the Colonel and then at Maria.

'Airman, with your permission, we'll come aboard.'

# Chapter Thirty-One

Brush wandered down the hall, headed for the computer area. He intended to have Fred hook him up with a video call.

'Early good morning, Major,' said Fred, a little surprised to see Brush at this hour.

'Doesn't qualify as early from what I've gotten used to lately. Think you could get me a visual connection with Glenda?'

'Sure. It's mid-afternoon in France, and as of a few minutes ago, they were in their digs.'

Fred rose and moved to a computer desk a few feet away. While Fred clicked keys on the desktop, Brush studied him. He was your average height, average looks, average medium sandy-brown-haired guy. *Someone who blends into the crowd,* thought Brush.

'You're up, Major.'

For a second, Brush closed his eyes as if he were testing the reality of Glenda's smiling face looking at him on the computer monitor. She reached up and touched the screen.

'Hi, babe. It's nice to see you live and in person. Well, not the sort of in-person I would prefer,' said Glenda.

'I missed everything about you. I'm not sure if I can say the same about ranching.'

'So, it's gratifying but hard work, *as Jim has always said*,' she recalled.

'Exactly. How do you know?'

'Superior psychic ability, mister.'

'Uh-huh. How's high finance?'

'Interesting and boring. Not getting us anyplace. I have to go. What's next might be more exciting. Can we talk tonight, and I'll explain?'

'Will try if I'm here. I don't know what the plan is yet. Miss you, babe.'

'Love you, big guy.'

'Me too, beautiful. Take care of yourself.' Brush wondered if she meant that since the finance ruse wasn't getting them anywhere, they were going to move from pencils and numbers to guns. *She'll clue me in later*,' he thought.

'Major,' said Fred, 'Sheilla just said they want you in the conference room.'

* * *

Marcel was confident that no one was observing him as he boarded the plane scheduled to fly to New Orleans. He bumped fists with his longtime legion buddy as he entered the plane.

'All good,' said Brian. 'No one has come inside until the pilots arrived this morning. We're off, boss, to a life of plenty.'

'Get some sleep, pal. At least seven hours before we touch down.'

To most people Moriac's caution would be overkill; to Marcel it was what allowed him to stay alive in the Dragoons. As they approached the Newfoundland coast, Marcel instructed the pilot to divert to Kansas City International Airport. The flight path would take them over Chicago, which was his real destination and where he would divert the flight to at the last minute possible. Anyone interested in tracking him would have a hard time adjusting to the last-minute change to a notoriously busy airport.

A private helicopter would be standing by to show them the sights of Chicago and the Lake Michigan waterfront. Marcel had meticulously plotted their helicopter route. He had studied the satellite image of the lab's location and how he would approach. The lab was in a nondescript building that could have been a small warehouse or office—1200 drab square feet of windowless space in the industrial suburbs several miles south of Chicago. He would spend hours observing before passing the virus to the lab geeks. Staying alive and defeating his enemies surpassed his need for comforts, showers, or clean sheets. The dragoons and their secret missions had ingrained the joy of defeating an enemy into his being.

Brian was a fool, but Marcel needed his ex-paratrooper buddy's help to execute his plan. Brian adored and worshiped Marcel and was content to do Marcel's bidding. He was proud that Ronno had adopted the nickname he had bestowed on him. Brian often daydreamed contentedly about being with him as they aged into retirement. The army had shown him the value of having buddies. He didn't need a woman. Have your way with them when needed, but as companions, a buddy was superior, as Ronno had taught him through the years.

Brian liked that the two would reap the money from this, their last mission, and go to central Vietnam along the coast. They would be warm and communicate in their native French tongue. *Turquoise seas, blue skies, swaying palms. Women to attend to their needs. A good place for them to grow old together,* he thought.

'I think we have enough evidence to shut their game down,' said Liam.

'As soon as we get confirmation from my boss, we'll be a go,' said Glenda.

'We won't have enough backup?' said Liam. But we have to move ASAP. We need to get in fast before Boucher hears from the local cops that we are gathering our forces. Too fast and we won't have enough bodies, and too slow and the surprise will be spoiled. It's damned if we do and damned if we don't.'

'You're right. They must have a lot of contacts with the local cops.'

'But we'll need them. We'll be stretched to the limit initially. Enough bodies to secure Ingram's part of the lab, but we'll need the locals to secure the outside and the rest of the château while we wait for your lab guy, HazMat, and more of my people to arrive.'

'You're convinced we shouldn't wait longer?' asked Glenda, knowing they couldn't but feeling she needed to ask.

'I've never been involved in an operation that was this understaffed. We were caught off guard, not expecting to find this big of a problem. We'll make do. And we'll probably take some flak when the higher-ups review. But we don't have a choice.

'I agree,' said Glenda. 'It's a risk, but one we need to take.'

'Yep, can't beat it to death; we do what we think is best,' he said with a certainty that belied his uncertainty.

'Something or someone might slip by us,' said Glenda, 'but we'll shut down the main threat.'

Jelle was odd but also brilliant in his own way. What set him apart was his outside-the-norm thinking. He thought around problems and then zeroed in for the kill. He acknowledged and followed his intuition. His instinct was telling him the plan—his plan—and that of Remilious was upside down. The missing researcher, a fact. His logical mind told him to trust facts. His intuition, his sixth sense. What disturbed him the most was the sudden disappearance of his assistant and Al-Qaeda-EIJ contact. *Where did Octavia disappear to? Why no communication?* Jelle couldn't reach her by phone late last night, and she didn't show up at the lab this morning. She had never even been late arriving in the past. He wanted to talk to her. He had decided he was almost willing to go to one of her dustbowl villages. He weighed the situation. His gut said big problem. His instinct said not to hesitate; execute your escape plan. Holding him back was the Somali and the young students he planned to infect and observe. 'Godverdomme,' he exclaimed as he stomped his foot and made two fists.

Self-preservation won the debate. He rushed to the lab. He injected a stimulant into Cigalle and removed the drip from his arm before wheeling the somnolent man into the glass observation booth. He pressed a button and allowed three young women to pass through a door and into the room. He hurried to another room and opened a locked closet. Everything he needed was packed neatly in a rucksack and a duffel bag. Looking at it made him sad. His past preparations would allow his escape from Remilious and their troubles but not give him what he had planned so long for. He cared nothing about the U.S. operation he had conceived. His only consolation would be the misery it would cause to the American sheep, not much brighter than his zombies. However, it was here with the rabid Somali his mind longed to be. *I must watch him in person and then I can leave.* He willed the Somali to revive. *Not acted on the Silver Screen, but in the flesh,* he repeated to himself. *Am I right?* he asked himself. *Stay a little longer and then decide?* His intuition screamed, get out now.

*  *  *

'We're understaffed,' restated Liam.

'It is what it is,' said Glenda, thinking they had already made that decision.

'The Château's labs are extensive. I'm only concerned about evidence getting destroyed before we can secure it.'

'Okay, the local gendarmes secure the doors. We get our doctor—Josh Ingram—to guide us to where the critical lab experiments are, and we secure them.'

'Too slow. I think we send our people in, using his diagrams and then let him show us and your weird lab guy where the illegal and harmful stuff is,' added Liam.

'Agreed, then we can decide what our next course of action is,' said Glenda, assuming her natural air of authority.

'Let's get super star lab jockey questioning Ingram while he's still in the air,' said Glenda.

Abenaa laughed, 'You mean your resident nut?'

Liam looked quizzically at Glenda.

Glenda closed her eyes and shook her head sideways before saying, 'He's a little eccentric, maybe more like a lot eccentric, but there is no one better to get to the bottom of what Remilious' labs are doing.' She looked up with her golden cat eyes at Abenaa. 'He's brilliant. We couldn't have anyone better for this.'

'I've only had the privilege of seeing him inebriated and with his face dyed by Indians in the jungle, so perhaps my opinion is, ah, skewed,' conceded Abenaa.

'Bring Ingram in. I'll get Nusmen on comm,' said Tom.

'I want to record this,' said Francine. 'She's right,' said Glenda. We can't miss anything. The devil is in the details.'

'Right you are. We're taking on a big company with political contacts,' said Liam.

'They might be short on cash, but they still have enough to make our lives difficult. You bet, we carefully document everything we do,' confirmed Glenda. 'We're at the endgame. Enough already. Enough covering our asses. Let's shut them down and get the top guy.'

'He's a terrorist, not just a corporate criminal. He'll be finished if we do our job right,' added Liam.

'Nusmen's on video,' said Liam. Everyone turned toward the monitor. Those who knew Nusmen mouths gaped, and their eyes widened. 'Wow,' said Glenda.

'Wow, what? You're always making faces at me. What now? Why am I here? I have my experiments. I don't want to be wherever I'm going. I want to go back.'

'Well, hello,' said Glenda. 'For a minute I thought there was a new Nus minus the Shurar tribal face markings. I'm surprised, is all. I thought you had them removed. Everyone, meet our secret bio-weapon with an attitude.'

'I don't have time for nonsense or worrying about what you think about my face. Where am I going?'

'You'll find out, and you will like it. Enough chitchat. We're time-sensitive.'

'I want to know.'

Glenda ignored him. 'This is Dr. Josh Ingram. Abenaa will translate his French. Doctor, as succinctly as you can, fill Nusmen in on what you told us.'

Josh Ingram didn't say anything.

'Dr. Ingram, no hesitation. Get on with it.'

'But I want ...,' Nusmen started to say.

Glenda didn't let him finish and said in a voice that shut Nusmen up, 'They engineered a virulent bird flu that can also infect humans. They are planning to kill chickens that lay eggs used for vaccines in the U.S., and on top of that, infect people with an engineered avian virus.'

'I think you have his attention,' said Abenaa.

Glenda shook her head. 'Now, quick as you can, inform Nusmen of the details of what the lab is doing and the exact locations of the experiments and personnel.' Abenaa translated as accurately as she could.

Josh Ingram proceeded to tell Nusmen about the bird flu research at the lab. Nusmen didn't nod off, but he looked bored. Then Dr. Ingram mentioned the RNA approach for H5N1 VLPs, from the co-expression of plasmids to developing a vaccine. Nusmen perked up a little.

'Are you getting all this, Nus?' asked Glenda.

'Yes, yes. That all of it, nothing else?'

Josh looked taken aback. 'None of this is news to you?'

'Some. Sort of interesting. Not groundbreaking stuff,' answered Nusmen.

'I'm shocked,' said Joshua. We're recombining a killer

zoonotic virus that could jump to humans, and you seem ... blasé. Je suis choqué!'

'You two are both nuts,' said Liam. 'What are you shocked about, Doctor? Pourquoi? Why are you doing it if you are so choqué?' asked Liam.

Joshua Ingram looked embarrassed. He had never understood how he had migrated down the path that led him to his present position. *Money*, he thought. *No, it wasn't only money.* 'Je ne me comprends pas,' he answered, looking at his lap. If he had known the plan was to spread the virus to the population of the Midwestern United States and then likely kill half the world's population, he would have been crushed. 'I thought we were finding a way to save people for this virus.'

'Back on point, everyone,' said Glenda, frustrated that time was short and the meeting was getting away from her.

'Okay,' said Nusmen in the most in-charge voice he could conjure up. 'Explain your lab setup like Glenda asked.'

'Better yet, draw a diagram on the whiteboard,' said Glenda.

'I've already given you a detailed map.'

'I want to see you draw it again. Which people are working on the transmissible flu and other viruses?'

'Like I said before, the whole place worked on this.'

'Humor me. One more time, as I said, I want to go over again who the bad guys are, not the worker bees.'

'Alright. But before I do, there's something I haven't mentioned.'

'I cautioned you about leaving anything out, Doctor. Well, spit it out.'

Ingram hesitated and finally said, 'Dr. Visser was experimenting with making the rabies virus more transmissible.'

Nusmen almost jumped out of his chair. 'What? What do you mean, more transmissible? How was he doing this?'

'Engineering it for a short latency period and transmissible through aerosols.

'How? Tell me how.'

'It's complicated and will take a while to explain.'

'You mean you have done this in your lab?'

'Exactly what I said,' a bit exasperated at repeating himself. 'We have an infected man in the lab.'

'Like with rabies!' exclaimed Nus.

'Again, yes.'

'You're keeping someone infected. Not treating them. Using them as a guinea pig?'

'And he exposed others.' Josh could not bring himself to say, "we" exposed the others.

'Jesus, fucking-a-Christ!' shouted Nusmen.

'Stop,' said Glenda. 'What are you so excited about?'

'There's no cure for rabies once symptoms manifest. Rabies is lethal. I've never heard of anyone using people as lab rats this way. It's freakin' fascinating.'

'Nusmen, you really are bonkers,' said Abenaa. They're making a virus to kill people with the avian flu, and you don't seem to mind. But with this rabies, you're all excited.'

'Huh?'

'You heard me.'

'Again, back on point. Is there anything else you've failed to tell us, Ingram?'

'No. I mean, my lab work didn't have anything to do with the rabies experiments.'

'You better not be lying to me, Doctor.'

Josh knew he had to be completely honest if he had any chance to survive this. 'Alright, I'm embarrassed, and I'm pissed that I had any involvement at all in the rabies experiments. It was my boss, that crazy Visser, who wanted the project. Some sort of childhood fantasy.'

'You leave anything else out, and our deal will evaporate in a puff right before your eyes. You got that?'

Josh couldn't bring himself to answer. He nodded.

'Put a yes in, or I'll make sure you spend your life in prison.'

'Yes. Yes, I understand.'

'Let's move forward,' said Glenda. 'Proceed with all the details and stand up and draw us a map of critical lab areas we should isolate first. Nusmen, stay quiet, observe, and make sure all the lab details make sense. We are going in there, and we need to secure the right areas.'

'And we don't want to die from rabies,' added Liam.

'You won't,' said Nusmen, rolling his eyes. *Imbecile.*

'You dumbass. He said it was transmissible.'

'Well, maybe,' acknowledged Nusmen.

Ingram proceeded to sketch out lab diagrams on the whiteboard, while the team asked questions. Glenda looked at Nusmen several times with a finger on her lips. To support Glenda, Abenaa used her death stare on

Nusmen twice. When Nusmen broke eye contact and looked down, Abenaa winked at Glenda.

'Alright, Nus. You can chime in now. Are the important areas that Dr. Ingram noted the ones we need to secure first?'

'I guess.'

'I don't want a guess. Yes, or no?'

'Okay, yes, but I need to see inside their labs to be sure.'

'You will soon enough. Liam will oversee corralling the bad guys into a separate area from the rest of the lab rats. The primary players, Liam, Abenaa, and I will interrogate now. We'll save the second-liners for questioning later, when we have more staff. Any questions?'

# Chapter Thirty-Two

'Only got a minute, if that,' said Glenda.

'Same here. I'm on a fast flyer to the state with all the S's,' said Brush.

'M-I-S-S-I-S-S-I-P-P-I,' said Glenda, rattling off the letters in quick succession with the appropriate pause after each double S, as every child learns early on in school. It is something that sticks through the years and easily rolls off the tongue.'

'That's it. Jackson in the multiple S state.'

'We might be separated by six hours, big guy, but at least we're now connected on the same mission. I've got ninety-two personnel who are loading up to secure the lab here. I gotta go.'

'Take care, sweet stuff. I mean it. Watch that beautiful body of yours. I can't stop the bleeding six hours away if you let more bullets find you.'

'No worries. Should be simple and it's the invisible bugs they're making that we need to worry about and on your end too, maybe. Really gotta go. Later. Love you,' as Glenda disconnected and quick-timed it to the car where Liam was waiting.

'Your lab guy is in a car headed to Château Noire,' said Liam.

'Okay, let's roll,' said Glenda.

Brush didn't know much about what the labs did at the Château Noir. Only the quick briefing he had just received as it pertained to the chicken flu and what the team had learned about the Remilious' plan to kill off the birds first and then possibly infect Americans with a deadly virus. What they didn't know was how much of the new viruses had been released in the U.S., or if any had been discharged. *What I'm going to find out, I guess,* he mused. He couldn't put his finger on it, but something was nagging at him. He'd never worried about Glenda before. She was as capable as a person could be. Was it that she had become a major part of his life, his fiancée, or maybe he loved her more or respected her more? His mind drifted to the restaurant floor at the top of the Seattle Space Needle, where she had taken three bullets from Najma. His mind's eye reminded him of how beautiful she was when he first saw her as an undercover agent. The image quickly shifted to her falling onto the restaurant floor, leaking blood from her wounds. He shook his head, dispelling the memory, which was immediately replaced with their many *addicted-to-each-other days* in the hospital afterward. He couldn't stay away from her then, and he didn't want to now.

Brush was the laid-back fighter who never even broke

a sweat worrying. It perplexed him that he was feeling jittery. He had never experienced anxiety before. Was it a premonition about Glenda? *I should be there with her,* he thought.

Dr. Jelle Visser felt more and more certain leaving was the right choice. All his senses told him it was. His reluctance, still, was not being able to observe his rabies experiment, as the virus ran its course in his subjects. His thoughts bounced back and forth. His real-life zombie was here, only a few rooms away. *I could take him with me. No, I couldn't control him even sedated,* he thought. As a new idea often happens, in a flash, it sprang into his mind. *I'll turn him loose. Maybe I'll hear something or even get to see him on the news.*

'Jim. I love Cherry almost like a sister, but I'm not sure yet that I trust her in civilization,' she paused and said, 'if I can call many places in the world civilized. What if she kills somebody? It's the only way of life she has known.'

'Could be said for all of us. We have two personas. If she doesn't understand that a guerrilla operation in the jungle is different from the normal streets of a city, she will have a problem.'

Maria stood silent for several seconds, thinking about

her new friend and her old friend. *Heather's gone, and I don't want to lose this one.* She nodded her acceptance, squeezed Jim's arm, and walked toward the plane's steps.

*She looks good,* thought Jim, dressed in FARC fatigues. He liked her hair. It had grown longer and remained as tousled as ever. A wild look that suited her. The blond highlights from her medium brown hair had vanished during her stay in Colombia. She's lost a little weight, too. *Not quite skinny yet.*

Maria turned and waved when she reached the steps to the plane. 'I no like her to go,' said Cherry.

'She'll come back. Her home has always been her work. Now she sees a different life is possible. I think she is too fond of it here and of you too, not to return.' Cherry smiled at what Jim had just said. She subconsciously rubbed his arm as she thought about her new friend and Jim.

He made his decision. He opened the door containing the rabid Somali and the four other infected captives before retreating to the lab's entrance door, where he could observe. Nothing. They all stood there. He motioned with his arm, but instead of exiting the door, the Somali stood listlessly, while the others pushed against the back wall. Jelle kicked the door next to him in frustration.

'She is nice,' said Pedro as the small jet taxied toward the runway.

Jim hesitated and said, 'She's your mom's oldest friend.' Knowing what he had just said wasn't anything they didn't already know.

Pedro looked at him and nodded.

Cherry put her arm around Pedro and pulled him to her. 'That means your mom was una persona muy buena.'

'Si.'

Jim reached down and took Tshui's hand. She hadn't looked away from the plane during its taxi or as it lifted into the sky. 'Time to explore the city, señoritas.'

'Maria's plane's ETA is 1400 at Meridian National Guard Base, near Jackson, Mississippi,' said Sheilla. 'Your transport leaves in forty minutes, putting your ETA about the same as hers. JP is the only one of Neilly's team available. He'll arrive before you. Teckie Tom and Abenaa are in France. JP was doing some sort of interpreting for the CIA in D.C., so we snagged him,' said Sheilla.

'I'll take JP, but I wish we could have Neilly's full team.'

'You've got Carter's best group.'

'Second best to Neilly is still not too shabby, eh.'

'Here's your schedule of people and timings. Carter's team will be back up and move to the points we planned unless you direct them differently. The HazMat crew will stay back until you need them, except for the two testers working with you. I talked to Dr. Dakine on the plane. She's been briefed by both Glenda and Nusmen. And Glenda has a message for you: there's no vaccine for this strain of avian flu. It's meant to be debilitating and deadly.'

'So that's the message?'

'No. The message was, and I quote, "You watch yourself, mister." She apparently wants to keep you in this world.'

Brush's eyes twinkled, and a big smile stretched across his face. Sheilla watched the stocky Canadian smiling at the message from Glenda. He was only four or five inches taller than she was. He was so different from slim Colonel Johnson, both in personality and appearance. She had the idea, early on, when she came to BWC that Brush was a bit cavalier. He never seemed serious and, with a nonchalant expression, *brushed* all worries to the side. She had been partially correct. He wasn't a worrier. He was easygoing. But she had at first missed the calm efficiency, good judgment, and battle skills that were second nature to him. She had been wrong about him.

Brush wondered what Sheilla was thinking as she disappeared into silence. While her mind was somewhere else, he thought about Glenda's ginger hair and fair skin, and then a small smile appeared as an image of her breasts formed. And then evaporated as he looked at Sheilla with her long red hair and petite body. Both are so very different except for their competence. As competent or more so than any man. He thought that in a complimentary way. He had always thought women were superior to men, just as Jim did. It was something they had discussed many times as they discussed prejudices. It was simply that he forgot about their gender. His grin widened as an image formed in his mind of Glenda. *She's competent all right, but she's all woman. I really got lucky.*

Sheilla came out of her deep thought trance and wondered what had caused Brush to grin. She threw it aside and asked, 'You all set then, Major?'

Brush nodded. 'Hey, thanks for the message. You made my day.'

'Supplies are loaded. I'll alert both HazMat and Carter to get a move on. You should be in Mississippi at 1400.'

Dr. Jelle Visser felt like a new man. No paunch, a shaved head, and his real but shorter height. And it was much more comfortable out of the lifter shoes that had caused him to walk funny. He hardly recognized himself in the mirror. He wore tan slacks, wire-rimmed round glasses, and an unworn Imperial College London hoodie. He had always admired the technology and medicine-oriented university partly because of its standing but mostly because it didn't show any humanity to staff and students. *Just my kind of place.* He had purchased the sweatshirt a long time ago on a trip to a conference in London. As far as he could remember, he had never worn any hooded sweatshirt before. *Incogonineeeeeto,* he said to himself chuckling at his, *ahhh* ... paragoge. He had to think for a minute what it was called, *nice word he thought,* and then he ran his hand over his smooth head and said in an assertive voice, 'Precision is no longer my game. I'll say and do whatever I want.'

The liposuction had gone quicker than he had anticipated, and he was a little sore. He still had over two hours before the TGV train went to Marseille, where he would board his cargo ship. *I wonder what the Somali is up to. I wanted them all outside. Idiots. Why wouldn't they move. I was giving them freedom. Maybe they did.* As disciplined as Visser was, he couldn't help himself. He turned the older silver Peugeot he had acquired two months ago under a fake company name back toward Château Noir.

It felt good to be back on a mission, thought Brush. The plane was like a second home. Relaxed, he closed his eyes.

Corporal Moriac was as relaxed as Major McGuire was on his plane. One flying east and the other west, they wouldn't cross paths in the air; still, they were inching closer on the map. Brush was flying to Mississippi with the HazMat and Carter's team. Moriac was speeding toward Chicago with Brian. Octavia was the only person who knew the real plan—where the lab was located. Her organization had arranged for the two university students to handle the virus. It worried Marcel to have them involved. He didn't trust anyone, especially terrorists. Two days, minimum, Visser had said were required for them to enhance the virus quantity. He would then rendezvous with a white supremacist that the EIJ had connections with and receive the supplies and weapons he required. He felt naked with only the two Glocks he smuggled into the U.S. on the plane, one for himself and the other for Brian.

# Chapter Thirty-Three

Heinrich marched back into his office so purposefully with his Germanic features that one might have thought he was a soldier. He dropped into his brown-leather swivel chair. He had hardly touched its glossy surface when he jumped up and ran down the hall and into a lab. Opening a cabinet door, he was surprised to see all the atomizers were gone. Perplexed, he went looking for Jelle to see if he knew anything about what had happened to them. Jelle wasn't in the lab. Heinrich knocked on his office door. After a few seconds, he opened it to an empty room. *Scheisse.* Slamming the door, Heinrich paged him and didn't receive a callback. Scheisse, shit, he cursed into the phone.

He couldn't ask Visser's assistant; Octavia had mysteriously disappeared too. Something didn't add up. He wondered if Al-Qaeda had kidnapped Jelle and taken him to some dust bowl village with his rabies virus and the flu atomizers. He wouldn't go there on his own, would he? *I need to check to see if the rabies virus is here.* Thinking it was the only thing that made sense. *Would it be gone too?* He jumped out of his chair again. Before he got past his desk, his door burst open. 'Heinrich, the Somali is out wandering the halls.'

'Scheisse. Go find him. I'll call security.' Heinrich called for the two goons who had escorted the Somali to the lab the first day. He paged Visser again. 'Verdammt! What the effin' hell is going on? Where are you, Visser?'

*This is not right. Something is dreadfully wrong.* Then he panicked. He grabbed his rucksack and loaded personal items and his lab notes into it. *These could send me to prison.* Packing made him feel better. Getting out of this place sent a wave of relief through his mind. He didn't want to be here any more than he did in some godforsaken dust-covered country. He ran down the hall to the steps. He shoved the heavy door to the outside open, slamming it into a woman in uniform and knocking her to the ground. Scheisse! *What is a polizist doing at the door?* As he looked at her, the two cops grabbed him and threw him down next to her. The woman looked over, with blood dripping from her lip and spat at him before she stood and kicked him in the stomach. *It's over. I'm too late, he said to himself. How could I be so stupid?*

'The bastard left me here,' he said as he groaned.

'Shut up,' said the woman officer, wiping the blood from her lower lip.

The two officers handcuffed him, jerked him up, and walked him back inside. The halls were suddenly filled with shouting. They escorted him to a room where Dr.

Joshua Ingram was standing next to two women, one tough-looking short-haired black woman and the other a buxom strawberry-redhead.

Josh looked away from Heinrich and said, 'He's one of the bad ones.'

Heinrich was so astonished that he looked straight at Dr. Ingram and said, 'Ficker. You're lying. Visser is the bad guy.'

Abenaa strode over and grabbed Heinrich's arm with a strength that surprised him. His thoughts roamed wildly through his brain, assessing the debacle he found himself in. The muscle-bound woman, none too gently, pushed him into an empty room, telling him to sit and not to move in German. He answered automatically in German. Abenaa sneered at him. 'German, huh? Don't get out of that chair.' Two uniformed officers entered and stood by the door as Abenaa walked out.

'There's a guy who just drove up close to the back entrance. As soon as he saw the cops, he wildly reversed and tried to drive off,' said Techie Tom.

'What do you mean, tried to drive off?' asked Glenda.

'I thought it might be prudent to stop him.'

'You shot him?'

'No, I, ah, shot his tire.'

'You shot his tire?'

'Yes, ma'am.'

Techie wasn't sure if he had done the right thing.

He smiled when she said, 'Well done, Tom. At least I think so. We'll find out for sure soon enough. I want you monitoring calls in and out of this place. Watch the car and driver. When Abenaa gets to you, come back with her and the driver.'

'Roger that.'

'Abenaa, find Techie outside and bring the bald guy he's watching back up here.

The room that had held Heinrich only a few minutes ago now held over two dozen people, including Benthal, Krasner, Christensen, and six officers.

'We have three rooms for interrogation with recorders ready,' said Liam.

'We need more if we're going to get this job done sooner rather than later,' said Glenda. 'Get someone started on setting up more.'

'Will do.'

'Dr. Ingram, Josh, of the people in this room, who knows the most?'

'Heinrich, Benthal, Krasner, and Christensen are the top lab scientists, and they were in on the rabies experiments, too. Heinrich is Visser's right-hand man. Visser's Middle Eastern assistant, Octavia Mustafa, disappeared a couple of days ago.'

'His what?' exclaimed Glenda.

'You didn't mention this before.'

'I didn't know it was important; I don't know much about her other than she was Dr. Visser's shadow. I always assumed she was just an assistant.'

'Maybe, we'll see. Who are we missing?'

'Dr. Visser and Mustafa are the only ones I see missing.'

'Why isn't he here?'

'I don't know. He's always here, except he wasn't this morning.'

Abenaa, along with Techie Tom, escorted the bald man into the room. 'You know that man, Josh?'

Josh glanced over as the two walked the man over.

'I've never seen him before.'

'Okay, folks. The place is locked down. Let's get started. Move Heinrich, Benthal, and Krasner into the three rooms we have now,' said Glenda. 'Abenaa, you take your pick of Benthal or Krasner. Colette and I will take the Heinrich guy first, then you can have him. I think he's the one who knows what we want.'

'Maybe, but so far, he's been playing the angry, silent guy.'

'Krasner then,' said Abenaa.

'We'll see. Liam gets Krasner then. Colette, I want you with me to interpret. The rest of you, get all these lab types identified and find out what time-sensitive experiments they're working on. I want Nusmen first escorted around with Dr. Ingram and then we'll look at what experiments need attending to. We don't want to lose any data at this point. One last thing: nobody leaves or goes back to work unless I approve it. If the lab staff are working on something critical or some procedure that needs their attentionyou come and ask me pronto. Okay, let's hustle, folks.'

'Heinrich, let me formally introduce myself. I used to be with the FBI, and now I work for another government organization.'

'CIA?

Glenda glared at him, 'Soon, one way or the other, you are going to enlighten me about everything that goes on in this lab. First, I want your full name and title.'

'Everyone just calls me Heinrich.'

'Full effing name. Got it?'

'Dr. Heinrich A. Müller, deputy lab director.'

'No middle name?'

'I don't use it.'

'Last chance, Adolf.'

Heinrich looked at the ceiling and said to himself, *she already knew*. 'Adolf,' my grandfather's name, and before you say anything, it has nothing to do with that Adolf. I guess you already know that and why I don't use it.'

'Don't mess with me. Answer my questions. You got it?'

'I've ...'

Glenda held her finger up to her lips. 'Shush. You answer and I'll decide if you are worth getting a deal.' Glenda set a bound folder on the table. On the cover, it had in bold letters Heinrich Adolf Müller. 'You are forty-three years old, never married, it says not gay, dedicated to your work with a master's degree and Ph.D. from Technische Universität München. This information is quite extensive, going back to July 16, 1958, the day you were born to Gisela Krüger. Your father, Wolfgang, as you know, is not your biological father.'

Heinrich's mouth dropped open. 'How ...'

'Shush. I'll ask the questions.'

Glenda put her hand karate chop style to her mouth with her index finger touching her lips. Behind it, a careful observer would detect a hint of a smile. 'This file was prepared by French and German intelligence services. You can see by the number of pages that it contains. I imagine all there is to know about your forty-three years on Earth. What it doesn't tell me is what exactly you do at the Château Noire's labs. I do know some of what's going on, of course, and before the next few days are over, I will know everything there is to know. I can assure you of that.'

'But you are not German or French. You are American,' said Heinrich.

Glenda continued. 'What you have to decide is how you want to spend the next forty-three years of your life.'

Heinrich almost rolled his eyes up, thinking, they don't have anything on me. Then he looked down at the folder and knew that was not true. They had everything on him and would squeeze whatever else they needed out of the others. His face went red as he thought, *Jelle Visser left me to take the fall.*

'Is this how you normally interrogate people?'

'No, I usually hook you up to an electric chair, supply a little voltage, pull your fingernails out, cut off your testicles one at a time, maybe remove a nose or an eye.' She turned to Colette. 'I don't think Heinrich will need any of that sort of motivation, not yet at least,' as she winked at Colette.

Heinrich thought she was kidding, but then, if this operation was CIA, French intelligence, or German intelligence, she might have the ability to do some of those things. He didn't need persuading any longer. Visser had fucked him. He would try to save himself.

'What if I talk ... ah, can you make a deal?'

'I have to tell you straight up; it will be tough. Do you know anything that the other lab staff can't provide me with?'

Heinrich at first thought that all he would have to do was to tell what Visser and Boucher had been up to, and not mention their connection with al-Qaeda and EIJ. 'What if I did know some things that would be of more interest to you and your CIA than you can get from anyone else?'

'I'll listen. It will have to be good. Test me.'

'Middle Eastern connections.'

'Maybe. Are you referring to the Somali, al-Qaeda, ELF, Mustafa, or? I need details.'

Heinrich was trying his best to look calm, pretending he wasn't nervous or scared. *Scheisse. I'm screwed. They already know. Maybe I have nothing to trade.*

'Actually.' He paused and bit his lip, not certain what he should say. *If I tell them, how do I know that they won't use it against me?*

'I'll be honest with you,' said Glenda. 'We want to get the top people. We want to know who is involved and precisely what the plan is in the U.S. We know there is a connection to the M.E., but I want your version? We're not interested in you if ...'

'Dr. Visser's gone,' Heinrich blurted out. 'He escaped and left me here.'

A knock on the door. Liam said, 'Can you step out for a minute?'

Glenda stood, not wanting to leave. She could sense

Heinrich was folding, *and what about Dr. Visser being gone? What did he mean?* 'This guy is going to talk,' said Glenda, 'and I was just about to hear what he could offer. This is important, right?'

'Bear with me.' Liam nodded. Henri, bring the little guy over. 'Let's go back into your room with this guy.'

Glenda looked puzzled but decided Liam must have a good reason.

'Heinrich, do you recognize this man?'

Heinrich looked as perplexed as Glenda.

Liam said, 'Introduce yourself.'

Jelle didn't respond.

'Look closely and tell me what you see,' said Liam.

Heinrich looked, shaking his head sideways, still not recognizing Visser.

Liam took a rolled-up polar fleece jacket and, while Henri held Visser's arms, he stuffed it on top of the stomach dressing and under Visser's shirt. 'Does this help any?' Visser grimaced as Liam had been none too gentle.

'Huh? Jelle, is that you?' said Heinrich, with his eyes and mouth wide open in astonishment.

'Don't say anything, Heinrich. Don't be stupid. They can't prove anything.'

'Get him out. I have a special room for him,' said Liam. 'I hope they didn't cut out his couilles with the stomach blubber. I'd hate to miss doing that myself,' as he herded Visser out the door.

'I wouldn't want to be the mysterious doctor. Liam loves his job and he's hard to control sometimes. I'll try to keep him away from you, Heinrich. So that is the missing

Visser. Okay, back to where we left off and now with new information. I expect that Dr. Visser can provide us with all that we need, leaving you,' she held up her arms, 'up in the air without a parachute.'

Heinrich closed his eyes. Visser would fuck him. He hated him, and he hated what this place was doing to him. 'I'll tell you everything. Can you help me?'

'Colette, stay in here. I'll be back in a minute.'

When Glenda came back into the room, she said, 'Give us everything you know, don't leave anything out, and I can get you something better than the firing squad. That's it.'

'Can I have an avocat, s'il vous plait?'

'All right, but keep in mind I don't have to provide you with a French lawyer. You give me everything you know, and I'll do my best to work a deal with you.'

'I don't think that's fair. I wasn't in charge here, but I was close to Visser, and I can help you. And I will. Please can't you help me?'

'Start talking. I'll send an avocate in and we'll see where we are.'

The French intelligence service assumed that some would ask for representatives and that there would also be agreements written in trade for information. They sent a small group of bilingual avocates to the Château Noire. None would prove to be entirely impartial defense representatives. What the team wanted to know were details about the infectiousness of the avian flu for humans: how fatal; what was the plan in the U.S. to spread it, and the connections to al Qaeda? For that, they would consider giving Heinrich a complete pass and a new life outside prison. As long as he spit out all the answers. Unfortunately for him, he knew practically no details about the U.S. operation.

'Excuse me, ma'am. Your lab specialist is here.'

'Keep talking, Heinrich. Colette, see if he's got anything worthwhile to say. I'll be back.'

'Yes, ma'am.'

Glenda looked at Nusmen standing and looking agitated. 'Your persona is even more impressive in person, Nus.'

Nusmen stood there like he didn't know what she was talking about. 'Where's the guy manifesting with rabies?'

'Get serious. That can wait.'

'Okay, okay, right, what do you want me to do then?'

'I want to get on with it. Talk to this Ingram guy, see the lab. And their research.'

'Okay,' said Nusmen.

'We'll get you a guide first and then go on a tour. I want a meeting with you in thirty minutes and then in two hours. Two fifteen-minute tours with Heinrich and one with Ingram. Then tell me which is the most cooperative. Take the one who can help you best and spend an hour and a half in the lab. Then I want your summary of what they are doing. After, you can investigate the rabies issue. We need to find out how serious their bird flu virus is for us in the U.S. And second, is there any danger to this rabies thing?

'Rabies is a 100 percent fatal. The H5N1 probably is mostly fatal.'

'Hmm. Okay, I want you to put together the story from what you see in the labs. I'll correlate it with what they fess up to in interrogation. You're the key in all this, Nus. You understand how important you are here? Is that all okay with you?'

Nusmen nodded, mulling over what she had said about how important he was.

'Take Dr. Ingram for the first fifteen minutes. Back here, and then you can take the other one on tour. Don't be a minute late. Got it?'

Nusmen nodded again.

'I want to hear you say it. You got it?'

Nusmen bobbed his head and then added, 'Yes.'

Glenda opened the door to Colette and Heinrich and poked her head in. 'Who's the best person to act as a guide for a lab tour?'

'I am,' said Heinrich.

'I'll be back.'

She opened the door to where Abenaa was hovering over Krasner. 'Ask your guy who's the best to give Nusmen here a lab tour, and I'll ask Ingram. Heinrich volunteered. I don't trust him.'

'You got it.'

'Nusmen looks almost normal,' said Abenaa.

'Different with his haircut sort of normal.'

'Are you getting anything from your guy?' asked Glenda.

'Krasner's a pussycat and scared shitless. He got pretty nervous when I told him what his future looked like. But he says he'll fully cooperate but wants an avocate before he'll say anything.'

'Heinrich wanted one too, but he's giving us the full story without; at least I think he is.'

'I thought he was going to be belligerent. How'd you get him to fess up so fast?'

'He knows we didn't just bust in with this sort of force on a fishing expedition. I put on my nice lady act mixed with a little tough talk and gave him the truth about his circumstances. Said I could save him from the firing squad, but not much else.'

'That sounds like a sweet-lady approach, alright. Except, do you think he's going to confess all with you saying you'll throw him in prison for life?'

'Truth is, I could get him a new life and no jail time if he gives up what the plan in the U.S. is. He's plenty worried.'

'And I would have put on my mean-Joe face on and hoped to scare the bejesus out of him.'

Glenda laughed. 'That face might have worked faster than my sweetie-pie look.'

'Okay, what's so funny, you two?' asked Liam.

'Nothing that can be shared,' said Glenda. 'I've got to get back in there and get his story. I need to get Nusmen and Ingram started. Have Douglas go with a recorder. Tell him to keep quiet and not let on he speaks French. And tell him the schedule and make sure that Nusmen stays on it. Maybe someone will let something interesting slip out. This is our best shot at finding out what they are up to. I want to have as much info as we can on the General's desk first thing in his morning.'

'Visser is in a secure, cold room.'

'Anything from Bethnal, Liam?'

'Bethnal says he never wanted to be involved, and he'll do whatever we want,' said Liam.

'Let's huddle up and compare notes in fifteen minutes and then again ninety minutes later. I should have Nusmen's summary by then.'

'Good idea,' Abenaa added.

'I want Josh Ingram to escort Nusmen first. Heinrich might be the best one as a guide, but I need to finish his statement first. I'll send Heinrich out to Nusmen and Douglas in fifteen minutes.'

'What are you going to do with the bald guy?' asked Abenaa.

'Let Visser sit. The more information we have before we interrogate him, the better.'

Glenda walked back to where Heinrich was talking, while Colette stood with her arms crossed, leaning against the wall.

Heinrich used his hand to brush up the front of his thick light brown hair and said, 'When do I get to talk to an avocate?' then he added, 'Please.'

As he was asking, the door opened and a man wearing a suit, carrying a briefcase, in his mid-thirties, well-groomed, with dark hair and complexion walked in.

'He has been made aware,' said Glenda, 'of what we may be able to do for him, depending on the information he provides. Then she turned to Heinrich. The choice is yours. After you've had your little talk, what I want you to focus on first is the terrorist attack in the U.S. I use *terrorist* to emphasize to you both how severe the consequences could be for you. After you tell us what you know about that, Heinrich, I want a detail of the lab experiments and every person's part in those experiments, including Dr. Visser and your boss, Boucher.'

* * *

'The staff are all saying Heinrich knew more than anyone except for Heinrich's boss, Dr. Visser,' said Liam.

Glenda sighed. 'If my fair-haired German is finished with his avocate, let's get someone with a tape recorder to follow him and Nusmen around the lab. I don't want to miss any details. And I don't want them taking forever. The advocat is going to tell him he can keep him out of prison if he cooperates fully. Let's bust a gut.'

'Your expression is ... um, interesting, quizzical, and uniquely American,' said Liam. 'The meaning is clear, nevertheless,' as he walked, shaking his head, toward Jelle Visser's room.'

Glenda said loud enough to penetrate Liam's mumbling while wondering what the heck he was carrying on about, 'Bring him in after I send the sans fair-haired boy out. He's the key player.'

Visser heard the woman call him 'the key player.' *Bad for me, he considered,* before he smiled as the game unfolded in his thoughts. He would have to give them the real key player. *Boucher is my key to a get-out-of-jail card. He's the one they want.*

As Heinrich was escorted out of the room, he couldn't take his eyes off the re-created Dr. Jelle Visser. The more he stared, the more he questioned if it really was Visser. *Is it him?* Confusion coursed through his mind; how did he change so much? Maybe it's a look-alike so Visser could escape. What if the real Visser left with the Al-Qaeda woman? This Visser's too short.

Visser's smile faded, and then he became angry. He kept asking himself, *how could I have been so stupid? All my plans: up in smoke.* Over and over, he asked himself the same question, if only I had kept on driving, or if that numbskull Drumheller hadn't been so fast with the liposuction I'd be approaching Marseille and my freedom boat. Now I'm doomed unless I can make a deal. He was enough of a realist to know how many crimes he had committed. There would be no deals, *unless, unless* he repeated to himself. Could he get off if he gave them all the information he had on Boucher? Maybe the Americans wanted to know about the plan there. *Of course, that's it. Or is it al-Qaeda and ELF?* There are my tapes. Maybe that and turning against al-Qaeda, or would that make him guilty as a terrorist conspirator? He was as confused as Heinrich had been about his new appearance. Heinrich had probably been spilling his guts, and the others had no backbone at all. *Do they need what I can tell them? Yes,* he thought. 'Yes,' he said out loud. 'Yes, they do.' *And I know more about the M.E. groups than Heinrich. And I've got all the recordings. Hah!* Boucher is the big prize, and Jelle knew he was the one that could deliver him.

Liam started Visser toward the door. 'He wants an avocate too.'

'All right, set him down and send one in.'

Liam knew which avocate Glenda wanted to use for the big fish.

'Tell the avocat to speed it up. Time's short. When he's ready, I'll get started on him,' said Glenda. 'I'll be out here getting the preliminary report from Nusmen.'

The avocat came out after a few minutes and motioned her in. 'He wants a deal, and he can give you the owner, Boucher, wrapped in a red satin bow. What can you offer him?'

Glenda was surprised. 'Let's hear what he has to say first.'

'He says he'll provide you with information that will allow you to take Boucher down. He's giving me some examples and if what he says is true—and I think it is—I expect you'll be interested.'

'Alright, I want the story.' Glenda walked into the comm room they had set up and called General Crystal. 'I don't like this, sir. This guy is a real slime, General. But it's probably what we need to get Boucher.'

'If we can nail Boucher and get what we need about the virus, we do it. But I don't want this guy turned loose on the world.'

Five hours later, General Crystal sat reading Dr. Jelle Visser's report. An initial assessment by several analysts accepted that all the important details jived with the other staff's statements. There seemed to be inconsequential inconsistencies. The General pushed the intercom for his PA, 'Have Bertrand and Martin come to my office.'

'One major piece of the puzzle missing from their statements is the details of the plan for the dispersal other than that there are lab techs and a lab at some unknown place in Illinois or Indiana,' said Bertrand as soon as he sat down and then added, 'Even less about this man, Moriac.'

'So, it's Illinois, not Mississippi?' said Martin.

'Looks that way.'

'I've only got a short biography for Marcel Moriac,' said Martin. 'He's apparently a tough character. Recon paratrooper in the French Legion. I read his official files. C'est un enfant terrible.'

'He is on his way to the U.S.,' said the General, 'and it seems he has in his possession a modified avian virus that will infect humans, according to the head of the lab. He said it would be at least another day before techs in America could generate a large enough quantity to effectively disperse it. Again, he asserts he does not know the location or where Marcel Moriac or the lab is. He says Boucher arranged everything personally in the U.S. Boucher is refusing to say anything except for the proverbial ...'

'Let me guess—No Comment.'

'Either this Visser is lying, or Boucher knows. My money is on Visser.'

'We should know soon where his plane is landing,' said Martin. 'They have to file a flight plan. But Boucher would not personally do anything, so this Visser is probably trying to deflect blame onto Boucher. Or he would have had someone make the arrangements for him. If so, who?'

'Makes sense,' said Will. 'Coordinate with Glenda.'

'We have the bare bones of what their intent is. I've instructed Glenda that we will need Remilious to double their efforts for a vaccine in case we can't stop the release.'

'You don't mean the company will benefit?' asked Martin.

'That's not the plan, but along with Nusmen looking over their shoulder, it's the best way to save lives if this gets into the population. We'll need a vaccine.'

Madge knocked and poked her head in the door. 'Would you like coffee, some snacks, and, of course, Earl Grey tea with milk for the deputy director?'

General Crystal smiled, 'Thanks for suggesting it, Madge.'

It had not taken Madge long to learn what the new CIA director liked and didn't like. In the short time since he had assumed the role, she had grown quite fond of him as well as learning his peculiarities, such as breezing right past mealtimes when he was working. She had known Bertrand and Martin much longer, and while she liked them both, the General was whom she had come to enjoy taking care of.

Madge walked through the door with an oversized silver tray loaded with an assortment of sandwiches and cookies. She was followed by another woman carrying a silver teapot and coffee pot. Madge, wearing a long gray knit dress, smiled at Bertrand as she sat his milk pitcher on the table.

'Thank you, Madge.'

'Milk in the tea business is a long-lived habit learned from his mother,' added Martin as he winked at Madge.

'It has been mentioned, sir.'

'You're razzing me,' said Bertrand, as he smiled at them. 'I guess I might have divulged it previously.'

Now it was Madge's turn to smile. 'Perhaps you have,' she said as she gave a slight nod and left the room.

'Let's get down to business,' said General Crystal.

A tap on the door. A man walked in and handed Martin a sheaf of papers and stood to the side. Martin scanned them. 'Full bio on Marcel Moriac. More details than the official French version. The short of it is, as we've already thought, he's a tough character. Lots of training and experience. All job and mission. Little or no compassion. Still, trusted by the soldiers he worked with. We've identified the plane we believe Moriac to be on. The original flight plan has been changed in mid-air. We're verifying the new landing with the FAA. Phil, get back in here as soon as you have the location.'

As Phil was leaving, an attractive woman with black, tight curly hair, breathing hard, appeared at the door and nodded as she handed a paper to him.

'Good work, Sam,' said Phil as he turned to Martin. 'Here's the landing location, ORD, Chicago O'Hare. Nothing verified yet on the passengers. We'll be checking the FBOs and their security cams.'

'Phil, get people to the FBOs,' said Martin. 'He's faked us out. Our teams are in Mississippi 1000 miles south.'

'Get them moving north,' boomed General Crystal.

'On it. I'll go back with you, Phil,' said Martin as he grabbed several cookies and headed through the door with Phil.

'I haven't seen the woman before,' said General Crystal.

'Martin recruited her from the NSA. She started yesterday. She prefers Sam to Samantha. Martin's high on her skillset.'

The General pushed the intercom button. 'Get Glenda for me.'

Madge kept her speaker volume ultra-low. Most of the time, she could hear the General's requests through the door, making the intercom superfluous. His overly loud voice certainly commanded attention, but it was the one thing about him she had found difficult to adjust to.

'Whatcha got, Nus?' asked Glenda, feeling far less casual than she sounded. She realized that how fast they moved here and what they found out could either save or destroy thousands of lives in the U.S. *Lucky that we moved in as fast as we did,* she thought.

An animated Nusmen said in an excited voice, 'Tons of cool stuff. This lab is fantastic ...'

'We're on a tight schedule, Nusmen. Get down to business.'

'Yeah, yeah,' sulked Nusmen. 'Alright,' he said as he flopped into a chair and hung his lanky leg over the it's arm. 'First off, this facility is not working on vaccines. Only on creating genetically modified viruses.'

Glenda stayed silent but raised her eyebrows as he talked.

'Two focuses: first, a bird flu that infects birds, jumps species to Homo sapiens with a high fatality rate, and the second project is rabies. As far as I can tell, the rabies research hasn't gotten very far. I can't even see what it is all about. The avian virus is modified for high transmissibility.'

'Okay, let's forget rabies and stay with the bird flu.'

'Most of the lab is dedicated to it. The rabies stuff seems to be a pet project of the jelly-roll guy. It's very interesting ...'

Glenda sighed.

Nusmen pursed his lips, 'Alright, jeez, I was.'

Glenda continued looking at him without any expression.

Nusmen rolled his eyes, 'What they have engineered is great. It's lethal. They modified the protein receptors for human-to-human transmission.'

'What can we do?'

'What do you mean?' asked Nusmen.

'A vaccine is the only way to prevent it, of course, right? Do they have one?'

'No.'

'Without a vaccine, it will easily be the biggest killer, the largest pandemic the world has ever seen. Killing hundreds of millions.'

'Let me get this straight. They developed a lethal, transmissible ...'

'Highly transmissible,' interjected Nusmen.

'Okay, a deadly, highly transmissible virus without concocting a vaccine?'

'Brilliant, huh?'

Glenda scowled.

'Well, I mean, what they did was brilliant. Labbies tell me ...'

'The what, the who, labbies?'

'The lab techs. Short for them.'

'Okay, okay, keep the conversation going forward.'

'... that any vaccine would be developed in their Marseille research facility.'

# Chapter Thirty-Four

The jet carrying Brush, JP, Maria's Hazmat team, and Carter's BWC-quick-response special ops SF had two hours before they arrived at Chicago's ORD airport: twenty-six highly skilled operatives, each with their special expertise. JP, the language polyglot, was the sole Special Forces member present from Neilly's team. Brush, the group leader, which was something he'd not experienced since Vietnam. Maria, the Hazmat team's leader, and Carter's BWC version of special forces, whose primary mission was to protect the Hazmat's personnel.

'Okay,' said Sheilla, 'the closest major egg facilities are far south, east, and west of Chicago, with only one close to the city. Most, however, are in Iowa. Others are in Indiana and Ohio. A smaller one is in Michigan.'

'They're all a long way from Chicago, except for the one not far northwest of the Windy City, eh?' said Brush.

'It's hard to figure out what he is up to,' said Sheilla. 'He's landing in the center of egg-laying heaven, but not close to any chicken farms. We've got nothing to go on. We need more information. Maybe Glenda will help us out there. Someone in the Remilious labs might know his plan.'

'Put me on with her and I'll see ...,' Brush started to say before Sheilla abruptly stopped him.

'Focus, Major. I know you want to talk to her.'

He grinned broadly, thinking, *she is that, but she is also now my fiancée.*

'I'm in touch with her. And I got a feeling you will be bumping into her soon enough. Besides, they would have called if they had any new information.'

'She's on her way here, Sheilla?'

'You guessed it, Major.'

Brush's mind drifted to what Sheilla had just said for him not to do, thinking about Glenda. He couldn't help it. Even the mention of Glenda caused an uncontrollable stirring in him. He hadn't seen her now for too many days. Thoughts of her and the slight vibration of his plane seat made it impossible to do as Sheilla had said, even if she hadn't meant anything like his current dilemma. *Jeez, that woman is attractive and special,* he thought. *No one has had this effect on me before.*

*She would say to me if she were here,* 'Focus, big guy.' And that's what I had better do.

'Are you there, Major?'

'Yeah, yeah, I'm here. Distracted thinking about Glenda for a moment.'

Sheilla wouldn't have had an inkling of how his thoughts affected him months ago. She kept her imagination at bay when she worked. When she was free to let her mind roam, the feelings of arousal she felt when she thought of Martin gave her pleasure, something she had never experienced before.

'Are you there, Sheilla?'

'Yes, sorry, just thinking is all.'

'Hmm. Maybe what you said is the answer. Chicago is a busy airport, not next door to the largest chicken farms but smack dab in the middle of them. And some of the biggest in the Midwest are within striking distance. He's cautious. He's a survivor. He won't give us any clues easily. A busy place is a good place to hide.'

'I agree. He's too cagey to land at his real destination. But where exactly would he head after ORD? How do we intercept him?'

'Best guess, eh, Shiella?

'Got to be Iowa, I think. Until we have something more to go on, it's just a guess and would be a wild goose chase. I'll do some plotting and try to put myself in his shoes and see what pops up,' added Sheilla. 'Stay with me, Major.' She sat thinking, spun in her chair, once, twice, three times. 'They told me a story once about how one of the ranch's reindeer had run off over the mountains behind the Wolf Canyon. Ironically, it was Christmas, and it was spotted and then chased through a small remote town by the locals. It hit the news, and everyone thought it was a SantaChristmas prank. That's how they heard about it at the ranch, on the news. Duanne dropped Jim off in sub-zero temps on a hiking path the reindeer had left the town on. There were tracks. He followed them all night only to come out on a road where Duanne picked him up and said a rancher had trapped her in his barn.'

'I've heard most of this story before,' said Brush.

'My point,' said Sheilla. 'Jim chased, and sometimes it might be better to intercept.'

'Are you sure you weren't in the army?

'Major, when you do catch up with this guy, by all reports, he's a tough guy. Be careful.'

'Yeah,' said Brush casually.

'I'm serious. I've got a bad feeling about this Marcel Moriac,' said Sheilla. 'You watch yourself and watch out for the team too.'

'Back to location: we've got nothing else to go on, so we follow your instincts. I'll buy what you suggest about getting somewhere and not tracking him. We map the likely targets; calculate the way a careful guy would approach and monitor. We'll start looking at that. Maybe before we touch down, there'll be some new info and we can change course again if it makes sense. While we've been palavering, I decided I had better check in with the General. Maybe the CIA has a better way to game what he'll likely do.'

'Sometimes all the distraction is a way to arrive at a solution,' said Brush. 'Palavering helps. I don't think he wants to be on the ground for longer than he has to be. Also, he wants to escape and leaving the same way he arrived is risky. My guess, he will stay close by and not head to states that keep him away from the border. Heading to Canada makes sense. What's on the way out of the country?'

Sheilla was happy thirty minutes later when she called Brush back, after liaising with Martin. 'Martin wanted to divert to Sioux Falls Regional Airport or Joe Foss Field, home of the 114<sup>th</sup> Fighter Wing. CIA thinks it is the most likely area for him. The more he talked, the more I became certain about Chicago.'

'What's at Sioux Falls?'

'Martin's idea. Got it from his team. Makes some sense. The biggest facilities are close by, and for us they would be able to provide plenty of support.'

'Good reason for him to stay away from there. Does it have to be a big breeder? Or will the virus spread from one to the other?'

'Don't know. No matter. Bertrand thinks and I agree Chicago.'

'Agreed, Sheilla. We go to ORD. Something tells me we are right.'

'I'll hang on and listen into your plans and assist if you need me.'

Brush sucked in a deep breath and bumped up his drill instructor voice, not quite to the level of the general's, 'Rise and shine kids, at least for those napping.' Carter elbowed the sergeant snoring next to him.

Brush looked at all of them crammed into the small jet. 'We're making a guess. Sheilla and I agree that the Windy City makes the best tactical place for him to insert. With the problem, there are not any of the big breeders in the immediate area. The biggest concentration is to the west and east. West in Iowa and east in Indiana.'

'Could be south in Illinois too, from the data I've seen,' added Carter.

'CIA thinks Iowa or South Dakota.'

'If we're smart, we should do the opposite of what those desk jockey pricks say,' said Carter. 'What about BWC?'

'Chicago's first choice. Here's what I want to do. We make up six teams of two: me and one of Carter's SF are one of those six teams. Maria and Carter figure out who is in each team. One Hazmat and one SF in each of the other teams. Captain, Maria, you stay with the reserves.' Both nodded.'

'Reserves will be a quick response to wherever.'

'Just so I'm clear,' asked Carter, 'Five teams of two and a sixth, counting you and my sergeant here in the field and the rest of us at the plane in reserve. What about ground transport?'

'BWC will get us whatever we need.'

'You got it Major,' said Sheilla over the video screen. 'A transport is bringing a comm team and their mobile equipment in. We'll have choppers at our disposal.'

Sheilla added, 'Glenda Stuart will be head of that ground group.'

'I think it's a good plan,' added Maria, a little surprised by Brush's authoritative style as she was used to Colonel Johnson making the decisions. Brush had always been the laid-back partner, never the leader. Maybe she had short-changed his ability all the time they had known each other. Then she continued, 'A good plan since we're shooting in the dark. And sure, it's dangerous without immediate backup for the small teams, but we cover more ground and still move fast to a new location.'

'I don't like it,' said Carter. 'The Marcel guy's a badass. Whoever bumps into him will have a tough fight. Our guys will have the disadvantage that the hunter always has and added to that: we could lose somebody spread that thin, two-person teams, no immediate back-up.'

'True,' said Brush, 'unless you have a better suggestion, Captain, that's the plan. Be vigilant. Sheilla will give us the seven most likely locations to scout before we land. Wolcott and myself, ah sorry, Buffalo will take the most likely. Carter, you assign each duo to the other five locations. Call sign will be Bird one, two, three, etc. Keep your comms live. BWC will be 'Eagle. If you get ambushed or need backup, switch your call sign to 'Chicken' one, two, three, etc., or click twice. Reserves will get to you ASAP.'

Carter swirled his head around. 'From what we read about this guy; nobody is going to get a chance to say anything if he spots you first. No screwing around, eyes and ears open. All of you, I know your capabilities, you all can take care of yourselves and one-on-one probably take this guy out, but let's not underrate him. I love you all too much to lose one of you.'

Brush laughed at the moans and mumbles throughout the plane. 'The boss loves us,' said Buffalo.

'Shut up, you buttholes,' said Carter, shaking his head with a faint smile.

# Chapter Thirty-Five

Brian glanced at Ronno from the back seat of their Eurocopter, thinking the man was a wonder and complimenting himself, as he had done many times, on having him as his best friend. In truth, he was more like a big brother. Before meeting Marcel, Brian had been a good soldier with superior fighting skills. Even so, he had always struggled to hide his lack of self-esteem. Marcel had immediately assessed Brian's need for an alter ego, someone to lead him when he lacked courage. Ronno found him useful and ignored his sometimes-obsequious manner. When they were a few miles north of the city, Moriac directed the pilot to fly east over Lake Michigan. And then instructed the pilot to descend and hug the wave tops. Twenty miles from the shoreline, Moriac flipped the transponder off.

'Why did you do that? We're still in a high-traffic zone and it can't turn it off.' He reached his hand out to turn it back on, and he felt the point of Marcel's Sykes double-edged seven-inch knife tip at his neck.

'Shut up.' Moriac was never one to waste words. 'Head southeast. Enter West Beach, Indiana, into your GPS.' The pilot hesitated. Moriac drove his knife into the pilot's leg just above the knee. The pilot screamed. Moriac gave him a hard, open-handed blow to the pilot's right-ear headphone that knocked the pilot's head sideways. 'Enter West Beach into your GPS.' The pilot, with his hand trembling, did as he was instructed.

'Dumb shit,' said Brian, as he reached forward and cuffed the pilot on the head. He then smirked as he slouched back in his rear seat, vicariously feeling the power Ronno had over people. He watched the man's shaky fingers enter the airport designation, 3HO, into the GPS. Blood ran down his leg. When he found Hobart Sky Ranch Airport, he stopped and read the page. 'There are NOTAMs. It is closed to all traffic. Shut down for repairs.'

Moriac pushed the knife point into the pilot's neck until a trickle of blood ran down. 'Okay,' said the pilot, visibly shaking as if he was sitting naked in a snowstorm.

'At the shoreline, I want you to turn east.' The pilot had hoped that this man would make a mistake and take them back into restricted airspace or fly too low over the city. With the transponder turned off, he couldn't punch the hijack code in. *How can I alert air traffic control?* His mind spun, finding no solutions. At their altitude and distance from the airport, they were not in restricted airspace. The awful realization occurred to him; does he need me? *What if he doesn't need me?*

Sergeant Moriac was competent enough to fly the chopper. He had flown many different choppers, mostly from the second seat where he sat now. This Eurocopter was a new model and Marcel watched the pilot and the controls to see what he might learn. He could have killed this middle-aged man in his white shirt and blue coat with his fancy gold epaulets, opened the door and sent him to a cold burial in the big lake. Instead, he watched the pilot, observing the intricacies of the new model. It was a little like a riddle, and he would spend a few more minutes at it. Marcel reached up and changed the radio frequencies. 'David Clarks are a better headset,' he said as he reached over, grabbing the pilot's flexible mic stem and severing it from the white Sony headset. The pilot closed his eyes as the knife came toward him. He dared a glance at the man's face and again asked himself if he was needed or if this man could fly. *But I'm still alive,* he thought.

Moriac could sense what the pilot was thinking. He knew the type. Hope turned them compliant. *Weak losers,* he thought. It was something he had said to himself many times before. Survival motivated their behavior, differing from Brian, his so-called buddy, whose weakness was motivated by a set of simple comingling needs of wanting to belong and be liked. Weakness of any kind disgusted Moriac.

He pointed his index finger left, and the pilot moved his gaze to the front, wondering what this man planned while he watched the shoreline come into sight. Below, the wave tops displayed small crescents of froth. As they neared the shore, ice fused the restless water to the snow-blanketed land. The white ground merged with the gray-white sky on the horizon. The land was flat, partly agricultural, and partly dilapidated houses, and oversized rusted industrial sites severed by a busy multilane highway with lines of trucks rolling on top of the concrete thread leading from urban Chicago, through Gary, Indiana, and continuing east in a straight line along the southern Lake Michigan shoreline.

* * *

'You've got my report. Everything is pretty zipped up here,' said Glenda. 'I think we have at least most of the full story and after the legal beavers add their confirmation, all we need to arrest Boucher. The Somali is being sedated at the Château's lab as he has no chance of survival. The others exposed were inoculated. All the disillusioned wannabe lab terrorists will probably feel lucky to be able to go home and live a normal life. Nusmen's enroute to the Marseille labs with Liam's lieutenant and five of his team. The French president called the lab director, Blackwell. My take after that conversation is the labbies are going to be no problem going the extra mile to exonerate their part in this.'

'Labbies?'

'Sorry, General. New word.'

'Uh huh, Nusmen, I'd wager.'

'Astute guess, sir!'

'I've heard it before. Go on.'

'Anyway, Blackwell was humble pie. The urgency was

instilled in him, and the president alluded to a national award if he produced results. The president's skilful with the stick, and even better with the reward. I could feel Blackwell jumping at it. The board has appointed Gabriel as interim director of Remilious.'

'I'll save saying, well done, until after we find a cure for the virus and stop the spread of the new strain,' said Will.

'Sir, I'm not a lab jockey, and we've interrogated everyone except Boucher. I want ...'

The General cut her off before she could finish and said, 'I want you back on the ground on this side of the pond. We're assembling some of your old team from when you pursued Najma and some of the same equipment. It's on the way as we speak. They should be in Chicago when you get there. The BWC teams and Brush will already be searching for Moriac. Their ETA is seventy minutes. Shake a leg, the plane's waiting for you.'

'Yes, sir. And thank you, General. Wait, how's my team getting there so fast? Where are they driving from?'

'They're not. They're in the air on a Hercules transport.'

'Our RV too?'

'Your Bus too. Good thing we're flying them as Mississippi was a mistake and if they'd headed there, it would take an age to get them up north. They will be spooling up their comms and coordinating with BWC by the time you land.'

'I'll start sorting this on the plane, sir.'

'Just so we're clear, this isn't about backing up Major

McGuire,' Will continued. 'He can take care of himself. You will be more effective there. I need your investigative skills on-site to stop the viral spread before it can be disseminated by Moriac or whoever else is there working with him. He's a loner, but don't assume that.'

'Got it, sir. What about the chickens?'

'Animal Plant Health Inspection is in full gear. No doubt millions of them will end up being exterminated. It'll decimate the egg-laying facilities and our vaccine production. That can't be helped, but your goal is to try to stop this before potentially millions of Americans die too. You will have full authority over the FBI. The local cops are being informed. Any trouble you contact me.'

'Understood, sir. Will I be coordinating with Animal Plant?'

'Maybe. Depends on where the infected facilities are. APHIS normally has nothing to do with the CIA and of course, they will have never heard of the BWC. The best is we can stop Moriac and be gone. We are out of our remit working on anything in the U.S.'

'FBI?'

'Large contingent assembly in Chicago and Midwest offices. With the extent of the threat, there will be a lot of manpower on the ground. Keep me informed.'

Glenda, Abenaa, Techie Tom, and their on-loan financial expert advisor boarded the plane bound for ORD. 'Are you dropping me off in DC?' asked Glen Adams.

'Afraid not. It's a shorter flight back to your offices from Chicago than Marseille via Paris on commercial. I appreciate all you have taught me and the help with

Remilious, but we're in a big bust hurry, and like I said, it would take you a lot longer to get hooked up with a flight from here than to go with us and catch a short hop from the Midwest.'

'Okay with me. And truth be told, I liked working with you and this group, and I'm going to miss the excitement a little. You need me again, I'm all yours.'

Before Glenda could answer, the headset was passed to her. 'What's up, Liam?' She listened for thirty seconds. 'Are you kidding me! How the hell did that happen?'

'No clue,' said Liam. We opened his door to interrogate him; the room was empty. No one saw anything. I don't know how he got out and how he could have gotten by the security on the doors.'

'Maybe the little creep is still in the Château?'

'We're searching and interrogating everyone inside and out. And before you say it, I know it's a problem. He's the key to tying up Boucher.'

'Merde, I'd better let my boss know.'

'Your French has improved!'

Glenda Rose turned toward the comms operator and said, 'Get General Crystal back.'

'Sir, you might want to take back any compliments about what we did at Remilious.' Abenaa looked at Glenda with a what's-up expression. Glenda looked at her lap, deep in thought for what seemed to her a long time. In reality, it was only a fraction of a second. Softly she said, 'I've just been told that Dr. Jelle Visser is not in the Château.' Then her normal confident voice returned, 'You want me back there?'

A slight pause followed before the General said, 'Liam and his team will handle it. Stopping the virus spread is the important job. I would assume that Sergeant Moriac knows that we've shut down the Château's labs. Whether he does or he doesn't, he's not the sort to stop in the middle of a mission.'

'No, but if he's expecting someone to come looking for him, it will make him more unpredictable.'

'That's why I want you there pronto with your old team. Sheilla and Martin will back you up. Stop him, ask for whatever you need, make it happen before he releases the modified virus.

'My information here says it will take a couple of days to reproduce any quantity. By the time we arrive, there might only be one day to locate one guy in a huge city, if he is in the city. And if what I hear is right about him, the FBI might be short an agent or two—or should I say, a reduction in manpower if they bump into him.'

* * *

It was hard for Jim to discern who was the most infatuated with Cuenca. Cherry, he supposed. Tshui had a wide-eyed look that might have been either interest, curiosity, fear, or something else entirely. Cherry constantly looked between her Ecuador travel book and the city. With eyes searching, exploring the city and the book, looking at people, she fired non-stop questions at Jim. Pedro saved his dad by answering the continuous litany, jumping in with answers to her relentless curiosity. Tshui's large, dark, burnt almond eyes purposely scanned, not darting from one thing to another as Cherry's did.

Passersby looked surreptitiously at them: the young, brown-skinned boy, the face-tattooed Shuar girl, the tall blue-eyed man, and the short black-haired, voluptuous Colombian who was obviously a tourist with her well-worn guidebook but could not shake the aura of her guerrilla heritage. The watchers sensed the soldier in her. There was no way to disguise the impact of the "family" on the Ecuadorians, regardless of status, or the expats, and local people walking on the street. No one said anything. No one overtly stared. Occasionally, a person would nod a greeting, which Jim could tell from their faces harbored an unstated question.

As the foursome stepped and stopped their way through the city, Jim motioned them to an outdoor café table. He moved a chair for Tshui next to him and carefully set her down. She sat, legs dangling, looking fearful. Jim picked up a menu. Before seeing the first item, a voice from behind him said, 'Discúlpe, señores y señoria.'

Cherry looked intently at the dark-haired, woman who wrested her eyes from Cherry's as though she was mesmerized and said, 'I don't mean to disturb your meal or intrude, but is it possible that the child is of Shuar descent?'

'¿Cuál es su interés?' asked Cherry, holding the woman again captive with her menacing guerrilla stare.

The woman recognized her authority, shifting her gaze down as she said, 'It is because I, too, am of the Shuar. Might I speak with her? It would give me pleasure to do so.' Cherry relaxed, allowing her eyes to soften. After several seconds of the woman talking in her native language, and with Tshui shyly answering, Jim asked, 'I would appreciate it if you could translate what you are saying,' as well as he could in Spanish. Pedro, you might need to interpret for me.

'Perdone, señor. I was so happy to speak to her that I have been rude and not introduced myself. And I speak a little English. Forgive me. It is giving me much pleasure to communicate in my natural tongue. My name is Sharupe,' as she delicately put out her hand to the Colonel. Pedro immediately stuck out his hand, introducing himself, and then Cherry, with slightly less exuberance, did the same.

Jim looked at Tshui first and then said, 'Sharupe,' nodding at the woman, then at a chair. Tshui gave Jim no sign that she had understood what he was asking. 'If you would please ask Tshui to confirm that she wouldn't mind if you joined us.' Jim watched her for any response, that the woman made her uncomfortable. From Tshui's expression, he couldn't help smiling. Tshui's grin was infectious. 'It seems that Tshui would be pleased if you did,' said Jim, motioning to the empty chair. Tshui grinned as Sharupe translated. Still, she inched closer to Jim.

Sharupe sat, casting a quick but thoughtful glance around the table. 'You are not typical tourists, nor, if you will allow me to say so, a typical family. I mean no disrespect,' she said inquiringly.

'No, I suppose not,' answered Jim. 'Pedro is my son. Cherry is a friend, and we are all friends of Tshui.'

'Permítame, señor, Tshui, from my conversation with

her, would think of you more as a father or even possibly she sees you as her protector shaman, possessing in our language "tsentsak" or magic that protects her. She is very afraid here amongst these unfamiliar tribes. She knows not who her enemies are, but she obviously cares for you and trusts you. Will you stay with her, seňor, or will you leave? I suspect you will leave. I wonder then what effect it will have on her. Please forgive me if I am intruding where I should not.'

Jim studied Sharupe, recognizing in her an acerbic mind. The thought of leaving Tshui had been disallowed from his conscious thoughts and what effect it might have on her. Sharupe's words forced them to the surface. All he knew now was that he felt a bond with the young girl, a responsibility.

'What do you suggest?'

Cherry had been wondering something similar. Jim had been very kind to her. She found him extremely attractive and wondered if it were possible that he felt attracted to her. Pedro, too, recognized the dilemma; in a different way, he had been attracted to Jim during their first encounter at the firefight in Guillermo's cartel head-quarters in Tubutama, Mexico. They all looked at Sharupe with rapt attention. Sharupe looked at Tshui's questioning eyes, then at Jim's for a long moment, and said, *yajá jíiminia nui nukap papíi miniakeame.* It is a line from one of my poems; translated loosely, it means something I feel from your eyes, behind your eyes, you hold a thousand tales.'

Pedro shouted, 'He does. My dad has many tales. You

are like my mother who is,' and then a sadness overcame him as he said, 'was a poet.'

Sharupe had not expected the conversation to drift toward grief and realized immediately that Pedro's mother, Jim's wife, was not here or had she been replaced by the woman named Cherry. A tragedy had happened. She was unsure what to say as she looked at Pedro with his sad, questioning eyes. Then she ventured, 'Pedro, in my culture, Tshui's culture. We never lose those close to us. They go to a different place, but they always remain by our side. You can feel her presence as we sit here, can you not?'

'I think of her all the time.'

'Then she is with you.'

'I want her to be. I miss her so much.'

'We have a word phrase, one of my favorites, "*enenteimjai chichasta.*" It's important to our culture and how we think.'

Tshui smiled shyly, hearing the words she had heard for as long as she could remember. Sharupe continued looking at Pedro, 'It means simply, speak from your heart, but as with many Shurar words, it is not quite as simple as that—perhaps more of an opening of one's heart or if you open your heart to her, you will feel her presence.'

'*Enenteimjai chichita,*' said Pedro, looking wonderingly at this petite woman with her tattooed face and dark hair, and oval brown eyes who seemed to understand his feelings, his grief, his missing.

'*Chichasta,*' said Sharupe. 'You learn quickly.'

'I would like to learn to talk to Tshui.'

'You will, I'm sure, señor.' Pedro smiled at her, happy that she called him señor. Sharupe looked at Jim. 'The question remains: when you leave, she will not understand. Her world is here.' Then she laughed. 'I mean, with her family, not here in the city. She knows nothing of the outside world or even that there is one. She will most likely remember this trip as a dream or spell cast transporting her to an imaginary place. You, Pedro, and Cherry might be the only real things in this place to her. Whether here or at her home, she will not understand you leaving her.'

Pedro and Cherry both looked at Jim, wondering what his response would be.

'Hmm,' said Jim. 'It's a conundrum with no obvious solution. One I should have understood earlier.'

'What will you do, Dad?'

'Do you have any suggestions, Sharupe?'

'You could stay, of course. But you won't. You can't take her. She would end like me, in a no man's land, I mean in a no woman's land, fitting nowhere, losing her identity and place in this world. One other thing, that is most obvious, our face markings are not understood in your culture. It is just barely possible for me to get by here in Cuenca. She would be seen elsewhere as an oddity.'

'I would protect her, Dad.'

'I know you would. We need a solution that is best for Tshui.'

Cherry smiled at Jim, moving her head back and forth, a slight smile on her face. She raised an eyebrow. 'Perhaps, Colonel, the solution is for you to stay and make a family here, no? She might become accustomed to you leaving her world for the spirit world and returning. You could take me and Pedro with you to see the places in the books you brought me, and we could then return.'

A mellifluous sadness flowed through Jim. The loss of Heather, worry about Pedro, and now he had placed Tshui in an impossible position. *Many men would be overjoyed to do what Cherry had just suggested.*

Pedro looked at Cherry. 'You be my new mom?' he asked. 'I think, Dad, it is a good solution,' he beamed.

For one of the first times in Jim's life, he felt his control of a situation suddenly deserting him. He could imagine Brush laughing at his predicament. Heather might even see the humor in its absurdity. Then, once again, sadness overcame him. Heather would worry about Tshui's feelings as much as he did.

'This is something that will take some thought,' he said at last. 'I think any man would be proud to have all of you as his family. And you are both my family and friends. Cherry, you and Jago are an item, just as I am and maybe always will be with Heather. As Sharupe said to Pedro, she remains with me too.'

'Ah, Jago. Forget him. He has another woman. He came back from Ecuador with her. That's life, no?'

Other women were the furthest thing from Jim's mind after Heather died. *And before,* he thought. He had never strayed, and embracing another woman immediately struck him as a betrayal to her, to Heather. Nevertheless, Cherry's offer caused him to have a fleeting thought about Maria and then Cherry. He looked at Cherry, seeing in her a voluptuous woman, one who understood that life is hard. And valued what one has. He thought back to when she became infatuated with Brush. A man's man that she could respect, an American with different prospects she had never thought about during her previous life as a guerrilla. But she had changed. Her mind bubbled with new thoughts. She was in a city. With the books Jim provided, she was vicariously experiencing other worlds. Growing. She was quickly realizing that another world existed outside the jungles of Colombia and Ecuador.

# Chapter Thirty-Six

'Martin, add as many people to your team as you need,' said General Crystal. 'CIA can only be supportive and not involved with the FBI, but I want unobstructed sharing with BWC,' as his eyes strayed to Martin's missing thumb. The one he had lost months ago at Guillermo's cartel headquarters in Mexico, courtesy of Najma. The same hacienda where days later Pedro and Lola, attempting their escape, had been saved by Jim during the assault to capture or kill Najma. Jim and Marilyn, the General's favorite helicopter pilot, had almost died, as had Najma.

Martin caught the eye movement to his missing thumb and smiled thinking about what the torture experience at the hands of Najma had brought him, a new reputation, a mystique, a new life meaning. 'We're checking all cams, logs, manifests, airport personnel, alerts to airport staff, private fixed base operators at airports, and the cops have been instructed to report directly to Glenda and the FBI and to not apprehend. We'll do everything we can staying off the radar but supporting.'

Now Bertrand shook his head. 'Keep at it, Martin. I need to sit down and put myself in this man's position and try to see what next steps he will probably choose. What makes the most sense for him as a plan, and he will surely have an escape route?' Bertrand stood and walked out the door, his mind already focused on categorizing the problem, melding his thoughts to that of Marcel Moriac, organizing the parts of the puzzle, and eventually resulting in the most likely scenarios. It was what Bertrand loved, what he was good at, and why he wanted nothing to do with replacing General Crystal as the CIA's director.

Liam hit the wall hard with the palm of his hand. 'Goddamn it. Mon Dieu. Where could the little bugger have gotten to? Zéro, rien, nada, nothing,' he said out loud, hoping for some idea to sink into his thoughts.

He opened the door. 'Everyone, in here now.'

All were as baffled as Liam as they sulked into the room. 'Knock off the sad-sack faces. Let's solve this,' said Liam angrily.

'We've been trying to do just that and can't find anything,' said Colette.

'Okay, let's quit beating ourselves up. What haven't we done?'

'What we know is that he didn't break out. He walked out. Someone let him out. And the same for how he got out of the Château. Who the fuck is the culprit?' asked Colette.

'Unless he's still here. Are any of the other staff missing?' asked Colette.

'No one,' said Liam.

Colette picked up on his look and raised her eyes to the ceiling. 'I meant before we showed up here. There was a woman who worked here who vanished.'

'So what?' asked Henri.

'We're at a dead end. Ne soyons pas stupides.'

'She's right,' said Liam, 'We're being stupid—I'm being stupid. So, what are you thinking, Colette?'

'I don't know. We've missed something.'

Bastian looked at his notebook and said, 'Octavia Mustafa.'

'What's her background?' asked Liam as he stared out the window. 'Middle Eastern, huh? What do we know about her?' he said, feeling as though at least they had something new to talk about.

'I have nothing on her,' said Bastian.

'Colette, see what you can find out from personnel records. Bas, see if intelligence knows anything about her. Renard and I will ask about her with the people here. Maybe nothing, but it's the best idea we've had.'

'Probablement rien,' said Colette, hoping she wasn't causing them to waste time on the chase of the savage goose. *Chasse à l'oie sauvage,* she repeated to herself.

'Let's get on it. We have to do something,' said Liam as he nodded to Colette.

* * *

Bertrand sat in his office as he had done many times before, doing something he not only liked but was good at, constructing the most likely scenario. And it was why he held the position of director of intelligence with the CIA, fitting pieces of puzzles together, solving mysteries with logic. Pick the problem apart and find a probable answer. *Let your mind work.* He's skilled, but he will want to move fast. In and out. So how does he cause as much damage as possible in the shortest time frame? Does he suspect people are after him? *Assume he does.* He will move linearly. He won't waste time backtracking. We know he's landed in Chicago and then so far; we don't know where he's got to. The biggest egg factories are both east and west of Chicago. Also, south. It makes no sense to land in the middle if he plans on spreading the virus only in one direction and not the other. *Or does it act as a diversion?* Where are the largest egg producers? They're in both directions. Which direction makes the most sense? Which way will he choose? Does he escape by leaving from Chicago O'Hare Airport? How many others are involved in his plan?

Bertrand was frozen in time with his thoughts for several minutes. It's a wrong assumption to limit this to egg-producing facilities. They've already infected chicken raisers, and no one will be able to track the source of the virus if it jumps species. And a big if, the avian flu virus has so far only infected a few humans. So, their engineered one is meant to be fatal and infectious to all humans. But is it only for humans or for all mammals? What if he doesn't go after only people but instead animals? What if it kills humans, livestock, pets, and birds—all animals—everything?

*I need to narrow it down. The variables are too wide-ranging. But then, has a puzzle ever been simple? Hmph, if they were, it wouldn't be any fun.*

Bertrand, the Indian born to an inferior-status family, named after a famous philosopher by his mother, sat for over two hours dissecting Moriac, his choices, and what he might do. He rose from his chair, knowing his conclusion was only a guess. He had massaged what they knew, reflected on Sergeant Marcel Moriac's background, and derived the best solution he could by assembling all the facts available. *Will it be right? We'll know soon enough.*

* * *

As they approached the ice-encrusted shoreline, Marcel shifted from watching the controls and gauges to looking for the small park. It should be deserted this time of year. Snow-covered humps, which on warm summer days where cream-white sand dunes speckled with sun lovers and children. His eyes flicked back and forth from the window to the GPS. The summer playground should be less than a mile up the shoreline. 'Continue east along the shoreline.' Marcel watched for signs of cars or vans that would indicate a police force, army, or government agents positioned near the rendezvous.

He spotted the grove of trees bordering the crystalline

dunes with a solitary dark-colored van parked as the driver had been instructed. As he neared, he scanned the surrounding area. Still, no sign of other vehicles or people. He saw no other car tracks leading from the parking entrance other than the ones left by the van. Nothing suspicious in the woods. He pointed out the landing zone to the pilot and told him to approach southeast to northwest over the treeless leaves. 'Turn and hover 100 feet behind the van,' said Marcel. 'Set it down when I say.'

Marcel assured himself there was no threat from the van or near it. Unless there were men inside, and he was about to find out soon enough if he was being betrayed. 'Set it down. Nose heading 240,' he commanded. Marcel, ever cautious, wanted an oblique position facing the rear of the van. 'Brian, check the van.'

As the helicopter churned a torrent of snow, partially obscuring the van, Moriac aimed his Glock toward its back door. Brian moved to the side of the van, motioning for the lone man to open the rear doors with his Glock. The van carried cargo and was otherwise empty.

Marcel continued to scan the area while Brian returned. Get the suitcases ready. The pilot dropped his eyes in relief, thinking that his unwanted passenger was going to depart. Brian set the cases outside and got back in.

Moriac smiled at the pilot. 'I want you to fly a reverse course back out over Lake Michigan. Climb to 1,000 feet ten miles from the shore. After you observe and make sure there are no boats or planes, descend to just above the water and hover until I signal you to return to pick me up. Brian, call when you are hovering. Hold that position. I'll signal when and where I want you to meet me.' The pilot's momentary relief deserted him. He wasn't rid of his passengers yet.

Blowing snow in all directions, the Eurocopter lifted, turned, and headed north past the shore and out over the expanse of Lake Michigan. The van pulled beside Marcel. He observed the driver closely as he jumped out. 'Load them,' he said as he stood several feet away, observing. On alert to any movement from the woods or dunes.

When the suitcases were loaded and Marcel was certain there was no one inside or out, he climbed into the front passenger seat and said, 'Drive over by that tall white tree and we'll get another container.'

The driver did as Marcel instructed. As they approached, he asked, 'Is the rest of my money in one of the cases?'

'It's been close to you all along. The money case is hidden in the woods in the container we are getting. I'll show you.' They stopped, got out, and the driver followed Marcel for several yards into the trees. Marcel turned and pointed to his left toward a dense group of bushes. 'It should be right there. Retrieve it.' The man walked past Marcel to where he had been instructed, thinking about all the money. He had a millisecond's realization of a nine-millimeter bullet impacting the back of his head and exiting the front, removing parts of his face.

# Chapter Thirty-Seven

Sheilla's monitor blinked on just as she finished one spin in her chair. 'Martin, nice to hear from you.'

'Likewise, Sheilla. Sitting with me are Bertrand and our new analyst recently of the National Security Agency, Sam. And we have a video connection to Ms. Stuart.'

'I'm bringing her up on my screen now. Hi, Glenda. And I see Abenaa there with you and others.'

'I thought it would be handy to have my group listen in while we devise a strategy. No General Crystal?' asked Glenda.

'He's been summoned to a congressional hearing, and as he said rather loudly, he would probably be there wasting most of the day.'

'Let's start,' said Bertrand. 'Ms. Stuart's flight has been redirected to Chicago ORD. The ground staff sent to Mississippi have been loaded into a transport and are also on their way.'

'We have Kitty, Brees, and Chen joining our video call,' interjected Martin.

'Nice to see you guys again,' said Glenda.

'Same here,' said Kitty. 'Differing from our last mission in Washington State and Idaho, this sounds like a pretty big deal. More important than tracking one radical woman terrorist.'

'She caused us trouble, but nothing like this problem could,' added Martin.

'Out mission code name is Souilimer,' said Bertrand.

'Cool,' said Sam. Remilious spelled backwords.

'Who thought that one up,' asked Brees.

'CIA's director of intelligence,' said Martin.

'Bertrand,' he added.

'It will be a few minutes before we are able to get Dr. Dakine added to this call,' said Bertrand. 'First, let's summarize the problem so all of us have the same information before looking at strategies. We've been fully briefed by the Centers for Disease Control on the potential severity of the virus we are dealing with. To put it in context, the CDC says the 1918 flu virus killed an astounding, estimates vary, but up to ninety million people, and the population was much less then. Up to this point, the avian influenza A virus has infected millions of wild and domestic birds outside the United States. Few cases have been reported in humans with the first a three-year-old in Hong Kong in 1997 with only mild symptoms. Glenda has been in France at a company called Remilious and will give us a briefing.'

'The Remilious lab has engineered two viral strains—

one that infects birds, including, of course, chickens, and the second mammals, including humans. The goal of the company's president is to kill the egg-laying chickens that provide eggs for the government's manufacture of vaccines. The second one is to cause a pandemic with people. It's a species of influenza A virus. Don't let the name lead you to believe this is just another flu. The information we have for the engineered $H5N1$ subtype would be fatal to humans. And highly transmissible. We are code-wording it Remilii. If released, the death toll could be in the hundreds of millions, perhaps even billions worldwide. I don't need to impress upon you the importance of stopping what would be the largest terrorist attack on the U.S. and its worldwide ramifications.'

'Glenda, there are no existing vaccines, right?' said Sheilla.

'Only ones of limited quality, and probably not efficacious. Remilious is the best equipped to develop and produce one. Nusmen says that the BWC is aware of the viruses potential and has been looking at the virus for the past two years. Puttering with it, according to him, which for any of you who do not know, is BWC's primary mission to research and find solutions to these types of problems. Barbara is gearing up for a 100-percent effort from BWC. The problem in most countries, including the U.S., is that the egg-based method of producing vaccines is used and Remilious will have severely disrupted that ability by infecting millions of egg-laying chickens. Remilious has been developing a non-egg-based method for producing vaccines, leaving them one step ahead of other drug companies.'

'Exotic plan,' added Martin. 'Kill the chickens that lay the eggs. No vaccine production except for Remilious. And then save humanity with a vaccine, at high prices, making the company rich.'

'Diabolical,' said Sheilla. 'Or better yet, hideous, since it rhymes with Remilious.'

'Ignominious, pitiless,' said Sam, looking a little sheepish. She shrugged, 'Words are my thing.'

'Yes, perfidious,' threw in Martin with a slight grin.

Bertrand almost said, let's get back on point, but he decided to let them wander for a few seconds before he added, 'Mysterious,' to their word game. *Sometimes a little levity eases the tensions,* he acknowledged to himself before taking the conversation back to the central issue. 'The chicken infection. and the egg disruption is a fait accompli.' 'What the president of Remilious did not figure on was us finding out about his plan, and he misevaluated the government's response to the issue. The French government has taken over Remilious' main lab in Marseille. Experts are being brought in, and BWC has Nusmen on-site there now. Our problem is preventing the introduction of the human version from entering the population. That is centered on one man, Marcel Moriac. He may be working alone or with a team. We have no details other than his flight diverted to Chicago and landed.'

'Will he continue his mission if you track the money he must be receiving and take it?' asked Sheilla.

'Possibly. From what we were able to find out from the

lead scientist's second in command at Remilious, which was little, as it appears he was not involved in the U.S. plan, Visser, the leader of the project, was the only one to know the full details of the plan in the U.S. Boucher may know, as Moriac appears to work directly for him. Moriac is accomplished, ruthless, and importantly cautious. As far as we can tell, he is maintaining no contact or receiving any instructions from Boucher or anyone at Remilious. He's our problem. Stopping him will stop the viral spread.'

'The timeline's short,' added Glenda. He's hours ahead of us, but he will need two days to increase the quantity. We have learned that there is a lab in the U.S. with two students recruited by and through the EIJ terrorist group to do this.

'Who did you get that information from?' asked Bree.

'Intercepts tracked by CIA from the EIJ.'

'We are working overtime together with NSA to get more intelligence information,' added Martin.

'The rub,' said Glenda, 'as of this minute we have no idea where this lab is or what the dispersal plan is. Our best hope is for Bertrand to do what he does best, to connect the pieces and predict the most probable future. He works magic, but this is a big ask. If no one else has anything to add, Bertrand, what do you propose?'

'We have very little to go on. CIA is searching all known databases for anyone connected to terrorist groups that are associated with chemical companies or universities and focusing on the Chicago area. My concept is that Sergeant Moriac will take the easiest way to spread the virus. Chicago Airport provides that and where I think we need to focus our search for him. If we can find the enhancement lab before he has enough quantity, then we stop the operation. Time is not on our side. We need to find him before he can place it where it will infect people. A major international airport, like Chicago International is, in my opinion, the most likely place.'

'That possibility is not something, I confess, we considered at BWC,' said Sheilla. 'We assumed he would be going to egg-laying facilities so that it will appear the virus mutated from a chicken site to humans.'

'There would be no way to prove that someone from one of the many chicken farms did not carry the virus to the airport,' said Bertrand.

Sheilla sighed. 'Bertrand, you are probably right. It's depressing that this guy could go to Chicago Airport or another airport, or to dozens of facilities. So many possibilities.'

'This makeshift lab is probably near Chicago O'Hare,' said Martin.

'Why not at a university if the virus is being enhanced by students?' asked Sheilla.

'It is possible,' responded Bertrand. 'Or it could be at a residence.'

'We have the FBI on the ground,' added Martin, 'following up leads at chemical facilities, the chemicals and equipment they would need, and universities and monitoring using an NSA keyword program.' 'NSA is searching all calls through to the U.S. that might be relevant. And BWC computer group is along with the CIA ... this cooperation is a first I might add.' He paused, 'It's an FBI ground operation but because of the EIJ and French involvement, the CIA is openly working to coordinate all the agencies. We need to find Moriac or this lab.'

'One more important thing,' added Bertrand. 'Katarina and FBI profilers all come to the same conclusion. Moriac is dangerous, cautious, and does not work with groups. He is as well trained as any of our Special Forces, having spent his career in the French Dragoons. He thinks linearly about what he wants to accomplish. He is a sociopath, brutal, single-minded, patient, with no fear, and efficient. Importantly, his primary concern will not be to survive like our last terrorist, Najma. He will accomplish what he intends by attacking full-on. He will not let the battle come to him. He will take it to you. So, don't assume we are chasing him. He will turn this around and be chasing you.'

* * *

Elie Katherine, better known as EK to her friends, looked out her window, smiling at the blue skies dotted with white cotton ball puffs. She put in her hearing aids. And wondered about her short hair she saw reflected in the glass. If it were longer, her hearing aids wouldn't show. *Easier short,* 'And you don't mind, do you, girl?' She reached down and petted her one blue-eyed border collie. Schatje was her constant companion, and her few friends said the love of her life. EK had taken early retirement as she had started to lose her hearing, and it began to affect her work at the University of Illinois Urbana-Champaign.

A paradox, a linguist who couldn't hear properly. She had never accumulated much money but had always loved sandy beaches and found she could afford a home along the south shore of Lake Michigan near Gary, Indiana. Many of the factories had closed, and the area was disintegrating, but it was affordable, and for Elie, in a great location.

'What do you say, girl? A beautiful day for a long beach walk.' Her small brick house on Maple Street was only a block and a half from the shore and dunes. They walked down Lake Shore Drive and took a public path to the beach. EK turned Schatje loose, as there was no one in sight. Even though Schatje still had energy, she would never stray far as she was as attached to EK as Elie was to her.

Elie breathed in the cold air hovering over the crystalline snow-covered beach and marvelled at the beauty of sparkling icy edges along the shore before they set off walking toward the deserted Beach Park and its dunes. After an hour, she said, 'I think a short break is in order, girl.' There's a log under that tree. Let's sit there for a while.'

She pulled out a bottle of water and a small bowl and poured some for Schatje. Between drinks, her best friend and companion was given several liver snacks that EK always carried. Schatje stiffened as she pointed down the beach. The soft breeze and stillness were interrupted by the sounds of a motor. A helicopter. Elie looked through the crisp air and spotted the dark spot on the horizon traveling just above the lake surface. It passed the shore and headed inland before looping back and disappearing behind the trees. 'Well, we don't see that every day, do we, girl? Ready when you are. Let's make tracks.'

They had walked toward the deserted Beach Park when the helicopter rose above the leafless trees, it reversed its earlier course, heading north out over the lake. The thumping sounds of the beating blades slowly disappeared. 'Glad to be rid of that awful invention,' said EK.

Schatje jerked her head toward the woods. She stood as frozen as the skeletal trees, then she whimpered. 'What was that crack sound? Is that what you heard? A gunshot? Probably a tree snapping with too much ice weighing it down.' EK looked at her watch. 'Perhaps we should head back. It will be lunchtime soon. I do hate to leave, don't you? It's so beautiful and clean out here. I know many people dislike it, but I love the cold and the snow. It's so peaceful this time of year.'

Marcel climbed into the black Ford three-quarter ton van. He opened his rucksack and removed two phones one with a taped label—Brian. The other labelled ORD. He dialed a code into the one labelled Brian. 'Au revoir, pal.' Moriac wiped his fingerprints off and tossed it out the window. Then he dialed an alphanumeric code into the one labelled ORD and pushed the call button.

'Chicago radio, Cessna November 68L.'

'68L, Chicago radio.'

'68L is 3,000 feet two miles north of Gary/Chicago

International. Ten miles to our NE was an explosion on the water.'

'Roger 68L.

Moriac wiped the phone of fingerprints and threw it out the window into the snow. He studied a map for a minute, memorizing the streets. The building that had been secured through Visser's assistant, Olivia, was approximately two miles away. He had previously selected a probable vantage point to observe the building. He didn't intend to approach it until later in the afternoon. The two lab specialists expected him at three. He would watch for any suspicious activity until four. That gave him a little over three hours before the prearranged time and one after.

He had lots of experience driving on sand, but not with snow on top. He gently touched the accelerator pedal and with one wheel making a minor lurch, the limited-slip differential kicked in and the van moved forward. He followed the tracks that the man had left when he drove in. After a few minutes of carefully negotiating the off-road portion, he turned right, still following the tire ruts to the park's entrance. Then he turned onto Lake Shore Drive. He was the only car on the road. Two younger kids and a mother walked by and waved. Then a lone woman with a black and white dog did the same. He didn't like being observed. And then he reasoned that by late tomorrow, he would be headed to the first egg facility, and no one would remember or know he had been here. The only time he would use his remaining phone would be to send the coordinates on a GPS locator that Boucher had installed to know that Moriac was following the plan. Of course, Moriac was not following the plan. This was meant to be the fourth stop, not the first. He would receive a ping when the one third of the three million dollars he had been promised had been successfully wired. He bit hard and flexed his jaw at the unnecessarily complicated precaution of Boucher and an ineffective one.

Before he approached Alabama Street where the lab was, he drove streets as far away as a mile, searching for any unusual cars, police, or vans. After an hour, he drove to his observation point. In the cases in the back of the van, he found the tripod and an 8x12 binocular. He extended the legs and placed it away from the window so he could look out without being observed. From his position, he could see the front entrance of the grimy gray-white cement-block building and, at an angle, one back corner. It was on a dead-end road. Behind the building was a storage yard for a defunct construction company. Derelict equipment and scrap littered the large, abandoned storage grounds. On the other side of the road, there was only trash and brambles.

The dead-end street would make it impossible to escape in the van if he was attacked. He confirmed his plan to park the van beyond the dead-end street in a neighborhood hidden from the lab. His sense told him that there would not be a problem. Ever cautious, he made a circuit around the neighborhood before he parked and approached the makeshift lab.

It was one p.m. when an old blue and white VW microbus pulled in front. Two men in their early twenties got out and looked around before unlocking a padlock on the door. Marcel could see a light seeping out through the open door. They moved fast, unloading several crates and boxes from the car. They scanned the area and disappeared inside the building.

'Sharupe, would you consider going back to the Shuar with us for a day or two? We could fly you in a helicopter and bring you back.'

She sat without speaking for a minute. 'Were you planning on only staying for a day or perhaps a little longer?'

'We hadn't decided. But if it's okay with the village, then longer.'

'They will welcome you, Colonel. That is not a problem. I am more worried that they would accept me. It is not my Shuar group, and to them, I have left the Shuar for Western ways. Will you return me to Cuenca if they do not want me there? And if they do, I would relish staying longer.'

'Happy to take you back, although I can't imagine them not accepting you, and it would be a great help for me to have someone to translate for all of us.'

Pedro looked expectantly at her. She didn't respond for several seconds. She nodded her head in affirmation and said while looking down, 'Si.' She raised her eyes and looked directly at Jim and then at Pedro. 'Yes, I will go with you.'

'Do you need to get anything to take?'
'It will not be necessary.'

'Doctor, my scientists want to know every detail of all your projects. Precisely how you engineered the avian virus to start with and how to make a vaccine to counter it. I know a great deal, and I have passed that information along. I have been provided with an additional list of questions.'

'Why not take me to your laboratory, and I will explain to them there?'

'If you answer all my questions and they are accurate, that will be the case.'

'Olivia, I have always been nice to you. You rescued me. Why don't you trust me?'

'First question. Tell me again exactly what the new gene sequence is?'

'I want assurances first.'

Visser felt the blow to the side of his head and the searing pain. His hands were pulled behind his back and snap-tied to the chair. His feet were tied to the chair's legs.

'You never had any intention of taking me away.'

'Hard or easy. Your choice. And just for your information. You were always a prick, and no, you did not treat me well.'

Olivia's two goons pulled Visser's pants down and took out a knife. 'It is very sharp,' she said. Then the man grabbed Visser's left ear. Visser instinctively pulled away. The ear stretched as far as it would go from his head, and the man effortlessly severed it, throwing it on the floor where Visser could see it.

'Are you ready to tell me what I want to know?'

Visser closed his eyes, trying to shut out the pain. The man grabbed his other ear.

'No more. No more. I'll tell you and work with you if you'll only take me away.'

'You haven't answered my first question yet.'

'If I tell you, you'll kill me.'

'Let's get this straight. We can kill you. You could be dead very soon. And as much as I would like to for the way you treated me, if you tell me what I want to know, then I shall consider your future. I want you to talk fast and accurately. She pushed the start button on a recorder. If you don't, we have several methods. As you are hesitant.' She nodded. The man pulled his head back, squeezing Visser's jaw and forced his mouth open. Olivia dropped several Ritalin and caffeine pills far back on his tongue. He swallowed involuntarily. Then the man held his mouth closed and from a small bottle she tapped a white powder into his nostril, forcing him to breathe the cocaine. 'Not the best stimulants, but it is what I could find to make sure you stay wide awake. The question for you is how much pain you want to endure before you die or if you cooperate go to our country. Your choice.'

She placed a glass vial of yellowish liquid on a table. 'You know what this is?' Visser shook his head. 'It is concentrated sulfuric acid. Very painful on skin, far more so in open wounds.' She took the vial and filled a glass eye dropper. She held it over his ear, and Visser jerked his head. The drops missed the raw flesh and instead fell on his bald head. He yelled in pain as the acid burned his scalp. Olivia smiled as the drops ran down toward his severed ear.

'That was unwise of you. Luckily, it is trickling along toward your ear and not your eyes.'

Visser screamed at the top of his lungs and cried as the drops touched the raw, bloody flesh and bubbled with a slight hiss. He saw red. He saw black-singed flesh. He couldn't believe this was happening.

'With the drugs, you will not be able to pass out and miss the fun.'

Visser was petrified and reeling in pain. His mind working frantically to find a way to survive.

'Unfortunately, we don't have much time. Answer my question.'

Visser didn't answer and Olivia nodded to the man.

The hesitation was costly. The man reached down and grabbed Visser's scrotum and penis and severed them. Visser screamed again for all he was worth before passing out. They revived him. 'Hmm, too painful, I see, even with the stimulants. Perhaps psychologically you didn't like losing your little manhood parts. I advise you to talk.' She dripped the acid into his belly button, filling the hole. 'When I add more, it will trickle down to help seal your new status as a eunuch. Perhaps sear is a better word.' She smiled. 'I think you know what that will feel like. I ask the first question again.'

Visser didn't hesitate this time. He talked frantically,

feeling the acid burning, willing it not to run to the gaping wound below. He held nothing back.

Olivia was sure she had received accurate information and all that she required. If it proved not to be accurate, she would soon endure what Visser just had.

'Visser, you are a fool. The ending would have been the same, but you could have skipped all the suffering.'

Olivia looked into his wide-open, petrified eyes and said, 'Bye, Mr. Nice Guy.' She poured the rest of the acid on the exposed flesh, while the man tipped his chair forward, adding the pooled acid to the wound. Visser howled as one of the goons held his head up while the other slid the knife across his throat. The scream stopped. Visser's last thought was that he didn't deserve this. Mindless zombies marched through his thoughts and faded.

# Chapter Thirty-Eight

Marcel took a padded case containing Visser's genetically engineered virus vial out of the van and pushed his way through the brambles with thorns gripping his clothes. When he saw the lab through the bushes, he set the case on the ground and covered it with leaf litter. He made a mental note of the exact spot and walked to the side of the building. Seeing nothing suspicious, he moved to the door and turned the handle. *The idiots had not locked the door.* He slowly pushed it open. Inside, the two students had their backs to him. Marcel scanned the room and walked in, closing the door. He watched them work on some glass equipment before he moved away from the door. He picked up a rusty piece of metal off a shelf and tossed it in the opposite corner from where he stood. The two dark-haired men's heads snapped toward the metal clattering on the cement floor. Then they saw him. 'You scared us. Who are you?'

From the rough look of the man, they thought they knew who he might be.

'I saw you enter the building. You're trespassing.'

'No, sir. We rented it.'

'Stand over here.' Marcel made them put their hands on the table and frisked them. They had only a small amount of money. He took out their identical Motorola cell phones and a set of car keys. He put the keys in his pocket. 'Is there an unlock code for these phones?'

'Why? No, I won't. It's private.'

With his left hand, Moriac squeezed the man's neck with his thumb, pushing hard on the jugular vein. He held it for several seconds and let go. 'Your code?'

'Three, six, nine, eight.'

Moriac opened the phones and looked at recent calls and text messages. There was nothing suspicious. 'Turn around. I'm supposed to meet you. Is your equipment set up?'

The young man started to ask who he was and then thought it was better to keep his mouth shut. 'It will only take a few minutes longer.'

'Are you using He-La?' Moriac used the word Visser had mentioned as a last check on the two men. They looked almost like twins: thin black hair, and caramel-brown skin.

'Yes, as we were instructed.'

'Both of you, come with me.' Marcel ushered them to the brambles and located the place where he had concealed the vial. He pushed the leaf litter off with his boot. 'Pick it up and get started.'

Moriac watched them for two hours. He had kept their phones and noticed nothing that would imply they were anything but two students with the knowledge necessary to enhance the virus's quantity. Satisfied, he walked to the delivery door and opened it. It was rusty and in need of lubrication, but he managed to push it up. He left and retraced his way through the bushes to the van. A few minutes later, he had it parked inside the building. He took their car keys and drove the microbus inside before closing the door. Neither Tarik nor his cousin Aabid dared say anything. They went about their business as fast as they could, wanting to be done and get away from this man.

Elie was strangely tired in the morning. She hadn't slept well and decided to stay in bed after making a strong cup of coffee split with half a mug of warm whole milk. Schatje was curled up on the bed next to her in her usual place. EK ruffled her companion's short brown mixed-gray hair, thinking they should get up. Instead, she continued to read a book she had never thought she would like, assuming it would be inaccurate, and instead was finding it quite interesting—*The First Word—The Search for the Origin of Language*. She looked at her watch that was resting on the maple bedside table. 'Almost time for the late morning news. Let's see what the weather is supposed to be. Will this overcast clear or not?'

She flicked on the TV with her remote. It was the

usual nothing interesting until a report appeared—'We report on the helicopter that exploded north of Gary yesterday. The Coast Guard is on site. There were no survivors. We have information from the wreckage and the Emergency Locator Transmitter that it was chartered yesterday at Chicago O'Hare for a tourist flight. The names of the passengers and crew have not been released pending notification of their families. The FAA would neither confirm nor deny the cause of the crash pending an investigation. The police have asked anyone sighting the helicopter, a white Eurocopter with the number N1462R, to phone 312-710-6477. Officers are standing by to take your call. Now here's Burke with the weather.'

'My oh my, Schatje. Do you think it is the one we saw? I suppose we should call. But we don't have much to say, and I think we can find better things to do with our time. Since you are the only one who had breakfast, I propose making something for lunch. Grilled cheese and a pickle, I think.'

Elie was pouring olive oil into a pan when the doorbell rang. 'Darn it anyway,' she said as she turned the burner off. 'That's enough, girl, shush.' She pulled her robe closed and looked out the window. Standing outside were two police officers, a man and a woman.

She stood behind the door and opened it a sliver. 'Yes?'

'Ma'am. We are making a routine door-to-door check to see if you saw a helicopter flying over yesterday?'

Elie was startled. 'I just saw something on the news.' She took a deep breath and said, 'As a matter of fact, I did see one flying over Beach Park yesterday. It was just before lunch.'

'Can we come in and get a statement?'

'Would you give me a minute to put something more appropriate on? I'll be right back.'

She could hear the officers talking on their radio, but not what they were saying. *Have to put my hearing aids in. What a bother.*

'Officer Rex and Hoskins are about to interview a woman at 26 Maple Street who says she saw a helicopter just before noon yesterday.'

* * *

'Our man didn't die in the crash,' said Glenda, fidgeting at her station on the bus. 'It's another ruse. Helicopters crash, they don't explode.'

'Unless it was a mishap with some explosives,' said Brees.

'We have hundreds of agents on the ground,' said Kitty, the second in command. Probably the most extensive manhunt I've been involved in and nada since he and his sidekick left ORD yesterday and the crash. Couldn't be the end of all this, could it? He blew himself up?'

'We assume not. We have to work on the assumption that he is still out there. My gut tells me he is, and the explosion is his work.'

Glenda turned toward Kitty, whose birth name was Caitlin. A name that she hated just as their tech Sept hated his real name—Septimus. Kitty's skin was transparent like her own. Glenda accepted that her strawberry blonde hair fit her complexion, but not why Kitty, who had dark hair, also had that type of skin color. Other than their complexions, the two looked nothing alike. Kitty was rail thin, while Glenda was well-rounded and curvy.

'Come on, everyone. What are we overlooking?'

Kitty shook her head.

Brees held up her hand and said, 'If the guy's alive, he can't just disappear. Why not plaster his face all over the news media?' She put her headset back on and listened to the FBI chatter.

'So, he's holed up someplace,' said Glenda for the tenth time. 'A place someone else arranged. A makeshift lab. Our only connection is the two Middle Eastern students who disappeared. NSA has not been able to trace any phone calls between them and Remilious or the EIJ. All dead ends. This repeating isn't getting us anywhere.'

'All we can do is wait,' added Kitty. If you are right, he is close by. The lab is close by. With all the agents in the area and local cops going house to house and the new smaller drones that Fort Huachuca sent us, we have a chance of spotting him when he breaks cover.'

Regurgitating the same information over and over was nauseating to Glenda. And saying *we're missing something is too, she said to herself*. 'What is it?' she said as she hit her desk in frustration. All four, Chen, Kitty, Brees, and Sept, briefly looked at her, knowing that she was feeling as impotent as they were. Then Glenda's thoughts turned to Brush. He was at the airport with Carter's and Dr. Dakine's HazMat team, testing for signs of the virus.

Glenda had decided not to drive there, even though Bertrand surmised that ORD would be the target. She chose to park the bus at Gary Airport, closer to where the chartered helicopter exploded.

Brees took one side of her headset off. 'Glenda, the labs have confirmed a C4 residue on the chopper wreckage. So far, no DNA or bodies. Divers and salvage crews have collected everything possible. It's too deep for divers to reach the bottom. The University of Chicago's Marine Biological Laboratories has a remote submersible being flown here from Lake Superior. It's expected in two hours.'

'So, we are confirmed that it was blown up. Not a big surprise. But by whom? My bet is on Moriac,' said Glenda.

Sept jumped up from his chair and high-fived the air. 'We got something. Local police are interviewing a woman that saw the helicopter.'

Chen scrunched up her lips and did a funny rolling with her mouth, thinking, *a woman is not a "that," but a woman "who saw the helicopter." Get your grammar right, Septious.*

'Something but not much,' said Glenda, 'but you never know where it will lead. Let's go hear what she has to say.'

Sept gave the driver the address. It was no more than fifteen minutes' drive away. Glenda blew a raspberry, drummed her fingers on the dash, and thought that even with all the frustrations of coming up blank with Moriac, she liked her crew. They had been great at chasing Najma into Idaho only a few weeks ago. She had thought about recruiting Brees for the BWC, but the jovial, energetic woman said she could not stand to be buried underground at the BWC labs. She was as sharp as they came and could have been an excellent assistant to Sheilla.

Two unmarked sedans and a police car were parked outside the one-story brick house at 26 Maple Street. As soon as the bus pulled in, the FBI agents dressed in their dark suit uniforms got out of their cars.

'Hope this leads to something,' said Glenda. Brees and Kitty gave her a thumbs-up.

'You two come in with me. I want to keep the dark suits out.'

They heard a bark as they walked up to the door. The female officer had remained inside, drinking coffee with Elie. Her partner was outside in their car. He radioed Rachael a heads-up that the hordes had arrived. She met them at the door just as they were about to knock.

Glenda introduced herself, Kitty, and Brees. Rachael ushered them into the living room where Elie was sitting on the sofa, wondering what she had gotten herself into. Schatje wiggled her tail and sniffed the new group before curling up next to Elie's feet.

Elie was pleased when Glenda Rose Stuart introduced herself as the agent in charge. Although she had never personally had a great deal of trouble with misogynists at her university, she was aware of how many women had. It was refreshing to see a woman in a position of authority sitting in her dining room.

After a few brief pleasantries and declining coffee, Glenda said, 'You were walking on the beach not far from here, and you spotted a helicopter?'

'We were having a water break near the park when a

helicopter flying from the west, low over the lake, turned inland and disappeared below the tree line. Several minutes later, as we were walking, it came into view again and headed north over the lake.'

Glenda was getting excited. *Maybe this will lead to something.* 'Do you think it landed when it disappeared behind the trees?'

'I don't know, but it could have.'

'What time did you see it?'

'It was just about eleven.'

Kitty asked, 'You didn't see it return or hear it again, ma'am?'

'I prefer to be addressed as EK. No. We decided to get lunch.'

'We?'

'Schatje and I.'

Glenda smiled, realizing that these two were a couple. 'She's a beautiful dog, EK. A border collie?' asked Brees.

'Yes, and most certainly, my best friend.'

'Then you left the beach and walked home. Did you see anyone or anything else?' asked Glenda.

'No, not really, just a mother and her daughter and a neighbor driving by. Well, I didn't recognize him as a local.'

'Can you describe him, where you were exactly, and the vehicle?'

'We were walking home on Lake Shore Drive, about a block west of my street. It was a black van, a Ford, I remember. I didn't get a good look at the driver. He didn't wave back, which is odd in this neighborhood. He had a rather broad head, as I recall, and he turned away from us. He didn't seem very friendly. Usually, everyone waves around here, as I said before.'

Glenda had trouble keeping her composure. 'Did the van have any marks or dents? Anything else you could say about the man? Was he alone? Wearing a hat, for instance? You didn't happen to see the license plate number?'

'No hat. No, I didn't see the plate. The van was dirty and had slush in the wheel wells. The only other thing I could add from my glimpse of him was that he had shortish hair, darkish, and looked rather coarse and unshaven. A rough character, I would say. Oh, and yes, he was alone.'

'Excellent. You've been a big help. Would you be willing to escort us to where you saw the helicopter? We could give you some lunch and we'll bring you back.'

'We would have to walk on the beach, but we could drive up the Beach Park entrance road if it's not too snow-covered. And of course, I must bring Schatje. Okay?'

'Come on, girl. We're going to be chauffeured back to the beach, and I can see out the window that the haze is clearing.'

They got in the back of one of the FBI cars. Brees and Kitty returned to the Bus and told the driver to follow. The procession of two FBI sedans, followed by the police car and the Bus caused quite a stir with several neighbors standing out on their porches and peering out windows, wondering what was going on.

EK pointed out where she had seen the van and its direction of travel. They drove by the path that EK and

Schatje had walked on to the beach and then to the park entrance road.

'There are tire tracks on the road. Kitty, get someone to take photos of the tread marks. Get the area blocked off.'

'On it.'

'Could you point out where the helicopter disappeared in the woods?'

EK pointed to the grove of trees.

'Glenda called Chen. 'Let's get a drone here ASAP. And I want a search crew on-site pronto.'

'Are you up for a walk, EK?'

'Love to. Can I ask you what is so important about all this?'

'EK, I'm sorry, I can't give you the details, but I can tell you it is of the utmost importance for our national security, and I must ask you not to speak to anyone else about it, and especially the press. We can't afford to let this man know we are looking for him. You have been such good help that I promise I will personally tell you the story when this is over. Is that okay with you?'

'Holy cow! It sounds very exciting.'

The policewoman, an FBI agent, Glenda, Schatje, and their prime witness, EK, followed the tracks toward the beach until they turned toward the woods.

Minutes later, the small-plane-sized drone flew over, moving toward the trees. Glenda directed it with Sept and gave Sheilla the background of the interview while they walked.

'The drone is imaging the place where the snow has been blown away and the vehicle tracks stopped. Footprints went into the woods. We're getting a hazy infrared image on the ground. Moving in closer to take a look-see. I can't be sure,' said the drone operator, 'because of the trees, but I would guess that since the IR source is stationary but still emitting some heat, it could be a body or possibly a recently dead animal.'

Incongruously, everyone in the van cheered. 'Finally, a clue,' said Kitty.

'A morbid one,' added Brees.

As they walked, EK said, 'We should be watchful in the woods. I heard a loud crack yesterday when a branch broke because of a heavy ice or snow load.'

Glenda looked at her, thinking, *a branch, or a gunshot.* Could it have been a gunshot? asked Glenda.

'It was my first thought. Then I dismissed it, thinking it was not likely. But yes, it could have been.'

The group followed the tire tracks until they came to where the helicopter had landed. Then they followed footprints, staying several feet to the side of them, a short distance into the woods. A man lay on his face, with his head surrounded by a halo of red snow.

Glenda immediately called the Bus. 'Chen, get forensics here ASAP. We have a body.'

Schatje started to run toward the body. 'Schatje, no. Come here. Elie patted Schatje. 'Good girl.'

'Thank you, Elie.'

It wasn't long before the area was cordoned off and swarming with FBI agents. A HazMat team arrived and found no evidence of a biological agent. The body was loaded onto a helicopter and shipped to a morgue where an FBI forensic pathologist waited for the corpse and Dr. Dakine's arrival.

The FBI identified the man and was compiling data about his life within minutes. He owned a black Ford van. The NSA and BWC computer teams, with help from the CIA, did a lightning-speed search for everything about him. Within an hour, they had full records of his phone calls, bank accounts, and life history. An agent found his phone in the snow. It was immediately shipped to their local Chicago lab for analysis.

'The helicopter with Moriac landed here. The dead man, Brad Roman, has had phone contact with the French country prefix. NSA is searching their database for recordings, and we should have them in a few minutes. A witness saw a man who was possibly Moriac driving a van. Unfortunately, there is no SAT coverage at the correct time. I'll keep you in the loop.'

'You're getting closer, Glenda,' said General Crystal.

'Progress,' added Martin.

'I love it when, out of the blue, all the pieces quit spinning hopelessly and start to fall into place,' said Sheilla.

Bertrand chuckled at Sheilla's comment and then his mind turned to the reality—they knew hardly anything more than they had hours ago. Perhaps they were a bit closer to finding Moriac. Or was it an illusion? They already knew he was in the area when they had twenty-four hours before he had enough of the virus to disseminate. Or at least that's what someone has estimated. If correct, time was almost gone, and they did not know where he was or precisely what he planned. It still made sense to Bertrand that he would go to where he could infect the most people. Glenda added the Gary/Chicago Airport to a possible place where he might release the modified virus, and soon it would be teeming with agents looking for the black van and Moriac. It was not as busy as Chicago O'Hare, but still a lot of people.

Glenda soon realized that Bertrand had moved past the elation of finding a piece of the puzzle and had refocused on the big picture.

# Chapter Thirty-Nine

'All drones are up. Everyone is on alert,' said Brees.

Kitty said, 'If we think he's alive, why don't we close down the area? Block it off to any outgoing cars and people.'

'We've discussed it. If we did, the gamble is that he sees us and releases it before you can capture him. It's too big an area with too high a population to close. You can't shut the airport and one of the largest cities in the U.S. It wouldn't work.'

'Martin's group evaluated it and concluded we could never do it. It was a plausible idea to consider, but it won't work. He's gotta move soon. The best hope is to spot him. The FBI has facial recognition set up on most of the outgoing roads.'

'We don't even know if he has a team or is working alone. It could be someone we'd never recognize who could take the virus to ORD or out of the area.'

'The enhancement time is up. But that's an illusion. There is nothing to say he needs an exact amount to release. In any event, he's going to have to move to do it, so I hope he does something stupid, or we spot him.'

'Like you said, unless he uses someone else,' said Kitty.

'He's made a couple of mistakes with the rendezvous location and blowing up the chopper. Let's hope he makes another one.'

* * *

'We are finished. The virus is in the atomizers,' said Tarik.

'Bien,' said Moriac.

'The last thing I want from you two is to load the cases that are in the Ford van into the Microbus and put the atomizers in, too. Put your stuff in the Ford van, glove box, under the seats, every bit of it.'

Tarik almost complained, but his desire to just get away from this man was too great.

'I don't need that box. You keep it. You can sell it and make some extra money.' Again, neither Tarik nor Aabid wanted to say anything. He was letting them leave. Their spirits rose. Moriac tossed them the van key and said, 'Drive safe.'

'Um. You too. Good luck.'

Aabid opened the door and jumped into the van. When they got around the corner, he slumped in the seat, kicked with his feet, and pounded on the dash. They both laughed. 'I thought we were goners, for sure,' said Tarik. 'Man, can you believe it? I've never been so scared.'

'I know we're not supposed to, but I want a drink. Let's celebrate our making fifty grand. Two days' work for that much money. And the EIJ will trust us now with more assignments, and we can make more moolah.'

Moriac had placed a tracker in the Ford van. He pulled out in the Microbus, closed the door, and followed them at a safe distance.

The two students were spotted as soon as they drove onto the entrance ramp of the westbound Indiana Tollway toward Chicago. The late afternoon traffic was mostly moving in the opposite direction.

'Why did you get on the freeway?' asked Tarik.

'I don't know. I just want to go fast and get as far away from that man as we can.'

'Me too, but I want to eat something. Get off onto the Highway 20 freeway and take the first exit; we'll get a McDonald's.'

'Good, a Big Mac meal for me. I'm starved too, now that you mention it.'

'You are forsaking your roots and turning into an American.'

Aabid slapped his cousin on the shoulder. 'Our secret.'

They were too elated to notice the cars following them and the highway closed 100 yards ahead. As they took the off-ramp and merged onto Highway 20, Tarik looked in his mirror and saw flashing lights. 'I didn't do anything. Why is he after us?' Ahead, the road was completely blocked by a barricade of vehicles and flashing lights. Suddenly, a helicopter was hovering in front of them. A loudspeaker said to stop your van. Behind them, there were dozens of marked and unmarked cars with flashing lights.

'What do we do?' asked Aabid.

'It's not us. They're only warning us of a problem ahead.'

'You're dreaming. Shit, the fucking guy turned us in.'

'Out of the vehicle.'

Tarik closed his eyes as he listened to the helicopter's loudspeaker ordering them to get out.

Moriac did something he rarely did—he smiled. He could see the van trapped below by dozens of vehicles as he approached the overpass. He pulled over to the side above Highway 20. He had a bird's-eye view of the action. He saw the helicopter and the two students get out and onto the ground. The cops started to move in and stopped.

As soon as they heard, Glenda ordered their driver to step on it. 'Our ETA is four minutes. Chen, tell Carter to secure the van, and then I want the HazMat team there before anyone else gets close to it. Tell the FBI and cops not to approach.

Moriac pulled a phone from his rucksack with a number two written on the tape label. The two kids were lying on the pavement, and no one was approaching them. Marcel realized, *they think the virus is in the van. They figured out what I did at the beach park.*

A dozen vehicles had stopped on the side of the over-pass, behind Moriac, to see what all the fuss was about. Several minutes went by, and a large bus pulled ahead of the blocked cars. Its top was loaded with comm discs. It was no ordinary RV. *Some sort of command vehicle,* Marcel said to himself.

Moriac looked around. He didn't feel in danger here as one cop car after another raced down the exit ramp behind him. He heard a familiar flap-flap sound, and to his surprise, an AS532 Cougar landed behind the van. A tac team rushed out and deployed in two lines on both sides of the French Eurocopter. The same kind he had deployed from many times in the Dragoons. They were followed out by the puffy, white-suited HazMat team.

The tactical team moved forward until they had surrounded the van. They cautiously opened the rear and front doors, and the sliding side door. The two students were frisked and cuffed. Carter reported, 'Clear.' The HazMat team moved to the black Ford with Dr. Dakine in the lead.

'Let the HazMat do its job,' said Glenda on the open channel.

'Approaching the vehicle,' reported Dakine.

'We're moving up,' said Glenda.

Moriac could sense the moment he had been waiting for was getting close. Glenda told the driver to move up behind the van. The driver drove forward and was about 100 feet away when she yelled, 'Stop. Everyone, use caution. Move away from the van. Moriac is not there. Is there a bomb disposal unit here? HazMat, move away until they clear the vehicle.' *What's the biggest danger, the virus, or booby traps?* wondered Glenda. *Who goes in first? Got to be the bomb squad.* 'Where's the bomb squad?'

'They're on the way, ma'am.'

'I want everyone to stand down. Move back. Now.'

Moriac sensed the caution. He keyed in the code and watched the massive explosion. The HazMat team and Carter's Fast Response team vanished in the inferno. Dozens of the closest FBI agents and police were killed or wounded, and her command bus shook and sustained minor damage from flying debris.

'Oh, my God,' said Brees.

'Is everyone okay?' asked Glenda.

Glenda looked at her monitor to see how the driver was. The driver, covered in blood, slumped in his seat behind the shattered windscreen.

# Chapter Forty

'The scene was a nightmare. Wreckage was blown in all directions. A smoldering van. A helicopter lying on its side like a dead cockroach. One pilot dead and the other critically injured. BWC lost eighteen people, Maria Dakine, five of her HazMat team, and everyone in Captain Carter's team. The FBI had eight agents killed and nineteen wounded. Our *Bus* driver is dead, and the two lab kids are not recognizable,' said Glenda.

'Jesus,' said Martin.

'And the lab kids won't be telling us their story about the virus or Moriac,' added Brush. 'I didn't know any of the HazMat except for Maria. I've seen this over and over —good people dying. She didn't deserve it.'

'The media rightfully are casting it as a terrorist attack, and somewhat unfairly, on some news sources, as a failure of the FBI,' said Martin.

With the military and so many agents and officers

involved, it did not take the reporters long to get information and discover that a woman agent was in charge. They were questioning was why an ex-FBI agent is in charge. Most of the news stories reported it as a tragedy. Two, however, were critical of the leadership, while one pointedly inferred that, as a woman, she was not capable.

The FBI PR department immediately responded saying Glenda was not in charge. She had special knowledge and was assisting the ground effort.

'Ignore the media, Glenda,' said General Crystal. It will get replaced soon by a new story. I've listened to the recordings from the scene. You tried to pull people back. You, we expected a virus, not a bomb.'

'I let the HazMat and Dr. Dakine go in.'

'You didn't. You sent the Quick Response Team in to secure the site. They did that. Carter knew better than to move his full group to the van without checking for explosives. It's a tragedy, and there will be a plethora of people saying how it could have been handled better. Most of those people would have done worse and have never been involved firsthand in situations like this. All you can do is evaluate rationally what you did and didn't do. Hindsight is not something we have the privilege of having when the battle heats up. Use it now to your advantage and as a learning experience. But don't accuse yourself. I know it's difficult.'

'I know you're right. But it's still bloody well hard. I was responsible, and it won't bring all those people back. Will it?'

'Something that all of us wish we could do. You lost a

battle. The worst thing you could do now is lose the war. You need to drop any remorse and get on with the mission. Find Moriac before he kills more, maybe hundreds of times more. Get on with it.'

The FBI identified the remains of Tarik and Aabid using DNA and dental records, and miraculously, a melted driver's license inside a wallet remained legible. Minutes after the ID was found, they had agents at Indiana University interviewing staff, students, and professors. Most importantly, they traced Tarik's and Aabid's car registrations. An all-points bulletin to notify the FBI, and do not apprehend, was circulated across the Midwest for a green Datsun 240Z and a blue and white 1983 Volkswagen Microbus. After the explosion, agents began reviewing videos of the incident. The same-colored VW Microbus was seen parked on the side of the overpass.

Brush arrived at the scene just as a tractor-trailer tow truck winched the *Bus* onto its bed. Glenda climbed into Brush's SUV rental car.

'I thought the glass had killed him, but it was a hunk of metal from the tail rotor that shattered the windshield and tore into his abdomen.

Brush scooted over as far as he could go in the Chevy Yukon and put his arm around Glenda. 'You okay?'

'No, but I got a job to do.'

'What can I do?'

'No pep talks, please. The General's given me enough. Just hold me for a minute and follow the tow truck. They said it's about three miles to a repair facility. The windshield needs to be replaced. My guys are still in the *Bus*.'

'I can't believe we lost Maria.' As your eye welled up. She struggled not to cry. 'She was truly a nice person and a special friend. I liked her, and it will be a blow to Jim. He was close to her, and she was Heather's best friend. All this makes me wonder what I am doing this for. If I am good enough.'

'You catch this guy, and you'll save a lot of lives. That's why you're doing this.'

Brush put the car in drive and followed the tow truck. Glenda sighed and was silent for several seconds. Then she reached over and touched Brush's arm. 'Apparently, she didn't have any family. They found a will on her desk at BWC and left her sailboat to Ben, with the moorage paid and a maintenance fund. I guess she thought he liked it when they went sailing together.'

'Ben doesn't have anything to speak of. She knew that besides liking him and not having any heirs. Nice thing to do for him. Now he has something of his own, a boat owner that doesn't have to worry about maintenance or moorage fees.'

'Thoughtful of her.'

'Yes, and one, I'm sure, he will always remember her for. We all will.'

'Don't you dare let anything happen to you. I couldn't cope without you.'

Brush listened and let her talk. He knew from experience that she was having a hard time not blaming herself. And it was better for her to get everything out.

'Thanks for listening, sweetheart. Aren't you supposed to be at the airport?'

Brush studied her for a few seconds. 'There are plenty of people at the airport. About a zillion FBI agents, and I think Moriac is somewhere close to here. I'd rather be here with you, eh.'

She leaned over and gave a kiss and a look that said without reservation that he was the love of her life and he needed to stay in her life. 'Step on it. I want to get back to the *Bus*. Brees, Kitty, and Chen are still inside working. I've got a job to do.'

Something nagged at Brush as he drove. Something she had just said. He couldn't put his finger on it.

'Glenda, the FBI,' said Brees, 'is searching the University of Indiana Northwest campus and the two students' digs for anything else that might be useful. I think a major effort will go into finding their contacts and how they are involved. Chen and Sept are focusing on video looking for their vehicles. Kitty is busy coordinating with the FBI, CIA, and BWC.'

* * *

Jim closed his eyes for several seconds. He looked at Pedro

and Cherry. They looked at him, wondering what it was that he had just heard.

'It's bad news. Maria was killed.'

'Mierda,' said Cherry as she pulled Pedro to her. '*Amo a esa dama*. She my best friend. This bad.' With all she had been through in her life, as tough as she was, a tear welled and beaded on her lower eyelid. She squeezed Pedro for almost a minute. Letting go of him would be letting go of Maria.

Jim looked at Pedro, sensing that the young boy would be at the end of what he could stand with his friends and family dying. Jim was no stranger to death, but a sudden feeling of aloneness passed through him. He had never felt this before—Heather, and now Maria. A lone tear drifted down his cheek. Pedro looked at his dad and started to bawl. It was as though all the past deaths he had been keeping inside spilled out. He had been holding every-thing in, and suddenly it flowed with full abandon from his whole being.

Tshui looked wide-eyed at Pedro.

'Sharupe, perhaps you could explain to Tshui that the woman that was on the helicopter and boarded the plane,' Jim uncharacteristically had to pause and regain his composure, ... 'and she was a close family friend who just died.'

Sharupe talked with Tshui for several minutes. Cherry, as upset as she was, consoled Pedro and desper-ately wanted to console the Colonel and be consoled by him. In a melodic voice, Sharupe said in her native language:

. . .

*ame áarma nuna mejentsat nukaka wakeraj*
  *aya takatsan nuk, antinkish atsutai nui*
  *chimiamu atsana tsunki,*
  *mamush-sha, ami yapí nukichi*
  *shinik mayai aínis weame*

It is from one of my poems. Loosely translated, it means:

*I want to caress your words*
  *without touching my lips*
  *where there are no wounds*
  *and no maskss to conceal your face.*

* * *

After humiliating his pursuers, Moriac had driven four miles down the freeway when he saw an oversized truck rest and fuel stop with a giant "J". He could see the sign a mile before he got to the exit. There were dozens of semi-tractor trailers parked and scattered in the parking area, people sleeping in their cars. He knew he needed to ditch the microbus. When he drove into the truck stop, he saw several hitchhikers standing near the exits. He scouted the parking area and drove away from the hubbub to where cars looked parked for the day. Among the cars, he spotted a dingy, unwashed white Chevy pickup with an old, uncared-for camper on the back. A light sliver seeped through a window curtain.

He pulled over close to it and got out. Moriac could hear someone inside. He knocked on the door. An old man with several days' growth of gray-white whiskers scowled as he opened the back door. 'You got nothing I want. I'm out here so as not to be bothered by nobody.'

Moriac hit the old man with a beefy fist in his solar plexus. The man doubled over and fell backward into the camper. Moriac climbed in and put his boot on the old man's protruding Adam's apple. He pressed down with his full 220 pounds, hearing crunching noises as the old man's cartilage and larynx collapsed. The travelling transient stopped breathing. Moriac surveyed the area out the back door. No one was close. He pulled the old man to the door and lifted him onto his shoulder. Using the camper as cover, he walked into the bushes and dropped the old guy.

*If I leave it here, they will find it and figure out what vehicle I took. But not for a few hours.*

The keys to the truck were on the dinette. Moriac switched his equipment cases out of the microbus into the camper. He started the truck and drove it to the fuel pumps, filled the tank with gas, and parked it closer to the convenience store. He returned to the microbus and drove to where the hitchhikers were waiting, hoping for a ride. There was a half tank of fuel. *Enough to get someone quite a way down the road,* he thought. 'Anybody going to Chicago?' Bill and Susie practically jumped toward Moriac. Susie said, 'We are. Can you give us a ride? Cool old VW bus.'

'Are you two trustworthy?'

'Why?' asked Susie.

'I've got a problem. My girlfriend and I were taking our two vehicles to Chicago. We had a fight, and she left with a truck driver. Now I'm stuck with both vehicles and only me to drive.'

'Are you French?' asked Susie.

'Born and raised near Marseille. But my dad moved here when I was fifteen. I still have a little of the accent, I guess. I can't give you a ride, but if I could trust you to drive my microbus to Chicago, I would appreciate it. You do drive, okay?'

'We started in Brooklyn and our car died not far from here. We can't pay right now to get it fixed, so we want to go to my mom's house in Chicago.'

'Well then, it looks as though we can help each other out. Give me the address of your mother. You two drive one of my vehicles, preferably the microbus, to your mom's house. I'll get someone to give me a ride and pick it up tomorrow. Deal?'

Bill didn't like the looks of Moriac. Still, he nodded when Susie looked at him and said, 'How much trouble can we get into, driving by ourselves?'

'Great. Super,' said Susie. 'We'll do it.'

Moriac got out and left the microbus running. If you please, write your address on something. Susie dug into her pack and took out a business card, turned it over, and wrote her mother's address on it.

'Take good care of it. I know it's old, but I'm partial to it.'

'We will. There aren't many of these around still. I know it must be special to you.'

Moriac said, 'Fuck them.' He pulled out of the truck stop, going back to where he had blown up the van. He drove by the overpass and took the next exit, under the freeway and back up on ramp, heading toward the scene. He pulled over not far from where he had parked in the microbus and looked down at the chaos. The oversized vehicle with all the comm devices on the roof was being loaded onto a truck.

'We might have him this time. The microbus was just spotted on the toll road headed toward Chicago,' Glenda yelled. Almost simultaneously, they received positive confirmation that it had been parked above the explosion site.

She ran down the steps of the *Bus* and saw Brush standing with a mechanic looking at a dark green sports car. 'Brush, we're on the road.'

They jumped in Brush's sport utility rental. 'A cam picked it up on the I-90 freeway. It's about three miles from here. I don't want to screw up again. Moriac switched vehicles with the uni students. He's in the VW.'

'Why is he still close to here, eh? It's been almost an hour since the explosion.'

'No idea.'

'Think, sweetie, doesn't make sense. He's writing the script that he wants you to follow.'

'Understood, but there's nothing else I can think to do. We've got a sighting; we need to chase it.'

'We have to find a way to get ahead of him if we want to put an end to this,' said Brush.

'Kitty, make sure the bomb squad is on-site as soon as the cops have the microbus boxed in and stay a safe distance away. I'm not making the same mistake again. The FBI is coming on the freeway three exits ahead and behind the current position of the vehicle. They'll stop the traffic behind them and in front. And somehow get the cars out. He won't be able to go anywhere.'

'It's not going to be him,' said Brush.

'I doubt it too.'

'You already had that figured out.'

'Not likely he would try the same thing twice. On the other hand, he might expect we would think that and set us up again.'

'It's probably not him, Kitty. Regardless, tell them to keep their distance. I don't want to see any more of the good guys blown up.'

'I will, but I don't think they will need much encouragement.'

Brush sat thinking, trying to latch onto some way to get ahead of this man. *The microbus is a timewaster. Is he going to come after Glenda? Take out command, and the troops are in disarray.*

Glenda toggled her radio. 'An FBI observer says there's

a man and a woman in the front seats of the vehicle. No sign of Moriac.'

'Funny that,' said Susie.

'Funny that, what?' asked Bill.

'I just looked back in the mirror and there are no cars behind us.'

'That's weird. Oh, oh. Look ahead now. There's a roadblock with a hell of a lot of flashing lights.'

'Something's wrong. They're moving the cars in front of us through single file. Suddenly we're like isolated in a huge empty freeway.'

'What's that?'

'It's an army vehicle,' said Bill.

'He's coming this way. What's going on?'

The car started thumping. 'I think we got a flat tire,' said Bill.

They didn't know that snipers had just shot both of their front tires and were about to shoot a metal-piercing round into their engine.

The rubber-wheeled armored vehicle pulled to a stop 100 feet in front of them. The blue and white microbus was the only vehicle on the freeway. There was a loud clank and their motor stopped. Two men wearing strange heavy suits and helmets lumbered out of the vehicle. One with an automatic weapon pointed at them and the other with a bullhorn and a pistol. On top of the armored car behind a steel plate was a machine gun aimed at them. 'Get out of the vehicle. Hands in the air.'

'Are they going to shoot us?' asked Susie.

Bill, who was a cop movie aficionado, said, 'No sudden movements, and hold your hands way up. Don't reach down or make any quick moves. We'll be okay.'

'Walk forward. Keep your hands up. Move it.'

Brush and Glenda zig-zagged their way through the stopped cars to get past the front of the roadblock. 'It's not Moriac. At least so far unless he's in the back of the microbus. Another decoy?' questioned Glenda.

'Probably,' said Brush. Minus the fireworks this time, I expect. He knows it will take us some time to clear the VW and we'll use a lot of extra being cautious.'

'Gives him time to get away. He's playing with us.'

'He had to be close to time the van explosion. He might be close now.'

'What about the microbus parked on the overpass when the van blew up? Was it this couple or was it Moriac?'

'Get the FBI to check out any likely vantage points while they clear the VW. Get the couple away from the vehicle. Find out how they ended up in the VW and if they can shed any light on what Moriac is driving.'

'Okay. Let's watch this to make sure there are no disasters. We'll get back to the *Bus* and wait for the report.'

Bill and Susie were ten feet away from the heavily padded bomb squad personnel. The man with the bullhorn was pointing a pistol at them. 'On the ground.' They were quickly handcuffed, jerked to their feet, searched, and walked back to the back of the Army vehicle.

'Who's in the back of the hippie bus?'

'Nobody. It's just us two. What did we do?' asked Susie, trying not to tremble. Bill knew enough to keep his mouth shut and let Susie, who was the chatty one, do the talking. *Talking might calm her down.*

'The two civilians are secure and away from the Vee-dub. The bomb squad is approaching it now.'

'You're right. I can feel it. A fakeout,' said Glenda. 'Let's make sure the microbus isn't going to explode and then get out of here. We can read what the couple had to say after they're interviewed.'

* * *

'Glenda, the windscreen is fixed, and the new driver is here,' said Kitty over the radio.

'Stay put, we're coming to you. I don't think there's anything else we can do here. We'll get the report soon. It was another time-wasting prank, this time thankfully without a bomb. I want to be ready to roll as soon as we get back to you. We're at least twenty minutes out with all this traffic.'

'Kitty, I need a breath of fresh air and some sunlight,' said Chen, 'and I want to go look at the fancy parked car outside.'

'I'll go out with you,' said Brees. 'I need some air and a stretch, too. As soon as the boss is back, we might not have another chance for a while.'

'No sweat, ten minutes, guys. I want you back and ready to roll when Glenda gets here.'

Moriac had followed the trailer'd command vehicle. And parked the camper on the far side of the repair facility. He spent several minutes scouting the area before he approached the *Bus* from behind an oversized building. He extended the tube of the light anti-tank weapon, flipped up the sight, and squeezed the trigger. A whoosh as the projectile left the tube and made its way to the *Bus*. Almost in slow motion, the sides of the *Bus* ballooned and burst into flames.

The shockwave hit Brees and Chen. 'Oh my God,' said Brees.

'Kitty, ETA is five minutes,' said Glenda. 'Kitty, do you hear me?'

# Chapter Forty-One

Moriac made his way back to I-94 and then drove south on Interstate 65. After about forty minutes, the commercial buildings and houses gave way to farms. He turned off at Roselawn and drove east, then south, on another rural road. He was searching for much the same thing that Najma had months earlier—a derelict farm, possibly with old people and few visitors.

Some might say he was overly cautious, but he wanted to eliminate another link and dump the camper in case the old derelict's body was found or someone had seen him at the truck stop. Most of the farms were well maintained: fields plowed, fences repaired, lawns mowed, livestock grazing or freshly fed with hay waiting as anxiously as the farmers for the spring grasses to grow.

He stopped and backed up. The fence posts were tilted, and several strands of rusty barbed wire were broken. The driveway showed no sign of being used, and there were no fresh tracks in the snow. He turned onto the road and drove to a small house with peeling paint overshadowed by old barn with a sagging roof. He reasoned someone was home as a porch light glowed in what was left of the late afternoon light.

The steps did not look like they would support his weight, but there was a newer ramp leading up to the porch. When the door opened, there was an old lady in a wheelchair holding a shotgun pointed at Moriac.

'What's your business?'

'My car is acting up, sputtering.'

'That's your problem. Nothing to do with me.'

'Sorry to have bothered you,' he said as he walked back down the ramp to the gravel driveway. Out of the corner of his eye, he saw her turn her wheelchair back into the house. He turned and shot her in the head. It was an easy shot from fifteen feet. He scrambled back up the ramp and pushed her inside, waiting for a minute, listening. There was no sound. He looked through the rest of the house—there was no one—she lived alone.

He started to doubt she had a car. If not, this was a wasted effort. A waste of time, *a precious commodity*. He opened the garage door. It was empty. He walked to the barn with the drooping roof. There was a sliding door. It slid easily. Inside was an old, oxidized, and dented brown Dodge pickup truck. The keys dangled from the ignition. It didn't start. The battery was dead.

In the truck bed, there was the usual toolbox. He opened it and found what he needed. He removed the dead battery and tossed it to the side. He drove the camper into the barn and put its battery in the Dodge. It started a little rough, and after a minute, the motor settled down to a smoother hum. The next problem—the tires. He remembered seeing a rusty compressor in the garage.

The tires, after sitting half-inflated for months, had formed flat spots. The lumpy ride, as he drove south on I-65, wasn't smoothing out. He was less than a half hour from Boucher's first money wire when the GPS would indicate he had arrived at one of the larger egg producers in Indiana. It was far from the largest in the U.S., but sufficient to infect thousands of chickens and a few people with the engineered transmissible virus. Boucher wanted the N1H5 to appear to have modified naturally in a chicken breeder's facility and then spread to people through its employees. Moriac's GPS gizmo would alert the bank he was at the site and the funds would automatically transfer to his account. He had thought many times he should alter the GPS locator so that it gave a false reading. *Boucher is deceiving himself, trying to make people believe the human virus came from an egg facility. I don't care. His money, his choice. I bought myself a little time. I need to get out of this country.*

'Now I've really messed up, Brush. She grabbed onto him and squeezed hard. I got Kitty and Sept killed. I should have put security out. Bertrand warned me that he would take the battle to us. I didn't listen. Am I losing it? I'm used to hunting, not being the prey. This fucked-up situation is all my fault.'

'You didn't get them killed, and it could have been any of us making the same decisions. He's using a different playbook than you've encountered before.'

'I just don't understand the difference in the military mindset.'

'No one would have expected that he would even know about the Bus. Is there someone helping him on our side?'

'A mole?' asked Glenda. 'There are hundreds of agents here. It's possible.'

'Not likely unless Boucher paid someone off. Which maybe isn't that unlikely. I doubt, however, he would anticipate that the FBI would be trying to stop this. He's responding to the situation. None of this was planned. Most likely if he was watching when he exploded the van, eh? The best place would be some high ground. What if he spotted you arriving at the scene from a higher vantage point? Saw all that garbage on the roof and somehow followed it back here.'

'Pretty brazen,' said Glenda, staring off at the twilight blue sliver between two metal buildings.'

Brush studied Glenda's face. 'That's who you are dealing with.'

Glenda Rose continued to stare blankly. *Am I out of my depth? Am I capable of running this operation? My only ability so far seems to be getting people killed.*

'I gotta get a handle on this. Is he going to keep attacking?'

'Protect your flanks. Hope he attacks so you can take him out, but I would wager he's done his damage and now he'll focus on his mission.'

'General, if you still want me to be in charge, and I wouldn't blame you if you don't, if you do, I want a military group like Nealy's. Preferably Nealy's A team. Can you get him here?'

'I've been thinking the same thing. It'll take a couple of hours to get them to you.'

Brush pulled her in close, tilted her head back, and looked straight into her red-rimmed moist bloodshot eyes. 'Beautiful, you are better than you realize. I've known Will Crystal since our time in Southeast Asia. And I know what he thinks of you. And he's right. He usually is. Battles go sideways.'

She swiped tears away angrily. 'Yeah. Okay. I have to be smarter, change my thinking. I don't want to keep losing people.'

Brush took hold of her shoulders. 'You better get this straight, babe. In a war, there are casualties. People die. Good people. You haven't lost the war. It's been costly for sure, but the first skirmishes are over and now you need to get him. If anybody can, it's you.'

'I'll never get over losing Kitty and Maria. I think Maria and I could have maybe even been good friends. She was kind, and she was smart,' she said, brushing away another tear. She was accomplished. I liked her.'

'Memories never go away. Sometimes they hide for a while. Jim told me Maria had assimilated into FARC village life and that she had become buddies with Cherry.

Hard to figure, the uneducated rebel with the Ivy League doctor.'

'A sexy lady with the hots for you, as I remember.'

'That's what I think about all the guys that I see glancing at you. Who in their right mind wouldn't want to go after you?'

'Enough already, enough feeling sorry for myself. Back to the mission. Talk to me. Think about what you would do. I'm going to replace Sept with Techie Tom. It'll be good to have both his military and tech skill sets. He can back up Chen. I want Abenaa to go with you. She grew on me in France. We got to know each other. We became friends. She can be a tough cookie, and then Glenda smiled for the first time since the explosions. We teased her about her warrior face.'

'Abenaa, go with me where?'

'First, what would you do?'

'You've got a lot of manpower. Put a team of observers in every location he might go. Don't have the FBI standing around in dark suits and sunglasses, with wires hanging out of their ears. Get them concealed at observation points. Radio check-ins every half hour. He will have another vehicle by now. Look for the man, not the vehicle.'

'I have a call in a few minutes with Bertrand. You think Boucher's butcher has gone back to Chicago International like Bertie originally guessed he would?'

'No. Why come down here and then head back unless it's part of his escape plan?'

Brush shook his head. 'Don't know. Cover all the possibilities. That's all you can do.'

'I don't think the airport, but it would be a nightmare if he does show up at ORD; I want you and Abenaa to get there. I'll stay here.'

Brush's first thought was—a bad idea. He's here somewhere, close. He didn't realize that Glenda wanted to separate them. She couldn't afford to have anyone else she cared about killed. And Bertrand could be right. He usually was. Brush could be instrumental at the airport. If she had reasoned it through, she would have realized that it was a bad idea.

* * *

'Stupid woman posting us out here,' said Tony. 'Nothing's going to happen in the boondocks. Zero. We're sitting here with our thumbs up our rears watching a bunch of birds.'

'Jesus, mate. It would be nice to hear something other than you're bitching. We're comfy enough in a warm truck. And big surprise, we could end up winning the lottery and be the guys that bust this guy.'

'Fat chance. There ain't gonna be any perps coming our way. One stupid command decision after another,' said Standish, with his characteristic smirk. 'All the action will be somewhere else.

'We've done stake-outs dozens of times. You're not wearing a suit or having a tie choking your Adam's apple. We're incognito in these farmer John tan canvas bibs, a beater truck, a thermos of coffee, and I sort of like our big boss. She's gutsy.'

'So, you think it's okay that the boss lady with big tits

who never made anything of herself in the FBI is now our head honcho? And sending us out here smelling chicken shit in these farmer threads is a good idea? It's a waste of time?'

'Jeez Louise, Tony. Besides all the moaning and groaning, you've turned into the world's biggest woman hater? A hard-core misogynist. Pour me some coffee and then do a grid search. And keep quiet.'

'We have twelve snipers. The question is, how do we deploy them?' asked Jack Hall, the second in charge of tactical. 'A hell of a lot more than a dozen places to choose from.'

McAfee, the agent in charge, who was Jack's immediate supervisor, looked up and said, 'Boss Stuart said to concentrate on the airport, and to not forget that our perp could go into attack mode again. She said to set up bait vehicles and agents.'

'That's a new one.'

'Keep them subtle, but ones that might attract his attention. Place them so the snipers can cover the bait vehicle and other likely places he might appear. Two birds with stone concept.'

'Techie, I'm putting you in charge of keeping the command van safe. It's nothing exotic like the *Bus*, but we're done losing people. It'll be me, Sept, Brees, you, and two SFs on the way—Roberta and Garcia.'

Tom smiled and said, 'Good. I hope that means we're getting all of my bros here?'

'We are. Those two were closer and could get here faster.'

# Chapter Forty-Two

oriac drove the roads surrounding the Victory egg-laying facility. It was rural; flat with straight roads forming grids built around white-painted farms. He saw nothing suspicious. He spotted a dirt track alongside a stubbly, frozen corn patch. At the end was a small cluster of leafless trees. He backed under their skeletal branches. The battered brown Dodge was well camouflaged with its rear directed toward the chicken houses.

Barren branches partially obscured the truck from the egg barns. More importantly, he had a clear view of the parking lot and entrance, which housed a small wooden shack with a light on. Marcel climbed into the pickup bed and opened one of his cases. He took out a standard camo cold-weather suit, gloves, and heavy boots. He planned to spend several hours observing the buildings and surrounding area from the truck bed.

He climbed back in the truck, warming up and

watching the road while looking for any sign that someone had observed him. After thirty minutes, he got in the pickup bed and covered the cases with blankets and quilts he had taken from the mobile transient's camper, with his night vision scope resting on a grungy pillow also courtesy of the old vagrant. He pulled a dark quilt over his head leaving only a small opening for the scope. With the patience learned in the legion, he slowly shifted so he could observe each quadrant around the truck. The leafless trees obscured much of his vision toward the road. There were just enough of them between the truck and the egg production building to provide camouflage.

After assuring himself there was no one watching him from his sides or behind, he focused his attention on the buildings and the parking lot. There were only about ten parked vehicles. Most were pickup trucks. As he slowly panned the night vision scope, something refracted light in one of the trucks. After a few seconds, he saw exhaust vapors drifting into the night sky. He continued to observe the reflection, only occasionally moving his gaze away to scan other areas. There were two men inside. Forty minutes later, the passenger door opened and one of the men stepped behind the truck. He was wearing farmer's clothes.

* * *

Jim put the phone down. 'Who call, Dad?'

'It was Brush.'

'I would say hi. Why you no let me?'

'Also, me,' said Cherry.

'Next time he calls, you can both say hello.'

After the phone call, Jim moved everyone from town back to the air base where sleeping quarters had been arranged.

After the children and Sharupe went to bed, Cherry asked, 'Now you tell me about phone call and what the problem is?'

Jim turned to Cherry. 'Details about how Maria died.'

'I want know.'

'An explosion.'

Cherry didn't say anything. She sat still, facing away from Jim. Then she turned. 'Tell me about bomb?'

Jim sighed. 'There is a man, a terrorist. She was investigating when a van containing explosives detonated.'

'Who detonate?'

'We don't know for certain. Best guess the man.'

'We go find this man. Leave at sunrise.'

Jim took her by the shoulders. She could feel the strength of his grasp. She could feel her attraction to him.

He held her dark eyes. She could see the hurt in his eyes. And then she felt a chill as the starlight glow died and his eyes turned to ice blue. 'You and the Major are two people I would like to have by my side when we find this man. But Pedro is doing good here. I need you to stay and be his protector.'

She glared at him. She wanted to punish this man for killing her friend. But she knew she had no choice. She knew she was incapable of persuading the Colonel. He didn't decide things on a whim. And it was hard to escape her history as a FARC rebel; she had learned to accept her fate was to do as she was ordered. She became resigned, although it still irritated her to stay. 'I do not wish it, but I will do as you say.' Her mind churned through a plethora of thoughts: hate for this man who had killed Maria; a feeling of wanting this man standing before her; not willing to accept the death of her friend; wishing it were not so; wanting revenge, wanting to be protected and cared for by someone, by a man, by this man.

'I leave in two hours. In the morning, a Captain Mobley will fly the four of you to the outskirts of the Shuar village.'

'You understand. There never be anyone like her in my life. I never dreamed of knowing or feeling friendship with someone like her.'

Jim thought Cherry started to choke up a little, but she held it back.

'She would have been a true friend and we would have done things together. Gone to places I am only dreaming about now. Things that were never in my thoughts before meeting you and her. Will you take me to one of the places in the books?' She hesitated before adding, 'Jim.' She had always called him Colonel. 'Will you show me your ranch —Norte Americana?'

Jim put his arms around Cherry, who enveloped him with her arms and body. He didn't answer. He wasn't sure how to. How to keep Cherry as a special friend and not more. They understood each other and the dark sides of life. He respected her. The gulf that had always separated Heather and him didn't exist with Cherry. After losing

Heather and Maria, he felt powerless in her grasp. It confused him. Her toughness, her understanding of the world, her softness. They held each other, both grappling with their separate feelings, before Cherry looked up into his blue eyes and said, 'What you do about little girl, Tshui?'

Jim shook his head. 'I don't have an answer.' He knew he couldn't take her to his world. Perhaps the only viable option, at least for Tshui, was to stay in hers and Cherry's world. An impossible decision. He would wait to see how the circumstances changed and hope a solution surfaced. First, he had business in the U.S. Maria had been an inseparable part of Heather. The two joined in their lives and spirits. *Both died because of me, my job, my enemies, my missions. Not entirely true with Maria, but still.* She had been as much a part of the BWC as he was. Her job was different. To save lives, not take them. She shouldn't have been exposed to dangers outside her realm of microbes.

* * *

Marcel saw nothing new of interest. He looked at his watch—0400 hours. He estimated the distance to the guard station and parking lot to be a little over a kilometer. There was a chain-link fence and little cover in the winter field to conceal his approach. He would use the long, narrow buildings as cover. He had expected security cameras and had seen none.

'If the breeze blows the exhaust under the car, we could die of carbon monoxide poisoning,' said Tony.

'Jesus Christ, Tony. First a Mr. Misogynist and now a Mr. Negativity. Think positive before you drive me crazy,' said the slim gray-haired Standish.

Moriac could hear their voices. He had cut a chain-link fence, approached behind the buildings, and circled into the parking lot. The guard was asleep in the shack. He didn't know for certain who these two were, but he couldn't release the virus with them sitting there. Ducking, he stayed below the vision of their outside mirrors. One of the men continued to talk.

The passenger's side door opened, and a large, slightly overweight man stretched his arms to the sky, rolled his neck, and strolled back to relieve himself. *Never-ending coffee, pee, more coffee, and more peeing. I gotta cut down. It can't be good living on caffeine and donuts.*

As he reached the back of the truck, he had no time to react. A beefy hand clasped his mouth. His legs collapsed. He felt Moriac's knee on his spine and heard it crack a fraction of a second before the ex-paratrooper ratcheted his neck until it too made a fatal crack. Moriac lowered him silently to the ground.

'Standish, I have to take a piss too.' Roy walked toward the back and turned away from the man he thought was Tony. Marcel almost chuckled before he broke both Tony's clavicles with a sharp downward blow and engulfed him with his beefy arms in a hammerlock until his breathing stopped. Moriac searched the men's pockets and took their guns and IDs. *Feds.* He put both men back in the truck and quietly closed the doors.

*The FBI doesn't know where I am, or they would have more than two men here. Where are they focusing? Doesn't matter if it's not where I am. And if not here, then it is not likely they will be where I am going.* Moriac would see what he could learn by monitoring the agents' radio. Time was short. The agents would have a reporting schedule. It would cause a response when they missed it.

He had brought supplies in a canvas rucksack from the truck, and he quickly put on his protective gear, took out an atomizer, and entered the egg facility. He sprayed several hatching areas, the doors, and anywhere humans might touch in the morning, methodically working his way outside. He was infecting chickens with the modified H5N1 virus, but the primary goal was to infect humans. The Remilious plan was that it would be assumed the virus had mutated in the birds. He moved to the guard shack. The man was dead to the world. *Or soon would be.* He slid a window open a few inches. Misted the interior and closed the window. He heard a voice on the radio as he retraced his path to the truck. He turned the volume up. The two agents had missed their check-in time.

'If you two bozos are asleep,' said McGovern, 'you can kiss your careers goodbye. Come on, talk to me,' said a male voice. 'It'll take the better part of two hours for someone to drive to you. Fortunately for you, I can spare them.'

He clicked the radio off. Standish doesn't miss check-ins. He turned to his deputy, DuToit. 'Alert command.

Get me a chopper. And I want a SWAT team in the air to Victory Hatchery, now! And another with the bio-HazMat. I want cameras and agents monitoring roads between here and Victory Farms. I'm tired of sitting here like a limp dick wondering if he is going to come after us again. I'm going after him.'

Glenda yelled, 'We might have his location! Two agents didn't check in at Victory Farms. Get me two drones to the facility and cover the roads. This time of night, there won't be much traffic.'

'Are we driving there?' asked Techie.

'Too slow. Instead, we monitor gas stations with cameras. Let SWAT do its job. Use the drones to get license numbers from any vehicles on the road. Bring up the maps of the area. Let's try to figure out where Moriac will go.'

'Could be any direction,' said Brees.

'Nope, he's got a plan. Look for other close facilities. For once, let's try to get ahead of him.' Glenda called Bertrand with the news. 'What do you think?'

'We've got two profilers standing by. Escape, infect, or attack. I'll get right back to you.'

Glenda called Sheilla. 'Any news about the virus anti-dote?' Nusmen said to leave him alone and let him work. We're working all out with Martin and the French intelligence, cleaning up the Remilious issues. I was just informed that Dr. Visser was found dead in a room in the Château. He was tortured, and it was gruesome, according to Liam. The Wolfpack, BWC, and CIA are gathering everything on the Egyptian terrorists and their apparent point person, Dr. Visser's assistant.'

'Thanks for the update. Gotta go.'

Seconds later, Bertrand called back. 'We don't have a unanimous opinion. One of the profilers thinks he will continue to be aggressive. I disagree. I don't think he will push his luck again. At least not right now, or unless he feels cornered.'

'Major McGuire suggested the same thing.'

'BWC's Katarina agrees too. If he's made the effort to infect a facility, knowing all the manpower and woman-power out there tracking him, he'll focus on whatever remains of his mission and then escape. You need people at all the egg hatcheries in the area. Pull some of the people from ORD. That does not make sense based on his last location. Leave it covered but get people to other airports, such as Indianapolis International. The FBI is sending you several hundred more agents.'

# Chapter Forty-Three

oriac, for one of the few times in his career, underestimated an enemy. He immediately recognized his mistake. Back at the old brown truck, he changed out of his protective gear after spraying the outside of the suit with bleach and started down the road. Six miles north of Victory Farms, a Super Puma heading south raced overhead. It was a different version of the one he had destroyed when he blew up the van. If he continued, he would be exposed on these country roads with little traffic. *Merde. Head back to the egg farm. They would not be looking for a vehicle going toward the facility but would focus on ones heading away.* He stopped under a train trestle. It wasn't much wider than two or three truck lengths. While he considered his options, he got out and walked to the edge, looking east at the first golden glow on the horizon. As he scanned the morning sky, he spotted a dark object high above him flying south. He identified it as a drone. *First time I've seen one in the wild.*

Based on when DuToit alerted Glenda about the Chicago agent in charge's suspicion that something was not right with the two observers at Victory Poultry Farms, 'Moriac could be as many as thirty or forty miles away from VF. One drone is about that distance north. Tom, until we get the second drone arrives, have it stay high and search for any vehicles headed away from Victory. Call every sighting with a plate number into the FBI. Keep it in the north sector. When the other drone gets there, have it stay on the south side.'

'Second drone is two minutes out,' said Techie, lifting one earpiece of his Bose headset to hear Glenda's conversation.

Glenda raised a hand for quiet, her fingers holding her headset tight to her ear. She scowled and clicked off. 'The two agents are down at the Victory egg-laying facility. A SWAT team and the FBI are searching the area. A security guard says he's been awake all night watching the grounds and hasn't seen anyone.'

Moriac spotted the second black drone moving faster to the south.

A minute later, another Super Puma rushed past, flying toward the chicken facility.

'A HazMat team is eight minutes away.'

'Techie, I want a live connection with the lead FBI agent on-site, the SWAT team, and the HazMat.'

'Will do, a couple of seconds, okay? SWAT found tracks in the snow headed across a field and are following them. The chopper is up with an observer over their position. You're live now with SWAT and HazMat. The FBI agent in charge, McGovern, is monitoring.'

Glenda listened as the SWAT team moved across the field. 'Spread out. Eyes on the trees and our six. Birdman, move to the woods and tell us what you see.'

'Tracks stop at the edge of the trees. Vehicle tire tracks lead away.'

'Moving up. Perp appears to have flown the coop.'

Glenda heard a couple of moans.

'Alright, all right. Focus. Let's not get ambushed.' He cranked his arm, and the SWAT members jogged to the edge of the trees.

'Confirmed. Perp's tracks stop where a vehicle was parked.'

Glenda said, 'Get the chopper to the end of this two-tracker and tell me which way the vehicle turned on the road.'

'HazMat, anything to report?'

'Copious quantities of virus in the egg-laying buildings and the guard shack. We have quarantined the site.'

'Nobody leaves. Keep me updated. Teckie, anything interesting from the drones?'

'Traffic's picking up. They've gone low enough to get plate numbers.'

'He's close; I can feel him.'

'Agent DuToit, I want roadblocks at fifty miles on every side of Victory Farms. And a second perimeter 100 miles back. Skeleton crews at the airports. I don't want local cops alone on any roadblocks in the fifty-mile perimeter. Fax the vehicle owners to me as they're identified.'

'We dispatched a lot of the ORD agents to other egg farms. We don't have the bodies for roadblocks. We have to use local law enforcement. Hold on. Correction, the new multitudes of agents and HazMatters have arrived.'

'I want every drivable way out of the fifty-mile radius covered. Use locals if you must. The same goes for every airport inside that circle.'

'He could still try to hoof it out,' said Techie. 'We could use the drones' IR for any warm bodies walking out.'

'Yes, and I'm thinking about whether the National Guard would help or hinder.'

Moriac slowed behind several other vehicles, mostly pickups, as they approached Victory Farms. The road ahead was blocked. He pulled to the side, turned his blinker on, and did a slow U-turn. He returned to a farm track he had noticed a few minutes ago alongside a large field. The snow-covered track led past the field and into a wooded area. The road ended at a small stream. The water was shallow. The ground on the other side was brushy, flat, and had no bank. He put the old truck in four-wheel drive and edged across the stream, up the shallow bank, and crept over deadfall, branches, and brush into the woods. He picked his way carefully. He moved into a dense over-grown area and stopped.

* * *

Glenda perused the sheets of the licenses and the owner's information. 'Okay, here's a pickup from the area where we lost Moriac. And another, a delivery truck.' She looked at Brees and said, 'Get agents to the two addresses. Chen, go over the list and see if you can find any other connections.'

Techie was pushing pins in a map at the locations of roadblocks surrounding Victory Farms. He looked at Glenda and said, 'Only three possible ways to enter the farm itself and a hell of a lot more roads to block at fifty and 100 miles.'

'How many?'

'A fifty-mile perimeter, sixty, counting all the minor roads and any drivable tracks across fields. And too many to count at 100 miles out.'

Glenda blew out some air through pursed lips, and with her index finger, rapidly flapped her lips up and down, making a bu, bu, bu, bu sound. Chen scrunched up her lips into one of her strange facial contortions in response. 'Damn, damn. We can't cover them all, and that makes it a wasted exercise. How many are set up now?'

'Fifteen and more setting up by the minute.'

'Focus on the fifty-mile roadblocks. Move agents in from the 100-mile ones and tell them to monitor all vehicle drivers as they drive. I repeat the faces.'

'You got it, boss.'

'Don't call me boss. Glenda will do when we're in here at home.'

'Miniature one compared to our old one,' added Chen.

Glenda stared at her for a second, thinking about Kitty and Sept in their destroyed command bus.

'All roadblocks at the inner perimeter are in place,' said Tom. Thanking himself that he didn't say boss again. He had always called his superiors boss.

'That happened fast?'

'Some were set up but hadn't called in, and others were close to being set up. If you don't mind me asking, what is your official title? In France, we called you by your finance cover name. Out in front of others is ma'am, okay?'

'I guess the official title is special agent in charge. And ma'am is okay. Glenda in here though.'

'Got it.'

'Boss,' shouted Brees. Two agents checking vehicle addresses found a dead woman in a wheelchair. They're searching the house and property. Shot in the back of the head. Hold on. They found an old white camper parked in a barn. The forensics team is on the way. From the VIN, it's registered to a Frank Mulray. The plates are missing. The woman has a Dodge pickup truck that has not been licensed for two years. They're waiting for the bomb squad to clear the camper.'

'Get a bulletin out on the Dodge truck and the camper license plate. Do not apprehend; notify the FBI if sighted.'

A few minutes later, Brees turned to Glenda. 'One of the roadblocks reports that a beat-up brown pickup did a U-turn near their roadblock. It didn't raise anyone's suspicion because it signaled and made a slow u-turn. They didn't look concerned.'

'They?'

'I could see who was in the car.'

'Focus the drones on the area. Get teams to look for fresh tracks that match the truck from the farm on any of the adjoining dirt roads. Any breaks in fences. Let's corner him. We're getting close. Get any FBI off any outer road-blocks in the other quadrants and move them up to ...' She stopped and did a mental calculation. 'Damn it, he could be thirty miles away by now. Assuming he's driving the speed limit. I'll wager he is. But he wouldn't risk staying on the open road. Would he?'

'Assuming he's the one in the brown pickup,' added Tom.

'Yeah. Get all the choppers searching and let's move our location up.'

'Major McGuire and Abenaa are flying on a chopper that left ORD. ETA is twenty minutes to us,' said Brees. 'Hold on, General Crystal just called.'

'Yes, sir.' She squinted her eyes at Techie Tom.

'Colonel Johnson is on his way to you. He's four hours from landing at Grissom Airbase north of Kokomo. About another hour before he joins you. I'm not happy about it, but he might be able to assist you.'

Glenda wondered if the General was bringing him in to replace her.

* * *

Marcel loaded his rucksack with what he thought he would need, including two atomizers. He stuffed a Ghillie suit in. Packing it around the weapons in the pack. He covered the truck with cut branches, dirt, and leaves. Always cautious, he did a quick wipe of the steering wheel and door handles and anything else he thought he had touched. He wanted to torch the truck, but it would be seen. He expertly set three booby traps. Possibly overdone, he could spare the ordinance. He could only carry so much ordinance on his back. He rigged a pressure release in the driver's side door. One on a timer set for four hours wedged by the fuel tank, and the third took more time, a pressure switch under the seat. He wanted to make sure the truck was destroyed and any evidence of fingerprints, DNA, or hair.

He was a mile away, heading north, jogging when he came to a road. He was getting sweaty. The weather was warming, and the snow was getting soft. Enough, he hoped, to melt it soon. The truck was obscured from the air, but not the tracks left walking in or the boot tracks he had left crossing the field. If the snow melted, they wouldn't know which way he had gone. He scanned the air and road and saw nothing. The road was clear of snow; he went west, increasing his pace. He reached a road junction and saw no cars and no drones overhead. He started to turn south toward Victory Farms when a car pulled out of a farm driveway and turned toward him.

He had little choice. He stood his ground at the four-way stop. A woman in a green Datsun stopped and rolled down her window. She was pretty, with light blonde hair, and deep blue eyes. 'Kinda cold out there for a hike. You lost or hitchin'?'

Marcel saw no other cars. He smiled and walked to the

car. Without hesitation, he used the heel of his left hand with a ramrod-straight blow, hitting Debra Krensky in the nose. She slumped unconscious in her seat with blood gushing. The force of the blow crushed all eight nasal bones and caused a minor fracture in the ethmoid bone protecting her brain. Then he heard a noise. In the back seat in a child's security chair was a young boy. He scanned the roads and quickly glanced at the sky for drones. He opened the door and pulled her out onto the asphalt as if she were weightless. He slammed his boot heel down on her face, doing what his palm blow had not: breaking the ethmoid bone, pushing it into her brain, and killing her. He grabbed her right foot and dragged her off the road into some brush. Then he pulled his French-made FAMAS bullpup auto rifle out of his rucksack along with two hand grenades and put them on the seat. He got back into the car and turned left, driving east. He changed his mind about going back to the egg hatchery for what he had assumed would be his last battle.

Little Rod was too young to understand what was going on. Still, something caused him to start bawling. Moriac reached back and hit him with a backhand that stunned the two-year-old. 'Join your mère if you wish?' The force of the blow knocked the two-year-old boy unconscious, which, for the moment, saved his life.

Debra's mother walked out of their driveway to check the mailbox. She glanced down the road and saw her daughter's car at the crossroad junction and a man getting into the driver's side. 'What the hell!' she exclaimed. She couldn't see Debra.

She dialed 911 and got the sheriff's office. 'Cynthia. My daughter just left the house with Rodney. I went out to check for mail and saw her car in the middle of Cushing and Stark Road. A man got into the driver's seat and turned west. I couldn't see her inside. Only this guy.'

'What did the man look like?'

'I didn't see his face, but he was big ... stout or burly, not fat.'

'I'll radio the sheriff. Don't worry, we'll find them and find out what happened.'

'Sheriff. Mrs. Krensky just called and saw a man driving away from the Cushing-Stark junction. He only said he was burly, not fat. Could this be the wanted man the FBI's after?'

'Could be. He's supposed to be in our vicinity. I'm about three miles from Stark Road. Five miles west of Cushing.' Cynthia could hear his siren wailing as he disconnected.

Techie turned to Glenda. 'The FBI picked up a 911 call. It sounds like it could be our guy stealing a green Datsun, license number 703DEH. Sticker 88 for Wabash County. The sheriff is trying to intercept on his own.'

'Call him off. Get agents on all possible roads. I want the area locked down so tight that smoke couldn't seep out.'

'Brees, get Brush.'

'What's your location?'

'We're not far from you, about two klicks.'

'Get here and pick me up. We've got a sighting that might be Moriac. I want in on this.'

'Chen, Brees, Tom, you know what to do. Converge with the drones. Set up roadblocks and keep me informed when I'm in the air. I think we might have this guy finally boxed in.'

Techie said, 'Fresh tracks in the snow on a two-track road. They're following them into the woods. They found the brown pickup camouflaged with brush.'

'It's about two miles from where the Datsun was reported hijacked.'

Chen said, 'We just intercepted a call from the sheriff, who said he was in pursuit of the Datsun.'

'Patch me through to him.'

'Sheriff, this is the senior agent in charge. Stand down. Do not intercept. Since you've alerted him. Stay back and keep him in sight. Do not approach him. There'll be road-blocks ahead. You got me?'

There was no answer.

Teckie turned toward Glenda. 'We intercepted this: deputies just called the sheriff and told him there was fresh blood on the pavement. They looked around and found Debra Krensky dead off the side of the road. It's the sheriff's niece, and he is known to be a bully and a hothead.'

Marcel saw the flashing lights in his rear-view mirror. As the sheriff's car approached, he signaled and stopped on the side of the road and slid the seat back as far as it would go. Sheriff Krensky slammed on his brakes and skidded to a stop just behind Moriac. He pushed himself out of the police cruiser, undid the snap on his holster, and grasped his Glock. It was halfway out when Marcel turned with his FAMAS 5.56 and placed a burst through the back window into the sheriff's midsection.

As luck would have it, he had stopped a few feet before a small road that went into a wooded area. Moriac jumped out of the car, opening the trunk. He lifted the heavyset sheriff, put him inside and closed the lid, scanned the area, and saw no one. He gunned the Datsun onto the dirt track and into the woods. He grabbed his rucksack. He opened the passenger door, reached over, pulled the pin on one of his grenades, and wedged it between the driver's door and the seat. Rod gained consciousness and started bawling. Moriac grinned at him as he got out and jogged back to the sheriff's car.

He found the siren and strobe light switches and turned them off. He did a U-turn and raced at 100 miles per hour in the opposite direction, going east. The road was mostly deserted. He only passed two cars. After five miles at a four-way stop, he turned north and saw a black GMC pickup. He could see no other cars. Turning on the flashing lights and siren, he stayed behind the truck until it stopped. He could see one man inside.

Tod grimaced, as he couldn't afford another ticket on his record. *Shit. What did I do? Fucking cops.* Moriac got out and walked up to Tod's GMC Sierra.

He started to say, hey, you're not wearing a uniform, you don't ... Moriac said, get out and put your hands where I can see them. Move back to my vehicle. Moriac reached into the cruiser, while not taking his eyes off the man, and pulled the trunk release lever.

'What did I do and why are you opening the trunk?'

'I have something to show you.'

'Where are you from, anyway? Not around here.'

Tod rolled his eyes and looked up.

Moriac jabbed his fingers into Tod's throat, pushed him into the trunk, and shot him in the head with his Beretta. He reached into Tod's pocket and pulled out his ID. He had to drive 100 yards before he found a side road past a stubbly cornfield and did what he had been doing all morning: drove the sheriff's car into the woods, hiding it as best he could, knowing that time was critical.

Back in Tod's truck, which was still running, he continued north, staying just under the speed limit.

# Chapter Forty-Four

Agent Ray Tanner opened the driver's side door of the brown pickup. 'Jeez, Ray, back away. Don't do anything. The bomb squad is on the way.'

'It'll be a hell of a long time before they get here. I'm just going to peek inside and check the registration. In thirty years, I've opened hundreds of cars and there's never been an explosion. Somebody's paranoid.'

'With this guy, we have a pretty good reason to be. Don't be stupid.'

Two more FBI agents walked toward the car. Rachael stopped and said, 'I'll catch up with you,' as she pulled her cell out. Her partner, Bob, saw Ray opening the door and yelled, 'Don't open that door. What's the matter with you?'

Ray opened the door with theatrical caution, jumped backward, threw up his hands, and shouted, 'Bam.' He turned around, looking at his partner and the agent who'd yelled at him to stop, spread his hands wide, and said, 'Big surprise, nothing blew up.'

'Yeah. Alright. Just leave it, will you,' said his partner.

Ray ignored him and turned back to the car, put his right hand on the seat, and reached over, opening the glove box with his left. He pulled out the old, dusty papers and said, 'Hey, the glove box didn't explode.'

'Your partner doesn't seem to care much for orders,' said Bob.

'He thinks he knows ... before he could finish the sentence, he was knocked backward to the ground as the pressure-release booby trap under the seat exploded when Ray lifted his hand. A fraction of a second later, it was followed by a much larger explosion when the C-4 next to the gas tank blew. Rachael felt the pressure wave from the second blast and looked on in horror as her partner's body skidded in the leaves fifty feet from her. There was no sign of the other two agents.'

Techie Tom touched Chen's arm and said, 'Tell the boss to wait.'

Glenda peered back into their van with questioning eyes as the Hueys' blades thumped outside.

'It's the brown pickup. Three more agents dead. Booby trapped according to the one agent that survived. No other details yet.'

'I told them to wait for the bomb squad. Damn it. Stupid, stupid, stupid.'

Glenda called McGovern. 'You tell your people that the next agent that disobeys my orders—I'll crucify, that is if they don't get blown away first. This is an army guy with special training. If everyone is too dense not to know that by now, bomb squad first!'

'Okay. I've got it. I agree with you. I shouldn't have to pass the message along, but I will. These guys are supposed to be smart.'

'Obviously, they've been fooling everyone.'

'A bomb squad won't be there for another thirty minutes,' said Tom.

'Won't help now. It's forensics' turn. Get them started.'

Brees said, 'You go, Glenda.'

Glenda walked away, shouting at the sky, 'How could they be so stupid!'

Brush watched Glenda, amused from inside the Huey, wondering what was going on to make her act like a crazy person, flailing her arms around. 'Whatcha think, Major?' said Abenaa.

'No idea. Looks pissed. Guess we'll find out in a few seconds.'

The general looked at the video screen in the CIA's secure comm room. Sitting with him were Martin, Bertrand, and Martin's new special assistant, Sam. An exceptional group, but as Will looked at the conference room at the BWC with the staff he had carefully recruited: Sheilla, Misa, Vidya, Katarina, and his long-time lab director, Barbara, he longed to be there and not here in DC. BWC was his home, his baby. He had grown the labs into what they were today. *I'm a research doctor.*

*How did I ever end up as director of the CIA?* he asked himself.

On the video conference, acting jittery, was Nusmen at Remilious' Marseille research laboratory. 'I need to get back to our experiments,' said Nusmen.

'You do, but first I want you to fill us in on any progress toward a vaccine,' asked General Crystal.

'We're working on it. DNA plasmid, probably. But there is another avenue, not a vaccine—monoclonal antibodies.'

'I want twice-daily reports. Anything else?'

'Maybe. We're trying to reverse engineer the alterations in the DNA they made that allows it to leap to humans.'

'Time is short,' said the General. 'I want those reports.'

'I don't have time for that.'

'Nusmen, you don't have to do everything yourself. Assign someone else to do it.'

'Oh, okay.'

'Now get back to your work.'

'Ah, thanks.'

'Sheilla, summarize where we are.'

'Moriac's release appears to be contained at Victory Farms. We don't know if he has released it elsewhere yet. And Moriac seems to have evaporated again. So, there are multiple places he could have released it.'

'Katarina or Bertrand, any new guesses about what Moriac will do?'

Katarina deferred to Bertrand, who said, 'My best guess at the moment is not much different from before—

where can he do the most damage? Airports make the most sense to me. Towns, malls, or cities just don't add up as transport hubs do for spreading the virus.'

'There are dozens of airports,' added Will.

Katarina added, 'I think we have to look at locations like airports but combined with what his likely escape route will be. And if there are any more chicken breeders, he might target.'

'She's correct,' said Bertrand. The man wants to accomplish his mission, and if cornered, he will fight to the end, but he doesn't want that. He wants his freedom. We assume he is doing this for money. He won't give up his life easily or without a reason. Escape routes—Canada is the only thing that makes sense.'

'Chicago airport and then north?' asked Sheilla.

'I don't think so now. One way, not a return trip to Chicago. The best option, I think, is Michigan. I can't see him heading east. It's closer, and there are several international airports; Detroit is the largest. And next to the CA border. They are not that far away from here. Check all private flights out of those, and charter helicopters.'

The General's PA knocked and walked in. 'General, the congressional members have been assembled. The CDC director is present.'

Will stood and walked out of the room.

'First, an update. We have a potentially serious biological threat. 'Weeks ago, the CIA was informed of a Somali with a connection to the Egyptian Islamic Jihad who was transported to France. We alerted French intelligence and set up an investigatory team in France near the site of a large international pharmaceutical company —Remilious. They are a world leader in pharma research. But they are in financial trouble for several reasons. Our investigations uncovered a serious issue—in a diabolical plot to save his company, the CEO planned to infect egg facilities in several states. And today with a modified high-pathogenicity type A H5N1 avian flu virus. Millions of birds are being exterminated under the supervision of APHIS. His goal was to make the company the best positioned for manufacturing a vaccine. They have been working on it for months. Further investigations led us to an even more troubling problem. The introduction to the U.S. of a modified avian flu virus that was highly transmissible and deadly to humans. The FBI has quarantined a medium-size facility in Indiana that was infected last night. We have known for some time that H5N1 was a potential danger if it jumped to humans. If that were to happen, it would probably have a devastating effect on the world's human population, as well as other species such as domestic cattle and wildlife.

'General,' a senator cut in, 'is a plague of some sort in the CIA's provenance?'

General Crystal looked at the group. 'Some of you, but not all, are aware of a biological research facility based in western Washington. One that I founded years ago.' Some members exchanged glances. One started to talk, and the General cut him off. 'Our mission is and was to prevent exactly this sort of terrorist attack.'

'This is astounding. A secret bio-weapon research facility on American soil.'

'Its function is to counter possible bioweapons, not to create them for use, but to find ways to stop them.'

'The Biological Warfare Center has just received samples of the virus that was released in Indiana late yesterday. The French government has appointed a new CEO of Remilious. The BWC has staff there working with them to create a vaccine. The president was briefed two hours ago. CDC Director Jennings will provide you with more details. Director.'

'I want to reiterate the possible seriousness of the threat. The avian flu is nearly 100% fatal in birds. There are several subtypes, and I have had a full explanation printed for you. The U.S. to this point has had several identified infections in various birds, all of which have been low pathogenicity. The high-pathogenicity, HP type, that we are dealing with has not been found previously in America.'

A congressman interjected, 'So why the concern?'

'I'll try to explain. Victory Farms will lose several million egg-laying hens, along with the other infected egg hatcheries, reducing our ability to produce vaccines.'

'So, we lose a few chickens and eggs,' added a congressman.'

'The difference is that the chickens in Indiana have been infected with the virus that can spread to people. If it is not contained, we could be facing a lethal pandemic, and we will have, at best, a reduced ability to produce vaccines.'

The congressman sensed the others' displeasure, and it irritated him all the more.

'To put this in perspective—the HP, or high-pathogen type, that has been released could kill tens of millions in the U.S. If this engineered HP strain is what we think it is, it could spread rapidly. Does that help answer your question?'

The congressman looked menacingly at the CDC director.

'It will take weeks, probably months, to develop vaccines and then produce them in quantity, and that is unlikely unless we find an alternative to egg-based vaccine production. And worse, RNA viruses mutate fast, suggesting that any vaccines will be at least partially ineffective by the time they are developed. Worst case, if it hits the general population, the world could lose up to half its population, four billion people, without an effective vaccine.

The same congressman who wondered what the concern was, jumped from his chair and shook his finger at the director. 'You are fear-mongering. What you say is folly, absurd. And you, General, are only making a case for your illegal research facility.'

Jennings said calmly, 'I'm afraid we aren't, Congressman. Otherwise, we would not have asked you here. If we are right, and I pray we may still be wrong, we will, of course, do everything we can to mitigate the situation, and with luck, stop this threat. Even so, it serves to illustrate the need for better preparation. We need a central cabinet-level agency to deal with threats like this. One that we have not experienced since the 1918 flu. If I may remind you, a virus that killed as many as ninety million people. Ignoring this would be to live in a fantasy.'

A senator spoke up and asked, 'I want to confirm that you see this as a worldwide threat, and not only a domestic one. And please tell us what you propose?'

'Geographical borders will not stop the spread. At this juncture, our only hope is the BWC, and oddly enough, the company responsible: Remilious. It has a head start on non-egg-based vaccine production.' For a few seconds, the group sat in complete silence before launching rapid-fire questions to each other, the General, and the CDC director.

Olivia sat in a very different, yet similar, briefing of EIJ leaders. 'We do not need to take this to the great Satan. We can attack them by sending infected people flying to America. We've tested it in the lab. It is fatal. It will spread rapidly from wherever we release it. The issue is how to protect our Muslim faithful?'

'General. Where do you want Nusmen?'

'Ask him where he thinks he can be the most effective, Sheilla.'

'Okay, will do. Sir, we're feeling impotent. Moriac is not using communication devices, so we can't track him.

The best thing we have going is to second-guess the man, a half day of satellite, and searching on video cameras. It hasn't helped much so far.'

'Barbara is coordinating with Nusmen. I want you to focus on the Jihadists, especially the EIJ. We have paid little attention to the missing assistant to Dr. Visser with the Middle East connection. Get the Huachuca hackers and our computer staff focused on them. What if they have the virus? They could infect the U.S. or Europe as easily as Remilious has.'

* * *

Brush sat with a map of the area on his lap. They had been informed that the sheriff had disappeared. They sat in a frost-covered cornfield stubble. One like hundreds of others throughout the Midwest. One, as it would turn out, was only minutes from the missing sheriff's patrol car.

Glenda was constantly on the radio, hoping, waiting for any news of Moriac. The first news that broke was a call to the sheriff's dispatcher. A couple birdwatching near their home had stumbled onto a car parked in the woods. They were about to ignore it when they heard a child crying. They had looked in the car, and a youngster sat squirming and flapping his arms in a child's seat. The couple yelled for his parents, assuming they were close by. Hearing no response, they pulled the child out. Susan and Bradley called 911. 'There's an upset kid in a car and no sign of the owner or parents. We don't know what to do,' said Susan.

'Move away from the car. Do not touch anything in it. Deputies and the FBI will be there in a few minutes.' Susan and Bradley didn't need much encouragement and walked several hundred feet back to the main road.

'Brees, you make sure that the bomb squad looks at that car before anyone else touches it. We are only a few minutes away by chopper. Let's get this bird in the air to their location now,' ordered Glenda Rose. Brush looked at her as if he were seeing a different Glenda. First excitable and now the authoritative commander. He smiled at her. He felt like a lucky guy to be her partner. Then he grinned, *no, more than that, her fiancé.*

The chopper arrived on the scene and spotted the couple holding a young child. The pilot circled the area and landed in the cornfield. Glenda jumped out with Abenaa and walked over to the couple. Brush stayed in the chopper, studying the map. *North, south, east, or west? Where would I head?*

The bomb squad had not been far away and arrived, followed by two FBI cars. Phil motioned everyone back and put a wheeled rover on the ground. Using toggles, he maneuvered it to the older Datsun. He used the cameras to look under the car and on all sides.

Phil had been demolition trained in the army. And he knew that the person he was up against would have been trained in demolitions. Military types were trained to be expedient; they would use tripwires, grenades with the pin pulled jammed in between a seat and a door, or possibly a pressure release antipersonnel mine. Possibly even a grenade with its release lever under a tire or a rock outside the car. He was putting his mindset back years to the war. People had already walked to the abandoned car. *So, a path is clear,* he said to himself. The rear door had been left open by Bradley. And Phil noted that the rear window had been broken. Phil, with the help of his assistant, put on his bulky protective suit. He walked in an awkward, lumbering way burdened by the heavy padded suit.

'What did he leave me this time? What sort of trick?' he asked the car.

'What's that, boss?' asked his assistant.

'Nothing. Talking to myself.'

He followed the path that he had sent his robotic camera on, feeling secure that there were no booby traps along that path. He used the mirror mounted on a retractable pole to check the undersides of the car again. Then, through the open door, he felt under the rear seats and along the seat edge on the far side of the closed door. He scanned the headliner and then moved the camera under the front seats. 'Nothing,' he said into his mic.

'Seeing the same as you. Looks clear so far. Phil moved the camera to the front and looked at the passenger door and seat. And there it was, a grenade between the door and the seat. He leaned over the seat and extracted it, holding the lever down. He passed it out to his assistant. Switching to a retractable pole mirror, he said, 'I don't see anything under the dash.' Then he scanned the accelerator and brake pedals. He cleared the rest of the interior. All that was left was the driver's side door, the trunk, and under the hood.

Phil hadn't seen anything with the camera or mirror

and opened the door. Another one. 'Oh no!' For a moment, it sat wedged above the seat back lever. Phil started to reach for the grenade. Before he could get to it, the lever snapped open, and the grenade fell to the ground. Phil threw off his glove and bent as fast as he could, scooped up the grenade, and backhanded it into the woods. Three seconds later, the grenade detonated. 'You okay, Phil?'

'Yeah. Tricky bastard. That might not be the end of it. *He seems to have lots of ordinance.* Nothing fancy, but an effective way to kill someone. He carefully lifted the hood and then moved to the trunk and inspected it, feeling the edges. He moved around to the driver's door and pushed the release button with his ungloved hand. It popped open and there was no explosion. He walked back to the trunk, cautiously opened it, and said, 'The sheriff is in the trunk. Multiple chest wounds.' Phil held his hand in front of the sheriff's open mouth. 'He's not breathing.'

'Give us the all clear and we'll send in forensics,' said Glenda.

'Give me a minute more. I want to make sure the body is not booby-trapped.'

* * *

Glenda moved back to the helicopter. 'Come on, guys. Drones and agents, a black-and-white sheriff's car, can't just disappear. He can't have gotten far.'

She looked at Brush. 'This bastard is still outsmarting me.'

'The sheriff's car is too obvious. He probably ditched it

by now. Have forensics try their best to determine which way he turned on the road. There's muddy ground back there. There has to be some on his tires.'

'Whichever way he went, it won't tell us where he's going.

'What do you have in mind?' asked Glenda.

'I'm not trying to second-guess what you think or decide, but I've studied the map. My guess—and that's all it is—he went north. I don't think he will head to Chicago.

Glenda stood rubbing her lower lip with her index finger. 'I'm listening.'

He can't drive over the big lake ... but he could take a boat. Not really an option and too slow, I doubt it. He'll want out of the country, and the Canadian border is closest on the east side of Michigan. We set up ambushes.'

'Where? How do you do that? He could be on dozens of roads.'

'In a war, you don't always know exactly where the enemy is. But you set up ambushes anyway. In likely places. No roadblocks advertising the cops are here. That's what I want to do. You do your own thing with the ground troops and drones. Maybe one of us will get lucky. And if his direction is north and we know his speed, there are not that many roads. I've marked where I think the best spots are.'

'As long as I have radio contact, I can operate from anywhere,' said Glenda. So far though, I've been useless. I'm surprised the General hasn't replaced me. Let's try it your way. I'll stick with you. Jim is on the way here; maybe he's replacing me.'

'Can you get me a half dozen teams of six?' asked Brush. 'And no suit types. SWAT or military? When Nielly's team gets here, he can split into two groups of six. Abenaa, you and I stay together with a sniper. That gives us ten teams.'

A chopper landed in the field. 'Jim, I expect.'

'He's not here to replace you, and the General wouldn't do that. Helping catch Maria's killer might make Jim feel better. Maybe help ease his grief about Heather. That's why he's here.

'While I was sitting here, we discussed ambush locations and, if you agree, we'll set them up. Any physical sightings by anyone, and we'll move or adjust as needed.'

Glenda squeezed his arm. 'Alright, Mister, let's give it a shot.'

# Chapter Forty-Five

'Y'ou okay Cherry, Pedro and Tshui?'

'All of us good. They happy, especially since we can communicate with Sharupe here. She teaches us words. I know hijo worries for you. And he ... we ... all miss you.'

Now Jim hesitated. It felt good when she referred to Pedro as his son and being happy. 'Thanks for watching out for them. I'm glad you are all okay. I'll be back as fast as I can.' He thought it best not to say he missed her.

'Wait, Colonel. No go from phone yet. You find Dr. Maria's killer?'

'Not yet, Cherry. I'll let you know when we do.'

'I want know he dead.' She wanted to add that she hoped to see him soon but instead stayed silent just as he had.

* * *

Brush looked at Jim as he stood by his chopper. He knew why he was here: to avenge Heather and Maria. Brush respected his long-term partner too much to wonder if he would use his best judgment. Right now, he and Glenda could use an experienced helping hand.

Jim nodded. 'Any new ideas?'

'None.'

Jim reached out and touched Glenda's shoulder. 'Let's get started then.'

'SWAT, and Neilly's two shippers, Roberta and Garcia should be here in a few—eighteen total,' said Brush. 'Glenda and myself will take Roberta, Jim, and Abenaa will take Garcia. Four teams from SWAT. That gives us six ambush sites. When Neilly arrives, we'll have ten.'

'What do you think? Let's cut that,' said Jim. 'We can set up at more places with groups of two. What do you think?'

'We keep it with three. We can spin off a team of two from each group if somewhere starts to look more promising and still leave one just in case, said Glenda.

'Okay, three each. Swats here. Let's tell them what we want. We can talk to Nielly and have him go directly to four locations, three bodies at each.'

'Brush, give SWAT their assignments,' said Glenda. Let's hustle up and get out there as soon as they're ready.'

'You got it.'

'Neilly's bringing two bodies to replace Abenaa and Techie?' said Jim.

'Good,' said Glenda. 'I want Abenaa in charge of one

of the ambushes and Techie needs to stay with the command vehicle and coordinate with Brees and Chen.'

Abenaa had remained silent. She scratched her cheek. 'They replacing me?'

'Kinda doubt it,' said Jim. 'The last time I talked to him, I got the impression that he thought you were as good as it gets.'

'They might need to, Jim,' said Glenda. 'That is if Abenaa is interested in heading up the quick response team for the BWC. We lost Carter and several of his crew.'

'I don't think Neilly will like that much,' said Jim.

'Yeah, he will. I think after this threat the General is going to push for a closer association between BWC and his SF.

'SWAT's briefed,' said Brush.

'Let's hit it,' said Glenda.

'Misa, you and Vidya work with the two hacker kids at Fort Huachuca,' said Sheilla, 'and take any that you want from my computer team. Figure out what's going on with the Remilious-Egyptian Jihad connection.'

'You keep them,' said Misa. 'The four of us are enough. You can better use them to hack into cameras for Glenda. Call me if you need me.'

Moriac looked at the fuel gauge. *Merde, less than a quarter tank.* He put on a baseball cap and pulled the hood up on his jacket. He had zigged his way by the shortest route to just south of the Michigan border with Indiana. As he entered LaGrange, he came to a traffic light. As he approached, it turned yellow. The red light seemed to go on forever with only a couple of cars driving through. Just beyond it, off Highway 20, was a Marathon gas station. He drove to the pump furthest from the station store and its probable cameras. With his face facing the ground, he inserted a fifty-dollar bill into the machine, selected regular, and filled the tank. He didn't want to look up as he assumed rightly that cameras were also mounted above the pumps. There was a click device on the nozzle that allowed him to leave and get back into the truck. Keeping his head down, but scanning with his eyes, he waited for the fuel to stop filling.

He pulled to the side next to some trees and watched the store. He searched for cameras and spotted one on the entrance overhang and two more above the fuel pumps. He could see a larger supermarket a block south. He needed supplies to last for several weeks. He guessed there was less likely to be CCTV at the market. At some point, he would have to chance it; *why not now?* He drove to the market. After loading four bags of groceries into the truck's passenger side, he thought, *at the first airport, I trade this truck in.* His intuition told him not to go to the main Detroit Airport as his optional plan called for. He studied the map.

Marcel angled back onto U.S. Route 20 at the light

and headed east. Stopped off to the side of the highway was a sheriff's car. He kept his head pointed straight ahead but watched the deputy in the white, blue-lettered patrol car with his eyes. The deputy was fiddling with something on his lap and never looked up. After two kilometers, Marcel turned north and then took the second road back west before turning in the direction he wanted to go: north onto Highway 9.

He would disseminate the virus at two more airports: Kalamazoo Battle Creek International and Grand Rapids Airport. He decided to switch his truck in the long-term parking lot at Kalamazoo Airport.

'The drone spotted the sheriff's car about a quarter mile north of where we just left the abandoned child,' said Glenda, looking at Brush.

'What do you think?' asked Brush.

'Stay with your plan. We can't accomplish anything at places where he has been.'

He smiled at her. 'That's what I would do. We're about twenty minutes from the main junction of Highway 94 and 131 southwest of Kalamazoo. Jim is taking the site west of us at Paw Paw and a SWAT to our east, at the four junctions near Battle Creek. Everyone should be in place in thirty minutes,' as they studied the map. 'When Neilly arrives, we'll have the main junctions from Lake Michigan near Benton Harbor all the way east to the outskirts of Detroit,' said Brush.

'And the FBI is covering all likely airports in northern Indiana and southern Michigan. Let's hope he's headed our way. Look, Brush, Major McGuire, and then she mouthed "sweetie pie." The General put me in charge, but this type of operation is in your area of expertise. I want you to direct this bit.'

'You sure you're okay with that?'

'It wasn't a request, Major, it was an order.'

'Understood. Let's keep each other whole, get this skirmish over with, take some time off together, and celebrate.'

'We have some plans to make. We might have another minor skirmish when we tell Will Crystal we're engaged. Do you really think he will want a married couple doing what we do?'

'If I know him, he will. We've been partners for a long time. I don't see the difference between partners and married partners. Unless we end up with three of us.'

'Maybe four of us, but that will be easy, Mister. You'll be staying home!'

'Hmm ... never thought about that. Back to business, I think, eh.'

'Okay, let's get this guy.'

'Tricky to spot him. It would be better if we could get some info on what his wheels are.'

'We might soon. The Bomb Squad disarmed booby traps and found a body in the trunk. No idea who yet, but forensics has already sent in fingerprints. Hopefully, they'll get an ID and car registered to the corpse. Unless he switches vehicles again.'

Brush turned to the SWAT as they flew toward his chosen site. 'This is a major intersection. A cloverleaf. The good news is the high embankment on the north side. Split the team. A two-man team on the east side of the 94 and one body on the west side. There's no airbase close, so we are going to Kalamazoo Airport and fuel up. After that, we'll set the bird down on top of the ridge and cover the north route. We've got two sniper rifles. You take one, he said to the SWAT team. Give it to whoever you think can best use it. We'll keep the other.'

As they flew to Kalamazoo International, Glenda said, 'It's like looking for a diamond in the Sahara. Too many minor secondary roads. It feels like we'll just be sitting out of the action.'

'In 'Nam, sometimes the favorite outcome was boredom. Although I can't ever remember being bored there for long.'

'I'm feeling fidgety. Not doing anything.'

'We don't know where he is, so you can't do anything, no matter where you are. This way we have a chance of intercepting him. Best we can do while BWC and CIA track him with drones and CCTV ...'

Glenda put her finger to her lip. 'Message coming in.' Techie said, 'They've ID'd the man in the trunk, and he only has one registered vehicle—a black GMC extra cab short bed. Indiana plate "In God We Trust," number 68A477.'

'Get it on the air.'

After fueling the chopper at the Kalamazoo FBO and telling the FBI to stay alert, they had almost reached the embankment above the cloverleaf when Sheilla called back.

'We've spotted the truck at a gas station in LaGrange, Indiana, just south of the Michigan border. Thirty minutes ago. He drove east. We'll keep looking for cameras in that direction.'

'Sheilla, I'm starting to understand this guy,' said Glenda. 'If he went east from the station, he's probably going to double back or change directions. Keep searching. Focus on north. We're staying put.'

Brush nodded, thinking she was adapting and getting into Moriac's head.

'We spotted him again. A weigh station camera on I-94. Could be headed to the Kalamazoo Battle Creek International Airport.'

Glenda looked at Brush. 'He got by us. Airport now.'

'Get one SWAT, Jim, and Abenaa there ASAP. Move the other SWAT teams to these junctions,' said Brush.

How many agents are at that airport?

'Two.' Glenda picked up her radio, 'Stay alert. Blend in. Moriac is reported close to you. We're on our way.'

'Ronno, as was his learned custom in the paratroopers, with the enemy not far behind, stayed calm and used caution. *Or are they now ahead of me?* he considered. He drove to the backside of the airport, parked behind some bushes, and walked through them to the eight-foot-high chain-link fence. He observed nothing suspicious, but it would be the departures and arrivals where the cops would be. Back into the truck, he drove to the cell phone waiting area. He scanned the entrance of the terminal. He only saw people waiting for rides or taxis. Then a man without a suitcase touched his ear and talked, holding his head toward his lapel.

*Are they staking out every airport? How many are there*

*here?* Moriac assumed they had not found him or knew his travel direction. *A team of two, or could it be more?* Then he heard the engine, followed by the rhythmic beat of a helicopter. Ever cautious, as he watched it approach, he jumped into the driver's seat, driving the truck under a tree.

Brush was scanning the area and saw the black pickup's tailgate disappear under a tree. 'I think I've got him outside the airport.' He pointed to where he saw the black pickup. Abenaa looked. 'I don't see him.'

'He just moved under a tree on the northwest side of the car park. You can see the rear end of the pickup protruding.'

Moriac sensed he had been found when the chopper slowed. He picked up his Bullpup assault rifle and stuffed it into his duffle bag with his remaining supplies and two atomizers. He pocketed his Beretta and sprinted into the woods, away from the terminal. After several minutes, he turned back toward the long-term parking area, jogging while staying in the trees. He needed a car.

Glenda said, 'We have Moriac spotted. Brees, have the locals and the FBI converge; cut off the exit road.'

'What do you think, Brush?'

'Hover next to the truck and I'll jump out.'

'Three of us will jump out, not just you,' said Abenaa.

'Wait, that's wrong, not here,' said Glenda. 'No more chasing like you said. We need to outguess him.' She keyed her headset, 'Get us to the airport parking lot.'

'You're right. Good call,' said Brush. 'He needs a vehicle. I didn't see any houses nearby where he could steal one. Get all agents and cops, anyone close to the airport here pronto. You're right, best guess, he'll bolt to the parking area and steal a car. Block the car park road and the airport exit and entrance road.'

Marcel risked exposure, stepping into the open out from under the trees. He had little choice and smashed the window of an older black and gray Chevy Suburban parked on the edge of the long-term outdoor lot. He grabbed the wires under the dash ignition and touched several until there was a connection and it started. He drove over the curb and into the woods. A hundred feet later, he burst out of the woods, bounding sideways onto the airport exit road.

Two sedans and a local police car blocked the exit road. Cars were coming from the airport behind him. Moriac dug in his bag and pulled out his 5.56 bullpup, three grenades, and his last light antitank weapon. Then he heard the helicopter behind and above. He extended the tube on the LAW. The helicopter was his biggest worry.

'Hard left now,' ordered Brush. The pilot didn't hesitate and within seconds they were separated from Moriac by dense trees. 'Head behind the roadblock, keeping out of sight of his black and gray Suburban.'

'Why the emergency bank?' asked Glenda.

Abenaa said, 'He extended a tube on a light anti-tank weapon. Chopper would have been his target.'

'You saw it too, then, Brush?' asked Glenda, wondering why she hadn't. It became patently obvious to her how their different career paths affected what they looked for and how they reacted.

Brush nodded, watching Moriac. 'Stay back from the road. Land in that cleared area on the other side of that red-leaved tree. Keep the RPMs up, and your eyes on me. I give you a signal to take off—no hesitation.'

The chopper was two feet off the ground when Brush jumped out with his MP5 and headed toward the woods and Moriac's truck. He had intended to attack Moriac from the trees by himself. As he ran, he heard noises behind him. Glenda and Abenaa were fifteen feet back. Abenaa carried an M16 with a collapsible stock, and Glenda held her Glock in her left hand and a radio in her right.

The helicopter disappeared before he could pop up the light anti-tank weapon's sight. He turned to the road-block and fired the LAW at the center vehicle. He had aimed for the back as low as he could, hoping to ignite the fuel tank. The police car erupted into flames, followed by both the others. He jumped into the driver's seat, floored the old Suburban to the left of the black smoke and flames, and drove over the curb back onto the exit road.

Glenda saw what was happening and stopped. Brush had meant to ambush Moriac in the woods. With Moriac driving off, Brush and Abenaa would be rushing back to the helicopter. She jogged back toward the chopper, shielding her eyes from the blowing debris.

Over the beating blades, she thought she heard something. *Who's shouting?* She looked to her rear and saw Brush sprinting toward her and waving his arms, then she saw the Suburban rushing at her. *He's going to run me down.*

Moriac thought about running over the woman who was jogging toward the helicopter. If he had known she was in command, he would have. But she wasn't his target. He intended to hijack the chopper. As he neared, it lifted and ducked its nose, heading away. Brush had twirled his hand in the air, and the pilot, a combat veteran, followed Brush's command without hesitation. It saved his and possibly Glenda's lives and kept Moriac stranded.

Marcel spun the Suburban as Glenda fired several shots. He raced back toward the road. A man and a dark-skinned woman were sprinting toward him.

Moriac skidded the Chevy to a stop. 'Down.' Brush hit the ground in front of Glenda. Bullets kicked up dust as Moriac fired. Brush aimed the MP5 at Moriac and fired short bursts. He alternated between Moriac's position, behind the hood, tires, and the gas tank. The Suburban tilted down as the tires lost their air.

He knew he had made another mistake. He should have hit the woman and kept driving away. He jumped into the driver's seat, keeping low. The window on the passenger side shattered.

*Experienced fighters. Short bursts, merde,* he thought.

He floored the accelerator. With two tires flat, the car pulled hard right, heading toward his three pursuers. Brush loaded a new clip and stood. He motioned Abenaa to move right. Glenda saw blood running down Brush's face and another spot getting larger on his shoulder.

Brush moved to his left. The Suburban would be

between him and Abenaa. It veered toward him. The tires shredded and flapped at the turf as the rims cut through the rubber.

Marcel Moriac saw his position and knew it wasn't good. When he thought the car might strike the man, he opened the door, pulling his weapons bag with him; he jumped out.

Abenaa zigzagged toward Moriac. She stopped and fired short bursts. Glenda hesitated, seeing Brush wounded, and then marched directly at Moriac, firing.

Marcel realized he was finally losing a battle. He had always known he would someday. He pulled the pin on a grenade, let go of the lever, counted to two, and lobbed it toward the man.

Brush saw what Moriac was doing and sprinted away from Glenda before diving to the ground. The grenade exploded fifteen feet behind him. Seconds later, Moriac threw a second one at Brush's prone body. The grenade was in mid-air by the time Brush scrambled up, ran three strides, and dove to the turf wishing it wasn't so flat and that there was at least some shallow depression. Shrapnel tore into his legs. Marcel had thrown the grenade only moments before another bullet struck him. The bag fell to the ground before he could grab the last grenade. He saw dozens of men running and driving vehicles toward him. He yelled and charged Abenaa. She stood her ground and smiled at him, the calm matador. As he neared, she lifted her M16, sighted on his heart, and squeezed the trigger. A click as the hammer fell on an empty chamber. 'Shit! Idiot!' She dropped the gun and pulled out her Ka-Bar.

The man running at her was a bull, spouting blood from multiple wounds, but dangerous. He outweighed her by sixty pounds. She saw him lurch as another bullet struck his back.

A fraction of a second before he reached her, she dropped to the grass, rolled sideways, and sliced his Achilles tendon. Moriac thudded to the ground. Abenaa moved like a cat leaping on top of him. She held her blade at his throat with both hands. 'Your choice, Monsieur.'

Others would have surrendered. It wasn't in Marcel's nature to consider anything but fighting. He slapped both of his hands toward the sides of her head. They weakly hit as she pushed the knife into his throat.

Glenda ran to Brush. He was bleeding from his head, shoulder, and legs. She dropped next to him. He smiled at her and shook his head before he said, 'Hi, beautiful.'

The helicopter pilot circled back after watching the firefight. He pushed the cyclic forward, racing to the Major, touching down twenty feet away from him. Two FBI agents appeared, and with Glenda, they loaded Brush into the chopper. Glenda knelt beside him as they sped toward the closest emergency room.

Sergeant First Class Marcel Moriac lay bloodied on his back with a Ka-Bar protruding from his throat. Abenaa stood over him, wondering what the outcome would have been in a one-on-one, hand-to-hand fight if he had not been seriously wounded. She would never know.

The End

# Epilogue

'Abenaa. You knew Najma killed Heather by pushing a knife into her larynx and spinal cord? Didn't you?' asked Glenda Rose.

'I heard that. Why?'

'Jim's on his way. I wondered if it would affect him, seeing Moriac killed the same way Najma killed her victims and Heather.'

'It was not like I chose to kill him that way. The man looked like a buffalo charging at me. I reacted.'

'Understood.'

'Is it a problem?'

'No. It's just something that crossed my mind. You did what you needed to. It might not have come out the same way here without you. And I meant what I said about heading up the Rapid Reaction Special Forces team at the BWC. We can loan you to Neilly when he needs you as long as you want to.'

'I really appreciate you making that offer. Can I think

about it? I would jump at it if it weren't for Neilly's team being the acme of my military career. The best of the best. It's hard to turn down what I've wanted since I joined SF and first heard about his A-team. They're a legend within Special Forces.'

'I understand. Don't feel rushed. We have people at BWC who can replace the team members that we lost. I don't know if there is a good replacement for Carter, but we can find one. Not someone as good as you, I'll bet. Replacing Dr. Dakine in HazMat will not be easy either, but that one is not up to me.'

'What's the latest on Brush?'

'He was doing okay when I left him. He's being transferred and should be at the University of Michigan Hospital by now.' Just as she finished saying that, they heard a helicopter approaching. 'Roger that,' Glenda said. 'It's Jim's bird. He picked up the forensics guys.'


Two days later in the Oval Office


'General Crystal, Director. You ran a slick operation,' said the chief of staff.

'A lot of good people killed,' said the General.

'That is never good,' added the president. 'However, from what you and the CDC have told me, you may have saved perhaps tens of millions of lives. That would never have happened without your insight and direction at the CIA.'

The General started to say something, but the president cut him off. 'Will, I'm accepting your resignation, not because you asked to resign, or you've performed poorly. Quite the opposite, but because I know your heart is at BWC. I now realize just how important it is to all our futures.'

'Thank you, Mr. President. I ...' the president held up his hand. 'There's more. I'm taking you out of the closet and making the Biological Warfare Center a full agency under the Department of Health and Human Services. It is not as top secret as it used to be, so why not go all the way. Congress has to give it their nod of approval, but after it is fully understood that millions of Americans could have been killed, I doubt there will be much resistance. Your skills and insight helped prevent what could have been a huge human disaster.'

'We were lucky that it was stopped in Indiana. Our computer techs are still busy working on the EIJ connection, along with the CIA and NSA. For now, we are on top of it. But it worries me.'

'So, it's not over.'

'You know the old army saying: It's not over till it's over.'

'Thank you, Mr. President. I appreciate it. We will hopefully continue to have a good working relationship with the CIA. Our IT group is good, maybe the best, but it is far better to have the weight of the CIA's tech working in synergy backing us up.'

'Your IT techs have an interesting moniker. I understand they call themselves the Wolf Pack. A group of hackers forced into army service.'

'And a couple of very special academics on the BWC staff,' added Will. 'One from England.'

'They hacked the EIJ's communication network?'

'They did indeed. If they hadn't, we wouldn't know about their plans to spread the virus in Europe, where it would not have taken long to reach us here and the rest of the world.'

'And I heard a rumor that they had hacked the CIA once upon a time.'

Will, for a moment, wasn't sure how to answer. He decided to risk honesty with the president. 'I can verify that rumor, sir.'

'I'll keep it under my hat, Will.'

'Thank you, Mr. President.'

'Just another part where you and your staff should be congratulated. I'm told that the chicken facilities in Indiana are secure, and the virus is destroyed.'

'It appears so. I hope so.'

'And it doesn't stop there. Your laboratory staff has developed a vaccine, and while all the nuances are a tad outside my field, you've found a new way of creating vaccines.'

'Yes, using both our laboratories in the U.S. and those of the French company's labs in Marseille.

'Will, one last thing. For your service at the CIA and BWC and for what's been accomplished with stopping this virus, I expect you here May 1.'

Will remained passive but had hoped he was done with traveling to Washington, at least for a few months.

The president continued, 'When I will be very pleased to present you with the Presidential Medal of Freedom.'

Will sat speechless and then said, 'Mr. President, is that allowed for a person in the military?'

'Rest assured, General, it is.'


Summer 2001—the BWC conference room


'Nusmen, you've accomplished something far exceeding our expectations at Remilious' lab in Marseille. And you stuck it out there. A non-egg-based vaccination is no small feat.'

For the first time in Nusmen's life, he realized he might have done something worthwhile, maybe even profound. He looked at the table, and a lone tear tumbled down his cheek. 'Thank you, General. Thank you for everything you've done for me.'

'It's going to be a transition for me to call you Dr. Nusmen,' said Sheilla. 'At least after some of the names that may have slipped out of my mouth during your tenure. I'm proud of you. A heartfelt congratulations! You're the man of the hour.'

'But I didn't really do it. A Ph.D., I mean.'

'Nus,' said Jim. 'I spent over three years in the Ph.D. program. You accomplished more at Remilious in less than six months than anyone I know of in any Ph.D. program. Your publications and discoveries have earned you an official doctorate at the U Dub. It's not honorary. You earned it. You deserve it. Congratulations.'

Everyone in the room yelled a heartfelt 'Hear, Hear.'

The wild-haired, eccentric beanpole had started at the labs essentially as a confined jailbird. Most thought of him as their resident nut. His personality had not changed, but now he had become one of the most valuable and respected people at the BWC.

Jim looked at Brush. 'Well, partner. You're racking up the wounds after all those years of being unscathed. Twenty-three more.'

'Ah, none that are serious, mostly bits of shrapnel, and maybe a lot easier to handle than having my arm inside a cow in the freezing winter at the ranch. Besides, Abenaa's the one who stopped him, although I hear the autopsy showed that Moriac had two nine-millimeter rounds lodged in his chest. So, it's our elite female team of Abenaa and Glenda who finished that job.'

# About the Author

RS Perry has written six psychological thrillers combining adventure, mystery, and romance. Dr Perry trained as a NASA Astrobiologist and founded an educational charity that explores issues of the environment and space. He is also the chairman of an educational company in the UK. He is a script writer and a member of the Writers Guild of America West in Los Angeles. And a director of Athene Films, a Vancouver based film company. In the pursuit of science and adventure, he has crossed the Atlantic in a small sailboat, plunged to the bottom of the Pacific in Alvin, the Woods Hole deep submersible, climbed in the Andes and the Himalayas, enjoyed the solitude of deserts from the Mojave to the Atacama, the Yukon, and explored the Amazon. He is a Vietnam veteran who is a trained fixed wing plane and helicopter pilot. He has a continuing fascination with the Earth's wild areas and their preservation. Educated at the University of Washington, he has held fellowships at University of Oxford and Imperial College London. He splits his time between New York City and London.